Heirs to the Kingdom

Book Eight

The Circle of Darkness
Of the Ravens of Berengar

Robin John Morgan

www.heirstothekingdom.com

First published (Paperback) in the UK in 2020 by Violet Circle Publishing.

Manchester, England, UK.

Print ISBN: 978-1-910299-26-5
Digital ISBN: 978-1-910299-29-6

British Library Cataloguing in Publication Data.
A catalogue record for this book is available from the British Library.

All papers used in the production of this book are sourced only from wood grown in sustainable forests.

www.violetcirclepublishing.co.uk

*Dedicated to the Memory of
Private William Morgan No.48836 16th Manchester Regiment.*

*His brave deeds, surrounded by his brothers in arms on Manchester
Hill, France, defended the rights and freedom of everyone.
March 21st 1918.*

*Freedom is the sole possession of those who have the courage to
defend it.*

(Pericles.)

I will never forget that day, it was the summer of 1971, and I was alone in the woodland close to the Old Mere. As I walked through the trees, I saw a figure in white, kneeling in front of an old and ancient Oak, I approached and I realised it was a woman, and asked what she was doing.

She got up off her knees, turned, and lowered her hood, and I saw that she was a young woman with the longest and reddest hair I had ever seen. She was not a local, and yet I was not afraid, she smiled, and I noticed how blue her eyes were. She told me she was praying and blessing the tree, it was very sacred, as it had been the first tree to be planted in this area, and had been raised from an acorn by her father.

I asked how can that be? She replied that although she looked young, she was older than my grandparents, and then she began to tell me of the history of this area and the world. I spent the day walking round the Mere with her, as she talked of witches and sorcerers, and tales of long ago.

I returned the day after but she had gone, it would be many years before I saw her again. I was much older and going grey, and she had not aged a day. That was when I realised that her tales which I had learned by heart, were not some story of myth, but were indeed the truth, and when she had told me at age nine, a circle of darkness would surround this place, I knew I had to act, and build the wall.

(Journal of Jake Alfred Loxley)

UNDERSTANDING

So many had died... Too many, but as hard as it was to carry, it was understood that this was the price that was paid for freedom. Not all of them were unknown faces, many were familiar from around the Stockade, some of them close friends and family, and at times it was difficult to shoulder the burden of their loss. Eric, Anthony, Martin, Lee, Scarlet, Ruby, Rose, Sinclair, Alley, and even his father, the list was etched deep within his mind, and yet he had no choice but to hide the pain of loss and continue.

Sat in the cathedral beside Rune, as the hours ticked by waiting in hope that William would not be added to the list, Robbie had time for deep thought. Before him pacing back and forth with an air of irritability, was the one person he blamed more than the others, for she was the sole cause of the pain and evil that had surrounded him since the moment he lifted an old bone horn, and blew a perfect pitch to become the Lord of Loxley.

Morgan le Fey was his enemy. His dislike for her ran deeper than any would ever truly understand, for she alone was the symbol of the greed and malice that had risen out of the ashes of the Red Death, and brought destruction to the lives of every peaceful person in the land. Was it not bad enough that millions had already died, had the people not suffered enough through those times of devastation and fear?

To simply survive had been the hardest task, but then they had to find the strength to rebuild what little they could, to protect the few who had made it out of the worst of times. Robbie's hate of her, and her family, had simmered for the past year, and it had grown into the fire that drove him forward, yet sat in the cathedral watching her pale face, and those red devious eyes, as they traced the unmoving figure of William on the floor, he knew that to hold his sword to her throat and scream out his anger at her, would not undo any of the pain and devastation she had brought to this land. It was a surprising thought, it was almost odd to think it, but he knew deep inside, killing her now would achieve nothing, the people would be free, but Will who was the real hope for the future would die, but he also understood that having faced twenty seven years of struggle, it would take another twenty to recover and undo all that her family had done.

It felt weird to be calmly sat watching her, and as she spoke to Judith, he began to realise that even though she was his enemy, he actually had no idea at all of whom she was, or where she had come from. His brain ticked through all he had learned of her, she was the daughter of a Saxon married to a Celtic queen. She was half-sister to the last true king of the land, and an apprentice to Merlin, and mother to Mason, but that was the sum total of all he really knew. The strange figure earlier had named her Berengar, but what did that mean? It was something he knew Runestone wanted desperately to know, for like him, she too needed to unravel the truth of this evil woman and defeat her with him. The simple truth was, like a phantom she had arisen out of the tales of yesteryear, and her past was hidden behind the darkness of her deeds.

He felt his frustration deep inside, because to discover the truth behind her devious acts, would lead him to victory, and possibly the only chance to change the course of everyone's lives for the better. What evil did she hide behind, what lies did she fear as to hide her past, and protect her family? There had to be something so terrible and evil somewhere in the line of her blood, that she had wiped away any chance of being discovered, but what did she hide?

A strong pulse appeared to travel through him, and for a moment he stiffened. Yes... That had to be it, that had to be the way forward, it was in that small insignificant moment when all became apparent to him, she was the key, or her past was the key, he was not sure why but he was sure, sure enough to understand that here before him lay the answers to everything.

Somewhere in the darkness of her past, were deeds that brought her family line out of the wilderness to his land, and she hid them well, in fact in his mind she hid them too well. His mind lit up and burst into action as the questions began to flow. Why change her family name? What did they do that would shame her? After all, as far as he could tell, Morgan had no scruples or morals when it came to taking anything she desired. Her family had mutilated and tortured, they had burned villages and towns, raped and imprisoned women in orphanages to breed an army. She had raised the dead, and created beasts of unnatural abilities, and yet still she guarded her past, so what was it she hid? What could be so terrible that even Morgan le Fey feared it being known?

He felt a power rise within him like it had at the city in Scarborough when he defeated Billy, was this some hidden power of Fae that had yet to show its hand? It felt that way, and it felt strong and righteous. Now he understood Runestone's obsession of late, she too was looking back trying to find the very same answers. He smiled to himself, she was so much better at this than him, but he knew in that moment that they both were right. This had to be the right path; this could be the only way to end all of the suffering. With Runestone at his side, he had to find out what lay in the heritage of Morgan, together they had to discover her hidden secrets, and then use them with force to defeat all of her devious and despicable family.

CHAPTER ONE

THE GREATEST FLAW

Deep at the heart of the Forest of Time, on a high peak overlooking the vast lake below, the Green Lord sat on a huge seat carven from the stone, his mind in deep thought. Recent events had given him much to be concerned over, and as he processed the moments of Runestone, and her actions, to rewrite the history of the last 30 years, he began to understand that the evil that had been committed by the family of Morgan le Fey was more than just a lucky set of circumstances.

His mind stretched back into ages that were nameless from the start of everything, as slowly he tried to understand the history that had brought evil into the purity of the world that had been built by his hand, and graced with the gifts of life from his beloved Eve. The world had been so innocent and pure as they both had given free will to the line of man, and watched as they wandered in wonder through the many different landscapes they had created. All had been utopian for such a long time, man had flourished in harmony with everything that had surrounded them, and both Eve and he had watched like proud parents, watched over by Albanlin and Tideguyde. Hearne paused for a second, and his dark eyes like fresh berries glanced to the sky. "Tideguyde!"

A memory flashed into his mind, where Eve sat on a rock with her feet in the cool water at the edge of a stream, deep within the Woodland Realm. She turned and smiled a caring loving smile at him and then paused. "What is it my Love?"

He stared momentarily as his thoughts cleared. "Your hair, you have changed the colour." Her bright violet eyes flickered with glee.

"Do you like it? I have been watching the trees and how their shapes change colour with the new season you created to match my aura, so I made my hair copy them."

Her hair was caught for a moment in the reflection of the sun in the water, and the deep copper red burned almost like fire edged with gold, casting glints of firelight across her pale skin. "It makes me feel happy, especially since Tide left, her mooning around seemed to affect me so deeply, I wanted the restful feelings of your trees."

She slipped her feet from the water and lifted herself off the rock, and stood before him with a questioning look in her eyes. "If you do not like it, I can change it back." He shook his head slowly as he looked upon her pale form surrounded by the long falls of her fiery hair.

"No, my dear you look more beautiful than anything I have seen."

She gave a bright smile and scampered across the grass to him, where she slipped into his arms, and he embraced her, as his thoughts gently strolled through his acute mind. He held her warm slight figure in his arms for a few moments, before she slid back and looked up at his lined face.

"What troubles you my Love?"

He shook his head, freeing him from his momentary thoughts, and looked down into her bright violet eyes that sparkled with life. "What is mooning?" She gave a giggle.

"It is a new word I have made just for Tide." Her face looked serious for a second. "She is so filled with some kind of feeling I do not understand, it is almost like there is something inside her that has crept in and stolen her joy, and I have no word for it, so I made a new one which seems to fit her... I call it mooning; I think it shall mean like the day and night, sometimes bright and sometimes dark, like the ball of light in the sky she lives within. It is alright to do this isn't it? If you do not like it I will stop."

The young green man of the trees smiled. "It is fine, and I think you are right, it does seem to sound like she has been of late, we shall add it to the words we use, and teach your brother the word and explain it to him."

Eve gave a big smile and lifted up on her toes and kissed him on the lips, and then with a giggle, she turned and skipped out of his embrace and ran back to the water's edge.

Back on his seat as the memory faded from his thoughts and with it the brief feeling of joy, Hearne considered the words of Eve.

"It is almost like there is something inside her that has crept in and stolen her joy."

He had thought of this moment many times in his long life, but never had he considered the true depths of the words of Eve before. Most of the time this particular thought had been the one he would use to lift his heavy heart, yet today it changed his thoughts a great deal.

The old lord now dressed in the colours of reds, yellows, and browns, stood up and stared out over the land and across the vast lake, as his mind turned in a new direction. After the death of Eleanor, he had spoken many times with Eve, they both accepted that at some point the fate of everything had changed, and the world of love and splendour they had created to live in total harmony had seen a form of evil creep in unnoticed. Albanlin had always cautioned them as to the power of the Merle, and how the darkness could creep into the soul undetected given a chance, but both he and Eve had always felt that it was man that was most susceptible. Man was flawed, all of them accepted that, yet it was the flaws of man that Eve loved so much, because it added to their life force, and gave them deeper qualities that made them so much more different from them or the Fae.

It had been those very flaws that had led them to believe that man needed the rule of a one true king, which had been why after great thought; the line of Uther had been chosen. For in his youth, Uther had lived the life of a warrior, yet he held great qualities that had been reflected in those around him, and he had with the guidance of Merlin, achieved many great deeds to benefit man and bring about order. It had been the daughter of the union of the Saxon with the line of the high Celts that had brought malice to the courts, and infected those around Arthur the son of Uther after his fall. Hearne gave it a moment to sink in; he had looked into Morgan and her deeds of treachery, against her half-brother and Merlin that had for the last thousand years preoccupied his mind in the direction of the lines of man, but what if he was wrong?

It had always been agreed that there had been a specific point in time when darkness made its way onto the Earth and into the lines of men. The Ruling Council had discussed it many times, and had exhausted every train of thought, until eventually they had all agreed that the time when true evil had entered the realm, had been when the council were preoccupied with the warring factions of men, and had decided to seat the first true king. Hearne suddenly felt a cold chill run down his spine, he could not be sure, but suddenly he knew that even with their superior powers and extended knowledge, the council had been fooled. The question that stayed bright in his mind was no longer when did the darkness infiltrate man, but how did the darkness find its way into man? He turned in front of his large stone seat and with a flash of bright green light, he was gone.

Gwendolyn was stood on her rock plateaux high above the white mountain of the First Realm, watching the realms as Watcher, when behind her the light flashed with an intense green. The air around her turned electric, and before she turned, she knew the identity of her visitor.

"My Lord Hearne, I am surprised, yet happy to see you here in this remote land, what service is required that would bring such a personal visit?" She turned to see the tall lord she was so fond of, and her breath caught in her throat as she saw the autumnal colours of his attire. "What has happened, why have you left the Woodland Realm?"

Hearne dismissed her question and he hurriedly crossed the large red circle burned into the rock floor and headed towards her. "That is of no consequence, White Circle I have great need of your insight on a matter that is far more important."

Gwendolyn noted the urgency of his voice, and the look on his stern, dark lined face.

"My Lord, I am always at your service in this world, and others, so pray tell me how can I assist you?"

His pace slowed as he got closer, and their eyes met. "I need to know of the darkness and its influence into the world." Gwendolyn gave a slight sigh and spoke quietly to herself.

"Surely not this again?"

"YES AGAIN!" His voice boomed loud and his anger showed, Gwendolyn gave a slight step back and bowed.

"My Lord, please forgive me, but I thought we had discussed this to its ends, and we were all settled on the outcome."

"Things have changed, and so I need you to confirm my thoughts."

Gwendolyn snapped her fingers, and a few feet away an elegant chair rose from the stone with a large round table, and on the opposite side a tree like stump grew out of the floor.

"My Lord please be seated and tell me of these changes, for we have spent many years on this puzzle, and if there really is new evidence, I would dearly wish to examine it."

When Hearne reached the table and sat down, it was filled with a lavish spread of meats, cheeses and breads, with decanters of a faintly blue coloured liquid. Gwendolyn poured the liquid into wooden goblets, as he sat and made himself comfortable. She slid the drink across the table towards him. Hearne took a drink and let the cool liquid quench his dry mouth.

"I need to show you something... Close your eyes."

Gwendolyn closed her eyes, and Hearne reached across the table, lifted his arm, and pushed two fingers gently onto Gwendolyn's eyelids. Her eyes burned brightly for a second, and then deep inside her mind, the pictures of Eve sat with her feet in the stream appeared, and she watched the close happy, personal memory, of a time long past. The pictures faded and Gwendolyn opened her eyes to see the expectant look on Hearne's face, his voice was softer. "Well?"

She shook her head. "My Lord I am sorry but I do not see what it is you want me to see, all I see is a precious and beautiful moment between the two people in whom we all felt their great love." He gave a nod of agreement.

"Precisely... That is exactly how it has always appeared to me, but listen carefully to her words. White Circle you know how perceptive she was, and yet at times she never truly understood her own perceptions, do you not spot what she saw and we did not?"

"I am not certain I understand, Eve had a big heart, I loved her as a sister, as did Tideguyde, it makes sense that Eve would feel the sadness of her friend, and want to find a way to cheer her up. My Lord we all know why Tideguyde felt sad, and we also know that soon after she left to find the one she loved, Erathome. This is not new information, it is the story of us all, and I may add it is one of the most revered stories of both lines of Fae as it led to our creation."

Hearne sat back and gave a hearty smile. "Precisely!"

Gwendolyn felt awkward, was her lord losing his perception? Could he not see that this was meaningless, and nothing he had shown her was new information? "My Lord I am sorry, but this changes nothing, I fear we will never truly know."

In many ways she expected to see his disappointment, but instead he just gave a wide smile and his dark eyes twinkled with delight. "It pleases me to know one of the sharpest minds of the council has also been blinded to the truth. For a moment I thought my great age was starting to decay my thoughts." She was happy he felt such relief, but as she watched him, she really did not understand the point he was trying to make.

"Maybe we should speak more plainly so that I can share the understanding you appear to have reached My Lord." His laugh was infectious, like the sound of water running across smooth stones.

"My dear friend, long have we struggled with this issue, and the moment was so scarce and so insignificant that with the sharpness of our minds, we missed the most important quality of those we created. Yet the one who struggled the most to reach our understanding and learn our language, was actually the one who spotted the most important moment in our history, and yet did not see the importance of it, for it was the love and compassion of Eve that has uncovered the moment all of us missed."

Gwendolyn gave a sigh. "And yet still I do not see it."

"Your white lord warned all of us of the dangers of the darkness; he made it clear that within the Merle were many things that sought to corrupt the lines of men. The danger has always been very real, which is why he created Merlin to walk amongst men as a watcher for its infections. Do you not see what we missed?" He leaned onto the table and stared into her eyes. "In our arrogance we were so concerned with the lines of men, we missed where the Merle first hit, and it was not Mankind."

It took several long moments before Gwendolyn began to understand the point that her green lord was making. Her insides churned; how could he think such things? Her breath shortened as her shock washed into her, her action was swift and her seat slid on the floor as she stood abruptly. "THIS IS MADNESS… HOW CAN YOU EVEN THINK THIS?"

Suddenly understanding her own behaviour, she gave a hard swallow and lowered her tone. "Forgive me My Lord, but surly you cannot be serious, I mean how can you even think this? Tideguyde is beyond reproach, she is one of the most revered figures within all the lines of Fae. Hell she was like a sister to both Eve and yourself, how can you even suggest she is the one who brought the darkness down to this and all the realms, have you any idea what to suggest this will do, or the damage it will cause?"

Hearne gave a chuckle. "I think I fully understand the significance of this White Circle."

Gwendolyn shook her head. "My Lord with all due respect I am not sure you do. If what you say is true, then you are suggesting that Tideguyde the single most important icon of all Fae was infected by the Merle, and as a result it was she alone that brought evil to all of us and every realm." She swallowed hard. "It was her garment that Rhiannon and Bridge my grandmother, were made from, and from them came both of the lines of the Fae. If you truly are serious about this… Then… Then… My Lord you are suggesting that all the Fae of both houses may be flawed?"

Gwendolyn dropped in her seat, which was some distance back from the table; she lowered her head as if utterly defeated. Hearne rose from his seat, and came round the table, and placed a soft lined hand onto her shoulder. "This is grave news indeed White Circle, but it may not be as bad as first seems. You must look back into the past for signs of treachery, but do not be too disheartened, for I feel that at some point Tideguyde realised herself what had happened, and maybe she tried to help undo what had befallen her." Gwendolyn lifted her saddened face to her lord.

"She did… How?" Hearne smiled.

"Did she not return her gifts and pass on a secret held only by the Fae Ofmoon to a Fae of Earth queen?" He patted her shoulder and turned, and walked towards the edge of the high cliff, where beyond he could see the sky filled with tiny coloured orbs of lights that represented the many different realms that he created with Eve. Gwendolyn sat still, not feeling she had the strength to stand. Hearne's voice was soft and yet it appeared to fill all the space surrounding them.

"Tideguyde had a big heart, she felt things very deeply. I would imagine realising that her moment of despair at the loss of her loved one, was also her greatest moment of weakness, when the Merle attacked and infected her, it must have caused her great pain. I think it is clear that when Sequana found her, she saw her chance to try and undo all that had befallen. If I am right, and I think I am, in that moment she realised that it was a part of her garment that had remained behind, for she saw it in the gifts bestowed upon Sequana, maybe then she realised that only a small percentage of Fae had been infected by her garment." He turned and looked back at Gwendolyn sat attentively watching him.

"I believe that a small part was passed to your grandmother Bridge, for she fell into a deep melancholy shortly before she died, and yet I have seen no sign of it within you White Circle or within your brother, so I feel that she realised what had happened and took that particular part of the Merle with her in death. As I think about it, now I understand why she chose not to return as a new born or continue in another form like you have. As for Rhiannon, there have been times when she has made bad decisions, and I have questioned them, as did your grandmother, so I fear there may be some trace in some of the lines of Fae Ofmoon, although I see none in her son or her granddaughters."

Gwendolyn was starting to understand his thinking. "But how did sending Sequana back to me help? My Lord all I learned was a greater sense of sight, and how to pass powers from one line to another, that is a secret of the Fae of Ofmoon which I have not shared with any other." He gave a nod and smiled at her.

"Sequana also gave you another gift that has been of great value to all the Fae. Was it not she who also shared the secrets of the veil? That as far as I am aware is a secret created by Tideguyde, it was her greatest power for she used it to exclude the whole realm of Ofmoon from the eyes of everyone, and yet the Fae of Earth appear to have learned it and used it. Do not forget when you were captured, your people used it to hide from the mortal Le Fey. I would even go as far as to say it has saved the line of your people for the coming of the next queen." It made a great deal of sense and Gwendolyn could not believe she had never worked it out before. Hearne turned back to look into the heavens above him.

"I also believe she gave you another gift you were not aware of."

"She did... What?"

He gave a smile as his eyes crossed the skies. "She gave you the gift of feeling the power of the Merle, and you passed it on to your children. Do you not find it strange that young Una has possibly the greatest powers of protection ever given to a single member of any of the lines of Fae? Did you not witness on this very rock, how Una gave protection to the sword bearer who was so far away? It was impossible for the most powerful member of the Green Circle to communicate with her, Runestone tried many times to contact Jett Amber and failed, and yet Una was able to wrap her in protection and keep her and the sword safe across an overwhelming distance. That was nothing short of miraculous for a member of a Fae of Earth line."

Hearne turned and began to walk slowly back towards her. "Tideguyde gave you the power to see beyond all of us and it prepared Runestone, Una gave the protection to Jett, you prevented the mortal Morgan from attacking a future line of your queen, and Sapphire found the strength to protect all of us, and is now the eyes of all worlds against the darkness that has grown within the line of Morgan. I feel she has played her part well to undo some of the evil caused in this world, and I think in time more of her aide will be revealed." He stopped short of Gwendolyn and gave a slight sigh.

"I also think there is one more answer to a question long held, but I see Runestone has already discovered the truth of that."

"There is, and what is that My Lord?"

He paused for a moment as if giving the matter more thought. "This is my true reason for my visit, you see, Runestone believes that the mortal Le Fey is from the line of Fae, I would even agree and go so far as to say if you look back far enough, you will find a member of the Fae Ofmoon at the start of her father's line. There is a line of the early Saxons that visited our shores of old that has been hidden from us for a very long time, but alas until we know who it is, it will be hard to track them and discover what deeds they have done. It is time we must explore this circle of darkness, and cast the light inside to reveal the truth."

Gwendolyn's words were almost a whisper. "She is Fae... How can that be? I feel foolish because as you know your daughter once suspected the same and I disagreed, but there was no evidence to prove it at the time. Although as I think it of it now, it does explain a great deal of her antics." He nodded in agreement.

"White Circle you have the time and space here to think, I came here to ask you to try and remember your times as queen, for there must be some event from the past that we missed. I would say at first it would have appeared as an odd insignificant moment, and yet knowing what we know now, it is a moment that will begin a trail of explanation. Take the time to think hard and try if you may to discover the seed that grew into the evil we know today."

Gwendolyn gave a solemn nod. "You have no need to ask My Lord, already I am searching through everything I can remember, to try and find some instance that may guide all of us."

"Then my time here is done, and now I must leave and speak with my daughter. You are still connected to your people; I have assured it, so use this time well and keep Sapphire, who will soon visit Florae, appraised of your thoughts, for she is in constant contact with Runestone who has great need of any help she can obtain. Until we next meet my trusted friend, stay safe and at peace."

Before she could even answer, the light around him flashed green and he was gone. Suddenly everything in the air around her felt empty and still, and Gwendolyn had no choice but to remain in her seat, her mind overwhelmed with the news and in turmoil. Everything she had ever believed as a queen of the Fae had been challenged, and she found it exceptionally unsettling.

It was true that Eve often spoke with Hearne of the mistakes of their past, both knew they had missed important parts of the puzzle, and in doing so they had allowed events to get out of control. They both felt the responsibility of the mistakes and errors of their youth, and somehow at some point they had been too involved in the world they had created to notice a fatal mistake. The sad thing was that their mistake was actually only a minor event. It was a simple moment unheard by the ears of the council, and within that moment something occurred that would change the future, and bring havoc and chaos to their greatest achievement. It was just a moment of passing, when all of the council sat planning the coming of Rhiannon to a new realm based at the first realm to be renamed Avalon, and in a blink of one eye, something profoundly important occurred, and it was the beginning of the darkest powers arrival in their world, and it happened in the centre of everything.

On the highest and flattest peak above Avalon, shining brightly in the sunlight stood an arbour of old black wood, crowned with a silver roof. Beneath it a long wooden table rested in the shade filled with metal instruments and piles of parchment, in front of which, a tall figure of a woman with long tatty dark hair, stood lost in her thought as she read from her endless notes.

A happy voice called out to her, and her eyes lifted to see the small slender figure of Ariel dressed in a deep burgundy dress, was walking, and smiling towards her. She lowered the parchment to the table as she smiled back, and slipped it into the large open black book, and then closed the cover to hide it. The approaching figure of Ariel waved, and Branna lifted a hand to wave back.

In the few minutes it took for Ariel to walk the distance to the shelter, Branna packed her large black book into her bag, and poured out two large silver goblets of wine. Ariel gave a pant as she came under the arbour, and Branna embraced her. "I saw the marshal this morning and I am sorry to hear about Bridget Violet, it appears the word is out on her health. She is a good queen, how is she, is there nothing that can be done to cure her melancholy? Her presence is missed in all the realms." Ariel gave a sad smile and took the goblet to quench her thirst from the walk in the hot sun.

"From what I have been told, she is unchanged, we fear for her now, and I think it is likely that Gwendolyn will soon take her place, but thank you for your concern. I have been ordered back to Florae, hopefully not for too long, but it is at least going to be a month. They are sending a marshal shortly, and I wanted to say goodbye before I left. I will miss you and your wild ways my love." Her soft grey eyes held the sadness of the moment, yet Branna smiled.

"It is probably better; I have been thinking a great deal of late, and I too will be leaving here." Ariel looked surprised; her heart began to beat rapidly deep within her.

"When... How... I mean your work is here, isn't it?" Branna walked back to the chair beside the table.

"It is finished for this place, for what good it has done me." She sat down and took a sip from her goblet; Ariel walked over and sat in the chair in front of her. Branna looked drained and tired. "I have done all I can here, but it matters little, Rhiannon has refused all of my requests for an audience, she is so bound up with Sequana, I fear my studies will never see the light of day." Ariel shook her head.

"You cannot give up; not after one hundred years of study, you have learned things here that we all should know about the darkness and what it contains." She leaned forward and took Branna's hands in hers. "Do not give up, stay here for soon the queen will descend and take up guardianship of this realm, it will be a new beginning where both lines of Fae unite for the first time in this new realm. The council will then have more time, and have great need of what you have learned. Branna you must wait and then present your findings, wait for my return and let me help you, I know I can get you influence."

Branna slipped her hands out from Ariel's and sat back in her chair, her voice was stern and harsh. "You know the queen has no tolerance for me or my kind, even now after years of hard work I am seen as inferior because I carry the mark of dark hair. I have told you so many times, she is short sighted, and will not listen to the wisdom of a Fae she deems unworthy. So I have decided to leave and take what I have learned with me, she will regret her favouring of those with lighter hair one day and see it for what it truly is, her weakness."

Ariel felt uncomfortable and she looked around, her voice lowered to a cautious tone. "Please I have told you before, you must not say such things, she is your queen." Branna scoffed.

"She is their queen not mine, remember the line of the Fae Ofmoon runs golden, and there is little tolerance for us sent down here on this Earth to build a realm for her. When she comes, we will remain here in the outer reaches of Avalon hidden from view so as not to offend her. You know it is true, we are a race apart Ariel. Bridget is warm and welcoming to all in Florae, and I would imagine Gwendolyn one day will be the same. You are lucky; your brown hair is not a curse to the Fae of Earth as it is to us here. All we are fit for is the toil of working underground out of sight, or out here in nowhere, so our darker hair does not offend the eyes of our blind queen." Ariel felt a pulse of fear run through her, the thought of losing her after all their time together, was simply too painful to even contemplate, and her voice quivered.

"Then come with me, I realise things look bleak for Bridget Violet, but I am sure when Gwendolyn is crowned, she will be fascinated in what you have learned. Branna please, you must travel back with me and present your findings to the House of Elders in Florae." She smiled but shook her head.

"No my love, I have thought a great deal of late, I want to see this world around us, I aim to travel and find a place where I belong and I am not seen as lesser because of my hair colour. Many of my race have travelled into the realm of men and found happiness, I too will follow that path, for I feel there are many things out there to please me."

Ariel thought her heart would break, and her eyes filled with tears. "I cannot bear the thought of us losing touch, I don't want you to leave, please I beg of you, return with me and live in my house as I have yours, my heart will break if I lose you." Branna smiled, her love for Ariel was also strong, but she knew this was the only way.

"Ariel you know of the love I hold for you, but I aim to do this. I do not belong here; we have both known always that my spirit is wilder than most others; it is time for me to break free and walk out into the world to find my destiny. Fear not for as soon as I find a place, I will send word to you in Florae, and you can come to me." Tears spilled onto Ariel's cheeks and a sob grew out of her throat.

"The world of men is still fierce and dark. I shall fear for you until I hear word from you." Branna rose from her seat and knelt before Ariel; she pulled her into a deep embrace and kissed her. Her dark eyes glistened with tears, as she smiled.

"Let me do this, let me fly free, and I shall return to you, for you are a part of who I have become, and I will not have us parted for long. I am hardly defenceless now am I? I have many skills and powers not given to the lines of men. I shall thrive as my fellow Fae have out there. Think of all you have taught me, not only will I survive, I can be of use to the lines of men." Ariel held her tightly in her arms and kissed her again as she wept.

Both of them held each other close for a long time, it was heart breaking for both of them, as they hugged and kissed, but as the time approached, Branna took Ariel by the hand and talked quietly of being brave and facing what would be the next chapter of their lives, and a reunion to come at a later date, and together they walked back down to the house where Ariel gathered her things.

When the marshal arrived to escort her to the exit of Avalon, so she could travel to Florae, Ariel broke down and sobbed bitterly as she said her goodbyes, and Branna tried her hardest to be brave, and hugged and kissed her farewell.

Finally, Ariel mounted her horse and set off, and Branna stood at the garden gate and watched as she disappeared out of view sobbing. Branna ran inside and threw herself on her bed and grabbed the sheets that still carried the scent of Ariel, and wept bitterly until she was exhausted and fell into a tearful sleep. The moment passed, and faded unnoticed into time, and the future of everyone was to see its effects.

When Rhiannon made her victorious arrival to the new Citadel on the Mount, a little over five moon cycle's later, Ariel had already returned to Florae and Branna had left Avalon forever. Turning her back on her own people, she entered the world of men armed with the advanced skills of a Fae of the Moon. Her years of study into the darkness of the Merle had already started to have its effects, and at first, she was unaware of the damage it had done to corrupt her. Branna had always had an unnatural interest in the Merle, and as Hearne had now discovered, it was due to a simple mistake that had allowed the Merle to infect one of the Fae's most revered icons, Tideguyde.

Without fully understanding at first, Hearne had been correct, and a small amount of the deadly Merle had implanted itself within the garment that remained from the departure of Tideguyde. Branna was one of a few who inherited some of it, and from the moment of her creation, she had been steered towards the Merle, which increased its hold with more exposure during her studies. As she hugged and kissed her lover goodbye, it was a turning point in her life, for at that time filled with the love she held for Ariel, she had been able to resist its influences. As Branna packed her things and Ariel departed, the following days and weeks would see its influence grow and strangle the love inside her.

The moment had passed unnoticed, and now her fate was sealed as the Merle infected every aspect of Branna, and began its long journey of turning her colder and more corrupted towards evil. In many ways Branna was already dead and gone when she left Avalon, all that was left was a shell of greed and desire with an insatiable appetite for destruction and power, she had not yet felt it, but once she did, there would be no turning back.

The window opened, and Robbie led the group through into the centre of the cathedral at Lincoln. All around were the groans and moans of the injured and dying, many of them monks, nuns, and vicars. Steph attended them with a group of novice nuns, she stood up as she saw Robbie approach, and she looked relieved.

"Glad you made it, its utter carnage in the back rooms, they are lying the dead out in the gardens at the back." She gave a long breath and wiped the sweat off her brow with her sleeve. "Treen has taken command outside, hell Robbie it was like a slaughter house when we got here, those vile monks were at the doors, but Treen has pushed them down the street a little, I tell you if this is the Christian Church why are we so worried about crowning Will with their consent?"

Robbie patted her arm. "The people who did this are not really members of this church, they are hired muscle who wear the cloth of a cross for their own convenience, keep Jade inside she can help with the healing. I am going to take a look outside and see what can be done; Sapphire will be here shortly with more troops from Loxley." She gave a weak smile and he patted her arm.

The Specialists fanned out round the cathedral, Big John looked sickened as he looked round, stood next to the imposing figure of Bear, who held a large silver axe in his hand. Everywhere they looked there were wounded and dying, and the cathedral echoed to the sounds of weeping and moans, Big John gave a long sigh.

"This ain't right."

Bear gave a nod, his face fixed on the young novice nuns, as he watched them binding the wounds of what he saw as old men, he lifted a hand to John's shoulder and gave it a squeeze. "You are right my friend, never have I seen a sight so abhorrent, these are but old men and young women who have been put to the sword, I feel there is a reckoning in need for this barbarous act." John looked to his side and the stern face of Bear.

"Aye, there is, and I reckon we are the ones to do it." Bear gave the slightest of smiles; he lifted his hand and gently patted John on the shoulder.

"Blood will spill this day my friend, and our swords and axe will sing as it flows. Together we will stand for these people and those who did this to them will pay with their lives."

It had been a very long day and his men were tired, they had slept little as they had waited out most of the night in the cathedral at Canterbury waiting to see if Will would live. Robbie's mind had been focused for most of the night on Morgan le Fey, but now it had turned towards Mason. For a year he had focused on his armies and done his best to thwart them, but now it felt like he had more clarity as the moment of truth came closer.

This would be Mason's first real test of the Woodlands resolve, Robbie knew other Cutter brigades were moving out of the stone city below Birmingham, and moving north towards Loxley. Mason had finally shown his hand, and Robbie had to a degree guessed his move. It was now his task to face what he knew would be impossible odds, and yet deep down inside he felt a strange calmness. Was this to be his fate? Was this the moment everything in his life had been heading towards?

This was the point of no return, he knew it, the fight for the end would finally start today, and swords would clash, blood would spill, and continue until only one side was left standing, there was no turning back, and as odd as he thought it was to think it, he felt relieved.

Robbie turned to his Specialists who were gathered behind him in rank. Rowan looked stern, his grey eyes fixed in his pale chiselled face, he gave a slight nod as Robbie looked at the faces of the others behind Rowan.

"Let's do this, this must not go unpunished, and when we are done, we will return to Loxley, rearm, and then take this fight to the feet of Knox." He turned and headed for the door.

Robbie walked out onto the roadway that led under the arch, and out onto the main street, and instantly the sounds of battle raged below him on the flat wild meadow. Treen had used the little she had well, and pushed back hard against the Brethren, she had made it to the bottom of the road, and was organising her men as they fanned out in ranks onto the wild fields below. The fighting was close quarters and brutal, as a large swarm of men in dark red tunics bearing an ornate golden cross fought hard against the woodsmen of Loxley.

The ground was littered with the dead, some of which Robbie recognised from within the ranks he had used on his last visit; Rowan came up at his side as he viewed the battle.

"The scouts say that there is a Cutter force less than an hour away, we will need a lot more men."

"They are coming Rowan, Sapphire has it in hand with John, they shall be here anytime."

"What do you want the Specialists to do?"

"Hold them back for a moment, I want to see what Mason has for us, two armies from the south feels wrong, he has something special in mind for us and I want to know what."

Behind them the bright orb of blue burst open, and a long line of troops came trudging through, and down the road to where Treen and her captains waited to direct them onto the field. Rune came slowly down the road and up to Robbie's side.

"It's finally started, I am not sure I believe it." He began to walk slowly down the road viewing the scene as he planned his next move.

"It is happening Rune; Mason has shown us his first hand. I want you to go back to Loxley with the wounded, take Jade, he has a lot of men, but we can deal with that, go and follow your leads on this Berengar family, there will be no crowning till all of this is over, so find me the means to kill her. I want her gone Rune, I want her out of the picture, so find me the way, and then all of Mason's cards will topple. No matter how hard it gets for us, dig deep and give me the means to end her, because if I have learned anything watching her slather over Will's body last night, she is the key to everything, Mason is also her pawn, and if he wins, she will slit his throat and take it all."

Rune looked surprised as she watched his dark eyes dart across the field as he took the measure of the battle; she moved in close and kissed his cheek. "You sound like your father." He shook his head.

"No... He was too focused on Mason, like everyone else they think he is the one in command, I have learned from my grandfather's notes, he knew of her long before she appeared to the rest of us, I am not sure how, but he saw this coming and built the Stockade. This can only end with her, so go find me that fairy, because she knows everything we need to kill Le Fey."

"Ok Robbie, I will tend to the wounded and then head back with Jade."

Far across the meadow and up the road a ways, a long line of soldiers dressed in black appeared, and began to troop towards the wide open plain. Robbie turned to Rowan and smiled. "Prepare the Specialists, we will be joining the Outlaws and driving a road through black vests. Treen, you have command of the Bowman from Loxley, we shall need a rain of arrows on black vests." She winked and gave a smile.

"I am already in the thinking of it."

Rowan turned and yelled his orders. "SPECIALISTS OF LOXLEY!"

They all snapped into rank, as the long lines of woodsmen from Loxley continued to pass them. Robbie pulled Destiny out of his scabbard, and held it high so the sun glinted off the blade, as he turned back to look at his faithful group and whispered under his breath.

"Stand by my men today My Lord Hearne."

With his sword held high, he began to walk the remainder of the road towards the battle field. The Specialist drew out their blades, and loaded their bows, and in file walked down the road behind him. As they entered the field, Robbie slid up his hood and the Specialists fanned out in a long row behind him and did the same. Robbie looked down at the blood stained grass and then back to the fight in front of him, and pointed his bright sword forward.

"SPECIALIST'S... CHARGE!"

CHAPTER TWO

BRANNA AND BERENGAR

High on the walls at Loxley the guard had been doubled, around the whole wall outside the stockade, woodsmen filled the trees, and at the gates there was a heavy atmosphere of tension. David Williams stood his watch with his best friend, and Sergeant, Henry. The sky was overcast but it was warm, and life appeared as normal as it had for years. In the distance there was a faint rumbling sound. "Looks like we may have some thunder Davie?"

"Not really Henry, look!"

Henry followed his gaze to the floor, where he saw the dirt and dust that had built up over the week, vibrate and fall through the cracks in the wooden floor. "Thunder does not shake the wood we are stood on Henry."

Henry continued to stare at the floor. "Then what the bloody hell causes that then?"

"What indeed my friend?" The rumble grew louder, and the floor began to shake harder, David screamed down the walls to his men. "HOLD ON TO SOMETHING NOW!"

He grabbed the wall in front of him, and looked out across the fields and trees, as the floor vibrated harder; Henry grabbed the wall as everything shook so violently, he almost fell backwards. "Shit Henry, look!"

In the distance across the valley, both of them stared in disbelief as a wall a hundred feet high grew out of the floor. It slowly pushed upwards into the sky, made of black, smooth, glistening stone, and David needed no one to tell him how far it stretched, as it came to a shuddering halt he knew.

"Well that's it Henry, we are well and truly boxed in, his witch has cornered us, and for Mason it's going to be like shooting fish in a barrel. Sound the alarm, Loxley is under attack."

Treen stood firm on the higher ground at the end of the road from the cathedral, her hood down and her long red hair flowing behind her in the breeze. At her side the smaller figure of Claire gripped her flags, and signalled across the battlefield, where Robbie and Rowan stood six feet apart fighting with their swords, as they cut and slashed their way through the constant stream of black or burgundy coloured, vested men.

Around them on the grass were the bodies of Woodsmen, Cutters, and members of the Brethren, one of which was still firmly grasping the hood of Robbie's torn cloak. He had lunged for Robbie dragging him backwards, only to watch his arm get severed, as Blades bounced up from behind him, and struck with lightning force across his arm, her second blade following across his chest and up most of his face. Her speed and agility had saved her leaders life, and as Robbie staggered forward to fight onward, he found Blades and Jett flanking him and Rowan.

All around them were screams of pain and the clash of steel, as what was a brutal punishing fight ensued. Flashes of light struck overhead as Maddy unleashed her arrows into the masses of black dressed Cutters, or Jay let go a volley of stinger arrows, which would explode sending scraps of cloth, dirt, and parts of Cutter into the air, to rain back down on the fight.

The floor below them was a thick matted mass of wild flowers and grasses, drenched in blood, stomped down into a thick red paste of mud that splattered and spurted, as the men stamped their feet heavily down to gain a better purchase on the land, in order to deal out their mighty blows. Around the edges of the chaos, wounded and dying soldiers, gripped the clumps of long grass, to pull themselves free of the thick blood soaked mud, and crawl on their stomachs as far from the battle as possible. Around the sides of the main road, Cutters, Woodsmen, and members of the Brethren lay wounded and dying, and they stared hopelessly into the open skies above them.

Bear and Wolfie fought side by side, Bear swinging his axe and long sword wildly round, as Wolfie growled and snarled at his enemies, as he hacked and cleaved his path through. It was a terrifying scene of carnage and mayhem, as the forces of the Woodland Realm forced their way forward inch by inch, over hours, clearing a wide band of open earth between their backs and the road that led back to the safety of the cathedral.

The fight was almost a stalemate, and something had to give, as Treen organised yet another new party of bowmen to aim and fire a volley of arrows into the back lines of the army of Cutters. The arrows left their bows in a thick thatch of dark lines, and shot high into the air, hovering for just a second, before tipping over and raining down at high speed into the furthest lines of men. Cutters screamed and wailed as they staggered, impaled by the deadly rain of long sharp Loxley arrows. Men tripped and fell, only to find others falling over them, crushing the wind from their lungs, as the burning pain of the arrows coursed through them.

Blades spun in the mud, her grunts and screams lost in the raging chaos around her, she brought her foot up, and kicked out at the man in front of her, to push back and give herself swinging space. One of the Brethren lunged from the side, and grabbed on to her swinging pony tail, he pulled back with all his might, and Blades felt her balance tilt backwards.

As she stepped back trying to slice through the man in front of her, a glint of white passed over her head and there was a scream from behind her, as Robbie side swiped with destiny lopping off the arm of the man hanging on to her hair. She stumbled and rolled backwards onto the dead behind her, and then with the flick of her feet, she sprung back up, and took two steps back. Hanging from her longer than normal hair was the hand of the man that had tried to pull her back, she shook her head, and then with the flick of one of her razor sharp swords, she thrust backwards and up, and her pony tail flew up into the air, and then down to the ground with a squelch, into the blood soaked mud.

Blades took a long breath, and seeing the man on the floor thrashing around screaming with a bloodied stump, she flicked her sword and ended his life, and then moved forward to re-join Robbie at his side, where she had to almost shout to be heard in the noise. "Thanks, I meant to trim it before we left." Robbie gave a smile as he lunged into two men despatching one, and pushing the other into Blades path.

"Think nothing of it; I think I prefer it short anyway."

Treen yelled out across the lines of bowmen to Jay, she had spotted the long line of rifle men as they trooped onto the field, from the roadway between the trees in the distance. Catching Jay's attention, she screamed. "IT EZZ THE RIFLES!"

She pointed with her longbow in the direction of the men. Treen knew that the fight was slowly moving in Loxley's favour, but rifles could change everything, and she had to get them stopped at all costs. Claire lifted her flags and frantically signalled across the field of battle.

Jay pushed her group into range not that far behind the fighting hoard, where they loaded their bows with strikers as quickly as they could. Her pale blue eyes scanned the group watching their every movement, as she gave out her orders and directed the line of fire. They stepped back and another volley of over a hundred arrows shot above the heads of the mass of fighting men. Treen watched the lines of men as they turned at the end of the road, and prepared to take their rifles off their shoulders. Arrows rained out of the sky and flashed and boomed, as the Cutters ignited and scattered and fell to the ground.

Hawk with his command had seen what was happening, and broke free to the far left flank, he signalled to Robbie who had stepped back from the fight to take a breath, and the bloodied and sweat streaked face of Robbie signalled back his approval. Robbie looked across the scene of devastation, as he took a greater stock of the fight, from the back. He shouted out his commands, and saw Ox and his group with Louisa break free to the right.

Rowan stumbled back and the gap in the men closed protecting him, his breath came in short bursts as he lifted his cloak and wiped away the blood and grime from his face, his cool grey eyes fixed on Robbie. "This is a tough fight my brother."

Robbie gave a long breath. "We always knew it would be, and this is just the start, but we have the edge, so trust in the power of Loxley, we will win this day." Rowan turned back to survey the scene.

"We have the advantage, but a long fight with no sleep has taken its toll I fear." He stretched out his aching arm. "I would have preferred a long night in a snug bed before facing this." Robbie patted his shoulder.

"Within the hour we will see the turn, and then my friend, it will be a soft bed at home, or gentle straw here tonight, either way I can guarantee you will sleep deep and safe." Rowan gave a smirk and spat the dirt from his mouth and smiled.

"Within the hour you say, I say let's push harder and end this in half the time." He lifted his sword and with a glint in his eye, Robbie smiled back at him, and both of them walked back towards the line of fighting men.

"Let's end this."

All over Loxley bells rang out, as the word from the gates moved swiftly round the stockade. The tall front gates saw five squads of bowman take up defending positions, as others trooped out along the walls either side of the tall wooden gates. Those on the roadway that ran up towards the large open square in front of the gates, panicked, and quickly pulled out weapons, as they waited to be hurried up the road and in through the gates to safety, several of their passengers sat frozen on their carts staring at the huge wall that had shuddered to a halt on the horizon, their hearts filled with fear.

Inside Loxley was chaos; Woodland Soldiers went into action taking up defensive positions. All along the high rough walls that were the protection of the town, Woodsmen, Bowmen, and Arms Men, swarmed up the ladders into position, all gates bar the large main gates were swung shut, as those outside were herded inside, and the large heavy timber reinforcing bars were dropped into place to hold them shut.

Inside the main hall in the centre of Loxley, Fuse was stood by the large table of coloured markers as he gave out his instructions. Haden sat at a table busy preparing the new orders from a large book that had been prepared in advance, as he finished each order, he handed it to a runner, who would sprint out of the hall onto a waiting horse and gallop off to the unit it was intended for.

The main door sprung open, and in walked the formidable figure of John Lox. He looked stern as he talked to one of his advisors, and walked at a fast pace towards the door at the back of the room to assume full command of the region in the absence of Robbie. Under his long black cloak, he wore his heavy sword, and had an axe slipped into his belt, he talked fast in a gruff voice, and those in the hall who were working frantically on their despatches, stepped quickly out of his way. Fuse gave another set of papers to one of the women and turned to follow John to the office, the young woman who looked very scared touched Fuse on the arm, and he turned and saw the fear in her eyes, his face softened and he smiled.

"Do not worry my dear, you are quite safe here, this has been planned for a very long time, so stay calm and breathe deep, for I am sure it will be a very long time before any Knox walks these paths, if at all, ever." She smiled and took a deep breath, Fuse gave another kind smile, and turned back towards the office, he hurried to catch up with John.

Somewhere back in the past, in the memory of mankind, and towards the south eastern border of Germany, Branna sat holding the reins of the horses as she trundled along in her caravan. It had been ten years in the world of men since she had left Avalon, and she had travelled far and wide across the water into new countries, and sampled the life of many cultures. Beside her sat a heavy set man called Boris; he had paid her for a ride to Bohemia his home. He was in his early twenties and had served as a good companion, and an even better lover on the long journey.

Branna had embraced her freedom, and had sampled much of life in her ten year travels. Free of the rules of her people and in the world of men, she had embraced her free lifestyle and had sampled many of the excess of men, she was a tough warrior as well as a learned scholar, and with her Fae abilities, it had been easy to outsmart many of the towns leaders and take full advantage of those within each village.

Leaving Avalon now felt like the smartest decision she had ever made, from the moment she snuck out via an open border in the far west of the realm, she had felt an inner strength grow within her, and her confidence slowly soared. It had been just days after leaving, when she had come across a hunter camping on the southern coast on the land, and he had invited her to share his meal. Over the meal he boasted of how he had sold the skins of many animals for a good purse of silver, understanding more and more of how the world of men worked helped Branna. The Hunter boasted of how the money attracted women, little did she realise that he had other ideas after sharing his meal, but as they ate, the Fae side of Branna began to feel his intent.

Branna did not want to kill, but when he decided he would rape her and tried to attack her, she was left with no choice, and after blinding him, the forces of the Merle rose up within her, and she killed him by crushing his head with a large stone. It sickened her, but as the day wore on she began to understand that she was in a world of cruel men who did not have the powers of the Fae, and that gave her the upper hand.

This was her first real act of evil, and although it was her hardest lesson, it became one she would over time savour more than any other. It was the first of many as she moved on, driven by her determination to prove herself in the world of men, and she eventually killed without emotion to lift her living standards and profit her own life. After many years she had built up a large hoard of gold and silver, and after spending four months with a traveller on the road with his horse drawn caravan, she slit his throat and took it for her own.

Her sexual conquests had been many, and she had quickly discovered a liking for the abundant feelings she experienced once she was out of Avalon with its rules and guidelines for everything in life. Behind her lay a trail of sexually gratified men and women, for Branna had discovered the pleasures of everyone. Her work on the darkness within the night sky had drawn her into the Merle, and whether or not she was aware of it, without realising, her Fae powers had become corrupted. Over the last ten years she had travelled, she found her hunger for more and more of the darker side of life was growing, and yet there was still one part of her that felt unfulfilled.

Her love of Ariel had been strong, and it had taken a good long while for her feelings to subside. Out in the wilds there had been several occasions when just for the briefest of moments, her Fae side fought the power of the Merle, and memories of her times with Ariel had flooded her mind. Branna knew she wanted to share her existence with another, but she was wise enough to know that it could not be with a member of the Fae, for the life she had grown to enjoy so much, would repulse any member of a Fae community. She had set her sights on finding a male she could meet as an equal, and yet to date, even though many men had satisfied her sexual needs, she had yet to meet one with the power to match her in combat. Little did she know that her fate was soon to change as she shared her journey with Boris to Bohemia.

She pulled on the reins and the horses slowed, as she pushed on the brake, and the caravan shuddered to a halt. Boris jerked in his seat; he had been dozing and was woken with a start. "What is it?"

Branna pointed to where the bank of the road fell away towards the river. "There is a man lay face down in the mud, I think he is hurt." She jumped down from her seat onto the road, as Boris leaned over to try and see.

Branna walked carefully down the bank towards the still figure, there was blood on the grass as she carefully approached, trying not to slip on the steep incline. Boris stood up as she bent down, and pulled back the cloak lined with thick matted fur, of what look like wolf pelt. Branna, seeing that he was face down, gripped at the green garment on the shoulder and gave a mighty pull; he was big and heavy set, and she had to yank him hard, before he rolled over revealing his shaved head and long plaited beard of soft brown.

This man was obviously a warrior of high standing, his belt and adornments were high quality gold, his sword was still in its scabbard and was of the highest quality, and yet it made no sense that he would be here alone, surely whoever had attacked him would have robbed him? Boris looked on as she moved across his body looking for the source of his wound, it was in his side, and it was clear it was deep and he had lost a lot of blood, she looked back to Boris who she had heard grunt with disapproval, he was stood at the top of the bank and he spat on the floor.

"Varisci scum, leave him to rot and let's get going, this road is not safe."

Branna did not understand. "Boris he is wounded, I cannot leave him here to die." Boris scowled.

"That is no man, he is the dog of all men, leave him to rot and do all of us a favour." He spat on the floor and turned back to the caravan.

"I care not who he is, look at his clothes, he is a man of wealth, I cannot leave him to die in the road, he may show us great gratitude and reward, now help me."

Boris turned reluctantly. "I will not." She felt her temper rising.

"You ride with me you help me." He pulled himself back up to the seat.

"I paid to ride with a beautiful woman for companionship, not to lift dogs off the road. The Varisci are devils hated by all the gods, why help him? He will not thank you; he will slit your throat and steal everything you have. I will not help any of that murderous thieving bastard's kind, if you want to save him, do it alone."

Boris sat back and watched as Branna struggled. The man was heavy, and it took her almost an hour for her to drag him up the bank, and onto the road behind the caravan. She unfolded the wooden step and unlocked the door and opened it wide, then using a shawl wrapped under his arms she dragged the body off the road and up into her small living space.

She felt exhausted once she had managed to lift him up and onto the bed, at the rear of her caravan. Once she was on board not really caring, Boris flicked the reins and drove the horses onwards leaving Branna alone with the heavy warrior to tend to his wounds.

He was dirty, and she could see the fever that burned on his brow, she stripped him down stopping as she looked at his naked muscle set body, she was impressed especially as she noted his manhood. "Wow I am sorry you are not awake, never have I seen such equipment." She giggled, as she cleaned his wound, and pulled her sewing kit towards her. His face burned, and she knew the struggle between life and death was to be his own.

Once she had tended his wound and tried to get him to drink the little of her potions as she could, it was growing dark, and Boris had pulled in for the night, and was building a fire to cook.

Branna covered him up after binding his wound and left him to his fight for life, from what she had seen of him, she knew he was strong, but only he could conquer his darkness alone now, and so she came out of the caravan and down the steps to where Boris was sat by the fire eating, she was not happy with his attitude, but she was intrigued. "Tell me of these Varisci?"

He scowled as he looked up at her. "I told you, they are murderous bastards, you can heal him and lay with him, if he does not rape you first, but he will still rob you and slit your throat. They are scum, demons in men's skins, they are hated by everyone." She looked back to her caravan and smiled.

"You can only rape what does not want to be taken; I would enjoy feeling him take me." She looked back to Boris who looked upset and she laughed. "Don't worry; it will take a long while before he is healed to full strength."

She pulled at the ties on her dress and it fell to the floor revealing her naked body, he gave a smile as she came towards him, and he pulled at his shirt to pull it over his head. She smiled as she knelt down and began to undo the threads of his pants. "I have lots of time and have not finished with you just yet."

There are some people, who no matter what kind of life they live, are destined not to be satisfied. It matters not that they have a safe and peaceful life living under the protection of another, or that they have a good livelihood, and want for very little, for they feel that they are entitled and deserve more.

Take a good long look at the world that surrounds you, little has changed in a thousand years, greed begets more greed, and the lust for power and control is everywhere. We are born to grow into school age, and we are taught to learn, as everyone must work to create the things we need, and also to earn the money to buy them. Everything has to be paid for, the water that falls free from the sky is owned by those with power, and we pay to have it. All land is owned, so we cannot walk out into a pleasant spot to build our own home, because the men of power have rules that say the land is not free, and neither are the trees and wild food that grow on it, as once was the case in the past.

We call ourselves free, but men of wealth and power own and control everything, including us. For although we believe we have the freedom to choose, we do not, we are caught in the mechanics of the men of power, who dictate what we learn so that we can work, and everything we make or sell, adds yet more money and power to them. We spend almost all our life working, and when we grow old, they throw us away and replace us with the young. It is the young who come fresh from learning, into the machine that drives the economies that has become mankind. The old are discarded, too old for much, we are left alone, no longer young enough to do the things we dreamed of in youth, worn out and left to fend for ourselves, but the men of power live on, clawing away and adding to their ever growing power and status.

It is often seen as the curse of the modern man. Since man created wealth and currency, he has been on a slippery slope that has allowed those who lust to control everything, especially the people. Millionaire is not a term coined for modern man, all of history is built upon them, as from the moment one man grew in stature, and was large enough to dictate the terms of a tribe, his road to the lust for wealth and power began to grow.

One such man was a mighty warrior born to the good hunter Vulgan, and named Berengar, and he became a legend within the tribe of the Varisci, a group of mountain men living in a region known then as Sachsen.

Berengar was a skilled fighter, and in his youth, he was a good natured boy, but the life of a hunter followed by the endless turf wars between the tribes changed him. There were few who could match him in combat, and when he was chosen to protect the tribe leader Grembald, his family were very proud, although even they did not see how the horrors he saw, and the lessons he would learn under the tyranny of one of the most vile tribal leaders to date, would change him forever.

Combat was almost a way of life in the hard days before the men of the crucifix journeyed into the western lands. It was a hard life living off the land, and hunting in the vast forested areas across the high lands of Sachsen. In the times marked by the sword and the blood of conflict, protecting what you had was an essential part of survival. Berengar was loyal to his tribe, and fought with bravery in the battles with those who wanted to steal the land, and take the stocks and supplies of the village.

Grembald was different; he wanted more than a few miles of territory to farm and hunt in, he wanted everything he saw. Slowly under his lead, the tribe moved from protection to the attack of other villages. Grembald encourage the killing of everyone, he raped and stole, and burned away his enemies, pulling in greater rewards to line his long house, and expand his territory.

Berengar was Grembald's second in command, and he was an impressionable young man, who soon grew accustomed to wealth, fine clothing, and wine. With Berengar as his protector, there were few who could stand up against Grembald, and disagree with his raids and the killing of innocents. Slowly the people of the tribe began to despise Berengar for protecting Grembald, who not only raided towns for his wealth, but demanded ever increasing tributes from his own people, and behind his back they plotted his downfall.

One spring when Grembald took his men into the lower valleys to raid some of the more affluent towns, the warriors came across a village where the men had left to hunt. The village was filled with women and children, and the few remaining men were either too old or too young to fight. Grembald pulled his men together to give out his orders, and as they sat in the trees and planned the slaughter of everyone things changed rapidly.

Enough was enough, and some of the men turned on them, and attacked without notice. Caught off guard, Berengar was stabbed in the back, and fell down a steep bank onto the river's edge. Grembald was slain and beheaded, and his men withdrew, and returned to their own village, high up the slopes to present their prize of Grembald's head, and select a new and fairer leader. Vulgan the father of Berengar, was by far the fairest, and although grief stricken to hear of his son's fate, he felt the greatest shame due to his son's behaviour, and he was chosen to lead the tribe.

Berengar's younger brothers were outraged and left the camp in search of him, whom they knew to be badly wounded. Yet as they reached the village outskirts, Vladimir and Otto found there was no trace of their brother. Someone back in the village said he had been dragged screaming into the underworld to pay for the evil he had supported, some say he was met by a spirit who cleansed his soul, and carried him away to a mystical land. After a long weary search for over a week along the river, they met a trader travelling from Bohemia who told them there was a traveller who swore that Berengar had been rescued by a mystical woman he knew by the name of Raven, and she had taken him and nursed him, and then travelled onto Bohemia with him.

Even back in the oldest times, Bohemia was rural, and travelling through it, there was a feeling it would change little as the years progressed. The people were kind, gentle, and simple living; they worked the land and crafted all they would ever require from the world that surrounded them. The country was beautiful, filled with valleys of lush green pastures and forests of evergreen mixed with deciduous trees. Wild flowers decorated every corner, and ran alongside the lanes and in deep drifts across fields, and for Branna who had travelled far since she had left Avalon, it came across as being paradise, and she felt a stirring within her to linger and enjoy the ease of pace. Boris who had been sulking for the last half of the journey wasted no time leaving her, and he took up with a cloth trader, and left Branna alone with the wounded warrior.

It was late spring, and Berengar had fought through his fever and was finally awake after burning with delirium for almost two weeks. Branna pulled in on the edge of a large village, into a pasture near by a fast flowing river. There was a plentiful supply of wood for the stove, and she found an abundance of rabbits and wild fruits and leaves she could stew for food.

Berengar was at first startled as he woke, but as he tried to sit, the searing pain from his insides soon convinced him to stay as he was and lie back and relax. He spoke Sachsen, and yet one of the gifts of the Fae Ofmoon was to understand all tongues, and so soon Branna sat and offered him a meal, and told him of how she discovered him lying half dead by the river, and had dragged him up to the caravan and given him the aid he would need to recover.

Berengar had no choice but to respectfully thank her, under the rule of his tribe, he owed his life to her, and it was a debt he could only pay off by saving hers. Branna was a skilled warrior, as he saw by the weapons she carried, and he knew that for now, he belonged to her until such time as he could recover the strength to find a way to pay back the life he owed her.

What began as mistrust grew into dependence. The wound took a long time to heal, and as frustrated as Berengar felt, he had no choice but accept his fate as he slowly recovered his strength, and over the time of his healing, he grew a fondness for the straight talking, hard edged member of the Fae. One night as he sat in front of the caravan next to the fire, having eaten a good solid meal and drunk a few large tankards of ale, something Branna had traded in the village for medicines, he slowly began to feel a sense of trust.

Finally, after many weeks of silence, he told Branna his story of how he had been betrayed by his own people and left for dead. Branna listened quietly, and when he had finished, she took a long taste of her ale and thought for a moment, before lifting her head to meet the fixed stare of Berengar.

"The way I see it, you must return and recover the strength you once held by making an example of all of those in the town that betrayed you. Grembald was leader, and you were a loyal warrior in his service, but you were also in service to the people of the town whom you protected. They betrayed you my friend, they must pay for their lack of trust in you. I would say grow to full strength and return, and take your anger out on those who deserve it."

Berengar shook his head. "It is of no use, I am but one man against a whole tribe, I can best most men, but alone against the Varisci, I will not prevail." Branna gave a smile.

"But you are not alone you have me." Berengar gave the first mighty laugh he had since he had awoken in the caravan, he slapped hard at his thigh as his bald head shone in the firelight, and his cheeks lifted to reveal the whiteness of his teeth. Branna did not at first understand the joke.

"You are a mightily fine woman Branna, such as I have never met before, but forgive me, for as much as I have learned about you, I fear that even for a woman of such skill with a sword, we would not last long against the tribesmen of my region. I truly am grateful for your kindness and offer of assistance." He smiled and she felt his attraction, for there was a glee mixed in with the formidable intensity of the fighter that radiated out, and she found it very alluring. Branna leaned forward and crawled slowly across to the sitting figure of the warrior.

"It appears amusing, and that is a good thing, for neither you nor your people are aware of the things I have learned in my life. None know of the powers I hold, and terrors I can unleash, for there in that plain looking caravan I have the means to wipe out all the Varisci and their enemies at once."

She lifted a hand and touched his cheek, her dark eyes twinkling with malice as his stared deep into hers. "Berengar if you swear here to me now that you will give me your loyalty, I can assure you that with me at your side the tribe will fall to their knees and beg for your pardon. From that moment you shall rule as no king ever has. Give yourself to me, and the world of men will kneel at your feet and whimper like the wounded animals they are."

His smile faded, as he looked into the depths of her dark black eyes. "Do not mock me woman, for you know I would hand over my soul for such a thing." She smiled.

"Then join your soul to mine, and I will show you how to do it."

For ten years Branna had travelled and seen as much of the world as she felt she had wanted. Through all of her travels she had delved deeper and deeper into the darkness that surrounded the world, and had been overwhelmed by its power and force. In the process of mastering the force of darkness, she had pushed her body to the limits, and as a result she had grown strong and powerful. Her lust for power and the excesses of life grew more intense, and although she could best most men in combat and drinking, her one desire was to meet a man who would match her lust and desire for power. As she rested on her knees before Berengar, she knew she had met the one man who shared the lust that ate at her insides. His eyes betrayed him as she looked deep into his soul, and saw the chaos at the heart of him, his desire for revenge was strong, and within that she knew she could see that finally she had met an equal.

That night as she lay with him and tore at his skin, bit him, and kissed him, she felt the raw power of this man of the Varisci as he pounded into her, and she knew her search for something powerful and a place in this world where she was an equal, was within the arms of this powerful warrior. After three hours of passion, as he lay in the grass with sweat on his brow, she summoned the Merle to reach down and touch her, and as it did, she took the tail feather of a mature raven and plunged it deeply into his chest.

Then with the tip red with his blood, as he gasped and strained from the intense pain, she drew on his skin the runes of power that would mark his soul, and connect him to her for eternity. In the darkness away from the eyes of the world, under a veil of total protection, Branna swore her pact with Berengar of the Varisci tribe, and as the darkness surrounded them, it seeped deep under their skin, and seduced their souls to become one united in the blackness.

This was the moment missed by those of power. No one would realise what the pairing of two of such power, hidden from sight within a circle of darkness, would bring in later years. It would take the Green Lord hundreds of years to finally understand that the bonding of these two would create a line so dark and corrupt; they would infect the world with malice. From that moment as the darkness began to seep into the world, the magic began to work and weave in a way unseen to create a line to match the darkness. The result would lead to a confrontation, but the outcome was still unseen, only time would finally tell who would rise victorious, and so the scene was set, and the world would have to silently watch and wait.

CHAPTER THREE

SEEKING UNDERSTANDING

Deep in the heart of the forest of time, the old lord of the woodland had completed his journey, and returned to his seat at the top of the highest mountain, where he sat in the seat of heavy stone, and viewed the worlds he had created with all of the ruling council. The changes within him were now complete, and his robes had coloured to the rich darkened red of a cold autumnal mornings leaves. His beard that had always appeared to be filled with the many hues of the green grasses, was now mustard yellow mixed with a soft hazel brown. His skin had paled to a faint grey brown, and yet his eyes still shone like berries at the end of summer, and held a slight twinkle that sparkled as he cast them onto the pool of crystal clear water before him.

Dropping his hand inside his pocket, he lifted out a daisy of the purest white with a rich buttercup yellow centre, and cast it gently into the pool. "Hear me my Daughter, for I have need of your words." The water gave a ripple and changed in colour to a pale mint green, and two bright blue eyes appeared within an old lined face.

"I hear you Father and centre of all things." Hearne smiled as the picture expanded and he saw the daughter who although now quite old, was still as precious and filled with life as he had known her in her youth when he swung her in his arms.

"Daughter speak to me of the events in your realms, for I fear the mistakes of our past will now show themselves to us, in the evil beset to the children of our line."

Opal sat quietly watching the autumnal face of her father in the large silver bowl at the centre of her circle. She had felt the wave of fear pass through all the realms, and had been watching the events at Loxley. "Father she has made the move we saw in a time unwritten, the black walls have risen, and Loxley is encircled within them."

Hearne understood, he had seen this in the blue orb given him by Cal in the woodland when Sapphire had given her life force to protect him. "Their plans remain unchanged as before, I truly see the wisdom of our Runestone, for things are very different now."

"They are Father, for Runestone is free in the world, and is in command of her powers, I feel her moving as I speak back to Loxley, as before, the dark powers cannot prevent her passage past the walls into her own realm. Sapphire has had trouble, but she is Fae and with Rune as her guide, she too has found a way in via the Mere, for that is also Fae land, and as centre of a Fae circle, Sapphire cannot be prevented from walking on any Fae territory. My daughter remains at the cathedral tending to the wounded, but she has a greater power than expected by Morgan, for Stephanie walks with her father's gifts and the Merle will never be a barrier to her. We have hope my father, Loxley is inconvenienced, but it is not the trap as it was before."

Hearne gave a small smile, and nodded his head slowly as he thought. "I feel their hope, but also their fears, although there is a new found confidence within my young wolf, for he is taking the fight to the snakes, and in that I feel his wisdom. But we must look deeper my daughter, for through all of this we have been blind, and there is still yet much work to be done. In one of our worlds a door remains open that powers the darkness, you must search as I will and help Runestone, for if we are to be victorious, we must understand more of the errors of the past and rectify them."

"I am already looking my Father, and I have set Sapphire on the path of discovery in the affairs of Morgan, Runestone I have no need to guide, she is already deeply connected to her table which seeks the source of the Merle in all the worlds, her heart beats as strong as my mother's, and it is her greatest guide in this matter."

"Her table seeks this Fae who is unknown to all of us, many answers may lie in this Ena, you must aide her in this search, for there I feel lay many answers."

"I will Father, fear not I too have asked questions of many, and sent them into the worlds to seek her out."

"This is good, you have done well, but there again I expected nothing less of you, go with peace and work for their cause, I shall seek the council of others in this matter and speak with you often." Opal smiled and blew a kiss to her father.

"Until then my Father and Lord, I shall do all I can."

The picture in the pool faded, and Hearne sat back in his seat, his mind playing back through time all of the events leading up to this moment, there was something that at the time appeared insignificant, and yet he understood more than ever, that whatever it was they missed it was the most important moment in all of their history.

Sapphire burst out of her blue window at the garden gate, Rune was already at the glass doors shouldering her bow. "What the hell has happened I felt this huge burst of something, to be honest I am not sure just what, and when I tried to jump towards it I was bounced back, so I homed in on you, I figured you would know?"

Rune stepped down the steps and gave a smile. "History it appears it trying to repeat itself, we have a wall around us." Sapphire looked shocked.

"What? How?" Rune came up to the gate.

"It has always been their plan Saff."

"But I thought it was unwritten?"

"It was, they are repeating themselves in this timeline that's all." Sapphire gave a long sigh.

"So it was all pointless?"

Rune smiled. "Not at all, look their plans will be similar whatever we do, it's been on their table always, but this time things are very different."

"In what way, I am not sure I follow you?" Rune stepped through the gate and patted Sapphire on the shoulder.

"Relax Saff, look the last time they did this, most of us were dead, trapped or lost, things are so different now and we are all together to deal with this. Let her think she has the upper hand, because I would think about now they are all giving each other warm fuzzy hugs, and patting each other on the backs, and for now I am happy to let them do that. Whilst they celebrate their minds are occupied away from us and we have work to do, and answers to seek. I was a little distracted by the cathedral, but I am home and the kids are safe and I am back on her trail."

"Wow you are a lot calmer than I am Rune, and to be honest the only thing warm and fuzzy in their camp is those foul dogs, I am not sure they like each other enough to be that nice. I must admit the thought of everyone here caught, walled in a box gives me the jitters." Rune lifted a small box out from her bag and handed it to her.

"Take this, it has the last of the blessings from Iona in it, go to the gates and then work your way round all the wall scattering the contents every 50 feet or so, that will open a clear path for all Fae to enter any aspect of Loxley they wish to, and strengthen the protections I have placed around us, then come straight back to me."

Sapphire nodded and opened her window, Rune turned to say something as Saff jumped into the light, there was a bright flash, and Sapphire came bouncing back through the window, and slid at speed across the grass with a squeal. Rune gave a chuckle. "I was about to say take a horse, but you jumped." She gave another giggle as she leaned down and gave the slightly dazed Saff a hand up. "Once you have scattered the pieces, you will be able to bounce all over Loxley, but before you do that, here for the time being is the only place you can jump to, as it is also Fae."

Sapphire shook the stars out of her head. "Yeah right... Ignore me I am stupid." Rune lifted her up and helped pat her down with a smile, then as Sapphire took the horse reins off the rail, Rune opened her bright purple window. "Hey Rune, how come you can jump anywhere?"

Standing in front of her window she turned back and gave a bright smile. "I am the Redstone Sapphire, no one can prevent me walking wherever I choose, it's kinda cool eh?"

Sapphire gave a giggle. "Yeah, pretty awesome." Rune stepped through the window and it closed behind her, Sapphire lifted herself up onto the horse, and set off at a gallop for the Sacred Wood Road.

Across the valley, the wall of high black stone cast a shadow onto the trees and wild flowers. For a while they had bobbed freely in the breeze, but with the addition of the wall, the breeze stopped and a melancholy of stillness covered the plant life. Those close to the wall shrivelled and died as the touch of the cold black surface drained the life right out of them.

High above on the battlements Mason Knox stood next to his General, Mark Richard Dale, a few feet away stood Dana and Lance. Dale watched Loxley through his binoculars with a satisfied smile on his face. "You were right Mason, look at them scurry around like ants in panic, I am glad we waited, this is so much better than I expected, we have all the rats in one basket."

Mason leaned on the wall, his long sleek white hair fluttered around his shoulders, against his heavy black cloak. "Well not all of them old pal, we do still have their leader bashing away at our little diversion in Lincoln, but that suits me fine, he will not be coming home any time soon." He gave a happy burst of laughter. Dale followed the lines of the tall wooden wall with his binoculars.

"They are acting exactly as planned and have deployed more guards to the walls, your mother has been very useful indeed, I can predict all of their movements now they are sealed inside."

"Yes, I must admit the old girl has finally got her act together and pulled off a good one, it took long enough. She gets far too involved with all their little comings and goings, I have told her many times, just get them in one place and then seal them in, it's always been the most sensible move, but she does insist on her interfering with everything they do." Dale nodded.

"Now we have them where we want them, I will overlook her more dramatic moments, let her do whatever she wants now, I am happy to focus on this part of the operation with no interference." Mason gave him a hearty pat on the back.

"Come on we have a fine feast awaiting us, you can stand here as often as you like now and plan your tactical game, tonight we celebrate the start of the end, and soon we will be building a great city on top of splinters, to mark the centre of our empire, and the ultimate defeat of our wood chopper."

Mason walked down the wall and stood beside Lance; he lifted his arm to his shoulder and pulled him into a soft squeeze. "Did I not tell you this would come? Look at your future boy, for it lies on what will be the ruins of what you see over there. Within the week you will walk on their graves, and lay the first stones of a new city of power, a power both of us will wield side by side."

Lance gave a smirk. "I cannot wait to bulldoze that foul pile of wood into the earth forever, I want a line of poles with the head of each them out front for the world to see what happens when you cross this family, only then will I feel the job is done and done properly. No one will ever stand against us again."

Mason gave a hearty laugh and winked at Dana. "Spoken like a true Knox." She smiled as he took her hand. "Come we have a feast and wine to celebrate, I am feeling quite in the spirit of celebration, so let's all dine and toast our success."

Mason was more jubilant than anyone had ever seen him, for him it was a defining moment, as he finally saw his years of planning fall into place. His dream was so close he could almost taste it, and it filled him with a feeling of excitement that he had never known before.

Steph sat at the side of the huge doors, with her back to the high smooth yellow stone wall, and sipped from the battered and dinted metal cup. Her hair was damp and hung limply to her shoulders, as she watched the men who had been relieved walking slowly under the archway into the cathedral grounds. All around her the floor was littered with men lying down after a hard fight, many had cuts and scratches which were being attended to by the novice nuns. The very badly wounded were placed on make shift stretchers and taken inside the large cooler building, which now resembled more of a hospital than place of worship.

Jay walked into the yard, and spotting Steph made her way through the resting woodsmen towards her. She had slipped off her tunic and waistcoat so she wore only a dark green vest to cool her down. Her usually sleek black hair was matted and wet and stuck to the sides of her face, she looked utterly exhausted as she slid down the wall beside Steph. "I am done for."

Steph lifted the bottle from her side and passed it to her. "Rough day for everyone by the look of it, how is it going out there?" Jay took a long swig from the bottle and poured some into her hand to wash the blood off her face.

"It's as scary as hell out there, I have seen some tough fighting with you guys, but those monks are insane. I hit one with three arrows and he still kept running at Rowan. It has calmed a little, we have pushed them back onto the road and they are caught in a cross fire from our other guys along each side of the road, they are retreating where they can." Steph gave a nod.

"Robbie wanted them there, how is he, have you seen him?"

"Yeah, he is ok, although he is madder than the monks; I have never seen him fight as hard. Rowan and he have really dished it back at the Cutters, I think it's the first time I have seen him match Jett stroke for stroke."

"We got word to him about Loxley, I am sure he feels the need to finish this and get back home." Jay turned and looked at Steph with a sad look.

"It's true then, there is a wall round the whole place, a few of us were not that certain?" Steph gave a nod.

"It wasn't unexpected Jay, Rune thought this would happen, we are all ready and prepared for this, Jess has abundant food stocks, and I think Mason thinks we are trapped outside, but he has underestimated Rune, she is there at the moment with John and Jess working things out with them, do not worry, there are doors inside Loxley no one knows about."

"So I will be able to see my mum, dad, and sister?" Steph patted her knee.

"Hey trust us, we are woodsmen." She gave a chuckle. "Morgan thinks she is in control, she has not realised yet that Rune is the one here who controls things, just watch and see." Steph got up and stretched her legs. "Jay you are one of us, we will all work our hardest to defeat them, I know at times it looks bleak, but believe me, all of this was seen coming and we have prepared. Strange as it may sound, this is the moment Robbie has wished for, because now is finally the time that he can lead our people to end all of the pain."

Jay gave a nod, and closed her eyes, and leaned back on the warm stone. "I feel so tired." Steph smiled.

"Up all night at Canterbury, and most of the day here, I am not surprised. I am needed inside, just relax and recover your strength; I would imagine the others will regroup here when it's done." Steph left Megan resting with the sweat dripping off her hair, and went back into the cathedral to continue tending the wounded. Megan gave a long breath and relaxed, a little sleep was all she needed.

The day was entering the early evening when the Cutters mixed with the Brethren, finally backed away down the road. From the wide open plain that ran from the base of the Cathedral right up each side the road leading east, the area was littered with the dead and wounded. Woodsmen ran round collecting the injured and ferrying them up the short hill to the medics inside the cathedral. Robbie with Rowan mustered his generals and they all gave their reports, it was clear to see that having the hooded man amongst them had boosted everyone's morale.

It had been several hours since the combat had ceased when an escort was spotted riding slowly towards the open clearing down the road. Four heavily set men rode bearing a long pole on which was tacked a white flag. Treen stood her ground at the end of the road, and waited for them to approach. Her right arm had a torn sleeve revealing a bandage on her arm where she had been cut, she looked tired and dirty, and her usually bouncy curls of her red hair, hung limp and dank. Her bright orange eyes surveyed the riders approaching, Hawk stood up with Maddy, and walked slowly towards her side, as the riders came closer and stopped.

The rider in the centre came forward; he was a large stocky man wearing a burgundy coloured tunic that bore the crest of a large golden ornate cross. His face was dirty and it was obvious he had been in the fight. On his side he wore a sword of high quality with a jewel encrusted hilt. He viewed Treen as he nudged his horse on, whilst the others waited quietly behind him. Treen felt the heels of her boots dig into the soft earth as her hand rested on the hilt of her sword. "Name yourself Cutter, what ezz it you are wanting here?"

The rider appeared calm as Bear and Big John observed him from the side of the road with great interest. Maddy and Hawk stood resolute slightly back from Treen as they stared at the rider waiting for his response, which appeared to be something he was giving great consideration too.

"I am Bart, and I am no Cutter Madam, and you are?" Treen gave a slight nod.

"I am General Du Luc of Morbihan, and commander of the armies to Lord Loxley, what ezz it you want Cutter?"

It was obvious the remark stung, and his horse sensing his discomfort moved slightly as he gripped hard at the reins, he adjusted his seat trying not to allow her insolence to sting, but it did, and it was obvious, his words held a little more grit than he was willing to show.

"I would seek an audience with your Lord of Loxley if he is here, we have injured and our dead to attend to as is our faith and our way, which may I remind you again General Du Luc, is not Cutter." Treen shrugged.

"You fight with Cutters, and smell like Cutters, you may ave a cross on your shirt, but in my mind you eez a Cutter. I will send your word to Lord Loxley who as you say ezz here, and if he wishes to accept your request, he will give you terms Cutter."

She carried a slight smirk as she saw the annoyance in his eyes, somewhere behind her she heard Robbie's voice, Brother Bart looked up to see the dirty figure of Robbie approaching with Rowan, Jett and Blades, all of them looked tired after the hard fight. Bart slipped his leg over the horse, and dropped to the ground, around him he heard the clatter of arrows as they rested on bows, and as he glanced to his side, he saw the long line of woodsmen who had appeared from nowhere all aiming at him.

Robbie walked past Treen, and patted her shoulder; he stopped four feet in front of Brother Bart who gave a short nod of respect. "My Lord, I am Brother

Bart, I seek your permission to collect our wounded and administer the rights of the dead."

Robbie gave a nod of respect back, his dark eyes taking the measure of the man before him. "Brother, your wounded are inside the cathedral being attended to, although I have no objections to unarmed members of your men collecting them. I can assure you they have been treated with respect, and given the best of care. As for your lost troops, again I have no problems with unarmed men collecting them, so you may perform whatever rights you are required to do for them. But I will state this clearly to you; no armed member of your forces will pass this point and live, so please ensure you honour the respect shown to you."

Bart was a little surprised, but he gave a nod of acceptance, and turned back to the men on horses. "Go back and provide the terms, organise a collection detail." He turned back towards Robbie. "I am grateful to you for the care that has been provided to my men, we shall honour your terms."

Robbie gave a nod back and turned to Rowan and Treen. "Pass the word back and ensure the wounded are gathered together and brought out of the cathedral to be collected by the Cutter detail." He turned back to Brother Bart who was watching with interest as the woodsmen across the wide plain were gathering up their own fallen. "Is there anything else you would require Brother?"

Bart was uncertain, he stared into Robbie's eyes, and it was obvious that he hated Robbie intensely. "Actually there is..." He stared for a moment as if looking for the right words. "Tell me this Lord of Loxley, why all this?" He licked his lips to wet them. "I mean you and your heathen followers have no interest in a house of God, so why bother defending something so meaningless to you? I am intrigued as to why you would lose the lives of so many to defend something that is merely stone and wood to you?"

Robbie smiled, he knew Bart was trying to work him out, he turned back to look at the splendour of the cathedral. "It is a little more than stone and wood Brother, it is a symbol of free people." He turned back to face the Brother. "You are a man of faith, the faith that built this building, I understand your point of view, but sadly I feel you completely miss our heathen views." Bart scowled at Robbie.

"And they are what exactly?" Robbie smiled.

"We may be heathen, but we stand for all the people, we defend those who cannot defend themselves. Your men of faith did unspeakable acts of slaughter in that building you prize so highly, and not I may add to heathens, but unarmed men of your own faith. The cathedral sits on the southern boundary of my realm, and as long as it does all people will be free to enter in peace under my protection, so may I advise you that your armed Brethren and Cutters are not welcome as long as you bear arms against the innocent, as I will always defend them. I hope Brother; you have an answer to your question?"

Robbie stepped back as Brother Bart gave him a deeper scowl, he turned back to his horse. "This is not over yet Loxley." Robbie turned back for a moment.

"I didn't think it was Brother. Stick to the terms and clear your people, break them and you will face swords against you."

"I understand, there is little need to repeat them." He climbed up onto his horse and pulled angrily at the reins. Robbie stepped back as Bart swung the horse round, and then kicked it hard into the sides, and galloped off back down the road. Jett gave a grunt.

"I wouldn't mind taking that sword from his cold dead hand, did you see the hilt, whoa that was pretty." Rowan gave a smile as he waited for Robbie.

Robbie stared down the road as he watched the soldiers of Mason and the church slowly withdraw; he gave a long sigh as if relieved for the moment. Rowan moved closer and lifted his hand to Robbie's shoulder. "Are you OK?"

Robbie gave a nod as he turned his head to see the endless fields of trampled mud, and red blood soaked water that had formed puddles between the dead and the dying. "This is such a waste Rowan." There really was little response, as he too observed the hundreds of dead from both sides that littered the fields; he gave a soft squeeze of Robbie's shoulder to reassure him, Robbie lifted his sleeve and wiped the side of his dirty face.

"Too many good men have been wounded or lost in battle. Too many mothers have wept at the loss of their sons, those left standing this day will call themselves the victors, but no one has won here, for if the price to be paid is the spilled blood of good men, then there can be no victory for anyone. War is caused by those few who yearn for greed or power, and their blood is always too precious to spill on the grass, so innocent men die in their place. Those that start wars always survive them with greater riches or power, and many families weep for the loss of their young. Tell me Rowan, where is the honour or victory in that?"

"We fight for neither of those things Robbie, we fight for survival, for if we lose, the likes of Mason will wipe us from this land forever." Robbie gave a silent nod and turned to face him.

"It is all we can do, but think about the cost in lives, I do not do this for money or power, and if I could choose now in this moment the result, it would be to resolve this without bloodshed."

"You have no argument here Robbie, but sadly Mason will never sit and talk, he aims to enslave everyone, and he aims to continue until he himself is taken down, what choice do we have?" Robbie shook his head.

"We have none. For now we tend to our wounded and supervise the rights of the dead. Watch the road and ensure they adhere to our arrangement." Rowan gave a nod.

"They will be back Robbie; you do know that don't you?" Robbie shook his head.

"Not soon, this was a test and we prevailed, they know they are in for a fight, this was Mason flexing a muscle to see how we would react." Robbie started to walk back towards the Cathedral. "Rowan, we need to finish up here and return to Loxley as quickly as possible, I will leave a strong force here under the command of Haughton, he understands how we shall play this here. I want all the Specialist's on Loxley turf for a short time, it is important we are seen at home by our own people, after that we have a wall to bring down, and in that I am hoping Rune has the answer."

"Yeah, I am with you. Just as a matter of interest, can we actually get back into Loxley, from what I heard there is a wall completely surrounding it?"

Robbie gave a laugh and patted Rowan on the back. "Rowan you disappoint me, walls fall, remember Dunnottar?" He gave a smile.

"How could any of us ever forget it?" He gave a shudder and Blades and Jett giggled as the group walked down the road back towards the safety of the old cathedral. Robbie finally felt like the battle was on, and after planning and waiting for so long, rather than worry, he actually felt relieved. This was not what he wanted, but he knew at least this was something he was well prepared for.

Robbie was right, neither the Brethren, nor the Cutters returned that day. As agreed, a Cutter force arrived, disarmed and brandishing white flags, to collect their dead and wounded. The Woodsmen helped lift the injured onto the carts which were instructed to park at the bottom of the road from the cathedral, and the wounded were carried out and helped up onto the long row of carts. Robbie deliberately kept the Cutters as far away from the cathedral as possible, as inside, the Specialists joined the Outlaws, and members of the church, to ship as many of the wounded to the House of Good Hope as was possible. Once Sister Carla and her crew were filled up to maximum, Robbie ordered the rest to be taken to Loxley.

As Steph oversaw the operation, most of the Specialists returned to Loxley to get a very well earned rest, apart from Treen, Maddy, and Blades with Fox, who all stayed to help organise the defence of Lincoln with General Haughton, and the Howling Wolves. By the time Robbie and Rowan arrived at the Village Hall, it was almost midnight and they were entering their thirty eighth hour without any sleep, and both of them looked exhausted.

Rowan sat next to the table covered with coloured markers, as Fuse who had been on duty for most of the day walked slowly round briefing Robbie. "As soon as it happened My Lord, we sent out riders to plot just how big and how far the wall extended, and as Scarlet said may happen, it is true, we are completely surrounded." Robbie gave a nod; Rune had warned him this might happen, so it was no surprise to him at all. He looked at the woodland to the east of Loxley.

"What about the escarpment?" Fuse took off his glasses to clean them and gave a knowing smile.

"I wondered if that would draw your attention. You are wise to look east My Lord, and indeed I think that is one place that Mason may have overextended his reach."

Fuse walked round the table where for the moment a series of pencil dots marked the places where they had been given confirmation of the exact location of the wall. "The problem with the escarpment is that it rises up above the level of Loxley, although from here we see little of it because it is tree lined, and of course we have a seventy foot wooden wall on our horizon." Rowan blinked his eyes awake and leaned forward in his seat, as Robbie got up and came round the table, Fuse pointed to the lowland below the escarpment.

"Clearly Mason does not really understand the lay of the land, or at least his mother does not. As both of you know the escarpment is a high wall of limestone and at its base is the buried remains of the old industrial city of Sheffield. It's a flat land for miles as it just collapsed into the earth. The thing is, Mason must have marked a line on a map without thinking of the contours of the land." Rowan understood as did Robbie, but Rowan was faster off the mark.

"So he built his wall on the flat land? The escarpment is far higher so it overlooks his wall."

"Precisely General. It may appear at first to not be that big a problem, after all Loxley is still enclosed, but it will allow us as they say, to see what they are doing." Robbie nodded.

"This is good; we will get a bird's eye view of their routine, and that I can really use to work out things like their guard rotation, which could be useful if we strike at them." Rowan got up out of his seat and came over to Robbie's side to get a closer look at the map.

"Bugger their routine Robbie, what I want to know is can we hit them from the escarpment? I mean we still have catapults; can we drop them a house warming gift or two?"

"What, like welcome to the neighbourhood.... Boom!" Rowan gave a smile.

"It won't hurt to look; can we get someone over there Fuse?"

"Already on it, the Night Strikers for now have been assigned under the watchful eye of Joe Whitmore, and have set off already, we felt they have been very busy as of late, so we have given them a lighter task, I feel it will rest them up for when the real action starts." Robbie agreed.

"Yeah, they have proved to be a very effective force, but we have had them all over the place at all hours of the day, some regular duty with long rest periods will help them, nice thinking Fuse. So we have Rayne in the northern woods, Davie is at the gate, and Joe with the Strikers has the east, I take it John is watching the west?" Fuse gave a nod as he watched Robbie looking at the map start to formulate a plan.

"All the Arms Men have wall duty, but there are far more on the west side My Lord, you are very astute indeed. Although I will add, that at this moment I feel they are watching everything we do, we have spotted their watchers on the walls, so I would suggest some rest; I think it is obvious they will try to work out our routine also before they strike. We have men out as we speak gathering as much information as possible, by tomorrow we will have every detail mapped out, and that will be the time to sit and plan our next move." Rowan gave a nod to Robbie as he looked up from the table.

"Good point, Ok I really need to get to bed, I have forgotten when I last closed my eyes, Skip is at home and we have night staff, so get some sleep yourself Fuse, you will have Skip and Treen back here tomorrow after they have rested up, and we will talk more with John." Robbie lifted his bow and bag, and swung his quiver onto his shoulder. "I will see you all in the morning, although if anything happens, send a rider or get one of Rune's family to wake her up and tell her."

Fuse gave a smile and a short bow. "Goodnight My Lord, goodnight General sleep well both of you, you do look exhausted."

Robbie and Rowan went out to where a stable boy waited with their horses; both of them mounted up, and began a gentle trot back up the dirt track to the Hawthorn lined lane that led up through the farm, and onto the Sacred Wood Road. Neither of them spoke much, possibly due to their sleepiness. When the track to the left appeared Rowan patted Robbie on the shoulder, and kicked his horse onward down the lane, as Robbie turned into the trees and headed for the Mere, and Rowan rode home to his warm bed and the waiting Jade.

When Robbie walked in through the glass doors to the house, he heard voices from the kitchen; he made his way wearily towards the door, as he heard Rune talking with Filomena the Fae helper from Iona. He opened the door as Rune asked the question; Filomena looked up smiled, and turned back to Rune who was sitting at the table with her.

"No Runestone, as far as I know there has never been any member in Florae called Ena. I know the name, it was used back in the old days before Bridget came from Erin, but since we forged the Isle of Florae, it was classed as too old, we embraced a more modern approach to names from that time, names more based in the minerals and flowers." Rune gave a smile to Robbie and got up and walked round the table to kiss his cheek.

"You look tired, go and sleep, I will be up shortly." He gave her a nod and turned in the doorway, and Rune turned back to Filomena. "What about Berengar is that a name you have heard before?"

Filomena thought for a moment. "I am not sure, I am sure I have heard it before, but that is not a name of Fae origin, although I am sure I have heard it, it was a very long time ago, I think I will have to give it some thought as I am going back a great many years. I am sure I remember hearing something, I will talk to Isolde tomorrow, she may remember it." Rune gave a nod.

"Ok then, I too am tired, I will call it a night and go and see the children before I get some sleep, thank you Filomena, you have been helpful." Filomena got up from her seat at the table.

"If there is nothing more, I will check the children and settle for the night." She walked round the kitchen towards the door as Rune put her cup in the sink, and as she went to open the door, she stopped and turned back to Runestone. "I am not sure this helps, but if I am right Ena in the old language, I think meant Fiery, you know sort of passionate, Isolde will know for sure, she has done a great deal of study on the old language." Rune thought for a moment.

"Well, it explains some of her behaviour; she was certainly passionate about getting even with Le Fey. Thanks, it does help a little." Filomena gave a smile and a small curtsy.

"Night Miss."

"Night Filomena, sleep well."

It had been a very long day, and as Rune locked the doors and turned down the oil lamps, she had a lot on her mind. Her experience with Morgan le Fey was very illuminating; her behaviour towards Hornet and her rage at this unknown member of the Fae interested her deeply. She found it odd that Ena had managed to hide herself for such a long time, and was something; it appeared to be, completely unknown to the rest of her kind. Her thoughts danced around inside her head as she walked onto the stairs and headed towards the children's room, where for a few moments she let her mind fade as she leaned on the door and watched her two children sleeping, they looked happy and innocent and she smiled.

When she finally slipped off her clothes and slid into bed, she felt the weariness creep over her, she curled into Robbie trying to hold her train of thought, but such was the relief of relaxing, without noticing, her thoughts slipped away and the veil of sleep took her, and she was snug, lost to her dreams beside her Hooded Man.

Through the night, the wind outside howled up the cliffs, and rattled the windows. The gate banged, and the trees shook their leaves as they danced on the sea breeze. Sapphire was in a deep sleep, her mind filled with pictures of things she knew nothing of. She felt herself running through a deep plant filled dark woodland, her heart racing and her head pounding, and then as quick as a flash she was somewhere else hiding behind dark heavily embroidered curtains, and the room that hid her was filled with the rough sadistic dialect of a language she had no understanding of, it appeared to wail in hate and pain, and then suddenly a familiar feeling rushed over her.

She ran along the side of water and up an alleyway into a crowded street, she was filled with fear and panic as she looked from side to side nervously. The houses and shops looked old and from some distant moment of the past. She walked quickly trying to avoid being noticed, as she wove into the groups of people all walking in her direction, somewhere faint behind her there was shouting and calling, but she kept her head down and kept on walking.

At the sound of running feet behind her, she sidestepped into a crowded store front and tried to blend with the others around her, her heart was racing and she could hear it in her ears. Then suddenly without warning a cool white hand gripped her forearm, she jumped with shock, and looked up into the dark black eyes of Morgan le Fey.

"Oooh... Shit!" Sapphire sat bolt upright in bed with a start, her heart racing and sweat on her brow. "Not again, oh will this dream never leave me?"

She sat for a moment regulating her breath and trying to regain her composure, slowly her breathing returned to normal as her head swam again. "What the hell does this mean, why does it always have to be her?"

She rolled back the covers and swung her legs out of bed, the thin curtains showed light, and she realised that what she had thought had just been a short rest, had in fact been the whole night, and the new day had started again. Outside the gate banged and the trees shook their leaves, she stood up and reached for her long blue pants, and then there came a strange tapping noise and for a moment she froze, her voice was nervous and quiet.

"What the hell is that?" The tapping came again. "Is that someone at the door? Who the hell could that be all the way up here on an uninhabited island? Sapphire why are you talking to yourself, oh bugger I am definitely going mad here alone, I am now talking to an imaginary me."

The tapping appeared again. "It is, it's the door... I know it's the door why am I telling myself? Well you are alone and afraid that's why." She gave her foot a stamp and picked up her bow. "Stop it... Just stop it you are sending yourself nuts Saff." She shook her head as if to clear the imaginary intruder and walked quietly to her bedroom door.

She opened the door and peered across the small kitchen towards the door with a small glass pane in it. There was a figure stood outside, and it was silhouetted through the small lace curtain across the small window. "Who the hell is that, I am miles away from everything, who the hell would travel so far to knock?" She whispered to herself.

It was a good question and one that made her very nervous, as she cautiously approached the door fastening her belt that held her sword on it. She looked at the silhouette. "Hello?"

"Oh Hello, for a moment I thought you were out." The voice was soft and a little gruff. Sapphire unlocked the door and pulled it slowly open.

"Gwynfor?" He stepped right in wearing a broad happy smile.

"Hello my dear, I brought waffles, Una told me they were very good and always promised to make me some, apparently one of the locals made them for her once, and she loved them so much she learned to make her own, although alas she never quite got round to it. Up popped Runestone and off you all trotted, so I thought well what a wonderful idea for a visiting gift for breakfast. Oh you have not already had it have you?" Sapphire stared in disbelief and looked back outside to see who may have brought him this far, but there was no one to be seen, she turned back to her guest more than a little confused.

"Gwynfor?" He gave a bright happy smile holding up his package, and stood right in the centre of her kitchen.

"We need to warm them, is the stove lit?" Sapphire stared not completely sure if this was real or another her visions.

"Gwynfor?"

"Yes my dear." She blinked.

"Gwynfor... I mean... How did you get here?" The ancient Celt with bright twinkling blue eyes gave another cheeky smile.

"I walked."

"Huh?" He looked round the room.

"Cosy place this, so glad I could finally get to see it." Sapphire gave her head another shake and tried to gather her wits.

"Gwynfor you were on Iona, how could you walk, it's all sea?" He gave a loud almost childish chuckle.

"I do love getting out and about, you know I spent over one hundred years in the cave, it's so much nicer visiting people and seeing the world, it's like having lots of little holidays. So are we eating? I believe butter and a little jam really make them worth the wait."

Sapphire closed the door behind her and walked over to him, he put down the package and embraced her warmly, and she gave him a big hug. It felt nice having another person in the house again. "I have no idea how you came so far alone, but I am really glad to see you." He gave a chuckle and stepped back to look at her.

"It pays to know a fairy or ten, it also helps that my sister was once the most powerful queen of Fae, and it is most certainly very nice to see you Sapphire my dear." She gave a huge smile, and he gave her a cheeky wink.

"We have a busy day ahead of us, but first I think waffles, I must admit I am rather excited at the prospect, sit yourself down and I will get the stove lit."

Gwynfor dropped his long blue cloak onto the back of the chair, and flicked his wrist at the stove, the logs within it instantly ignited, and he gave another cheeky wink. "As I said, powerful sister and all that, you pick up all sorts of tricks growing up beside her." Sapphire smiled.

"You said busy day, has something been planned?" He stopped as he lifted down a pan and laid it on the stove.

"You are the centre of your circle and have lived in secret for most of your life, and so yes, today is going to be very busy, for there is much to see and much to learn."

Sapphire did not quite understand. "In what way do you mean Gwynfor, because I have my table here in the house and I have learned a great deal from it?" He gave a nod as he opened the package and dropped two large waffles into the pan to heat.

"I would say that alone you have done remarkably well, but there are things hidden within you that only others of your line can expose, and considering what is happening in the world... well let's just say, that today you need to meet your own people for the first time, after all one day you will educate their new queen."

Sapphire sat at the table and still did not fully understand what he meant, he was a lovely old man who she was immensely fond of, but at times she felt he talked in circles that she did not understand, although the thought had occurred to her that Gwynfor would love the company of Fagan, somehow, they seemed ideally suited.

"My own people? Sorry Gwynfor, maybe it's me, but I am completely lost, I know my own people, I was with them all day yesterday."

He gave her a big smile. "Not those people, I know they are your people, it's just... well you are a part of a very big family and to date you have not been to see them, so I thought I would take the time to give you the tour, and let you see them for yourself. You know I am not really sure you know this, but as you are a centre you can go there whenever you want."

She still was not clear. "Gwynfor what are you talking about, go where?"

He lifted a hot waffle out of the pan and slipped it onto a plate on the side dresser. "Eat it whilst it's hot... now where were we... Oh yes go where? Florae of course, after all it is technically your home now, and you will be there quite a lot when the new queen comes, so you had better get the lay of the land now while you are learning." Sapphire was completely surprised.

"Florae? You mean the realm where you all came from the night Iona was born?"

He sat down with a smile and lifted his waffle. "That's the place... Oh I say Una was right, these are absolutely scrumptious, come on eat it while it's hot, we have a lot to do today."

It had thundered all night, as the rain hammered down all around the small group huddled under the sheet cast over a rope, and tied between two trees. Close to one of the trunks surrounded by a small ring of stones, a small fire flickered as the rain dripped onto the hot rocks causing them to fizz and spit. It was an hour before dawn, and Ben was fast asleep curled in his blanket, huddled close to the sleeping figure of Martin. The Sage sat motionless, his eyes twitching, as deep within the centre of his mind, he stood under the giant trees of the hidden realm talking to Opal, while his little companion Leaf, stood quietly watching the long road through the forest, to the dark brooding sinister castle in the distance.

Opal gave a smile as she cupped her pale white hand to his cheek. "William, you are far too hard on yourself, I feel my father was right to ease some of your suffering, you have earned this gift in all that you have done in his cause, for never forget, it is his cause that Robbie and Runestone are fighting for."

He gave a faint smile. "There is still a great deal to be done, and with London lost I fear I have made mistakes that might cost us a high price in the south." Opal gently shook her head.

"A great many lives were saved in London, they have travelled through New Avon back to health, and they will be ready when the fight comes. You showed great wisdom going to your father's store, and as we speak Silas has organised many men, and goods are flowing in secret on the sea, and around the coast to Philip and Loxley. The sea captain has transported many goods to aid our cause to Lancaster, and over land to Robbie; he will have explosives, and good steel due to your efforts. I fear you are far harder on yourself than others, so rest your mind and seek out this man in the trees who controls many who would be well suited to your cause. I feel the time is coming my green friend when you should take the full measure of Loxley and walk with ease into your destiny."

He looked confused. "Is that not what I am already doing?" Opal gave another chuckle and dropped her hand.

"William you were raised in Loxley, and I may add not by just anyone, you were raised by the side of the Hooded Man by his own family, whether you believe it or not, you were raised to one day be a leader of men."

In many ways it surprised him, although he understood what Opal meant, from the moment Robbie had been made a lord at Loxley, he had always felt like he had been side lined. Opal understood his thoughts and shook her head slightly then smiled.

"Robbie was always intended to lead the men of Loxley, but you were trained to stand beside him and share the burden, whether you know it or not, inside you is a woodsman of great quality. Embrace it William, dig down deep to what your instincts are telling you, for there lies the power to lead many men. Gather an army of many and take them to challenge the power of your father in the south, he will never expect a large force to strike him from the rear, for that now is your task and your destiny. It is no coincidence that Runestone sent you the one man you trusted within the ranks of your father's army."

It made a great deal of sense; Martin had been the one man at Dunnottar he had spoken to most before he left to take up his role at Craigevar to protect Alice. He had indeed been very surprised to see Martin ride into his camp back in Wales, and had felt great comfort in the trees knowing that Martin was at his side. He was a well trained general who knew everything about the fighting tactics of his father's Cutter army, and he knew with Martin beside him, they would be able to predict and outsmart their enemy as they had in London. He looked into the pale blue eyes of Opal, and he felt that same sense of understanding he had felt many times during his talks with Runestone. "I will do my best to help Loxley, you have my word."

"I have never doubted it William, and I feel now is the time to leave the past behind, never forget what has been and gone can never define who you are, it is what you do now that will change the world around you. It is drawing late, so go and be what you are destined to be, leave with this coming dawn and allow all you have learned to guide your fate. Walk with peace in your heart, and if you doubt yourself, lift up your hood and pick up an arrow and fit it to the string of your bow, I am sure then you will know what you have always meant to have been, and it will guide you true."

The Sage stepped back and gave a regal bow. "My Lady of the Woods I shall not fail you, I shall find this man of many names, and I shall lead those he enslaves back to the trees they belong under." Opal gave a broad smile and lifted her white hood over her head hiding most of her face.

"Go my green friend, for I feel this day will bear many fruits."

Taking Leaf by the hand, the Sage turned onto the path and walked quickly away, Opal stood for a while and watched him go with his brightly coloured companion.

"Walk true my green friend, and my father will walk beside you."

CHAPTER FOUR

WHISPERING WATER

As the first light of the day settled into a warm and pleasant sun, Sapphire accompanied by Gwynfor, travelled to the southern end of the Violet Isle, and arrived at the well of youth. Stood on a mound of grass covered pale grey stone, Sapphire breathed in the fresh sea air, as her hair fluttered around her shoulders. Before her was a structure, almost pear shaped, and made from the same stone as surrounded her, she looked around not understanding how this could be an entrance to anywhere.

Gwynfor gave her a cheeky smile, as his long white robes flapped in the breeze behind him. "Not sure how we do this? Well, that is completely understandable; I mean not everyone can travel to Florae."

"They cannot?" He winked and turned towards the structure before him.

"Only a Fae of true heart and spirit may walk from here into the homeland. There is magic here older than anything built by the hands of man, it would take someone of great power to fool this door my dear, for this was built by the hand of Bridge, first queen of our people." Sapphire gave a soft smile.

"You say our people, but I have no knowledge of such things, this is all I have ever known."

Gwynfor took her hand in his. "Then my dear, it is time we changed all of that." He gave her hand a gentle tug, and stepped forward towards the structure, and as he did so, just for a moment Sapphire saw the soft blue light that flowed from the earth around her, and before she even realised, she was stood on a circle of white stone set within a circle of trees and looking out across a tree lined lake.

She blinked and turned to look back. Behind was a huge wall of pale stone, and she lifted her head to see she was stood at the base of a huge mountain capped with a peak of white. Gwynfor, who had let go of her hand, had walked to the edge of the stone circle, and turned to look up and get a better view as he watched

Sapphire gazing up, he smiled a happy smile. "That my dear is Mount Bridge; it is the heart of this kingdom and the source of all the life that thrives on these isles."

Sapphire turned to see him smiling at her. "Isles? Is Florae an island?" He gave a happy chuckle.

"Well, if I am honest, aren't all places? If you think about it even the land locked countries are but part of a large island, but yes, Florae is comprised of nine islands. Come we still have a walk before us, and as we journey, I shall fill you in."

Gwynfor stepped off the stone and onto the soft grass, it was clear there was a worn path where the grass was thinner, and he followed it through the trees. Sapphire hurried to catch up, and walked at his side as he began to tell her of what to her was a mysterious land. She had been told of Florae many times in her life, but it had always been a reference to just the place, she had never really been given any detail, but thinking about it, her mother was of the line of the Green Circle, so she understood she would know little of it. Gwynfor appeared to be in very high spirits as he trundled along chatting happily like a bird on a summer's morn.

"As you can see dawn is just arriving, you will find the world of men has sunrise a good four hours before us, the day comes a little later to our islands. Now where was I? Oh yes islands. Florae is but one of nine, we have Okuta, Braken, Sora, Nin, Ruba, Ada, Nen, Petra, and the main isle, which we obviously refer to as Florae Isle. The centre of the island is a deep basin at the foot of Kivi, the other large mountain range, which once we get to the end of this path you will see as we clear the trees."

Sapphire walked along looking round at the tall trees which appeared similar to those in her own world, below in the shade as would be expected grew many kinds of ferns and grasses, some she recognised and others looked strange to her.

Gwynfor noticed her looking round and continued to talk happily. "There are many similarities to the world of men, but we have a slightly different approach than they do. Life here is simple and is balanced with all living things. Whereas those Ofmoon dig in the soil for gems and metals, we do not, we never dig deeper than a foot, we tend the land with care and nurture the earth, and work with it rather than force our will on it. There are few roads and many tracks, the few roads we have are naturally occurring ones where the stone rises up to push the grass aside, the biggest of which is the Causeway, which you will walk upon this day. It runs from the centre of the city and the Royal Lodge, right down to the coast in one long straight line, and is primarily our transportation route for trade."

Sapphire who was feeling a combination of excitement and strangeness turned to him. "You have trade? With each other or with other races?" Gwynfor gave a giggle.

"We trade with many, never forget my dear that the lines of the Fae have spread into all worlds. We bring balance and reason to the lines of others; we are the peace makers of many worlds. But to answer your question, there are doorways to all the realms within these isles, one on each island will take you to a different place, the gate we just used goes to the world of men and are the most travelled, but we have an entrance to every kingdom within the nine islands. You will learn them all in time. Now where was I?"

"Not everything is the same as the world of men, and roads."

"Oh yes... This land and its people approach things differently. You see my dear, life here evolves around the life of everything, the seasons of our life are the same as everything else, and so in order to balance them we have thirteen months set across three seasons. We have Lambolc, followed by Helio, which are four of our months long, and then we have Gleefall the season of falling leaves and snow. Our months are divided into twenty eight days, with our last month of twenty nine days. Our year begins with Lambolc, which in the world you know would be February and Spring, Helio is what you would know as Summer, and Gleefall is our Winter, which is long and cold."

Sapphire gave a nod doing her best to try and absorb everything Gwynfor told her into her head. "So we are currently in summer, which is Helio?"

"Absolutely, you will find Helio is a little warmer than your summer, it does get quite hot at times, although we do have far more rainfall than I think you will be used to."

Sapphire gave a giggle. "I grew up at Callanish, I am not sure you would get more rain than that." Gwynfor chuckled.

"Hmm, I see, maybe you will acclimatise a lot quicker than I thought then."

The trees began to thin out, and Sapphire could see ahead of her a large expanse of water, and what looked like a huge wooden bridge, Gwynfor's pace quickened, and Sapphire picked up her pace to stay at his side, she was very impressed that for what looked like a very old man, he was very spritely indeed.

As the trees fell away, Sapphire found herself at what looked like the base of a huge valley. Across the bottom of the valley was a long vast lake, and she could just about see the other side in the distance. To her left she saw a second high mountain rise up in the distance, it was not as pointed as Mt Bridge which was behind her, it was more a long range with two smaller peaks at either end, both of which were capped with snow. Everything for as far as the eye could see was covered in a thick carpet of trees, made up of every shade of green known to any living soul. The air was crisp and clear, and as she walked onto the grass, she felt the warmth as the sun came up over the trees to her right and warmed her face. "Wow this place is beautiful."

The small very old and wrinkled figure of Gwynfor in his white robes, stood smiling before her at what was a slight incline up onto a massive timber built bridge. The bridge was wide enough to allow two carts to pass with ease as it spanned across the lake before them. "This place as you call it is home Sapphire, and yes, there is no other land I have walked more beautiful." He turned and walked from the hard dirt path onto the bridge. "Come along, you will like this."

Sapphire found it hard to move, she was so enjoying the moment, but as Gwynfor turned onto the bridge, she took a long look behind her at the path and the trees so as not to forget, and then hurried to catch up with him. The bridge was heavily built, and yet every aspect of it was carved with ornate flowers and swirls. The hand rails along each side were waist high, and the top rail was carved with elaborate symbols that appeared almost runic. Sapphire walked close and ran her finger softly along them as to feel the smooth letters. "These look so beautiful, what are they?"

"Those my dear are the symbols of your line; they are Fae runes. Along both sides of this bridge, they tell the story of your line and how the Fae were given the charge of this realm by Eve and Hearne. Although we have many scrolls that list the time and life of our people, when I built this bridge, I wanted something to remind every passer by of our rich history."

Sapphire stopped. "You built this?"

Gwynfor gave a chuckle. "I did indeed, in my youth I built many things, the shaping of wood has been my greatest achievement, and you will find many things in these isles shaped by my hand." There was a tone of great pride in his voice, and it was clear by the look on Sapphire's face, he enjoyed her appreciation of it.

"Gwynfor this truly is a work of artistry, you have a gifted hand there is no mistake. This lake it spans, does it have a name?"

"It is the Lake of Bridge." Sapphire gave a chuckle.

"Please tell me this is not Bridge's Bridge?" He gave a loud guffaw of laughter.

"No my dear, I can assure you it is nameless." They moved on and he began to chuckle. "I have never really thought of that before, you have much humour my dear."

Sapphire gave a giggle. "I assume not everything is named after Bridget Violet?" He shook his head and tried to suppress his giggles.

"In the early days many things were built in honour of our queen, but even she tired of it, and asked them to find other titles for the things we built. My grandmother found it a little tiresome; she would roll her eyes as if to say not another one." He gave a happy giggle.

Sapphire smiled. "I forget at times who you are, I forget she was your grandmother, and Gwendolyn was your sister. It must be hard to know they have passed into other realms and left you here."

Gwynfor gave a nod of appreciation. "I have lived a wonderful life, I had very loving grandparents, parents, and a deeply caring sister, I loved them all very much, but if I am honest the one I miss most is my father. My father taught me everything I know about the working of the grain; he was very gifted and many of the things he built still stand to this day, I worked at his side for many a year listening to his laughter and good humour, to be honest my dear, I think of him every day and have done since his passing many years ago."

They walked for almost an hour along the bridge, and then took another track through the trees that brought them to the top of a high plateau. Sapphire looked out from the trees across what was a wide basin far below her. A path wove down through the trees in a meandering way that considered the right angle at which to descend safely, and wove between the many trees and high wooden houses.

This was her first chance to see the realm and those who lived within it, and she was surprised to see how each home fitted into an area within the trees. The houses were all very triangular in their construction, and looked like huge roofs under which each house had several floors. The front ends were mainly glass with balconies that were railed, to prevent people from falling the great height from the upper floors, and like the bridge, she had crossed a little time ago, all of them were covered with ornate and elaborate carvings. The thing that struck her the most was the colour of the timber, it was green and mottled, almost as if it was coloured by many shades of moss, and such was the colour, they all blended perfectly into their surroundings. When they did come across areas of the path where the trees thinned and she could glimpse out across the wide basin, it was almost impossible to spot the houses on the far side within the trees.

The houses appeared to be built on stilts or on flat outcrops of stone, in places there could be four or five, all of them with neatly arranged gardens, some of which were raised beds of earth in elaborately carved wooden boxes. All of them contained food and flowers, all around her she could hear the voices of many birds as they sang in the trees above her. The people who she could see going about their daily routines wore clothes of a simple nature, such as flowing skirts and tops, all of them in hues of greens, rusts, and brown. At times she only noticed people when they moved, as they too blended beautifully into their landscape. Dressed in a dark royal blue, and wearing pants with white boots, she felt a little out of place as so far, she had not encountered one female not wearing a skirt of wide flowing fabric.

Gwynfor leaned into her and spoke quietly. "Our people are very colourful when they celebrate their rituals, then you will see colours so bright, it is like a rainbow came to life, here you are who you are, and your clothes show that you are of a high status and a highly valued member of this community. Opal was very shrewd in her choice of gifts, that bow you carry is made from a timber only grown on these isles, I would question how a member of the Green Circle could acquire such a prize, for that timber never leaves these shores." He gave a giggle. "She is cunning there is no denying."

By the time they reached the bottom of the incline and stepped out onto the pasture, and a worn hard dirt track, they had been walking for well over two hours. Sapphire's legs ached a little, and she felt warm in the hot sun of mid morning. Gwynfor pointed to a large pointed triangular building a little further ahead. "Almost there, we shall take a rest and have a drink, and something to eat before we move on, you will be pleased to know, we shall travel by cart up the causeway to our destination."

Sapphire gave a sigh of relief. "Just where are we going, you have not exactly named the place we are journeying to?"

"Have I not? Oh my dear, I am so sorry, it quite slipped my mind, we shall travel to the centre of this realm. and the house of my father at the Royal Lodge."

Within a few minutes they sat in the shade of the large logged building, sipping tea and eating warm muffins filled with thick butter and raspberry preserve. Sapphire ate greedily revelling in the taste of the food, as Gwynfor continued to chatter about the size and design of the building. "It's the snow load you see, come the winter months it's not uncommon to get a good six feet of snow, well as you know snow has a lot of weight in it, so my father decided it would be better served to make these tall steep sided triangular buildings, it does somewhat make sense, as all the snow just slides off to the side out of harm's way."

Sapphire swallowed noting the design and attention to detail, as this building had small flowers carved on everything, from the doors and windows right up to the steep sloped sides of the roof. Every aspect of the building was decorated, and somehow it felt appropriate, and in tune with the soft hues of green wood dye that coloured them. "I think these dwellings are very beautiful, I have never seen anything like them before."

"We have a great deal of time during the Gleefall, and so while the land sleeps, we use the time for working indoors with wood. All these houses are decorated by those who live in them; I feel it truly reflects the personalities of the people who live within them." Sapphire had felt that, she had noted the subtle changes from house to house.

Sapphire finished her food and sat drinking, as she looked out across the landscape. Being down on the lower floor of the basin; she got a better chance to observe this world that everyone referred to as her home. She could clearly see it was indeed a very wide basin, surrounded by sloping rocks covered in trees on to which there were thousands of homes built. Across the basin floor there were as many trees, and it was littered with houses, but she could also see there were large areas of fields filled with plants that were being grown for food. Sheep, pigs, and goats wandered freely in the abundant pastures of straw coloured grasses, and the many colours of the wild flowers. It felt idyllic and restful, and it was very clear that here was a people based totally in the earth, living their lives using only what surrounded them, and many of the things she saw reminded her a great deal of Loxley. "Robbie would love this place."

Gwynfor gave a nod. "I have thought many times how a man of his skills would be valued here, but his time to visit has not yet arrived, that time will come when he is much less pressured and free of the toil of battle."

"Do your people... I mean our people not approve of fighting?"

"We are peacemakers, we know of the ways of war and can be skilled in combat if pushed, but the taking of life is a sacred undertaking, and not one we do with relish."

"But you kill animals for food." Gwynfor nodded.

"Indeed we do, but it is always done with sadness, and we kneel before the lifeless body and give our thanks that such a life was given to us to sustain our life, we also eat many fruits, seeds and plants to ensure we kill as little as possible."

The sound of hooves thumped up the track towards them, and Sapphire turned to see who approached. Along the track came a rider in white pulling behind her two other empty horses. The clothing of the rider was a dazzling white, and it took a moment for it to register with Sapphire who it was. "CRYSTAL?"

Her horse came to a gentle trot as she pulled closer, and as the horse came to a standstill. With a big smile she slipped her leg over the saddle and dropped to the ground to embrace her. "Well met cousin, how are you enjoying being in your homeland?" She slipped back and gave a bow to Gwynfor. "My Lord of the Isle, the lord at the house felt it would be swifter to use horses rather than carts." He gave a chuckle and pulled her close.

"Hello, and well met my dear, as always his wisdom is illuminating, is everything arranged?"

"It is My Lord, all we need is our teacher, and we will finally be ready for the new era to commence." Sapphire was so surprised.

"Why are you here, how did you get here, when you were with all of us at the cathedral?"

Crystal smiled. "I am stationed here now, I have visited many times, and last night after we returned to Loxley I came here to prepare. I feel you forget cousin; my sister is queen at Avalon, and I am now the ambassador to Florae on behalf of my people."

"So you will be here when I visit?" Crystal gave a smile.

"I will be more than just here, you will lodge with me, and I shall be your guide here. It was decided some time ago by Merlin and my father that there will be a great period of adjustment for you, and so what better than someone who has lived in both worlds to aid you in the ways of the Fae here." Sapphire almost jumped in the air.

"This is wonderful news, I was so afraid I would be alone here, but just knowing you will be here is fantastic." Gwynfor pulled over the horses, and excitedly Sapphire sprang up into the saddle next to Crystal.

"You forget your line cousin, do not forget Una, Maddy and Melanie are also half Fae as is Treen and Jaz, I am sure we shall have many house guests once you are settled."

Gwynfor pulled his horse around. "We have much to do, let us make haste and head for the causeway." With that he gave his horse a nudge, and then rode off closely followed by Sapphire and Crystal.

The Causeway was a long road of exposed stone. Here the stone had risen up in a line that ran from the coast, to the centre of the huge basin that contained the central city of Florae. Either side the grass banked up just an inch and rolled away towards the fields and meadows, leaving a roughly shaped line of exposed rock. It was a much longer ride than Sapphire expected, and as she looked down the long road at all the trees and flowers surrounding the countless homes and official buildings, she started to understand the true size and scale of the place. When she had been told Florae was an island, she had thought it was maybe five miles or so long, but being here in the centre it was easy to see that actually it was a very large island indeed of possibly fifty to a hundred miles.

As they approached the Royal Lodge, the roadway separated around what looked like a waterfall that fell in a perfect circle down below the ground, into what Sapphire assumed was some vast underground lake. Three rivers ran up to and under the road before emptying their contents down into the deep perfectly circular hole. She tried to look down inside to see where the bottom was but it was very dark down there.

They slowed their pace and cantered the last few yards to the front of the lodge that was sat before the hill, which ran up to the top plateau lined with many houses and official looking buildings. The Royal Lodge was massive, and far bigger than any of the other buildings she had seen. Like all the other buildings it was a huge pent sloping into the floor, the only difference being that whereas most of the other buildings, had between three and four floors, the Royal Lodge had seven that rose up high above her to the last large triangular window at the very top. From the floor there were twenty steps up to a big wooden deck that stretched a good fifty feet out from the front of the building. Guards dressed in a rich green took their horses with a bow, and then escorted them up the steps towards the entrance doors, which were carved with two figures who she could only assume were Gwynfor's grandparents, Bridget and Malcolm.

Inside Sapphire caught her breath. Like the outside everything was made of heavily carved wood, small faces and figurines decorated every edge and rail to be seen. Down the long sides of what was a huge hall way, arched windows ten feet wide glazed with pale blue glass showed vistas on the deck filled with fountains and carved wooden statues. The whole far end wall was the same pale blue glass and the effect was such, the light seemed to flow like an aura around everything. It was so big and so vast she was utterly lost for words, and she saw in the very centre of the room were two very impressive and heavily carved seats, surrounded by wooden posts on which hung thick deep violet ribbon. Crystal leaned into her. "That is the throne of Iona, and one day she will take it and rule this kingdom and all the Fae of Earth."

Sapphire found it hard to find any words at all; she was completely overwhelmed by it all, and as she took a deep breath, her words almost whispered out of her. "I am not sure I belong in somewhere so wonderful, I am just a simple girl of the stones."

"I seem to remember a young girl before her coronation saying something similar, and yet she grew to be the most powerful queen our people have known to date. You should worry less and trust in the blood of your grandmother, for it flows in your veins also my Teacher."

Sapphire turned to see a tall silver haired man dressed in pale blue, she felt relieved to see he wore pants and a shirt of high quality, and had on pale grey boots. He gave a regal bow. "My lords and ladies." He looked into the bright blue eyes of Sapphire and she saw the kindness in his pale green eyes. "May I introduce myself, I am Lord Bade, and scribe to this royal household."

"I am Sapph...."

"Lady Sapphire of Callanish, and teacher to the queen of Fae. If I may, we have pressing business, and I would wish to escort you, for I feel your doubt, and so will relieve it by allowing you to see for yourself."

He gave a kind smile as he took Sapphire's hand, slipped it into the crease of his arm, and began to lead her across the huge inner hall.

Crystal and Gwynfor followed a few paces behind, as Bade guided Sapphire through an open door onto a wooden stairway, leading them below the level of the hall and into what she assumed was the area below the deck that surrounded the Royal Lodge. The temperature fell slightly, at which point Sapphire realised they had dropped below the level of the outside, Bade held her arm gently as he guided her.

"Fear not Teacher, for we are descending into what were natural caves when we first arrived, into a chamber that once the queen is crowned, will be specifically for her use only. It will be your task to instruct her as she approaches the right age, and here we have a chamber that you will find of great use, for it will show you the history of our people."

Sapphire who had grown increasingly nervous gave a slight gasp of relief. "I have no knowledge of the ways of Fae, I am sure it is a mistake that I should train Iona." He gave a small laugh.

"You alone were chosen by the previous Queen Gwendolyn, you must have some faith and trust the blood within you, for everything you will require has been with you since birth, and after all, you are the centre of the circle of sight, which is proof enough to all of us you have the tools required to prepare the next queen."

"Oh I hope so, this all feels like so much to take in."

"This is your first day, you will have eighteen more of the years of man to prepare, so trust in your line, for even though you do not feel quite so much as at home as maybe you do in your cottage on Callanish, soon you will see that the people are very excited to know you have arrived, and maybe then as you adjust you will believe me... Here we are the chamber of the queen."

Sapphire stood in a large chamber at least twelve feet high and a good twenty feet wide. The walls were smooth polished grey stone, and along the walls torches burned to light the way. At the far end of the chamber there was a tunnel that appeared to lead to what looked like a waterfall of shimmering light. Just inside the tunnel was what appeared to be a porch like structure, it had four tall posts on to which was a pent roof, Sapphire could not quite understand it and looked to her guide, he gave her a smile.

"From here on in I can only guard the stair, you must continue with the Lord of the Isle and Lady Crystal." He stepped back as Crystal came to her side and walked her towards the curious looking porch.

"Sapphire in front of you is an object of great magic not unsimilar to your table, it is known as the whispering water. Do you remember as we arrived, the point where all the rivers met and poured into a huge hole in the centre of the Causeway?"

Sapphire gave a nod as they approached and she heard the rushing of the water. "Well all that water that has flowed in from every corner of this land, and it drops down and lands on a huge table of stone. It was built by my line Ofmoon for Bridget Violet, and below that table of stone is a seat. The water will flow down completely surrounding you in a perfect circle, and if you take the seat and ask, it will provide you the answers to all of the history and customs of your people."

Sapphire gave a breath of relief. "Really?" Crystal gave a titter.

"Don't sound so desperate, did you honestly think you would be unaided in these tasks?"

"I don't know what to think, this place and up there it is a lot to take in for just a day, I mean I have spent weeks with my table and only now I am getting to really understand it." Crystal patted her shoulder.

"You worry too much, just relax, this water knows more than your table, and there is no Fae alive or act from the Fae past that can hide from it." Sapphire stopped and looked at Crystal's eyes that seemed to glow even brighter in the dim light.

"No Fae alive, do you mean Ena?" Crystal winked.

"There is no rule to say you have to use everything to train the queen, and after all, is it not prudent to ensure her survival by using the history of your people?"

Her heart suddenly started to beat faster, as she realised that the one point that was defeating Rune was in her grasp. They arrived at the strange looking porch, and Gwynfor gave it a push. Sapphire watched as it slipped effortlessly towards the wall of cascading water at the end of the tunnel. The porch slid into the water separating it, and Sapphire saw the inside of the waterfall, which was a perfect circle of stone on which four decorated pillars of stone held up the table of stone above. The water poured all around the room like a bright shimmering curtain, and right in the centre was a seat of stone. Gwynfor lifted a blue cushion from a large wooden box.

"Here, there is no need to be uncomfortable... Off you go then."

"What?" He smiled.

"Come on under the porch to keep dry, take the seat and introduce yourself, have no fear we will push the porch back to you when you are ready." He took her bow and rested it against the wall, then handed her the cushion.

Her heart beat faster as she took the cushion, and then stepped onto the wooden deck of the moving porch. She walked nervously along under the wall of water that had separated, and stepped onto the round wet surface of the stone floor. The water rang loud in her ears as she walked cautiously towards the seat, and as she turned to sit, she saw Gwynfor and Crystal smile, as they pulled the porch back towards them, and suddenly the curtain of water fell down obscuring them from view and everything went silent.

It was like being surrounded by a curtain of silver light and the silence was total, which felt odd as she knew that there were thousands of gallons of water cascading past her. The wall gave a flash of blue and she jumped, and through the curtain a figure dressed in white with a blue sash around her waist walked onto the table before her. "Greetings child of the White Circle."

The shadowy figure of Gwendolyn gave a bow. "My time is done, and soon all of the deeds of my life will pass, and the new queen shall walk our lands to rule. You have been chosen and charged with the tasks of our people to help her to learn and understand all that is expected of a queen of Fae line. I chose you above all others to be her teacher, believe in yourself, for today all that I have given to you in the gifts of our line will shine from within you. Trust me and trust yourself Sapphire of the White Circle, for you shall see many things here to guide you and the new queen to follow. Simply ask the whispering falls, and you will find what you seek."

Before she could ask a question the figure of Gwendolyn faded away, and left her in silence sat on the stone seat staring at the water. Sapphire could hear her heart beating in her ears; she licked her lips and swallowed as she tried to think of a good question. "Oh dear this all feels too much."

"Ask and learn." The quiet whisper made her jump and she looked around.

"Who said that?" There was no one there, just her alone.

"Ask, we are here to serve." Sapphire swallowed hard.

"Ok this is the weirdest thing ever, and I have been to other realms to get Jett."

"Ask."

Sapphire settled in her seat and thought for a moment, she looked at the wall of water that surrounded her, and then gathering all her bravery, she leaned forward and in a quiet voice she whispered. "Tell me of Ena."

"Ooh good question.... Good question indeed Teacher."

The day for Sapphire had been a long one, she felt exhausted as she had seen, and been given more information than she could process. Having witnessed the Whispering Falls, she had left the chamber, and after a brief tour of the Royal Lodge, where she had been given access to the Hall of Scribes by Bade, where she marvelled at a room filled with pigeon holes from floor to ceiling containing scrolls, she was finally taken up the slope behind the Royal Lodge, to her shared accommodation by Crystal.

Crystal had a pent shaped, three storey house on thick stilts. The bottom story was a kitchen and workshop, and the second floor was a huge spacious living room with a wood burning stove. Above was the loft which comprised of two bedrooms, one either end of the house, both of which had huge windows and glass doors that led out onto a balcony. Sapphire was really happy to know she would be staying with Crystal, she had been afraid that her lack of knowledge of what were after all her own people, may give the impression she was not worthy of the role of teacher to the queen to come. She rested her bag on her bed and went back down the wooden stairs to the living space, where Crystal waited on the balcony at a small table filled with hot food. She gratefully sat down and noticed a third plate at the table. "Do we have a guest?"

Crystal smiled. "Of a sort... Tila who has cooked this meal shall be joining us shortly; she is just getting the wine."

Sapphire had thought there was only the two of them. "Is she a maid or something?" Crystal gave a mighty chuckle.

"I would not let her hear you say that, she is my life partner." Sapphire suddenly felt stupid.

"Sorry Chris, I did not realise, I am sorry." She smiled.

"Nothing to be sorry about, to be really honest there are not that many that know. We have been friends for many years, but as you know, I could not touch without my gloves, so we have been close but not together for a long time. When Rune lifted the curse off me and gave me the power to control it, well I suppose I took the leap, she is Fae like yourself."

It felt odd to hear Crystal refer to Saff as Fae, she had spent so much time in the human world she had forgotten that her parents were both of Fae descent. Crystal sat down and joined her at the table. "She visited us a great deal on the farm at the doorway to Avalon, and it was Tila who found us the gap to get out before Mason walled us off. When I got sent here as ambassador, she organised this house and gave hers to a friend so we could be together."

Sapphire felt happy for Crystal, she remembered Rune at Dunnottar and how emotional it had made Crystal, and now she fully understood what Rune had actually done for her.

"That is really sweet; I hope you will both be very happy."

Tila arrived with a large stone jug shortly after, and sat at the table with a big smile. She was younger than Crystal with long brown hair and hazel eyes; she was very pretty and smiled a great deal, it was clear to see how happy she was. She leaned over the table to pour the wine into Sapphire's stone goblet.

"This is the good stuff, it's brewed from Birch sap and Elder, so take it easy, it sort of creeps up on you if you let it." She sat back in her chair and raised her goblet. "Seeing as this is our first official guest at a meal, here is to you Teacher."

"Please call me Saff, I do find the teacher thing a little strange." Tila gave a giggle and took a drink as the others followed.

"Saff it is... So come on spill the rocks." Crystal moved a little closer.

"Yeah, do not keep us waiting; you looked terrified when you came out of that chamber. What was it like?" Sapphire gave a frown.

"How do you mean?" Tila gave a gasp.

"Saff you have been in the one place every Fae here is dying to know about, so come on don't be shy, we want to know everything, what is it really like to sit in the chamber of the Whispering Falls?" Crystal nodded and gave her all of her attention. Sapphire smiled and took a long drink from her goblet.

"It was pretty weird, but there again it was mind blowing. I heard this really soft voice, and it was so soothing, but at first I was not sure if it was in my head or actually happening." Tila rested her head on her hands and stared intently, her voice was almost as quiet as the whisper in the chamber.

"Oh wow... and what did you do then?" Crystal was equally as quiet and still, and Sapphire felt the excitement build inside her, it was clear to see as the two other girls watched.

"I was a little nervous, but I remembered the cathedral and the Fae that caught us out, so I was thinking should I risk it, and then it just came out of me, and I asked it who is Ena." Tila's eyes sparkled.

"Oh wow... and what did it say... You know if you are allowed to say anything that is." Sapphire gave a small giggle.

"It was so amazing, the voice just whispered back to me, good question, and then suddenly pictures just appeared on the walls or water or whatever it is. The whisper began to tell me all about her, and how her mother was raped by the grandfather of the Dark One, and she took her revenge and stabbed him and fled the castle. Later she found out she was pregnant and had a child in secret, hidden amongst some travellers. It was a really amazing story of how she evaded capture for ten years, and then one day when she was out hunting, she got herself caught in a bear trap and wrestled to free herself. Before she could get free, she was captured and taken back to the castle where the Dark One's grandfather had survived, but he was crippled as a result of her attack, and she was thrown into their deepest dungeon to rot. I tell you it was really gripping stuff I was riveted." Crystal was equally as fascinated.

"So what happened to Ena, was she raised by the travellers?" Sapphire nodded.

"Yeah, she swore to avenge her mother when she was old enough, and then left the travellers to travel alone, she came to the shores of England as she had heard of the marriage of Victor the Dark One's father, and she has been casting a veil over herself ever since and learning her magic as she has looked into defeating the line of Dark One ever since."

Tila looked lost in her thoughts as she rested on her elbows, her bright hazel eyes sparkling in the candlelight. "Wow." She smiled at Saff. "You are so lucky."

Crystal sat back in her seat and lifted her goblet. "Rune will be happy to hear that news, you will head back tomorrow I take it?" Sapphire gave a nod.

"Yes I will, I am really tired, so I thought I would get a good night's sleep here and then travel back tomorrow, I think I need to process everything before I sit with Rune, if that is alright." Crystal gave a nod.

"Of course it's alright, Saff this is also your home, you can do as you please here. I will travel back with you. I will need to report back to Rune myself, so have a good meal, take in the sights as we do have a bird's eye view of the place, and then get a good night's rest, we will make a start about mid-day, as I have a few things to attend to in the morn."

The rest of the evening moved slowly onward, the three of them ate a good meal, and all helped to clear away the dishes and clean up, then they sat back on the balcony and talked. Tila was Fae of Earth, and so she was a great help to Sapphire as she sat and explained about the world of the Fae and the life they lead in more detail. For Sapphire everything appeared so strange and new, but as she asked her questions and got her answers, she felt more and more relaxed, and she began to really enjoy the thought of calling this place home as well as Callanish.

CHAPTER FIVE

THE PREPARATION OF LOXLEY

Earlier that morning, whilst Sapphire journeyed into her new life and duties within the realm of Florae, and the morning grew into the bright sunshine of the realm of the fairies, back in the woodland to the east of Canterbury, the small group of three led by the Sage, had risen to find the weather was far less appealing.

The leaves shook as the water danced across them and fell to earth, Ben sat close to the small fire and watched the steam, as it wafted up from the coffee pot spout, and was dragged away over the grass by the breeze. Above him the rain pelted down onto the canvass and drummed in his ears, Martin sat behind him eating the fresh bread and berries, as the Sage sat motionless, his blue eyes fixed on the trees within the birch like skin of his face. Ben breathed a sigh. "Are we staying here today Martin?"

Martin looked out at the torrents of rain as they drifted through the trees. "While it is this heavy Ben, there will be little hope of finding anything, tracks will be washed away and any signs of disturbance will be shaken and flattened by the water, there will be little we can do to track in this."

Ben gave another long sigh, and slipped back from the fire under the protection of the canvass, he lifted his blanket and pulled it around his shoulders, and watched the long stream of water that flowed from the corner of the canvass down to the mud, where it had formed a large puddle.

The cloud was dark and brooding as it lingered above them, and Ben pulled the blanket closer round him, what had felt like a new adventure was rapidly becoming the drudgery of normality. It was nice being just the three of them again, but for Ben, London had provided many distractions and things of interest, since they had arrived on the coast, life had become a long struggle cutting through brambles and heavy undergrowth, followed by the heavy rain, and somehow it did not feel like a very good start.

The Sage looked like he was almost in a trance, he had not been as talkative as usual, and it was almost as if he had been trapped in his own deep thoughts. Ben watched him sat at the edge of their shelter, almost as still as a statue staring at nothing, and he could only wonder just what it was that was going through his mind. He relaxed feeling the warmth of his blanket, at least he was nice and dry, and above him the canvass thundered as the rain appeared to be falling harder. It drummed loudly and the run off on the corner began to speed up, as it ran off the cover, and streamed splashing into what was already a big puddle that was starting to move away from them in a small stream on the ground, as it sloped away from them.

The Sage stiffened and his head finally moved very slowly, Ben peered over the top of the blanket as he watched. It was almost as if the Sage could hear something, but the pounding water above them was growing so loud, he felt that was not possible, but the Sage did appear to be trying to understand something. He lifted his arm slowly and Martin noticed, Ben looked slightly back at Martin. "What is it?"

The Sage who had been sat on the floor lined with soft cut fern, moved onto his haunches, as he tried to focus on something that Ben could not see or hear. Martin smiled and raised a hand as if to tell Ben to keep quiet, he could see Martin was focused solely on the Sage, who rose slightly and slid back his hood. Martin stood up and lifted his bow, Ben still could hear nothing but the pounding rain, but he trusted the Sage and his keen senses, so he unwrapped his blanket, and lifted his own bow off the floor, and slid a small brown feathered arrow out of his sling. Martin moved quietly up to the side of the Sage. "What is it?"

The Sage lifted a finger and pointed into the trees to the left of them. "We are not alone; someone or something is coming this way." Martin gave a nod and spoke quietly.

"I hear nothing but rain, what do you need?" The Sage turned and looked at Ben watching them holding his bow with an arrow fitted to the string.

"Keep Ben in the shelter, you go to ground close to him on the left and watch the camp, I will move out across the front of the camp into those trees over there, if anything comes in, you have the front, and I will have the back, stay sharp." Martin gave a nod and moved back to organise Ben, the Sage lifted his hood and walked out into the pouring rain.

Several long tense moments later, Ben sat alone crouched down behind their packs, his bow just a few inches from his hand. He peeped over the top of Martin's large pack at the place where the Sage had thought whatever it was would arrive. He could hear his heart thumping in his ears in rhythm with the falling rain, but that was all he could hear. He had been so warm and snug, but now a cool shiver ran down his back, and he could feel the hairs slightly shift on the back of his neck, and then finally he heard it.

Branches snapped and cracked, it was faint at first, but as he focused and strained his ears, the sound came again, and it was clearer and louder. He gave a little shudder and tried to sink as low as he could, but still be able to see the trees to his left. The crack of a branch was louder, and he froze waiting for whatever it was to reveal itself, and then with a loud crack through the rain he heard a soft whimper, and then a figure stumbled and staggered out from between two tall slender Alder and into view.

Just for a second his heart stopped, as his brain raced and he realised what he was looking at. More out of surprise he stood up, and his eyes met the dark brown frightened eyes of a woman who was covered in mud and soaked to the skin. Realising she had wandered right into a camp, she panicked and turned, Ben shouted. "No Wait!"

As she turned, she was confronted by the Sage as he moved towards her, she stumbled and tried to turn away as he closed in on her, and as she twisted Martin raced across the small cleared space to cut her off. With a loud terrified scream, the Sage was on her, but she swung wildly, and any hope he had of gripping her evaded him. Martin closed ground fast, and as she tried to swerve past him, she screamed again even louder. She twisted trying to avoid her captors, and Martin had little choice but to throw his arms wide, and then close them tightly around her. She screamed and wailed, and thrashed in his arms, kicking and slapping him hard, he shouted as loud as he could that he meant her no harm, but she continued to resist capture and fought with all her strength.

Ben ran over as Martin slipped and both crashed to the floor, but his grip was firm, and even though she thrashed with all her might to wriggle free, she was caught and she knew it. Her struggle and screams ceased as quickly as they had first started, and she went limp as Martin lay on his back holding her tight in front of him, and she burst into tears and cried. Ben felt a tug at his heart, as he watched the Sage crouch down at her side, he wiped the tangled hair from her face, which clung to it in the pouring rain, and he tried his best to smile and show he meant her no harm. "Shush, you have no fear here; we do not wish to harm you."

He wiped back more of her hair as the rain splashed down on her face, and Martin loosened his grip slightly, she opened her eyes and blinked the water off her eyelids, the Sage drew a cloth from his pocket and wiped her face. He gave Martin a nod, and he sat up pulling his arms away and let her sit, and she looked blankly at the Sage.

"Who are you? You should not be here; if the Coker finds out he will capture or kill you." The Sage gave her another reassuring smile, her lip still trembled and her hands shook as she took the cloth from the Sage and lifted it back to her face.

"I am known as the Master Sage, and this is Martin, and our little friend there is Ben, we are seeking a man who is known for his many names." She stopped wiping her face and a look of fear crossed her face again.

"Why do you seek this man, do you have business with him?" The Sage pointed to the canvass shelter and the fire.

"Come you are soaked, sit by the fire, we have food and hot drinks." She shook her head.

"First tell me your business with this man." Martin stood up soaked to his skin and covered in mud, the Sage looked at the soaked woman.

"This man I believe has many followers, and I want to convince him to aide me by taking up arms, and joining the cause of the Hooded Man." He stood up and offered a hand, and she started to laugh, it confused both the Sage and Ben. The Sage frowned. "I fail to see why that is amusing." She took his hand and appeared to relax as she gave another chuckle.

"You say he has many followers, you are mistaken, what he has is many captives of which up until last night I was one of them. I am Ester by the way, and if you really want to convince this man you want his prisoners, I hope you brought a lot of gold, because you have nowhere near enough men to persuade him otherwise."

It was quiet in the house at Robbie's Mere, when Robbie came slowly down the stairs and into his living room. As always in the kitchen there were sounds of life, so he made his way towards the door. The door swung open revealing the long heavy table, at which sat a rather exhausted looking Rowan, sipping at a cup of what looked like some kind of tea. Robbie stepped through to reveal Jade sat with Louisa; they both looked up as he headed to the stove and the large copper kettle. "Mornin Robbie."

"Morning Guys." Jade lifted a spoon to her mouth and he looked down at her bowl.

"What the hell is that?" The small earthen bowl contained a strange brownish paste, dotted with greenish bits. Louisa gave a chuckle as Jade looked up at him pulling the spoon out of her mouth.

"It's Porridge." Robbie had to look twice at it as she scooped a second sticky mound onto her spoon.

"That don't look like any porridge I have ever made." Louisa smiled as Jade loaded the spoon into her mouth.

"It's a recipe for expectant women Robbie, your grandmother gave it her to try." He glanced at the bowl then at Louisa.

"Why is it brown, shouldn't it be a sort of creamy oatmeal colour?" She gave a giggle.

"It is made with Beech Meal." A memory of being a boy came to him of Beth handing him a bowl, he realised what Jade was eating, it was made from the nuts of the Beech tree, he gave a nod.

"Right yeah, I remember, but what are the green bits?" Jade lifted the spoon up towards his face.

"It's Gherkins with garlic and nutmeg, you want some?" He felt his stomach twist as the smell hit his nose, and he took a step back, lifting his hand to the spoon.

"No thanks, I am suddenly not that hungry." Louisa gave a giggle.

"Yeah, we kind of lost our appetite too." Jade pushed the spoon in her mouth, and muttered between chews.

"More for me then, it's lovely."

Robbie poured his drink and made his way round the table towards Rowan, and as far from the stench of Jade's food as possible. He patted Rowan's shoulder as he sat down. "You look tired."

Rowan gave a nod as he looked up. "I am, it was a hard fight yesterday." He put his cup down and stretched his arm out. "I have not had an ache in my arm like this for a long while."

Robbie understood, it had been a longer day than he had wished for, most of the group had not had much sleep, as they had all been at the cathedral, and as soon as they had got back expecting to rest, they had been called to Lincoln and its defence. "How are they?"

"Like us, washed out and exhausted." Louisa nodded as she looked down the table.

"I was up at the farm at first light, Big John looked tired but he is ok, from what he said Keith and Rafe were really knackered when they got back, and he said Jay was still in bed, which was odd for her, as she is always up before the rest of them. Beth said she had left Alice and Bear asleep and got the little one up. Skip is at the hall, but he has left Treen at home." Robbie gave a nod as he sipped from his cup and felt the taste jolt his taste buds back into life.

"We are on home turf, so until Mason acts, they can rest up." Jade looked up from her bowl.

"We really are cut off then?" He gave a nod.

"Yeah Pebbles, he has his wall all the way round Loxley. No one is going out, and no one is getting in." She looked a little pale and tried to smile.

"But we will be Ok Robbie... Won't we?" He gave a smile.

"We are not done with just yet; we knew this would happen and are well prepared. From what I saw last night, which is not a huge amount I must admit, but I think he has already made one big mistake." Rowan turned to him.

"He has what?" Robbie winked.

"One door." Rowan frowned.

"I don't follow, how do you mean?" Robbie sat back in his seat.

"From what I saw last night on Fuse's table, he has built a wall around the whole five mile square of the stockade, and although I know not all the scouts were back last night, it looked to me like the only way in is that big gate across the valley from our gates. One way in and one way out, which means he is going to hit us all at once from the front."

"Yeah but Robbie he has cannons, what if he just plans to bomb us from the walls?" Jade had a good point, but Robbie could not see it, he had lay in bed thinking until he fell asleep last night, and at first, he had thought the same thing. He gave his head a shake.

"I doubt it Pebbles, firstly he is too far away for his cannons to hit us from the front wall. The north is too thickly wooded, the east is below us at the bottom of the escarpment, and if he fires from the west, well there he is high up on the moor. He could rain bombs down on us, but what use would that be without a gateway to push troops through. Plus he would mainly just hit farm land; we have no real buildings to damage on that side apart from the windmill at the valley floor."

It made sense to Rowan. "Well we have more eyes on him than ever before, all the walls have double troops on them and the reserve forces are placed all over Loxley, so whatever he has in mind we are ready to deal with it."

"He will wait." Louisa looked at him.

"You think he will try to starve us out?" Robbie shook his head.

"No he has had his spies in here, which we know, so he will know about the food stores and the weapons we have stashed. I think he will try to preserve those if it comes down to it for his own people. No, I think he will wait for all his army to gather, we will finally have everything he has in one place."

Rowan agreed. "Yeah, I see that, but they will be right on our doorstep." Robbie stood up, and patted Rowan on the arm.

"Mason is a man who will savour his victory, he has planned this for many years, he thinks he is now in control, and I aim to let him. We have work to do, let's go and see what Fuse has for us." He looked at Louisa. "Get your boys together, I want the people to see them in the town, same goes for the Specialists Pebbles. I want them out and about in full view, talk of that wall will be buzzing around making people nervous and afraid, let's show em we are home and on the watch for them." She nodded.

"Will do Robbie."

"Where is Rune?"

"She left earlier with mum; I think they are having a look round at things." He gave her a nod.

"Ok then, time to make a show for Loxley."

All over Loxley there was lots of activity. The appearance of the wall had done more than get the gossips going, everyone was talking and they were all afraid and worried. In the centre of the stockade all along the roadside tents had appeared almost overnight as soldiers poured in from everywhere. John Lox had withdrawn a large part of their external forces inside the walls, and most of the woodland forces that remained outside were now strategically placed within the woodland close to Loxley.

Jess Lox called all the farm staff in for a meeting in the court yard, and instructed everyone to start pulling in as many crops from the fields as was possible. The order was given that anything ripe or ready was to be gathered and brought to the stores, where more units had been placed, Loxley was on lock down and rationing was being implemented. Harry hid four undocumented barrels of wine in his loft, just in case. The postal office was closed, all mail ceased with the wall, and Rags and Lucy were given a desk in the Village Hall, where they took on the roles of coordinating all the military orders across the whole of the Loxley forces. A long line of rider's dressed in blue Loxley Postal Office uniforms sat waiting for despatches.

Alice and Anne Kirk had the shop open, but had dropped the tin size of their loaves so that they could produce more loaves but also ration their ingredients. Agatha as always was too busy gossiping to do much, so Melissa was in the shop explaining to all the customers that Loxley was now on rations, and she could only allow them a percentage of their normal orders. Alf Smith put extra locks on his meat lockers, and pinned up the official poster explaining the new rationing quantities allowed each day to each family. Reuben Stein appeared unconcerned, his shoes were a necessity, although he knew there would be little hide available for shoes if the campaign went on long enough.

The road outside the gates was busy, as those who lived close to Loxley packed their things onto carts, and headed for the safety of the walls. The gates were manned with treble the units, and all along the road the soldiers kept watch, as they guarded all those heading inside to safety. The people had never seen such a presence of their military, and this had been planned by David Williams, and his sergeant Henry, to make a good show for those across the valley who may be watching. It was a clear signal to Mason Knox that Loxley was prepared and ready, and would not be going down without a fight.

By mid morning the activity around the stockade was at fever pitch, and into it rode Robbie and Rowan much to the surprise of Agatha, who had been telling everyone he had not returned from Lincoln. Robbie sat proud on his snow white horse, his long emerald cloak bearing the golden wolves head crest on his left shoulder. Rowan sat beside him wearing his long blue cloak bearing the Loxley crest sat on a dappled grey mare. Both of them looked commanding and ready for anything, and all those who watched them felt a strong sense of ease in just knowing that Lord Loxley was amongst them. No one noticed that under their cloaks they wore the same clothes from the day previous and were caked in mud, neither had worn their best cloaks since their weddings. It served the purpose Robbie had wanted it to, and as they made their way down the main street and round through the market towards the Village Hall, it sent a clear message to everyone as to who was in charge.

At the Village Hall, Robbie and Rowan dismounted from their horses and tied them to the fence, as they turned to head inside, Rowan tapped Robbie on the shoulder. "I think you have a guest." Robbie turned to see Bishop Stevens with Father Warren hurrying towards them, the father gave a wave, and Robbie waited, Rowan gave a sigh of impatience. "What can they want now?" Robbie noted Rowan's attitude, and smiled as the bishop came gasping towards him.

"Oh dear, I am not used to so much walking up hill, please Lord Loxley I am aware you are busy, but if I could have a short word." Robbie gave a nod.

"I take it My Lord Bishop your accommodation is satisfactory?" The bishop paused to gather his breath; he gave a resounding nod.

"Yes My Lord, to be honest it has greatly exceeded my expectations." He took another long gasp of air. "No what I would wish to talk to you about is my aide Simon, I have not heard from him, and considering the business of yesterday, I wished to enquire if you had come across him?" Rowan cut in.

"We did, he was hanging in your office from the wall, his throat and stomach slit, and his entails hanging to the floor." The bishop recoiled in shock as Robbie turned to see the cold expression on Rowan's face, he turned back to the bishop who had pulled his handkerchief to his mouth and looked as if he was about to faint. Father Warren gripped the bishop's arm to steady him.

"I am sorry Bishop, but as my general has stated, he was killed in the fight." Rowan gave a long sigh.

"More like butchered." The bishop gave a stifled cry from behind his hankie, Robbie turned to Rowan.

"Simon was a valuable asset to the bishop and his working assistant; the bishop was very fond of him." Rowan looked unrepentant and looked at the bishop.

"My Lord of Loxley is too generous Lord Bishop, you were warned this would happen, we were quite clear about the Brethren, but you made the choice to side with no one and chose to ignore good advice, and as a result almost two thirds of the people in that cathedral were butchered to death. I am sorry if this truth offends you, but that is the reality of the likes of Mason Knox, if you still wish to talk terms with him." Rowan lifted his arm and pointed to the gates of the stockade. "You will find him not an hours walk over there." Robbie lifted his hand.

"Ok Rowan enough." Rowan looked defiant.

"Is it though Robbie? We told him to clear everyone out and leave the place to Mason, we offered everyone a safe place here, and now they lie brutally butchered and dead for no other reason than this man chose to try and talk to that mad man over there. You were warned Bishop what Mason would do, we told you the kind of man he was." Rowan looked at the Bishop and Father Warren.

"I walked round your place of worship yesterday listening to the cries of pain and suffering of wounded old men and young women. I took my sword outside with my men, and I watched good soldiers die by my side as they defended your precious church against other Christians. I lost count of the men who attacked us wearing that precious cross you wear round your own neck, and they were brutal and sadistic, and I cut them down as they fought alongside black vested Cutters, and I did it for those poor bastards lay wounded or dead in your precious building. Again, I am sorry Bishop if this offends you, but it is honest, and the facts, and that is the life we all face until we take that maniac across the way down." Father Warren lifted his hand.

"Please General enough, the bishop is very distressed, you have painted a very graphic picture of your experience, I am sure the bishop has heard enough." Rowan took a deep breath and conceded with a nod.

"I wish no offence, but I saw things in your church no man should see." Father Warren held onto the bishop and gave a nod of acceptance.

"It may not appear like it, but we are very grateful for the assistance the men of Loxley gave to our people, they shall be remembered in our prayers." It was too much for Rowan and he turned towards the hall.

"I will make sure I tell the loved ones of my lost comrades that when I meet their families later, that they are in your thoughts." He walked off towards the hall; Robbie gave a long sigh as he looked at the bishop.

"I am truly sorry for your loss; we did everything we could to save as many as possible. Many of your wounded were taken to the House of Good Hope for treatment; you will find some in our hospital, if you require anything at all please do not hesitate to ask Bowman Jersey and I will ensure you have what you need."

The old Bishop gave a nod and removed the handkerchief from his mouth.

"We are very grateful for your assistance; I hope you understand that My Lord?" Robbie gave a weak smile.

"I hope you understand that my general lost good men yesterday, he is not wrong, we saw things no man should see, it does have its effects on all of us." The bishop gave a nod; he looked much older than he had at their last meeting.

"I understand My Lord, and I know of General Loxley, he is highly regarded by everyone, and I do understand to have witnessed such things is very upsetting. I hold no malice towards him, if anything I respect his honesty. Your men will be remembered, they gave the ultimate sacrifice to save our people, and I can assure you they will never be forgotten."

Robbie put out his hand and shook the bishop's hand. "I am sure all the families of my men will greatly appreciate that, again my sympathies for your loss, I am sorry but I have important duties to attend to, but please remember anything you may need, just ask."

Father Warren gave a respectful nod as Robbie shook his hand, and then turned to walk into the Village Hall to view the map and what updates Fuse had added. Father Warren with the bishop turned and walked slowly back towards the hotel.

In the Village Hall it was all hands on deck, Skip was back with Fuse, Treen had a circle of despatch girls around her as she gave her orders, and for the first time Rayne and Gwynne had joined the team as they liaised with all the commanders of the forces out in the trees. Out on the training field new tents had been set up, and a force of several thousand Caerleon troops took their orders from a scarlet cloaked Jett Amber. The school yard had been taken over much to Maggs dismay, and new recruits were under instruction from Jay and Rigger, who had groups making explosive arrows. In the centre of the farm yard, Beth and John Lox coordinated the heavily sweating young woodsmen who were carrying large barrels of arrows up to the yard to be distributed around the soldiers. Carts arrived to be loaded and then when given instruction by Beth, they would head off to all the units that now completely filled all the walls around the town. Inside the barn, Bobby Thorn organised the distribution of extra swords. He had filled out a little working with John and had grown several inches. His arms glistened from the heat of the forge, as he sized up each member of the woodland forces that patiently waited in line to receive a new sword. Bobby would look them up and down and then without asking, he would turn to the racks and pull out a sword. He balanced it in his hand, and then gave it a swipe, before handing it over for the new soldier to test the weight.

In the midst of everything the Outlaws headed by Louisa and Ox walked around to ensure the peace. A few scuffles had broken out, but soon ended when Ox waded in with Tiny to lift the quarrelling men by the scruff of their jerseys and stare at them in a menacing way.

Hornet was busy on her printing press producing the new rationing leaflets, in the back of her shop Jimmy Perkins was sulking, as he again had been told he was too young to join the Bowmen, so Judith gave him the job of boiling the Oak apples in water filled with rusty nails, to cook new ink. In the hospital Una and Madeline were helping out stocking up the shelves and preparing beds for an influx of new casualties, as the nurses went over their orders and prepared for the worst. Gaynor was sat quietly next to William's bed as he slept having been treated by Alice earlier before she left to return to the farm.

Bear walked with Rafe and Keith, through the ranks of the new incoming

Woodsmen going over their positions for when the call came. A plan had been coordinated ready and every unit had a place within the stockade that would be their duty to defend. When the alarm bells rang out, all units would report to a specific place, no matter what time of day it was.

Wagons shipped logs for the watch lights to all the walls, which were loaded into large metal baskets on tall posts for extra light after dark. Other wagons ferried large barrels of water all along the walls to provide refreshment, and put out fires in case of cannon hits. Women who were too old to join the armed forces volunteered their services making bandages and splints ready. They patched uniforms and fixed tents, which considering the drizzle of the day would at least ensure everyone had a dry place to rest.

It was probably the busiest time that Loxley had ever known, as people swarmed like ants in every direction, and yet in all the chaos there was one thing that no one appeared to have noticed. Runestone, Stephanie and Melanie were absent.

Across the valley on the other side of the wall built by Mason Knox, Stephanie sat in the long grass with her eyes closed, while her large pad rested on her leg. Her hand holding a fine charcoal, sketched slowly as she drew down the lines of the image in her head. A few feet away Melanie sat with her legs crossed, and her eyes closed as her thoughts connected with a hawk flying high in the sky. As the hawk hovered above Mason's wall, everything it could see was pictured in Melanie's mind. Steph who was connected to her, could see the same images, and guided her thoughts to the charcoal in her hand, and she drew finally detail pictures of every section that Mason had built. At her side carefully held in the grass under a cloak, were several large and very detailed drawings of the road in, the gateway, and every dimension of the walls, including the positions of every group of troops. This would be the most important information that could be gathered for Robbie and Fuse at the Village Hall.

In another realm lost in the trees and hidden by a thick wall of dense green foliage, two bright blue eyes peered into a large bowl of silver containing water. Sat crossed legged on her heavy wooden stump; Opal watched carefully as events unfolded. "Well, well, little fairy, what brings you back from the dead, and why are you flitting about like a cat with flees?"

Opal watched Gwendolyn as she jumped to Carnac to consult her table, and then bounced to the Forest of Time. "Oh dear something has put a breeze up your skirt that is for sure. What has happened that would make you so jumpy I wonder?"

CHAPTER SIX

ESTER AND ARIEL

Ester sat by the fire beneath the shelter shivering, Ben lifted a dry blanket and placed it across her shoulders. She smiled at him and gave a nod of appreciation as the Sage handed her a steaming bowl and a spoon. "Here eat this; it will warm you from the inside."

Ester took the bowl gratefully and began to wolf down the food; Martin gave a startled look as he stood dripping just inside the shelter. "I would slow down Miss; you will give yourself a stomach ache." She looked up apologetically.

"Sorry it has been many days since I have eaten, and my last meal was just bread." Ben appeared shocked. He looked at the Sage who was studying his new guest.

"Did you hear that? Just bread..." The Sage gave a laugh.

"See how we spoil you young Master Winters; your belly is filled with stews and fine meat, while this poor soul lives only on bread." Ester gave a smile.

"Stale and hard at that too." Ben screwed up his face.

"Eww... I would die if I had to live on stale bread." Martin chuckled.

"You would die I fear if we missed breakfast." Ester looked up from her bowl.

"How many more of you are there?" The Sage looked at her intently.

"None. We do not need more, this Coker you have spoken of, will give me what I need, it has been seen." Ester shook her head.

"You are a fool; he is a powerful man and he has many more powerful men to back him." She looked round at Ben then Martin. "I see you have stout heart, but if what you say is truly what you desire, then you will not succeed, unless you have some kind of magic that will enchant all his men at the same time."

The Sage smiled. "Let's just say I have friends in high places, and should my need be great enough, they will come to my aid to help me convince this man Coker it is in his best interests to do as I ask." She looked doubtful.

"Why do you need these people, are you not just looking to put them to work as he has?" The Sage shook his head.

"As I said, I am raising an army, and I need free people to help me fight back a man far worse than Coker, I aim to help defeat Mason Knox." Ester stared at him; her spoon of steaming stew held frozen in front of her face.

"Mason Knox, you mean the man that sent the Cutters to cut down our people? Who are you... are you the Hooded Man returned?" Ben gave a giggle.

"No silly, he is Master Sage." The Sage stood up and turned his back to Ester, he looked out across the woodland, where the rain still hammered down into the soft moist earth.

"I am not the Hooded Man, but I once had the honour of being his hunting companion." Ben gave a gasp.

"You did?" The Sage turned to see Ben staring at him with even more adoration; even Ester had stopped eating and was looking more than a little surprised.

"Robert of Loxley is a man I called friend, and at this moment he is fighting to protect the lives of every free man in this land, I aim to aid him by raising an army to join with his and defeat Mason Knox. This Coker has many captives I can use if they wish to fight for their freedom, the battle will be fierce and we will lose many lives, but if it ends with every survivor having a life of free will, then it will not be in vain. Tell me Ester, would your people join me if I can defeat this Coker?" Ester stared at him as if she was trying to work him out, her words were spoken slowly.

"What you ask is the wish of all of my people, but what you say is insane. Coker is a vile brutal giant of a man, he fights with a huge two handed sword, believe me I have seen him cleave many men bigger than you into two from the head to the legs, and watched them fall into two halves on the bloody ground. You may or may not be who you say, but to face him with just your two companions would be folly." Martin gave a nod.

"Aye, but if he does do it, then would your people join with us?" Ester shrugged.

"I know some who would, as for the others I cannot speak for them." Martin gave a sniffle and pulled a rag from his pocket to wipe his face and nose, he looked at the Sage.

"Looks like it will be our job to convince them then." The Sage nodded and looked at Ester.

"Can you show me where to find him?" She took another spoon of food into her mouth and chewed for a second as if thinking it over.

"I think you are insane, and I must admit all I want is to run as far from here as possible, but aye, I think I will, if only to know for sure that you mean what you say. If Coker is gonna get what is coming to him, I wanna be there to see it and smile."

The Sage turned back to view the woodland. "Then it is settled, we finish our meal and strike camp, and then Ester, you will take me to meet with this Coker, and from there we shall take aid to the Hooded Man."

Sapphire walked into the wide green protected circle, deep within the hidden realm with Cal holding her hand. Opal as always sat as still as a rock on her long fallen tree stump staring into a bowl of silver filled with water, she did not move a muscle. "Welcome back Sapphire, what news do you bring of the realm of your people?" She looked up and smiled.

It never ceased to amaze Saff how Opal knew everything, despite handing most of her powers to Runestone.

"I am well and I have not been with Robbie for a day." Opal winked.

"I speak not of the Woodland Realm, but of your realm Florae." Saff smiled as she sat beside the old woman and rested her yellow wooden bow on the trunk beside her.

"Is there anything you do not see?" Opal gave a chuckle.

"Considering these past times, I would say plenty, but there again; I do tend to notice more than is probably good for me." She clicked her fingers and a mound rose out of the ground with a tall glass decanter of pink liquid and two fine glasses. "Much is happening Sapphire, I fear I must watch and do what I can from here to help preserve what we fight for, I take it this is not a social visit?" Sapphire gave a giggle.

"I do come to see you, but alas I have a question which would help me inform Rune much better than I currently can."

"So the waters revealed more than you bargained for." Sapphire gave a gasp.

"See, is there nothing you cannot watch?" Opal lifted the decanter and poured out the liquid into the two glasses.

"These are dangerous times Sapphire, what we seek is a secret that will go to the heart of all the Dark One has tried to hide, we must tread lightly so as not to alert her. For if she suspects just for a moment, she will turn on all of us with great anger, you must be vigilant and protect yourself." She handed Sapphire the glass. "Sadly that tiresome fairy Rhiannon made it impossible to see inside the waters, so tell me, what did it tell you?" Sapphire took a sip of her drink.

"I asked it who was Ena."

"Good girl, thinking on your feet in the heart of Florae, that is the spirit. So we know this Ena is Fae, the question is of what kind?" Sapphire understood.

"That is what I am not sure of, you see it told me her mother was Ariel, and she was raped by one of Le Fey's family, who I think may have been at least part Fae also, so I think Ena could be part both. The question is who is Ariel?" Opal nodded.

"Good question, and if I am right, she must be Earth. Let me think a moment, I remember something about an Ariel in Avalon." Opal looked down at the water in the bowl, Sapphire leaned over to see, but the water was clear. Opal gave a titter.

"This bowl is very special, it was made by my father and is for my eyes only, I find it ensures those who peep see little." Sapphire sat back straight and chuckled.

"And you call fairies for keeping their secrets." Opal stared at the water.

"Hmm that is it, Ariel was an ambassador from Florae based in Avalon before the queen arrived, and there was a scandal around her, I remember hearing about it at the time."

"You do?" Opal sat upright and turned to Sapphire.

"I do... From what I can remember, Rhiannon accused her of inviting the Merle into Avalon, it was all fiddlesticks of course, I remember my mother saying so, she thought Rhiannon was over reacting, and tried to consult her brother, but as is always the case, he had wandered off deep into the Merle and could not be found for years."

"What happened?"

"If I am right she returned to Florae under house arrest, according to Bridget who spoke to my mother, Rhiannon was livid and demanded Bridget release her back to Avalon to face trial, but Bridget refused stating that it was impossible for Ariel to do such a deed considering who her mother was, and the protections that had been placed on her as a child."

Sapphire was confused. "Protections... I am not sure I understand you, and who was her mother?" Opal looked surprised.

"Someone in Florae really must bring you up to date on your history girl. Enaria was and is possibly still the strongest mystic to come from any Fae line; it was Enaria who instructed Sequana. I met her once, she was quite lovely, I was just a young girl and she was so sweet, she charmed a flower and it crystallised into sugar candy for me, I thought at the time it was the most amazing thing I ever saw, or tasted... yes she was lovely."

Opal fell silent a lost look on her face as if she was re-living this important moment of her long life. Sapphire sat quietly watching. Opal looked up after a few moments and her eyes of brilliant sapphire blue met Sapphire's. "So there you have it, Ariel was a powerful member of your line, so if Ena truly is her daughter, then that explains why no one has seen or heard of her, she will be quite powerful."

Sapphire gave it some thought. "It does kind of make some sense; I mean she has even prevented Rune from seeing her. If her mother placed protections on her, then they would be in her blood, like the protections in the blood of Iona, yes?" Opal gave a nod.

"Yes indeed, those kinds of protections are the hardest ones to combat, this Ena you seek, if she truly is the daughter of Ariel or granddaughter of Enaria, then she has a powerful force inside her to ensure her survival. It is very old Fae magic indeed." Sapphire gave a sigh.

"It makes no sense at all to me." Opal gave a laugh.

"Give it time, you are just starting to really see the full picture of your race, fairies are a complicated lot." She gave a nod.

"The thing is, I do not understand why knowing of the blood line protection, Rhiannon would make such an accusation, she is revered as possibly the most knowledgeable member of both lines of Fae. You see what I mean; none of this makes any sense at all." Opal touched her hand and smiled.

"It makes far more sense than you realise, let me explain something." Opal shifted in her seat and got comfortable. "Rhiannon is a very political animal, she is a master negotiator, and I would say she also knows it. It is true that she is the oldest member of both Fae races, after all she is one of the first two ever created on this earth. Bridget sadly passed, which was a great loss to the world, my mother held her in the highest esteem for she believed that Bridget was the wiser of the two queens." Sapphire felt a spike of surprise.

"She was?" Opal gave a nod.

"Oh yes indeed, you see Sapphire what you are not seeing is the fact that you know little of Fae history, but I do as I was there. I was very young, just a child running naked through the Forest of Time, but I remember many conversations of the events of those times, and the one that caused the greatest stir was about Bridget and Rhiannon."

"It was?"

"Yes indeed, you see, Bridget challenged Rhiannon about the treatment of her people, she accused her of being short sighted and arrogant in the way she treated the Fae Ofmoon. Bridget said that the Fae Ofmoon ran only gold in her eyes, meaning she favoured those of golden hair over those of other colours; it caused a massive row and a very big stir, which divided the Fae and created distrust between the two queens. The high white lord was very angry about it, and he demanded they meet and talk to repair the unity of the two Fae, which of course they did, but things were never the same between Bridget and Rhiannon after that. Some even say that Rhiannon accused Ariel only because she was close to Bridget, as Bridget raised her like a daughter after the death of her greatest friend, Ariel's mother."

It made some sense to Sapphire. "So Rhiannon had her pride hurt and hit back at Bridget?" Opal smiled.

"She did indeed, Gwendolyn worked very hard to repair the rift between the two races in her early years as queen, but I must admit there have been many times I have watched Gwen and noted how carefully she would tread around Rhiannon. Gwen was devoted to her grandmother, and I always thought she never truly trusted Rhiannon because of all that. The Fae have always been the balance between races and the peace makers, especially the Fae of Earth, but Gwen was no fool, she united the Fae stronger than ever, but I have never doubted that she listened very carefully to her grandmother, and as a result Gwen protected her people with all of whom she was, she drove me insane at times, but I have always respected her for the way she protected her people." Sapphire gave a nod.

"I could use her wisdom now, my people are two completely different races, and I want very badly to protect them both."

"Go talk to her then." Sapphire gave a frown.

"How, she has passed from the realm forever?" Opal gave a chuckle.

"Forever is a long time Sapphire, and sometimes not everything is as it first appears. Remember knowledge is power, and Gwendolyn was very powerful, I would say walk in the Forest of Time and think of her, it is a vast place with many secrets, you may be surprised at what you will learn."

Opal patted her lap, and then stood up. "I feel food and thought will be of great advantage." She clicked her fingers and there was the fire with the familiar pot hanging above it filled with a bubbling meaty broth. Sapphire had already spent most of her evening eating with Crystal and Tila, and yet sat watching the fire and the bubbling pot, she suddenly felt starving. Opal ladled out the broth into two polished wooden bowls, and grabbed two large freshly baked cobs. "Eat up, we never turn down a chance to eat, after all, the way our lives tend to twist and turn, you never know when the next meal will be."

The food was hot and meaty, and had the flavouring of some very aromatic herb that Sapphire had never tasted before. It tasted wonderful and warmed her insides, she had not felt so relaxed and at ease like she did for some time. Tearing at her bread, she looked at the old lined face of Opal. "How do you do it... you know, live here alone like this? You appear so content; do you not miss our world?"

Opal smiled. "Sometimes... I miss the children, but there again I also watch them in my seeing water, so in a way I am still a part of everything they do. Never forget I also have many other children here to care for, and they are remarkably good company." She pointed to Cal who was sat in a circle of four other Sandlings across the grass from them.

"It's funny really, it's a question each one who visits eventually asks, I suppose they do not really understand as this place was once a prison for me during the age of sleep. They have never truly understood that this was also my first home with the man I loved very much." She gave a chuckle. "My father thought I was never going to settle down, I was quite wild in my youth. I always told him I was happy to wait for the one whom I could truly feel equal too; even now I am uncertain he fully understood that." She took Sapphire by the hand.

"I think we know when the right one comes, I have seen so many who swore blacks white that this one was the right one, but I could feel inside them that they hoped more than they actually knew it for sure. When I met Leenard, I knew, suddenly everything felt a little more precious to me, and being beside him made everything here bearable, do you understand that?"

Sapphire nodded and smiled. "Yes that makes so much sense, I thought I truly loved Keith, but since we have been apart, I have found that although I did love him, and I still do, it was not the big love that I thought it was at first."

"Precisely. I saw it in Jade when she first met Rowan, I always had faith that she would find herself the right man, her mother often doubted there was a man that could cope with her. I think she forgot how she fought me when Peter first came on the scene, maybe it is a Green Circle thing with the women of our line. She was terrible you know, ranting and screaming about how much she loved him." She gave a giggle. "I used to provoke her on purpose, just to rile up her passions. She had been so quiet and studious up until then, and then boom, out came all these wonderful and beautiful feelings from somewhere deep inside her, it was a wonderful time for her." Sapphire just sat listening and smiling.

"What happened then?" Opal sighed.

"She bought a motorcycle off Pete and ran off with him."

"What?" Opal gave a cackle of a laugh, as she saw the sudden surprise on Sapphire's face.

"It was the best thing she ever did; she went out of that dreary castle. and lived life to the full, and she tasted the world as it should be and never looked back. With Harry and Maggs, her and Peter had a wonderful time, simply living and laughing, and I may add getting up to quite a bit of mischief."

"You don't mind then?"

"Good grief no, I have seen too many people who are afraid to live because they thought others would disapprove, life should be about knowing what life is, and feeling it in every fibre of your bones. That has always been the problem with mankind; they turned from nature and invented too many rules and standards to live by, and then sat and judged each other. It's fiddlesticks Sapphire, go out there and live, taste the world, feel its energy, make love and laugh, and everyday accept and take joy in the wonder of this beautiful creation we called life. Too many people die with regrets and wish they had done more, take my advice, don't be one of them."

"I won't be." Opal smiled.

"You know I hear fairy men make excellent lovers, and you if I may say so, have a lovely body. They say they have good staying power, it sounds intriguing." Sapphire turned scarlet, and Opal stood up and gave out a large belly laugh, she shrugged her shoulders. "No harm in finding out is there?" She gave another deep belly laugh, as Sapphire's face went a deeper shade of beetroot red.

CHAPTER SEVEN

UNDERSTANDINGS

The roadway ran up from the valley floor, and then split as it levelled off, before dividing left and right. To the right, the road continued straight, its right side flanked with fields of wild flowers and long grasses, parted only by the mounds of yellow Gorse shrubs and scattered Birch trees, as it sloped gently down the hill towards the river. To the left, the road climbed up the gentle slope that led towards the gates of Loxley, where the wide heavy banks of mixed evergreen and deciduous trees, grew thickly hiding the tall wooden walls that formed the front defences of the stockade.

At the top of the slope where the ground levelled out, there was a huge area of hard compacted earth, forming a square, and the only way into the open gates of the town. After a day of crammed carts making their way into the protection of the town, a strange and eerie silence had descended.

The air was filled with the pungent scent of the drying earth from the previous day's rain, and the slight breeze wafted the smell of resin from the tall evergreens across the gates.

Jade sat at the top of the incline on the edge of the square, her boots in the thick grass that sloped away before her to the lower road, at her side sat the large frame of the old woodsman Joe Whitmore, both of them shrouded in their brown hooded cloaks as they used the few sparse blackberry and Rose Bay Willow Herb as cover, to watch the high black wall in the distance.

Joe pulled his binoculars away from his face. "There is movement on the wall, but there is bugger all happening." Jade turned, her bright green eyes staring out from under the hood that cast shade over most of her face.

"What you reckon, will they come out soon?" He stared into the distance, his body almost as still as a large rock.

"I dunno littlun, he has played a smart game to date, but this, well I'll be buggered what his game is here?" It surprised her.

"What you think his plan is daft, Joe he has all of us trapped, that seems pretty smart to me, I mean it's not like we can go anywhere is it?" Joe pursed his lips, stretching his old brown skin across his chin and tightening his neck.

"If you ask me, this is folly, I mean ok we are stuck, but why a wall?" Jade gave a slight gasp.

"Why a wall? Joe, he has us trapped, all he has to do is come through them gates and send everything he has at us, and we will be in a full frontal war, I mean come on Joe it's a pretty smart idea." Joe shook his head and gave a snort up his nose; he rolled his tongue around inside his mouth and spat into the grass.

"It is not what I would do, and too be honest it ain't how he has played the game so far. Look at the moors, he used all his flanks and a full on attack, no this does not feel like his doing, and if you ask me it's a bloody big mistake." Jade turned, her hood slipping back revealing some of her long blonde curly locks.

"How?" He gave a smirk.

"Don't be in such a rush to judge, hell littlun have you forgotten all I taught you?"

He nodded back towards the tall wall in the distance. "Look at them hills, he has to firstly get all his men out of them huge gates, and if he has as many as we think he does, well that ain't gonna be anything like a quiet task. Then he has to march em over moor and meadow, there are roads over yonder too, so he will have to get all of em over the walls, and you know them roads, some of em are so high in scrub, they will have to pick their way over. Even if he had a million men, it would take him days to get em all in order, and then they will have to cross the river and climb this hill ere before finally running up this slope to the gates. Come on girl you are no slouch; how many could you take out with a good bow at range?" Jade turned back to view the hills before her.

"Yeah, I guess so, I mean we have the best archers in the land, I reckon we could cut a lot down before they even got close to the walls." She turned quickly and her voice rose slightly. "Don't forget he has cannons?"

Joe shook his head. "He can have cannons and guns for all I care, he would need bloody big guns to hit us from that side of the water, I still reckon we have the best odds, I could hide twenty thousand men over yonder and they wouldn't see em until they were stepped on."

His old brown rough hand patted her on the shoulder. "You worry too much; first of all, we will see the buggers coming long afore we meet em. You need to spend more time in these trees and reacquaint yourself with em, you have lost your smell for them, as for these here walls behind us, Old Jake knew what he was doing when he picked this place to build a front gate, no bugger will walk past them while we still breathe."

Jade gave a sigh of relief. "I knew you would take the measure of them for me,

I do worry Joe, I love Loxley and I don't want it ruining. My life is so much better now than it was when I came to you to train." The old man smiled.

"It's that belly full of baby, it's got all your natural juices running backwards and making you feel womanly, they do that to you for a while. Look all of us love this place and we are dedicated to it, and so we will fight for what we have because to us it's everything. You think that lot over yonder care about here, they don't give a shit, they ain't fighting for something they love, to them this is just another dust up, they have no say in fighting."

"What you don't think they want to fight us?" Her surprise made him smile.

"Look what did I tell you at the cabin; don't you remember ought I told you?" She shook her head.

"I remember everything and I have used it to help Robbie." She sounded a little hurt, and he softened a little.

"I told you, them lot over yonder are just like us, don't you remember? Like us they are farmers, woodcutters and traders, the problem is they are not from these parts, and the only difference between them and us is that they chose the wrong vest, and this place ain't their home. They don't have the sort of fire in their bellies like we do." The memory of the long conversations they had just over a year ago in his old wooden hut, deep in the forest came to her thoughts, her voice was softer and tinged with affection.

"I remember." He gave a nod.

"Just keep that in your thoughts, and when you sight that bow think of it and hit em in the leg or the arm." She frowned.

"What we don't kill em?" He shook his head.

"Only if we have to, the way I see it, if we fill that side over yonder with wounded, they will writhe and moan and cause chaos, and they will also get a chance to get away from here and back to their loved ones. Think about it, he has a right tough job on his hands, so let's make it harder, because I will bet my last bit those buggers would rather be home by a decent fire, a good woman and pot of hot stew on the stove, than be here getting shot at by us. No littlun, we hurt em, and make him tie himself in knots dragging em out of the way. I reckon a little pain, then a trip home is a much better option for them than trying to kick us off this rock." Jade smiled.

"You sound like Robbie." He smirked.

"He is my sister's boy and well taught, he is a bright one for sure, there ain't any doubt about that."

Jade smiled as she looked out over the valley. "I feel better talking to you; I always knew you would understand all this better than some of the others... Oh and by the way, my juices are fine, I ain't all womanly and all that other girlie stuff." She gave a snort. "I am a woodsman, and I am not that pregnant, Rowan says it is not even as big as an egg yet, so how can all my juices be going backwards?" Joe gave a deep rumble of a laugh, and lifted his arm and patted her with affection on the top of the hood.

"Aye littlun, you ain't like many women I know, but never the less you are a woman even if you still refuse to see it. Them old boots of your dads hide it well, but I bet when them things come off, Rowan sees you less like a bloke and more like a woman... And never forget I was at your wedding, fool yourself all you like, but that weren't no bloke in that dress that day, even if you were wearing your boots." He chuckled.

As the morning rose above the mountains deep in the heart of the realm of Florae, Sapphire woke with a start in her large soft bed. She opened her eyes to see the smiling face of Tila sat in the chair near the huge triangular windows. "Good morning."

Sapphire sat up and rubbed her eyes, trying to focus on her new strange surroundings. She gave a yawn and turned to Tila. "Is it morning? I feel like I have not slept a wink." Tila smiled as she stood up and then walked over to the small table, set back against the sloping wall of the long room. She lifted a tall thin wooden jug and poured water from it into a glass.

"Walking in the dream worlds always does that to me too, here drink this and your thoughts will clear." She turned and walked to Sapphire, who sat watching her in her bed. Saff looked up at her, a puzzled look on her face.

"You know about the other worlds?" Tila gave a small chuckle and returned to her seat.

"You are Fae, and yet you know so little of your true identity, I can see why Crystal asked me to watch over you." Sapphire took a long sip from the glass, and as soon as the cold crisp water touched her lips, she felt warmth run into her, and her mind began to clear.

"I know nothing of this world, these people or this life." Tila gave a nod.

"I know of the fears your mother held, there was a time when all of us lived with the same fears, I think she hid your true identity to protect you, as she had no idea if we would ever unlock and leave this realm again, and in the realm of men, ignorance was your greatest protection." Sapphire understood, but somehow felt she had a right to have been taught more.

"She did try to tell me a lot of things on the boat to the mainland when we travelled to meet Una, but it was not a long trip so we had little time, apart from that she gave me small amounts about the things hidden within me when I was younger, and a long list of things I must never show anyone in the world of men. I wish she had prepared me better for all of this."

"It is understandable, she knew to control your gifts would ensure that the dark raven never discovered you, at that time this realm was sealed as it had been for many years. Many suffered in other worlds unable to return home, Gwendolyn knew that if she was killed, the raven would never be able to hurt anyone from here, as her power lived on here in this realm until the new queen was born. You were destined to be a centre of a circle, so your mother isolated you far away from prying eyes to keep you as safe as possible; it's not unsimilar to what we endured here alone, locked in our own realm." Sapphire turned and slipped her feet off the bed so that she faced Tila full on.

"I understand that, although I feel very much isolated still from all the realms now."

"I think that is natural, but as you learn more, you will find that you will gain a great sense of belonging to all the realms you walk." She stood up. "I will make us something to eat while you dress and then we can talk more, Crystal wants me to aid you in your understanding, so look to me if you have questions and doubts, and I will do what I can to help you feel more at home here in what is the realm of your line." She smiled and walked towards the door; Sapphire stood up.

"I have a lot of questions; I fear I may bore you with all of them." Tila gave a chuckle.

"I am a historian of our people; I doubt you will, although I may bore you with endless answers and over explanation, even Crystal thinks at times I talk too much."

Sapphire gave a smile, Tila was very likeable and as she reached for her clothes, she felt a little more relieved, yesterday had been a long and intense day, even now her mind was filled with a million questions. There was something comforting about knowing Crystal had asked Tila to help her adjust, in her mind she thought maybe the transformation into Florae culture would be a little smoother than she first expected.

Tila went down the stairs to prepare some food, which consisted of breads and fruits, and when she returned to the living space, she found Sapphire seated in her seat from the night before. Sapphire smiled as Tila walked towards her. "The sun is up; I don't have a lot of time, before I return to meet with Rune." Tila placed the oval wooden tray containing their breakfast on the table.

"Don't forget, we have a different time here to the world of men, trust me we have hours before anyone in that world rises from their beds." Sapphire gave a nod and lifted a roll of bread from the table.

"Yeah, I think Gwynfor said something about that yesterday... I am not sure I will ever learn all this stuff." Tila gave a chuckle.

"Relax you have years to understand all this stuff." She lifted a wooden beaker from the table and took a swig. "There is much to learn, and as they say there is no time like the here and now, so how about I begin where we began earlier?" Sapphire nodded.

"OK then, what will we talk about?" Tila smiled.

"Well for starters dream walking, I take it you do not really understand the process." Sapphire gave a nod.

"Not really no... I understand I travel there, it's just that whenever I come back, I am in bed." Tila thought for a moment, and then leaned forward toward the table and lifted a rosy red apple and sat back. Taking a small knife from the tray she began to cut thin slices off the fruit and slip them into her mouth as she began to speak.

"A Fae is basically two forms, there is the form you are sat in before me, and there is also another form, which others would probably call an ethereal like form."

"You mean like a spirit, a ghost?" Tila gave a little laugh.

"Well, if my understanding of the world of men is right, a ghost is the lost spirit of a dead person, so no not like that. For us this form is more a fluid form, like a water or gas, and we can slip with ease between the two. We can control it to travel to other places, the difference being that in this form we also feel whole and complete." Sapphire gave nod of understanding.

"Sort of like being in two places at once."

"Yeah, something like that. The thing is we all dream walk, if I am honest no one really knows why, it is just one of those gifts we all have. Now what is different is that we all have one realm in which we can walk in this dream state, yours is actually the coolest as it is the Realm of Dreams. You feel whole because when you are there, all that remains here is your physical body, literally just the bones and meat, which looks like you are sleeping. The person you are on the inside, sort of the invisible part of all of us that contains the good stuff like memories and thoughts etc, you know our true self? That travels to the realm with you, which is why you feel complete. Green Circle have it too, they call it their essence, but it is pretty much the same thing. I think it has something to do with the power of Eve, because it was her life force that was placed in all of us." Sapphire understood, Tila actually made far more sense than Rune when she explained it.

"But men have the same life force, yet they cannot do it." Tila agreed.

"Yes they do, and too be honest there are a few who use meditation in order to achieve this, but on the whole most men are not enlightened enough and so have not done it, so we think that somehow they can only achieve this after death, as their life force is somehow stuck to their meat and bones." It gave Sapphire a shudder to think of it. Tila chewed on her apple. "True Fae use this form to also change and move their physical body, I am sure you have heard of, or seen some of us turn into a small orb of light and zip off through the air. What all of you do not see is that what happens is our physical being shrinks to a very small size which is surrounded by energy, and so it looks to the observer like a ball of light."

"Yes, I think Isolde did it once to get out of the way, I was never so sure. You say true Fae, are there false Fae?" Tila gave a giggle.

"You are funny." She gave another giggle. "True Fae are pure with both parents being full Fae. You see you are only half Fae as you are from the union of a Fae and a line of men. Your mother is the daughter of a queen of Fae, but your father was a lord of high birth. To be honest looking at you, I would say you are about ninety percent Fae, your mother's line is powerful, and so I think you got far more than other mixed race Fae would get."

It gave Sapphire a lot to think about, she had never really looked at herself that way. "I doubt you could transform, but that does not really matter for you because you can make windows, something full Fae do not really do, I think it has something to do with you being a centre of a circle, although I did know a few ordinary other Fae who could do it."

It made a lot of sense and for the first time in her life Sapphire began to understand how she could have travelled over the Bridge of Sequana, and also that her windows as she saw them, were actually a projection of who she was. Tila made a lot of sense, and again it explained how Rune could appear to other people at the same time as being with her. In her mind because Rune was so powerful, she had the ability to do it whilst awake. She looked towards Tila, who she noticed was smiling at her.

"What?"

"I can almost see your brain making sense of it; I think you are really starting to understand how different you are from all those people who have surrounded you all your life." Sapphire smiled.

"It takes a little mental gymnastics, but yes, I think I finally am starting to understand parts of me."

For the rest of the morning Sapphire sat with Tila, asking questions and getting some very important answers. Tila had been right, she did tend to over explain everything, but Sapphire found all of it helpful. She learned how the Fae were very skilled with weapons, Tila admitted that she had advanced fighting skills, but she also explained how the elders had forbidden them from combat unless it was in defence of their own people. The taking of life was seen as a very serious act and considering the Fae of Earth had sworn to work towards peace between all races; to take a life in an unjust way had serious consequences.

The Fae of Earth were also highly educated in the crafts of the earth, and were very skilled in herb lore and the curing of all the races. Not only did they know all the plant forms of their own realms, but they had sent members of the Fae to all the worlds to learn all their plant lore too, and so were advanced in their skills of healing. Tila did note how they had withdrawn from the realm of men in the past when their elders learned of man's dealings with compounds not of the plant kingdom as cures, and had for a time called men barbaric for their treatment of each other with cures that had to be paid for with money.

Tila named many skills from communicating with animals, to charming fish. Some could make fire with a simple touch, others could recover burned out lands by making the plant life grow faster, but the one thing that really caught Sapphire's attention was when Tila talked of Sandlings, or Dream Weavers as she referred to them. "Yes, yes there are old tales that some Fae decided to collect dreams after they departed the worldly realms. It is said that they were born into a new form and had the ability to keep their gift of becoming orbs. The rumours and you have to understand this has never been proven, are that they would drift around collecting happiness to craft into dreams, which they then attributed to an individual. At the right time, they would then send those dreams in Fae form to visit the individual and soak into them, at which point the dream became a reality." Sapphire was thrilled to think that Cal was just like her, Tila gave a small scowl.

"The dark raven we think learned this secret, and she captures them and does wicked and cruel things to them, and creates those ghastly monsters of all darkness that I think you people named Darkmares. Crystal told me about them and the trouble you all had with them, I hate that vile woman, how could she be so evil as to corrupt such a pure and beautiful spirit being?" Sapphire felt a cold chill run down her spine.

"I know, they were vile things and the terror they caused was terrible to see, I have no idea how you could take something as beautiful as my Cal and do that to them. I would die if she caught and hurt him, she is vile, you are right, and her Houlen are just as bad." Tila gave a shudder and looked round.

"Best not say that word here." Sapphire looked a little surprised.

"Why is it a Fae swear word?" Tila shook her head.

"It's not, but it may as well be, many of our kind have suffered from those beasts of darkness, they terrify many here. The word you see is a Fae word, it means dark hole, actually the correct pronunciation would be Hole Dark, but most just say it as dark hole."

"Dark hole?" Tila nodded.

"Yeah, we do not go below the surface, for there are tales of hidden magic from the start of time buried in all lands. Fae Ofmoon dig deep within the earth, many times we have advised their queen not to do so, but they desire those things that can be crafted into items of great glory. It is said many a strange power has been found down there." Tila leaned in and lowered her voice to a whisper.

"It has been said often that the queen of the moon does not favour those of dark hair, because they go below and they are infected with the strange things that live deep in the earth, it is said it is those members of the Fae that the dark raven hunts to make her evil beings, which is why they are named Dark Hole in the tongue of the Fae Ofmoon." That was a real eye opener for Sapphire.

"That word is Fae Ofmoon?" Tila nodded with a very serious look on her face, but said nothing more. "I had no idea, but actually it does make sense, because my aunt told us Rhiannon sought them out and killed all of them." Tila took a deep breath, and then released it slowly as if to calm herself.

"We all fear them, it is said she killed them to stop word of their existence from being known outside of the realm of Avalon, it does make a lot of sense."

"She appears to know far more than she lets on, I wonder what else she knows." Tila gave her head a little shake.

"Be wary Saff, that is not a line of investigation you want to take, there have been many things said in the past, and all of them brought down pain and great woes, trust me, if you have questions to help Rune find this Ena, stay away from her. I have heard many things that concern me when it comes to the golden queen." Tila looked concerned and Sapphire felt her apprehension.

"But we need to find this Ena, it's almost like she never existed, and yet the water told me she does, what if she is Fae Ofmoon, wont Amethyst or Rhiannon be able to find her for us?"

"That could be dangerous Saff, listen to me, Rhiannon has many secrets and she does not like outsiders asking about them. There is a tale of a woman Bade once loved who accused Rhiannon of many things, and she vanished out of thin air never to be seen or heard of again. It caused a lot of trouble for the first queen and also for Gwendolyn when she was new to the throne. Rhiannon is very powerful and not to be messed with, I would say if you are looking for help, stay as far from Avalon as you can."

There was something in the way Tila spoke, something about her tone, she was very serious and if Sapphire was right, she was also afraid, all the time they had been talking she had been leaning forward talking almost in a whisper. Tila looked round to ensure there was no one in ear shot looking very worried indeed, she sat back up straight in her chair and her voice returned to normal.

"I fear her so much that I never mention anything to Crystal, after all she is her granddaughter and also my lover. I am no fool Sapphire, I am powerful and greatly skilled in my own defence, but there are some things no one should ever mention, and her secrets no matter what they are, I feel are best left exactly that." Sapphire gave a frightened nod.

"I hear you, fear not I have enough trouble staying out of the Dark One's reach, I can assure you I have no intention of upsetting any other." Tila relaxed in her seat.

"It's better for all of us... Good, you are as smart as I thought you were."

CHAPTER EIGHT

HOME

By the time the rain eased it was noon. Ester calmed down as she talked to the Sage and Martin, and she told them the story of how her small town had fought hard to survive after the fall of everything. They established trade by managing the large woodland on the outskirts of town, using the fast growing birch trees, they made charcoal. It had taken a few difficult years to recover the town to a stable living standard, but the production of charcoal had been the saviour of the town, as it allowed them to trade with farmers for extra food, to add to what was hunted and gathered. Their biggest mistake came when they started to supply the forces of Mason.

Five years ago, a soldier had wandered into town and arranged to make a big purchase. The town's folk were all delighted, and believed this would be the saving grace for all of them. For two years trade with the soldiers had been going well, but it rapidly turned into a nightmare, when a Cutter raiding party attacked them and took control of everything. That had been three years ago, and they had been enslaved ever since working for the Cutters, who made them expand their operation to supply only Mason's forces. Ester was reluctant to elaborate, but she made it very clear that all the women had suffered greatly at the hands of their new masters.

They walked for almost two hours; Ester had not lied when she had told them she had scrambled through the woodland in the dark all night. It was not long before the stone walls covered in moss and ferns began to appear in amongst the trees, to mark what had once been a country lane, Ester stopped and pointed. "It is about another mile down this road, it is easy to tell when you are close as the road has been cleared to get the carts up it." She turned and pointed into the trees. "The coast lies that way, and that is the route I took, everyone is locked behind a high fence at night on what used to be a sports field, although now it is just a large enclosure filled with shacks made from scraps." The Sage looked round.

"Ok so where do I find this Coker and his men?"

"Next to the sports field is an old factory, it is one of a few buildings that were not destroyed by the bad weather after the fall of everything. Most of the town is all around but it is nothing more than crumbled ruins, the road is reasonably clear and runs straight to the factory. The ground floor has many workshops where we make candles and cloth and other stuff, Coker and his men live on the next floor, we scavenged a lot of things from the towns all around that were hit hard, and set up rooms for each family, but they threw us out and took them for themselves."

Martin walked forward a few paces, he sniffed the air and turned back to face Ester, she had appeared alright walking towards this place, but now she had a look of fear and she shook slightly.

Martin eyed the Sage, and then turned his gaze back to Ester. "You say that the charcoal ovens are across the other side of the town, and that ten men will have to stay with them all night to watch over them?" Ester gave a nod.

"They work us all till dusk, and then bring us back and lock us in the enclosure for the night." Martin gave a nod and looked at the Sage. "If he has over fifty armed men, it would make sense to use the workers when they are free." Ester shook her head.

"No, you must be very careful, some of them have guns. Anyone who tries to run gets shot; they never leave the workers alone for a minute." Martin scratched his tatty grey hair, his green eyes burned in his tanned face.

"Arrows unlike guns make little sound; I take it they have a position from which they watch in groups?" Ester gave a nod; Ben looked at Martin then back to the Sage.

"If we find the ones furthest away from the others, can we not take them out and move in that way?" The Sage looked down at Ben.

"I would say Master Winter's you have the making of a plan, I must admit though, a visit from Sapphire about now would help." He crouched down on the dirt and looked at Ester. "Can you draw me a rough plan of this factory and the field, and exactly where the wood cookers are?" She looked a little confused and crouched down at his side.

"You do know this is insane, don't you? There are only four of us, and he has up to a hundred depending on where his cart men are." The Sage smiled.

"You would be surprised what a hand full of good men and a surprise attack can achieve, believe me, I have done madder things." Ester shook her head, and started to sketch a rough map in the dirt of where everything was in relation to each other.

Around Loxley little had changed from the morning, the whole of the stockade was a hive of activity as Father Warren walked round the side of Alf the Butcher's, towards the cake shop. Never in any of his time at Loxley, had he seen so many carts and horses, moving up and down the roadway, in between the two sets of shops. Agatha stood as usual at her gate and gave him a solemn nod as he approached the front of the Cake Shop. Anne Kirk was out in a flash, wiping her hands on her apron looking somewhat hot and red in the face. "Good afternoon Father, I did not know you were calling by, I was going to send your loaf over to your new lodgings." Warren gave a courteous smile.

"Oh I say, there is no need for that Miss Kirk, you are busy enough, plus I think I have rather enjoyed being out in the air, we had somewhat of a long night last night indoors, it's nice to take the air and clear my head." Anne looked a little saddened.

"We were ever so sorry to hear about your friends, awful business with those Cutters and such, killing in a cathedral, I tell you it's simply disgraceful it is. Alice was quite distressed when the news came in." Father Warren looked saddened.

"It was a terrible business you are right, so many wounded or lost, we will be having a small service of remembrance at the hotel at some point, so everyone can say a few words and pray for our lost brothers and sisters." Anne gave a mournful sigh, and patted his hand.

"I can assure you Alice and I, will offer our respects and say a prayer for everyone."

"Well, that would be very good of you, and I am sure the bishop and the council would appreciate it a great deal."

Anne moved round to the father's side and leaned back a little, to see Agatha leaning onto the dividing wall trying to listen in to her conversation; she gave a slight smirk, and pushed the father gently in the back, her voice rose a little louder. "Oh, so the bishop and his party are still here, I thought they had intended to go to York. Come on inside father and I will find you a nice fresh loaf, we have just taken a good new batch out of the oven, and you can tell me all about it."

Anne escorted the father through the door inside the shop, stopping only to note the sigh of annoyance from Agatha as she peered round the edge of the wall, annoyed that yet again, Anne had got to the good news first. She gave a long sigh and scowled down the street, before turning back towards the cheese shop doorway. "MELISSA!!"

Rune returned with Steph and Melanie, and as they entered the Village Hall, Rune hung back to watch from the doorway. Loxley in many ways appeared normal, the streets were full, the market was busy, on the field men were training, and yet all the extra tents, and new influx of the soldiers from the surrounding woodland, appeared to add another layer of noise and action. "It feels strange seeing this place so full, doesn't it?"

"What... Oh Rob, sorry I was lost in thought." Robbie had come out of the hall, and was stood beside her, she looked up at his side profile and noted how stern his face looked, he was worried about home, she sensed it, but knew it was natural; everyone in Loxley that day had to be hiding their fears. The threat that had hung in the air for so long had now grown larger than life, and was right across the valley. Rune slipped her arm round him.

"We will make it through you know?" He gave a slight note of recognition.

"I know, but how many of them will? Think about it, we really do not know what he is going to throw at us, and all these fighters, look at them Rune, look how young they are, and yet here they are preparing for the fight of our lives. Too many of our young have already suffered because of one man's greed and lust for control, I cannot help but wonder if there was anyone who has stood in the past before all of the wars of man, and asked the same question. We slaughter the young for what exactly, to prove we are right, or to say no to some maniac? All of this is senseless, Mason had all of Cornwall and Devon, he built a wall and was the hero who saved his people, why the hell couldn't he have stayed behind it?"

She pulled him tight and snuggled into him. "You have read everything your grandfather wrote in his notes about this place; he saw this coming because he understood that there are men like Mason who will never be content. You are right, he had all of that land behind his wall, but you fail to see that some men just cannot settle with what they have. The more you give them, the more they will demand, history is filled with them, it is part of what the human being has become. Some lead, some follow, some give and others take, it is why man has out competed everything else to rule the animal kingdom. I know it feels odd, but it is also why there has been some form of stability and order, everyone has played their role."

"Mankind is stupid." Rune gave a smile.

"They can be, but you must understand that there is so much more to all of us." He turned his face and glanced down at her.

"Like what?"

"Love, compassion, empathy, kindness, Rob these are also great qualities that exist in everyone, and I may add, they are also good reasons to resist the Masons of this world." Robbie gave a sigh and then leaned down and kissed her forehead.

"You missed hope." She gave a giggle as she released him.

"No, I didn't, there wasn't a need to say that, I already feel it pulsating quite strongly inside you, so knowing you have that already, there was no need to include it." He turned and pulled her back into his arms and kissed her softly.

"You are too wise for one so young Runestone Sapphire." Her radiantly blue eyes stared up into his as she smiled at him.

"Hey I keep telling you, trust me I know stuff." With a giggle she wriggled free and stepped back. "I need to head home and go to my table; I have things I need to see." He understood.

"Ena?" She gave a sigh.

"Not yet, she is out there somewhere and I will find her, I am hoping Sapphire will discover something, she should be back later. I have no idea how she is hiding from us; I know I am missing something; I just don't know what, but it will come to me so don't worry, one way or the other, I am planning to meet and talk to this Ena and find out just exactly who she is."

"Ok keep looking, I am going to be here a while there is a lot to be done, I have no idea when I will be home." She stepped back and stood on her tip toes to kiss him.

"I understand, just make sure you eat and get a little rest, you still look very tired, and remind Rowan to do the same, you two are doing too much, we have a massive staff so please take some time for yourselves, we have a big fight coming and us girls want our men fit and ready." He gave a smile and nodded whilst rolling his eyes.

"We will I promise, kiss the kids for me." She turned to walk towards the horses tied up at the side and lifted her hand to wave.

"I will, have no fear, and if you need me, tell one of the family to contact me." The horse boy aided her up onto the white horse, and she pulled on the reins and blew him a kiss. "See you later."

Robbie watched as she turned the horse and then trotted on to the lane that led up towards the Hawthorn lined lane and the farm, he turned and took a few more moments to watch the scene of the busiest he had seen Loxley, and then with hands slipped into his pockets, turned and headed back towards the doors and the chaotic Village Hall.

Sapphire and Tila were still talking and laughing when Crystal arrived back at the house. "Are we ready then?" Sapphire looked up at her.

"What...Are we going now?" Crystal gave a nod.

"Yeah, I thought you wanted to get back to Rune?" Tila jumped up as Sapphire looked at Crystal.

"Whoopee I will grab my pack." She ran across the room to the stairs; Sapphire felt a little confused.

"Is Tila coming with us?"

"Hmm, she got special permission from the elders; they felt it was important to keep your induction back into the Fae going even when you were outside Florae."

"Your Elders do know we are walking into a war zone, don't they? It is just her people are not allowed to take unnecessary life, and we could be walking into combat." Crystal gave a chuckle.

"You do realise they are not just her people, but yours as well? Don't worry about Tila her orders are to protect you at all costs, even if it means deadly force, you are very important to all Fae now." It felt odd to hear it.

The thumping on the stairs announced Tila's return, she walked across the room with a loose green back pack on, and over her shoulder she had a very soft light cloak of rusty brown. Her clothes were several shades of green, and over her green blouse she had a long soft brown leather waistcoat. Sapphire looked at her clothing and felt that somehow with her long brown hair and hazel eyes she would be able to blend into any woodland. She gave a smile as she walked towards a tall cupboard near the stairs downward. "Won't be a minute."

Opening the door Sapphire saw a long highly polished bow, which she gently lifted out, Sapphire marvelled to see it had silver designs inlaid into the wood. Tila pulled out a belt and swung it round her waist, on which she noted the very finely crafted sword and a matching dagger, as well as a small knife similar to that of Robbie's woodsman type. She gave another smile. "Ready?" Crystal shook her head.

"Honestly you were our ambassador for years; you would think you had never left Florae before."

"I know but it's been ages since I left here, and I have heard so much about Loxley, it's all your fault, you tell such good stories when you return, so I am excited to see it for myself." Crystal gave a giggle, and Sapphire smiled at such a cheeky look on Tila's face.

Ten minutes later they all had their bags and belongings, and stood in the living quarters ready to leave. Sapphire shouldered her bag as Crystal lifted hers. "Ok so do we go by horse or cart?" Tila gave a frown.

"What do you mean?" Sapphire shrugged.

"You know back to the passage that leads to Iona." Tila had a strange look for a moment and then smiled.

"I thought you were going to use a window, I am dying to see it, Chris says yours is blue, I have never seen a blue one before they are usually white or yellow."

"Oh, I didn't know I could use it here." Crystal gave her a smile.

"You can use it anywhere; Gwynfor brought you in via the passage because you have never been here before, and so he knew you would not know where to go. Just think of Loxley as you usually do and open it there." Sapphire turned in the centre of the room and her blue circular window opened up in front of her.

"Oh wow that is really pretty." She gave a smile at Tila, and stepped through onto the deep green grass of Robbie's Mere as Rune was dismounting off her horse, Rune gave a smile.

"Nice timing." Behind Sapphire Tila and Crystal walked through the window and it closed behind them.

Tila slowly turned round in a circle, as Sapphire walked towards Rune. "Oh wow, this place is beautiful." Sapphire turned back to Crystal and Tila.

"This is Tila; she is Crystal's life partner." Rune gave a huge smile as Crystal walked towards her.

"I am so delighted you finally brought her here to meet us." She gave a nod towards Tila who was watching. "Welcome to our home Tila, it is lovely to finally meet you after hearing so much about you." Tila appeared to stiffen and then shot down into a very regal bow.

"My Lady of Life, I am honoured to be a guest in your realm." Rune gave a smile.

"This is my home Tila, and you are very welcome, but please here I am simply Runestone, no one here stands on formalities, but I do thank you for such an honourable and sincere welcome." Tila looked a little awkward.

"I felt as a member of my race I should show you respect, after all you are also the mother to our new queen. If you don't mind, may I enquire if she is here?" Rune looked pleased.

"She is indeed; would you like to meet her?" Tila looked like she was about to explode, her eyes sparkled with excitement, and her voice became quite squeaky.

"Can I?" Rune gave a giggle, as did Sapphire and Crystal.

"I am sure that can be arranged. Come and I shall take you to her." Tila walked quickly over to Rune, who took her by the arm and walked her through the gate towards the house. Sapphire and Crystal gave a giggle and followed behind smiling.

CHAPTER NINE

HELPFUL FRIENDS

Hidden in the trees on the other side of what had once been a small town, surrounded by the remains of crumbled buildings, now clothed in moss and weeds, long rows of circular brick built charcoal ovens gave off wisps of smoke. The grime covered and rag dressed workers, shovelled dirt on to the top of the earth mounded up on the ovens, where deep inside the embers of the cut birch smouldered black in the searing heat.

Around the whole area was a ten foot chain link fence, with barbed wire strewn across the top. Set back in the trees behind a low wall, Ester lay beside the Sage, and watched the captives shovel earth or cut new wood ready for the next set of burning. Several ovens were open; their huge metal round lids stood up against the fence opposite, fresh wood was being cut and dropped inside. Guards walked up and down on the perimeter of the fence with crossbows and guns, inside the fenced area, there were four guards with wooden batons.

Martin leaned over from a few feet away. "Those inside have no weapons, they will not give us any trouble, but there are a lot on the outer fence, and they are all in view of each other, this is not going to be easy in day light." The Sage stared forward, his bark like skin blending into the shady surroundings.

"We won't have much of a choice; tell me Ester, what will happen when the day ends?"

"They line up and the gates are opened, then they walk in file back to the camp, ten usually remain for the night watch." The Sage considered her words carefully.

"Do the guards walk on either side of them to keep them in line?" She nodded.

"Yes... Although they stay a good distance away, they can raise a gun and shoot quickly if anyone breaks free, we have lost too many that way."

"Ok I have seen enough, let's get back to Ben, and we can work out just how we are going to do this."

Ester turned on the floor. "You are still going to do this then? You do know there are far more men back at the camp." The Sage winked.

"We won't be alone by then though, will we? We will have plenty of free men to help us." She smiled and shook her head slowly.

"I still am not sure if this is bravery or stupidity." Martin gave a soft chuckle.

"It's a little of both I think, but we have found it does seem to do the trick."

The three of them slipped back across the rough floor, and melted into the trees to head back towards Ben without a sound.

Tila crouched on the floor, her face flat to the soft carpet as Isolde lifted Iona from her crib. Crystal gave a giggle. "What the hell Tila you said you wanted to see your queen; you won't see much looking at the carpet." Rune and Saff gave a loud chuckle, as a mumbled voice came from underneath the huddled figure.

"She is a queen more powerful than Gwendolyn, I feel her power, and it is bound within a circle of deep violet, I am not worthy enough to look upon her, for I am only a simple cleric in the House of Scribes." Crystal turned to Sapphire.

"See I told you, she has not been out for a while." Sapphire started to giggle.

"Don't be mean; this is obviously very important to her."

"Yes you, don't be mean, this means everything, I see her force in my mind and she has such beautiful gifts, I see a golden tree set within the stars of Enaria on a sea of blue." Rune pricked up her ears, as Saff and Crystal sniggered more, she looked at Tila.

"What are the stars of Enaria?" Isolde held Iona close as she gurgled in her arms.

"They are twelve stars made by her husband and filled with secrets of the true power of the Fae of Earth."

Isolde looked down and scowled at Tila. "None outside of our kingdom of Florae are supposed to know of them." More muffles came from the floor.

"I am sorry, I got scared when I saw them in my mind, none of you understand." Rune walked into the room and took Iona out of Isolde's arms. She sat down on the floor in front of Tila.

"All of you leave us." Crystal looked at Sapphire who motioned it was alright, and both of them withdrew slowly into the corridor, and then turned to walk to the stairs, Crystal looked at Sapphire.

"What was all that about?" Sapphire shrugged her shoulders.

"Why ask me? You probably know more about Florae and the Fae of Earth than I do."

"Good point, I suppose we will have to wait. Fancy a coffee? It's the one thing I have missed whilst in Florae; I do wish they would start growing beans." They headed onto the stairs.

"Maybe you should ask Jess, she is always taking cuttings to increase the stocks, I am sure she could spare a few?" Crystal gave an approving nod.

"Good idea, maybe I will."

Runestone sat on the floor and lifted Iona close to the still crouched and slightly shaking Tila. Iona gave a happy squeak and reached forward with her tiny hands. Rune lowered her slowly to touch Tila's hair. From deep underneath the mass of cloak came a soft gasp. Rune smiled. "We are alone and you have nothing to fear here. Iona Violet future queen of the Fae of Earth, may I introduce you to Tila, clerk in your house of scrolls." Tila looked up.

"It is Scribes." Her breath caught in her throat as she came face to face with her future queen. Tears filled her eyes, and streaked down her face as she suddenly sat up.

"My Queen, please forgive me but you are so beautiful." Rune smiled as more tears ran down Tila's face, and she began to cry, and mumble. "We have waited so long in hope for this time, and now you are here, I have no words to use that are worthy enough, accept my sword and my loyalty are yours for as long as I shall live." Rune wanted to smile but felt it best she didn't.

"Tila of the Fae you have honoured your queen greatly." Tila swallowed hard.

"Do you think so?" Rune smiled.

"Yes indeed." She held Iona out to her. "Would you like to hold her?" Tila shot backwards and up to her feet stepping away a look of sheer terror on her face.

"Oh dear on Ninian's toes no I cannot." Rune gave a giggle as Tila shook with utter fright. "What if I dropped her?" She looked absolutely distraught, and as if she was about to unravel. "I mean we have waited so long and if I dropped her.... Oh oh oh lords of the council, I could kill my queen." Rune could do nothing but start to laugh, as Tila took another step backwards towards the door, she pulled Iona close and got up off the floor.

"I am quite sure my daughter is in safe hands, come sit on the bed." Tila shook from head to foot.

"I am really not sure My Lady; I can be clumsy at times." Before she had a chance to say another word, Rune pulled her over and sat her on the end of the small bed, and gently placed Iona into her arms. Iona looked up at Tila with huge violet eyes and gurgled; Tila burst into tears and looked at Rune.

"She is beautiful, oh My Lady you have honoured me beyond life." Rune smiled, and turned to the next crib.

"This is her brother, my son Halbert." And she lifted him out of the crib and turned to face Tila, who was staring down at Iona lost in time, and gently rocking her.

Crystal sat in the kitchen holding her cup, and kept looking up at the ceiling in the direction of the nursery, Sapphire gave a chuckle.

"Chris she is fine."

"Oh, I don't know Saff, I have never seen her like that before, it's not at all like her."

"Relax Rune is with her, it is her future queen, you know how much they loved Gwendolyn, well judging by that, I think it's safe to say they are going to love Iona far more."

"Yeah, I suppose so, it was a big deal for Amethyst when she took her seat, the people partied for days."

"How is Amethyst, I sort of miss her, we use to have a lot of time together on the road." Crystal gave a sad smile.

"I miss her too, although she and James seem really happy. Amy has made a lot of changes, I am not sure gran is completely happy, but at the end of the day it is her realm to rule now." Sapphire's ears pricked up, Tila had told her to avoid the subject of Rhiannon, but she could not help but wonder if Amethyst would rule differently.

"Why would your gran not be happy?" Crystal looked a little worried.

"Family stuff I think, Amy is not known for old ways, she has a more modern approach, I think there has been some friction." Sapphire gave a shrug.

"You know what they say, new broom makes for a good clean out, maybe she needed to make things run in her style, I mean it must have been expected, I would assume Iona will make big changes too when she takes the crown."

"Yeah probably."

Upstairs Rune sat on the floor of the nursery with a much calmer Tila. Iona appeared very content in her arms, and having got over the fact that this was her future queen; she relaxed more and just enjoyed cradling the infant in her arms. Rune smiled as she looked on.

"I have heard the name Enaria before you mentioned it earlier, was she very well known?" Tila looked up and gave a blink.

"Er...Oh yeah, she is possibly the most famous seer of the lines of Fae, in Florae she is greatly admired, she dedicated her life to our people and as a result it cost her exactly that. We have a room as tribute to her in the House of Scribes." Rune nodded as she listened to show her understanding.

"I always thought Sequana was the most famous seer of the Fae." Tila shook her head.

"If you listen to those Ofmoon she was, but they are just boasting, Enaria was Sequana's teacher, and considering she was of a different race of Fae, she did not teach her everything, like all Fae, we too have our secrets."

"So I have heard, tell me Tila, you say you saw a symbol of a golden tree on a pale blue background, surrounded by twelve golden stars, how did you see that?" Tila shrugged.

"I saw your daughter and felt a strong presence, and then the picture came to my mind, why do you ask?" Rune thought for a moment.

"I too have seen that symbol on my table; I believe it is the symbol that will mark Iona's own table of power." Tila nodded in agreement.

"It does make sense, she has great power already, she will need the most powerful Fae table to handle what she has flowing through her, yeah it makes sense to have Enaria's stars on it." Rune was confused for a second, but Tila was very relaxed.

"Why Enaria's stars, would she not be better to use the table of Gwendolyn?" Tila looked up and thought for a second, she considered the proposition and then shook her head.

"Not really, I can see why you would think that though."

"You can, why?" Tila gave a smile.

"Well it is true that Enaria created the star of protection that Gwendolyn used to protect the White Circle, but you see the circle that will develop around Iona will be far more powerful, and so Enaria's twelve stars of life and death are really the only symbols strong enough to handle the kind of power a violet circle will create."

"Enaria sounds like she was far more powerful than any of us have heard before, although I have to ask, how did she die?"

Tila looked sad for a moment. "It is such a sad tale. The story is that Enaria sensed that something was wrong after Tideguyde disappeared, so she made the journey up to the moon; this was right at the beginning of the Fae, and it was just before Rhiannon was given her seat on the moon so it's a very long time ago. She never really said what happened whilst she was there, but something terrified her, and she returned in a bad way. She went straight to Bridget Violet to report it, but fell sick on the way. Her husband sent for help and when Bridget turned up, Enaria begged her to get her daughter away from her, which was really odd because she doted on her daughter. Anyhow Bridget left with her daughter, and a few days later Enaria died, her husband died about a month after, so Bridget had little choice but to raise Ariel as one of her own. Enaria was very close to Bridget, it was often said they were more like sisters than friends."

Rune listened intently, she understood this was a story told within the Fae only, and it gave her a great deal to think about.

"So what happened to her daughter?"

"She became a Scribe in the house and the first historian of the Fae, most of what I have studied was written by her back on Erin. When we came to Florae, it was Ariel who actually designed and oversaw the building of the new house of Scribes. Bridget sent her as an ambassador to Avalon shortly after when it was being built, but her and Rhiannon did not see eye to eye, there was a bit of a scandal and she came home to Florae where she became a researcher. It's a bit sketchy and people do not often talk about it, it is kind of awkward apparently, but at some point, of which no one is really sure, she just disappeared and she has never been seen since."

Rune rolled her eyes. "How peculiar, you would have thought that the daughter of someone so powerful would have been more accountable to the realm." Tila shrugged.

"Bade knew her and worked with her." She gave a sly smile. "One or two of the older members of the council once told me they thought he was madly in love with her, I did ask him once and he got really angry, so I have kept my mouth shut since." She gave a little giggle.

Rune gave a chuckle. "Unrequited love can do that." Tila sniggered.

They played with the children for a good while, when suddenly Rune looked up at Tila. "What is Ninian's Toes?" Tila gave a loud guffaw.

"It's an old story from Fae. Ninian was the son of Bridget, Gwendolyn's Father, and when he was teaching Gwynfor woodwork, he slipped and dropped an axe, and it cut off three of his toes."

"Ouch!" Tila nodded with a smile.

"Bade seemed to think that they were important, so he had them preserved and placed in a glass case in the House of Scribes. Everyone gets to see them when they work there, and to be honest it's quite shocking when you see them, because Bade kept the axe as well and it's in the box with them. Honestly the first time I saw them it terrified me, as he mounted the axe in a piece of wood like it had fallen onto it and sunk in, and then lined the toes up exactly as he found them."

"Good Grief that sounds awful." Tila gave a giggle.

"It is, honestly they look so scary and shocking, so now it has become a sort of private joke in the house as we work, if something surprises or shocks us, we always say 'On Ninian's Toes." She gave another giggle and Rune joined in with her.

It was over an hour later when Rune appeared at the kitchen door. She walked in and lifted the pot and poured a tea, then came and sat at the table. Sapphire could feel a need growing within Rune, as she looked across the table at Crystal.

"I left Tila with the children; she is lovely Crystal; I really like her. She asked if you would go up to her, I am assuming you will be staying here with us whilst you are here, your room is already prepared for the both of you, so settle in and relax until we are all needed." Crystal gave a wide smile.

"It's good to be back, and thanks...You know for being so sweet with Tila." Rune gave a beautiful smile.

"You are always welcome you know that, and so is your lovely companion."

"Thanks Rune." Crystal got up and placed her cup in the pot sink, she left the room and went upstairs, Rune waited until she heard her walk along the corridor upstairs, and then holding her mug she stood up so quickly, her chair slid back on the floor making Sapphire jump.

"C'mon, table, now." She turned and left the room quickly, Sapphire had to glug her last few mouthfuls down as quickly as she could, and then followed Rune out of the kitchen, across the top of the living space to the small door under the stairs. As fast as she could, she made her way down the narrow stone steps, and by the time she reached the room below, Rune was sat with her hands on her table that bore the huge twenty pointed violet star. Mist was already swirling across its surface as Sapphire made it to her seat. Rune looked up her eyes filled with deep violet light.

"Hurry sit down and place your hands on the table, I want to see and hear everything that happened to you in Florae, somehow I feel it is of great importance."

Sapphire looked at the table and placed her flat palms onto the cold cool surface, instantly her eyes exploded with blue light, and the images of her and Gwynfor rose out of the table for Rune to view.

CHAPTER TEN

UNKNOWN FACTORS

The day slowly drew on as Ester sat with the Sage, Martin, and Ben, and watched her friends toil at the charcoal ovens. Several times a Cutter beat one of the workers with his baton, and on each occasion the Sage noticed how Ester would flinch and shudder. The look on her face alone, told him that she too had endured such punishment at some point in the past.

As Ester watched, Martin and the Sage planned how they could separate the guards from the captive workers. The Sage knew that he had to get the workers free to aid him; otherwise he would be walking into a large group of Cutters alone. They carefully worked out a plan, and mapped out the whole area, and when the time finally came with the ringing of a work bell, both of them moved into action. Martin took Ben, who had become a sufficient archer in London, and Ester stayed close to the Sage.

They separated, one to take up defence on the right of the gateway out, and the other team to the left. The guards separated either side and cocked their rifles, leaving a wide gap along the road that led back to their fenced off quarters and the old factory. One guard checked to ensure all was well, and then approached the gate, as the workers locked inside the compound of the burners, formed a long line. From the cover of the trees, the Sage looked across the wide area at the assembled workers, they looked exhausted, dirty and beat, and deep inside he silently prayed that the power of the green lord would be with him and with the captives. Twenty guards prepared, and he lifted his bow, on the other side of the compound Martin and Ben both lifted their bows loaded and ready, Martin breathed out slowly.

"Remember Ben, you take the ones from the end of the line back towards the gate, and I will start at the gate and meet you in the middle, and no matter what happens, keep shooting, Ester and the Sage will be depending on it." Ben looked a little nervous but gave a nod.

With no spare bow, all Ester could do was watch, and yet her keen eyes would be vital to the Sage who slipped two arrows onto his bow. "Been a while since I did this, let's hope I remember what I was taught."

The guard lifted the large lock and inserted a key, and then with a soft click it came away from the gate, and the guard swung it back. He cocked his rifle, and then using the barrel he waved the first men inside, out through the gate. Martin began to count slowly, and Ben lifted his bow and waited for his cue. Across the way the Sage slowly counted in time, and held his bow ready, as the workers began to walk slowly out through the gate. Ester's heart beat in rhythm to the soft quiet counting of the Sage, and she scanned left and right to watch the movements of all of the guards. The Sage's voice almost a whisper, as he reached nineteen then twenty, as soon as the number left his lips, his bow gave a soft twang, followed by a whoosh of wind, and two arrows came of the trees and separated in mid flight.

The guard at the gate crumpled dropping his rifle, and the second guard took a hit to the side of his neck, not quite as on target as the Sage had wanted, but it had the right effect. He quickly loaded his bow and shot straight and hard at the third guard. Across the other side two guards fell dead, and the workers realised what was happening.

As the Sage went for his fourth guard, the workers scrambled for the wounded and dead guards' weapons. This was exactly as the Sage had planned, although he had little time to concern himself, as there was a sudden rush of workers, the guards sprang into action raising their weapons at the scattering mass. The Sage felt the pressure as he loaded again, but as his bow came up; Ester suddenly bolted from cover and ran towards the gates.

One of the guards saw her and turned his rifle towards her, and the Sage spotting him, aimed and fired and went straight into reloading. The arrow hit the guard in the chest and pushed him backwards, as his gun went off shooting upward into the air. The workers with recovered rifles knelt down and joined in the fight, as they aimed and fired at the rest of the guards, who scattered for cover. Martin and Ben had little time as one of the guards realised that they were under attack from an unseen enemy, and turned to fire at them from the cover of an old broken wall.

Bullets whistled into the trees close by, and twice Ben dropped his arrow, as he ducked when a bullet hit a nearby tree spraying splinters all over him. Martin felt the pressure as the sweat formed on his brow under his hood, but repeatedly loaded and fired. Fights broke out with a few of the guards with batons as they tried to beat back the workers still inside the charcoal yard, and found they faced three workers at a time. They were beaten down to the floor, where the workers hit them with spades, and one worker lifted a large felling axe, and struck hard and deep on one guard, who had attempted to club him.

It was a well sprung surprise attack, but it was not a quiet one, gun shots and the roars of the free workers, combined with blood curdling screams of the guards, as the workers attacked, and beat them, which was loud and chaotic. The Sage was under no illusions that the Cutters back at the camp would now be well aware of what was happening.

Ester started to call out names as she ran forward waving a rifle, individuals within the group noticed her and stopped to look at her, and slowly over a few hectic minutes, calmness descended as the free men realised that even though she had escaped, she had returned and brought help.

All the guards lay bloodied and dead when the Sage walked out of the trees with his bow still loaded. Ester had a small group around her as she hurriedly explained the situation, and the rest of the crowd of workers murmured the story back to those out of ear shot. All of them stared at the Sage with his long green hooded coat, and his strange bark like skin, so much so that no one noticed Martin and Ben who had emerged from the trees behind them.

As the Sage approached the group they parted, to reveal a large muscular man hugging Ester tightly. He noticed the Sage and turned towards him releasing Ester from his grip, she saw the Sage, and still wearing a large smile she pointed to him.

"Dad this is the man who helped me, he is the Master Sage." The man turned as the Sage halted a few paces from him. Ester looked to the Sage. "Master Sage this is my dad, everyone calls him Dutch."

The large man who was dressed in a filthy vest, covered with a tatty patched shirt held out his dirty hand. His eyes were dark, and looked out from a dirty and what also appeared tanned leathery happy face. Dutch offered his hand, and spoke good English, but it had the flavour of a distinct accent. "I owe you a debt of gratitude, and I thank you for protecting my daughter." The Sage gave a nod.

"As much as I would like to stand and talk, this isn't over yet, none of you are safe, and I believe you have other captives? We could have more of them here at any moment, so I would say let's hold off on the pleasantries and get organised, otherwise your freedom may be short lived." Dutch gave a nod and turned to a small group behind him.

"Taylor, Euan, go watch the road and let us know if anyone comes." Two of the pack separated, and ran to the end of the road where it turned towards the camp to watch, Dutch turned back to the Sage. "OK what you got in mind?"

The Sage looked at Ben. "Go and collect our things for us." He turned to look at Ester. "Could you help him for me?" She smiled and gave a nod, and then followed Ben back into the trees. The Sage looked at Martin. "Dutch this is my number two Martin, and the way I see it, you know this place better than any, so quickly fill us in on where this camp is exactly, and what we face there."

Sat with Sapphire, alone in the room of the table of Runestone, as the pictures rose and fell revealing Florae, Runestone listened to every word that was spoken carefully. Patiently watching and taking in as much detail of the people of Sapphire's true race, it was a fascinating experience; she had rarely seen such a place of wonder and beauty. Her meeting with Bade was of great interest to Rune, but nothing prepared her for the Whispering Falls. She leaned on her table, as she watched Sapphire looking afraid and nervous, sit in her seat alone in the strange room, with the strange almost mystical voice that whispered from the water to her.

Rune screwed up her eyes and stared at the water, she noticed something. "Freeze." The pictures above her table froze instantly, and Rune stood up to lean over her table and study the image. "Hmm, now that is interesting."

Sapphire was staring at the picture; she had been there and noticed nothing. Slowly she moved to Rune's side. "What is it?"

Rune lifted her hand and pointed with a finger containing a ring with a stone of sapphire on it. "Look carefully, do you not see that?" Sapphire shook her head.

"I see nothing, what is it you see?" Rune turned her eyes still filled with violet light.

"Expand." The picture grew in size, and Rune traced the outline within the water. "I see a woman, and it looks like she is made up of clear water, surely you see that Saff?" Sapphire stared at the water and gave her eyes a slight squint, and then she saw it.

"Lords of all the stars I see it, but who is it?" Rune shook her head.

"I would have thought it would be Bridget, but I have seen drawings of her and that is not her, what else do you see Saff?"

Sapphire strained her eyes to try and see more. "I see only a woman, nothing more." Rune nodded.

"Yes, but what is she wearing?" Sapphire scanned the transparent image as best as she could.

"She looks like all the Fae in Florae, they pretty much all dress like that." Rune gave a smile.

"But do they all wear a belt of stars?" Sapphire looked again and then she saw them.

"Ok I see them, but why does it matter what she wears on her belt, I have one similar mum gave me with moons on it, why is it important, it's just a belt Rune?" Rune slipped back to her seat still looking at the image floating above her table.

"Do you remember the table of Iona?" Sapphire looked back towards her.

"I try not too, that was not a good time for me I was so afraid."

"It is a table with a golden tree on it surrounded by twelve golden stars, set on a blue background." Sapphire gave a nod.

"Yeah, I remember it now you think of it, why is that important?" Rune relaxed in her seat.

"It has bothered me a lot since we returned to this timeline, I don't know why but I see it in my mind a lot, why would Iona use those particular symbols? I mean Gwendolyn's table is a red star on a white background." Sapphire thought of her last visit to the table, she remembered it well.

"You know now that you mention it, I get what you mean. Although the golden tree is part of the line of Eve and Hearne, and she will be the joining of two lines, but I must admit why gold stars when the Fae use the red star as their protection?" Rune sat as still as a post as Sapphire watched her, understanding that she was deep in thought. Rune blinked and then looked back up at her.

"Tila talked of the stars of life and death, and Isolde appeared to be uncomfortable about it, I wonder, are those stars the same ones, and if they are, who would wear them on their belt?"

Sapphire shrugged. "Stars have always symbolised the heavens, maybe they have some significance to them."

"Or maybe they are also the symbols of a mystic?" Sapphire had no idea.

"Honestly Rune when it comes to the Fae, you probably know more than I do."

"Ok let's watch the rest of your time in these falls and see what else we can spot."

Sapphire returned to her seat as Rune instructed the pictures to continue, and heard herself ask the question followed by the strange voice that whispered, 'good question.'

The story of Ariel, the mother of Ena unfolded, and revealed how she was raped by Morgana's grandfather Otto, and in her revenge, she stabbed him and fled the castle. Lost in the woodlands that surrounded the castle, she was saved by a group of travellers, where she discovered she was with child. The child she bore, was female, and Ariel remained with the travellers until one day whilst out with her daughter who was ten years old, she stepped on a trap that bit deep into her leg. The sound of horses alerted her to the oncoming soldiers and being unable to free her leg, she told her daughter to escape and run back to the camp. After many tears and a parting of great love and sadness, her daughter escaped, and Ariel was taken captive and returned to the castle to face Otto who had survived, but had been crippled.

The final seconds of Sapphire's time in the room of the Whispering Waters, the strange quiet voice told her this. "In those parting moments, Ariel placed a charm on her daughter using very old magic, and since that moment, her daughter has been lost and hidden from all the Fae, until the moment that she revealed herself to Runestone in the cathedral, and it was within those moments, that her past and her truth was revealed to all."

As it ended, Rune watched the pictures fade and then turned to Sapphire. "This room of water, they told you it can account for all of the history of the Fae, yes?" Sapphire gave a nod.

"Yeah, it is apparently the entire history of the race." Rune looked puzzled.

"The thing is Saff; it told you that it knew nothing from that moment that Ariel disappeared from sight, yes?" Again, Saff gave a nod.

"You saw everything I saw Rune." Rune gave the moment some thought.

"How could these waters only learn her story once she appeared in the cathedral, it makes no sense, she is a fully grown woman?" Sapphire shook her head.

"She wore a veil all her life, you know more about those than I do." Rune nodded quietly as she thought, and her words were more to herself than Sapphire.

"So tell me this then, if that was during the life time of Morgan le Fey's grandfather, and we think this Ariel could be her mother, how did Morgan know Ena's name when she saw her? I saw the face of Morgan, and she was shocked to see her, and she named her in her surprise and I may add recognition of her." Sapphire had not thought of it at all.

"You know that is a really good point, how did Morgan know her?"

"Well considering the Fae could not see her, just how did Morgan know her, I think this Ena has a few Fae tricks that even the Fae are unaware of, because Morgan could only have recognised her if she had met her in the past, so how could Morgan see what the powerful waters did not see?" Sapphire shook her head.

"I have no idea; to be honest most of this makes no sense at all to me."

The pictures faded away from the table and it became the large twenty pointed violet star again. Rune's eyes returned to normal as she sat in thought for a moment before looking at Saff who appeared to be equally lost in thought. "My grandmother always said the Fae had far too many secrets, I must admit I am starting to get really annoyed with it, I need more information, and I think it is about time that the Fae started to answer a few questions. I think a meeting with a member of their council is in order, the Fae need to understand that as much as they like to live secluded in their realm, eventually Morgan is going to get around to seeking them out, I think it is time for a little straight talking." She got up out of her seat.

"Somehow Isolde knows something, and for once I think it is time, she gave away more than her silence, there is no coincidence her and Filomena were selected for this post guarding their queen, I want answers, the life of everyone here depends on it."

Sapphire looked confused. "They are just hand maidens to a queen Rune, what could they possibly know?" Rune gave a sly smile.

"Oh, I think they are far more than just simple handmaidens, and I think they know far more than they let on. Things here are getting serious, and if they want to protect their queen for a future of their line, then they need to cough up some answers and soon, because the way things are going, Loxley could fall if we do not find a way to stop Morgan."

"Don't you mean Mason?"

"No Robbie thinks Morgan is the key to all of this, and I trust his gut feelings, somehow this Ena, Berengar, and the Fae are all connected, and all of that leads right to Morgan, and I aim to find out exactly what that connection is and then sever it. If she falls, I think everything will fall with her, and that Sapphire, is our task."

Rune stood up and started to walk towards the steps that led back up to the house, the table gave a pulse of violet light, and she stopped as Sapphire stood up and turned back to look at the table. Out of the centre pictures flooded into the air of the Sage sat in the trees with a woman neither of them knew. Rune stood still for a moment and watched as he fired two arrows at a row of Cutters. Men dressed in dirty rags and covered in soot broke from a long line and began to fight as Cutters fired rifles at them. Rune reacted.

"It looks like our green friend is in some sort of trouble. Quickly, go and get Crystal and Tila, he may need assistance, I will follow you up in a second." Sapphire headed for the steps as Rune watched the fight unfold. "Sound." The room filled with sounds of the fight, and she watched intently as the men overpowered the Cutter guards, then she watched as the Sage was introduced to a man named Dutch, and listened to their exchange. Understanding he was facing almost impossible odds she left her table, and headed upstairs to where Crystal and Tila were organising their weapons with Sapphire.

As she grabbed her bow and two sets of arrows, Sapphire asked. "Shall I alert the others?"

Rune turned shouldering her arrows. "No we can deal with this one; I would like to keep things a little quiet around our green friend." Sapphire understood and smiled.

"OK give me a moment to locate him properly and then we can jump to him." Rune shook her head.

"We land close by but not directly at his location, I want to size things up before we go in blind." She looked at Tila. "I know your code, but be aware these Cutters will kill you on sight, sometimes to wound is not enough to keep them down, can you deal with that?" She gave a nod.

"I know my duty, you have no need to fear for me, I am trained better than you realise." Rune gave a nod and took a long breath.

"Ok then let's go." Sapphire's blue window burst into life, and expanded out in front of them, and as quick as a flash, they all headed through it at a good pace.

CHAPTER ELEVEN

STANDOFF

As the road led away from the charcoal burners, it turned left on what had once been a crossroads. The years of decay, combined with the power of nature left alone to take control, had completely covered two of the roads that joined the junction. The only way clear was what had now become one road that turned at a right angle, with tall trees and thick scrub either side, broken only occasionally by the remains of sections of wall, comprised of weed strewn crumbling bricks.

Dutch knew this road well, and so took the lead role in guiding the freed captives and the party of the Sage, towards the large factory that was the focal point of the town. It was slow going, as both he and the Sage knew that the rest of the Cutters would be waiting for them.

They kept as close to the side of the road as possible, using the thick matted shrubs and young trees as protection. Dutch spoke softly to the Sage who moved behind him, on the edge of the roadway as he leaned into the trees and scrub as cover. His accent rang softly of a combination of good English, and that of his native land of Holland.

"We face many, you must understand that the man who leads them is ruthless, he will not barter with you, so be aware, I am not walking you towards a negotiation, this is a fight, and we will be greatly outnumbered, but the lives of hundreds of men with their wives and children are at stake."

The Sage was more than aware of what he faced; Ester had filled him in well on their journey through the woodlands, and then sat in the trees. Observing the burners and the captives work, he had taken stock of the operation. "I am under no illusions here; your daughter has given me a lot of detail about your life here." Dutch smirked.

"Life? This is not a life, this is a living hell, it is a better chance of life that we will fight for this day."

The Sage looked ahead, the road was longer than he had expected, there was still at least two hundred yards before he saw the opening to the left, where he knew the old factory was situated. His senses were at full power, but he couldn't detect any signs at all of any Cutters, and it worried him a little. He had expected them to come at him with a full force, and their absence increased his apprehension.

He looked behind him; Martin was a few feet away with the man who he knew was called Taylor, behind him was a line of thirty men. He had counted forty at the compound, but their confrontation of the Cutters had cost them already. Martin winked and moved a little quicker to close the gap between them.

"This guy Taylor tells me that the Cutters all live inside the factory on the second floor, he has warned me to be aware of the top windows, they are broken and make a good advantage spot for the rifle men, so keep your wits about you, these guys have a big advantage over us with guns, keep your head down."

He understood, as it had been on his mind all day. His only consolation was that he had timed the Cutters with their rifles, and discovered he could load, aim, and fire his bow a lot quicker than they could reload their side action bolt loading mechanisms on their rifles.

The trees here were very tall, and their canopies met together high above the road, lowering the light, which hampered his chances of seeing if anything was lurking in the bushes. He slipped his hood up hoping to break the dappled spots of bright light and improve his vision, as his eyes adjusted to the dimmer light conditions. He had an arrow on his string just in case, and felt the pressure of the ground below his feet, as his sense of self heightened. He did not like this part of the road; it was a great place for an ambush. He noticed Dutch had slowed a little, and he ran his eyes along the edge of the road, as they adjusted to make sure they were safe, and at that point he noticed a slight sparkle. The Sage tapped Dutch on the shoulder, and gave the signal to Martin to stop, and the group came to a halt and stood back into the thick growth.

Slipping past Dutch, he crouched and made his way carefully to what he at first thought was metal, and was very surprised to discover it wasn't. The sun was glinting off a frozen boot; he scanned into the thick undergrowth and saw the frozen corpse of a Cutter. Martin's voice whispered just behind him. "What the hell, I have seen that before; remember Dunnottar and the frozen bodies?"

The Sage looked back and gave a nod. "The woman in white from the Specialists?" Martin gave a shrug.

"Who else do we know of who kills like that? It must be her, have you heard anything from Sapphire?"

"No, not for a while, well not since the lock up, let's hope she is around somewhere, we will need all the help we can get."

"I bloody hope so, to be honest, this feels like walking into a huge trap, knowing Sapphire is lurking about gives me a little hope, and we are going to need as much of it as we can get. You I trust, and whatever the Green Lord told you I have faith in, but these guys here are partially unarmed and pretty tired, this is going to really stretch us you know that don't you?"

It was almost impossible to see the Sage's face below his hood; his bark like face was lost in the shadow, the hood twitched. "Martin the key to this is to identify this man they call the Coker, take him down and the rest should topple, he will be my mark from the moment we are discovered, and yes these guys may not be armed as well as I would wish, but every time we take a man out, we will have the satisfaction of knowing we have a free man to take the dropped weapons. Relax my friend all is not lost." Martin nodded.

"Well, if Sapphire has brought Miss Freeze with her that will work nicely for us, she can take several at a time, and Sapphire is no slouch with a bow."

"Precisely, I have no idea where they are, but I feel this was a signal meant for us, and I mean let's be honest Martin, this is a sign both of us would understand." He gave a sniff and looked round.

"Bit of a bloody chilling way of letting us know they are here, no pun intended." The Sage gave a chuckle.

"Kind of takes the fun out of a warm welcome, don't it?" Martin patted his shoulder.

"Oh dear, you really need to work on your humour. Ok let's get on with this whilst I am feeling more confident, whatever it is we face, we might as well go look at it and deal with whatever they throw at us."

The factory was set in the centre of what was once a large car park. All the way around the building was a huge open space of cracked concrete and tar, where dandelion and horse's tails grew up through the cracks from the earth below. What had been neat hedges at one time, creating an attractive border around the parking space, had become areas of tall unkempt, wild bushes and trees, where long plumes of tatty white and blue Buddleia plumes, hung by the hundreds attracting masses of red butterflies. The building was once a modern machine factory of red brick and glass, with a pale blue metal polished roof, but now the roof was old and had rusty patches, which over time had created a dark reddish brown series of streaks all over it from the endless battering of the rain.

What had once been a wall of darkened glass was now a series of frameworks, with peeled paint and dark grey dirty broken shards of glass. The second floor was clearly visible as a thick concrete beamed floor, was set back a few inches from the glass wall. On one side of the huge building, a smashed canopy hung over what had been a loading bay, for the long articulated trucks that had transported the goods from here to wherever it needed to be. The factory was a smashed and broken relic of a bygone age, a symbol of what had once been the shining example of the modern world of technology. Now it was simply the living space of a group of violent and sadistic men who feared nothing, and brutalised all who would disagree with them.

How many people had died here, or been raped at the hands of these men of evil it was unclear, but as the Sage looked out from the cover of trees at it, he knew that oppression was the tool of control, and even though he had nowhere near enough men for this fight, he knew that to walk away would bring more death and despair to this place. The fact that there were no guards at all on the road where it joined to the factory site concerned him, what was this Coker up to? He really did not understand, but there were absolutely no signs of life anywhere. Dutch leaned in to him.

"Behind the building set back a way, is the old sports ground, which is where he holds all the captives. It has a fence around it and razor wire, it normally has rows of guards that walk up and down, but I cannot see any signs of life, what do we do?" The Sage smiled.

"I have a plan... Trust me?" Martin looked at him.

"Oh shit!" Dutch looked worried and Martin explained. "If he says trust me, it's usually some insane idea, and no matter what you say, he is going to do it no matter what." The Sage patted Martin on the shoulder.

"Have faith this may give us the edge we need... Ok this is what we are going to do."

On the second floor hidden from view, a Cutter watched the road. The day was warm and humid now the rain had stopped, and even in the shade it felt close and oppressive. He was tall and skinny and his black tunic hung dirty and lank from his shoulders. His hair was dark and greasy, and it was hard to even imagine it had ever been blonde. His skin was tanned above his bristled cheeks and chin, yet his pale eyes were sharp and observant. Out of sight from the road, in the shade of the broken windows, he watched as a lone figure walked out from the treeline into plain view.

The Cutter went rigid and tense; his right arm came up and frantically waved to the gathered group, who stood many feet behind him out of sight. A few moved forward to try and get a better look at what they expected to be at least forty men, so it came as some surprise to see just a single figure dressed in a long green coat, that had a heavy hood pulled up over the head. He simply stood alone in plain view holding a loaded bow; it made no sense at all to them. The Sage stood in clear view waiting, but for what?

Set back out of sight, Tila watched with Crystal, not entirely understanding what was happening. "What is he doing, is he insane he is a sitting duck there?" Crystal was equally as interested in the Sage.

"Honestly I have no idea, I have heard a lot about this guy, but up until now I have not seen him in action." Tila shook her head.

"If this is his plan, he is going to die pretty quickly, shouldn't we do something?" Crystal shook her head, which was hidden beneath the folds of a dark green cloak.

"Rune says trust him and wait, I am sure she will let me know if we have to step in."

Out in the middle of the exposed square of weed riddled concrete, the Sage remained frozen on the same spot. The Cutters were unsure, somewhere in the back of the factory a voice rumbled and grated to those on watch.

"Well, what is he doing?" The tall thin watcher looked behind him into the darkness, and shook his head then shrugged. "Nothing...I mean he is just stood there doing nothing, should I shoot him?"

There was a long pause in the darkness of the upper floor of the factory, and then a response came.

"Do nothing until I say so, I will deal with this."

Martin watched nervously from within the trees next to Dutch and Taylor. Dutch leaned over to him. "When you said your friend did insane things, I was not sure what to believe, but now...Well I think in future I will take you at your word. What exactly is his plan here, because I honestly have no idea what to do next?" Martin gave a long sigh.

"This guy has a faith in the green world you may never understand, but the one thing I know about him is he has great intuition. I will say one thing though, make sure all of your armed men are ready, this could kick off real fast, and he will need us to respond quickly."

Dutch gave a nod and looked down the line of his men to ensure they were all ready, he could see the same confusion in their eyes as was in his thoughts. From the loading bay at the side of the factory there was movement, and Dutch tensed.

The Sage stood quite still holding his bow, as several hundred yards away he watched a long line of captives dressed in rags walk out from the loading bay. Behind them obscured by the captives, he could see the black vested men of a Cutter Brigade walk out parallel. The line stretched wide across the empty concrete space, and the Sage counted twenty five captives, some women, a few children and the rest men.

From nowhere a deep voice boomed out. "What is it you want stranger?" The Sage stood motionless, the sun behind him, with his pale blue eyes peering out from below his hood.

"The Green Lord has sent me to collect his people." The voice of the Sage was loud and clear, Martin noted that his finger pulled back a little on his bow string.

The voice from behind the captives bellowed back. "There is nothing here for you or your so called lord, you have cost me enough this day, leave now and everyone will live, if you stay you will die."

The Sage took five paces forward. "My orders are not to leave until these people are free."

From inside the factory there came the sounds of laughter, another sharper but higher toned voice shouted from somewhere inside. "You are crazy, we know you only have a few men with guns, but we outnumber you ten to one." More laughter followed. The Sage narrowed his eyes.

"I am instructed to speak to a man known as the Coker, I have been told to tell him that he must free these people or suffer the consequences." More laughter erupted inside, and then a large voice boomed out from somewhere on the lower floor.

"KILL THE HOSTAGES!"

Behind the lined up captives rifles cocked, the Sage saw the faces of fear on those lined up as he noticed the movement of the Cutters taking aim. He stared into the eyes of a terrified woman who shook in her boots, and tears formed in her pleading eyes. The Sage noted her look and then softly shook his head. Martin tapped Dutch on the shoulder. "That is his signal get ready."

Panic ran into the faces of those lined up as they prepared for their final moment, the Cutters behind them took aim, and pushed their fingers onto their triggers. From four different directions arrows whipped through the air, the first Cutter took a green feathered arrow to the chest, then the second, the third got hit with a white feathered arrow, and as quickly as they aimed ready to fire, they jerked backwards and fell to the floor.

As the arrows arrived at speed, the Sage suddenly ran forward, and screamed at the row of captives. "RUN...RUN THAT WAY!" He pointed with his arrow and then refitted it to his bow. The captives unable to understand what was happening panicked, they looked from left to right, then noticing a few heading towards the tree line far across the yard, they all turned in unison and began to run for the trees.

A Cutter stepped out from the loading bay and lifted his rifle to shoot, up came the bow of the Sage, as he sprinted towards the factory wall, and within a second, he unleashed his arrow, and hit the guard square in the chest. The captives screamed and wailed in fear, as they ran terrified towards the trees, and saw a figure they knew step out and call them forward.

At the front of the factory, as the Cutters on the first level came up into view to take aim, a long silver arrow came out of nowhere; it hit the floor at the base of the factory wall, and it began to spray out a long plume of white. In an instant, ice ran up the frame and expanded outwards, quickly filling the gaps in the frame where glass had once been. Before any Cutter could shoot, they found themselves stepping back to avoid the thick mass of ice that filled the whole of the front of the building sealing the entrance and top windows.

The Sage had his right shoulder pressed into the brick wall of the factory side, his bow lifted in front of him, and his eye peered down the arrow loaded on his bow string, as he observed the open side of the loading bay, looking for any target that presented itself. The loud deep voice inside the factory gave a roar of a laugh.

"You bluff well, but there is no victory here for you man of green, do you think me so stupid as not to be prepared?"

On the opposite side of road that crossed the entrance to the factory, the trees parted and a whole troop of black vested Cutters appeared. They went down on their knees and brought up their rifles.

"Looks like we have a standoff man of green, where will you run to now, my men have you in their sights give it up, you are valiant there is no doubt, but even your men can not prevent your death now." The Sage turned to look back and saw the three rows of Cutters all aiming their rifles at him.

The Laughter inside continued, and then the voice boomed out again. "I have more men in the compound with the rest of the people here, surrender or I will order every man woman and child killed." Dutch panicked in the trees.

"My wife is there, and Ester is on her way to help them." Martin raised his palm.

"Calm down, we are not done yet, we have others here who will help." Dutch looked confused.

"You said it was just you few." Martin gave a smile.

"Have faith, we do the Green Lords bidding, he sent aid you will see." Dutch looked unsure.

"Your man is trapped and a sitting target, you ask too much Martin, I cannot gamble with my family. I see green tipped arrows and white tipped arrows, but I see no shooters, how many men extra do you have because we need at least a hundred?" Martin shook his head.

"Our aid comes straight from Loxley, you will be surprised what a small number can achieve, hold your nerve, this day is not done with yet, now lift your rifle and get ready, it will go down fast."

Martin was not wrong. Rune sat quietly in the wooden shack of Dutch with his wife, who looked very afraid. Her eyes flickered with violet light as she watched and felt the events happening all around her. Outside Cutters walked up and down the lines of rough built dwellings having ordered all the inhabitants inside. The door opened and a Cutter barged in, Dutch's wife blinked, and a sword of flame ignited, and the Cutter stood frozen his faced filled with shock. Rune sat motionless her arm extended holding her sword of knowledge. He grunted and she retracted her arm, and the Cutter fell backwards through the door and back into the street.

Forty feet behind the Sage, the floor gave a shudder and the long flowers of the trees and shrubs shook out their pollen. All the plant life began to vibrate and stretch, and then exploded into accelerated growth. The long flower bed filled with a thick dense layer of green new growth, making it impossible for the men on the road to see the Sage. Martin tapped Dutch on the shoulder.

"Now, take your men into that cover and start shooting."

From the trees on the far side of the wide concrete car park, men ran out and fired at the Cutters blocking the exit, they ran as fast as they could towards the newly expanded cover of the trees. The Cutters on the road scattered or fell to the floor to take aim, and the true fight for the captives began.

Sliding slowly along the wall, the Sage aimed his arrow ready to fire at any movement. A Rifle appeared at the edge of the wall and he froze. The head and upper body of a Cutter moved slowly into view and the Sage fired, there was a muffled grunt, the rifle hit the floor and went off, and then the Cutter fell forward dead on the floor, an arrow firmly imbedded in his forehead.

The Sage moved forward scanning the whole length of the side of the building, as he edged towards the open side of the loading bay. At the far end of the building, he saw a yellow coloured bow wave on the end of a blue clad arm, there was a slight movement of something followed by a swish of long auburn hair, and he smiled as he recognised the signal from Sapphire.

She came cautiously round the corner and flattened herself to the wall. Behind her seven rough looking men in black sat tied and gagged, and slightly dazed. The Sage gave a nod to assure her he was aware of her, and she smiled, and then began to move from the opposite end of the building towards him, and the other side of the open space that was once a loading bay. He quickened his pace relieved to know she had not abandoned him.

At the corner, the Sage leaned back against the wall and tried his best to listen, but the rifle shots going off at the far end of the property where Dutch and his men fired at the Cutters in the road, made it impossible to hear anything. Sapphire gave a little whistle and he looked to her, where she had reached the corner. From her pocket she pulled out a small round silver object, it was a small mirror set. She opened it up and held it in front of her to use it to see round the corner into the loading bay. The Sage watched and waited for her response. She rested her bow on the wall, and then watched the mirror and looked to him and held up four fingers, and then pointed to his side of the bay, and put two fingers down.

He understood that on the loading dock just round the corner there were two Cutters, so slowly he slid as close as he could to the corner and leaned on the very edge so he could quickly glance. As he did so both rifles fired, and the brickwork at the side of his head exploded as the bullets ricocheted off the wall, spraying dust all over his shoulder. The moment the Cutters fired, Sapphire side stepped forward one pace with her bow loaded, and then twisted to face the opposite side of the dock and shot her arrow. There was a shriek of surprise as she leapt back against the wall, and two rifles fired hitting the wall corner close to her face.

The Sage winked and lifted three fingers. Sapphire lifted two arrows out of her sling on her side and then with her arm outstretched, she moved them close to the corner of the wall. The Sage pulled on the string of his bow, where his arrow sat waiting. As she pushed the feathers into view, once again the rifles fired. Not waiting a second, the Sage jerked round, lifted the bow and saw a large Cutter behind a crate on Sapphire's side of the dock. He sighted the arrow, and fired with good pace, then swung back behind the cover of the corner of the wall.

Inside the loading dock his arrow hit the Cutter in the forehead, and he shot backwards crashing into a stack of metal drums. The clatter of the metal drums as they scattered said it all, and Sapphire smiled and lifted two fingers.

Ester and Ben made it to the fence where she had escaped the previous night. The hole was small, and no problem for Ben, the only trouble was the four men that had accompanied them. They gathered round each side, and grabbed the two small loose parts of the fence and heaved with all their might to tear the metal links apart. It took some effort, but finally after a really hard tug, the links separated and the hole expanded. Ester was the first one through leading the way with her rifle, Ben followed with a loaded bow, the other four had not managed to get a weapon, so carried heavy lengths of a branch they had broken off a tree to use as clubs.

Ben was really surprised to see a maze of rough built shacks, thrown together from every type of old wood and branches, covered with sheets of old plastic or canvass. Ester ran fast from corner to corner, checking each section or alleyway, for they were not much wider than two people's width, to ensure it was free of guards. A Cutter stepped out of a doorway, but Ben was fast with his bow and hit the man in the shoulder, he dropped his rifle and yelled, but within seconds two of the men with them set upon him, and clubbed him where he lay, and another member of their party had a rifle.

So, it continued from alleyway to alleyway, dodging and weaving as they went, Ben had no idea where they were going; he just kept a few paces behind Ester, and remained alert to shoot if required. Finally, they reached a doorway of a small hut built from reclaimed timber planks, and as they approached, the door opened, and Ben almost stumbled when he saw who was stood there holding the door open for them to run in. Rune smiled as he shot past into a darkened room, where one small window provided very little light. The door closed as Ester embraced her tearful mother, and Ben turned to face Rune, and went down on one knee. "My Lady of the Woods."

"Greetings Master Winters, you have grown since we last saw each other." He looked up surprised.

"I have? I did not think you noticed me." Rune gave a chuckle.

"I notice everyone, especially one who is such a treasured companion of the Master Sage." Ben appeared flattered, and gave a smile as he noted the looks of awe on the faces of the other men. Even this far south and in an isolated part of the country, almost everyone had heard of the Hooded Man and his wife the Lady of the Woods.

Ester gave a bow towards Runestone. "My Lady, thank you for protecting my mother, I am in your debt." All the others gave several nods of agreement. Rune looked at Ester, she was small in comparison to Rune, her face was pale and white, streaked with dirt, and it was clear she was under nourished, and yet her brown eyes sparkled with defiance.

"I am grateful to you for guiding the Master Sage here, I know it was not an easy task to return once you had escaped, it was a very brave act, and one I felt should be rewarded." Ester looked surprised.

Ben gave a grin. "See I told you she knows everything." Rune looked at the other men.

"From what I can tell, there are thirty guards walking round the camp, you need to gather all the men who can fight, and then we can attack from the inside." One of the men gave a sniff, and wiped his nose on his sleeve.

"No disrespect, but even if we get all the guards, we are still locked in, and out there is Coker and the rest of his men." The others nodded in agreement; Rune smiled.

"I know of similar groups who have taken out far more men with less, have faith my friends, we are not alone, there are more here than you know of, and they have skills to match this man Coker, the gates will open, I can assure it. We need to get everyone in here free, which will give us greater numbers, and then we join the others outside this prison, and fight for the freedom of everyone here."

They did not look completely sure, but gave a hesitant nod of agreement, Rune smiled. "Right then, we go house by house until we have everyone, and remember every dropped weapon is more strength to this side."

The biggest problem faced by Rune and her party was fear. Years of brutal abuse had broken the will of the people, and many cowered behind closed doors afraid to fight. Ester did her best to convince each person she encountered in their ram shack dwellings, but the group grew much slowly than she wanted. Each time they encountered a Cutter, there was a drawn out battle to take more space, but even though Rune knew that she could easily overcome all of the Cutters, she knew the importance of allowing each person to claim their right to freedom.

Robbie had often talked about how important it was that the people of the Woodland Realm understood that to do nothing would lead to their destruction, he knew that every man would have to stand up and be counted before the end; for that was the only way they would ever defeat the power of Mason Knox. So alleyway by alleyway, and house by house, the group slowly moved and expanded in size.

Outside the captive's compound, the Cutters held their position on the edge of the road. They moved back to the trees and fired at Dutch and his group, it was a stalemate, and neither party moved. Martin knew something drastic had to happen in order for there to be any real change. The one thing he was well aware of, the rifles his group were firing, would eventually run out of bullets, and at which point, he had no idea how they would overcome the Cutters.

After what felt like an age, Sapphire and the Sage finally won their game of cat and mouse, and made it onto the loading dock. The two remaining Cutters had worked out their tactics, and had made it difficult for Sapphire or the Sage to find them. Feeling relieved to be on the dock, they made it towards a doorway, only to find that the long corridor to the main factory floor was guarded.

High above the loading bay, Crystal and Tila walked across the roof, as Crystal scanned the inside trying to read the situation below. "Saff needs our help." Tila gave a nod.

"Where is she?"

"Right below us." Tila looked at the sheet metal roof.

"Can we get through this and drop down?" Crystal looked at the floor below her feet.

"We can, the problem is that if I drop you in there, you will have to drop for two floors, you might not make it as there are a lot of Cutters there, and I think they have hostages, so I cannot risk freezing everything, we will need another way in."

The Sage pulled back as the door frame erupted, and yet more splinters exploded out all over them as the bullets tore into it. "This is useless, there are too many, and with rifles as well, we have no chance of making it up that corridor. What about your window, is there not a way you could place me on the other side of the corridor?" Sapphire brushed yet more flecks of wood splinters off her shoulder.

"It is hard for me to navigate the inside in my mind, the place is full of metal, and the people inside are scattered everywhere, I am really not sure who is Cutter and who is hostage, there is not a safe place I can put you. They will see the light of the window before you walk through, I am sorry but at the moment it would be far too dangerous for you." He gave a long sigh and leaned back against the wall.

"We are caught in a standoff; there must be a way to move forward."

Sapphire shrugged and leant back on the wall on her side. "Unless you have a map of all this places weakest points, I am not sure we are going to get inside at all, this Coker knows how to defend a place well, I am starting to understand how he managed to take over this town and rule it, considering how many captives are here."

Across the way in front of Martin and Dutch, the Cutters were firing repeatedly, Martin took a long breath and looked to each side, where all through the undergrowth, the freed men who had acquired rifles fired and reloaded. He turned to Dutch as a bullet whizzed above his head.

"We are going to run out of bullets, tell your men to slow down and aim with greater care because once those guns are empty, they will charge us. Just go for easy targets and hold your fire until you have a clean shot."

Dutch turned and whistled, Taylor who was lay down ten yards up the line, popped his head up, and Dutch signalled to tell them to slow their firing down, Taylor gave a nod and then started to tell those around him. High up on the roof Crystal could see the problem better, she loaded her bow and took aim, Tila watched from her side as she tilted her bow upwards judging the distance, and then released the silver arrow.

The arrow shot upward at great speed, and then appeared to stop in mid-air just for a second; it tilted, and then raced to earth between the Cutters on the ground, and Martin in the trees. Tila watched as it hit the concrete and embedded itself, and then sprayed out a long plume of white. Instantly a thick wall extended on both sides of the arrow, preventing both of the parties from seeing each other and the firing stopped, as neither side had anything to aim at, but a tall white wall. Crystal gave a nod. "Ok that will give the others a moment to plan, we need to get down and see what we can do inside."

The roof of the building appeared to lurch, Crystal staggered, and then an almighty explosion erupted out of the front of the building, blasting frozen chunks of ice and metal into the air. Tila slid back and fell on her back, as she was blown off her feet, and she landed heavily and rolled right off the edge of the rooftop. Crystal lurched across towards her, diving flat on to her stomach, and snatched her arm just in time, as Tila gave a squeal and felt her arm yank upwards.

She looked up at the white gloved hand gripping tightly to her wrist, as her legs swung wildly below her.

Crystal gave a gasp, Tila was a lot heavier than she expected, she screwed up her face as she strained to hold her, and slipped forward slightly on the smooth metal. She could just make out Tila's features as she looked at her hanging, with a frightened look on her face. "Don't let go." Crystal gave another gasp.

"My glove... Pull it off." Tila did not quite understand at first. Crystal felt the pull on her arm. "My glove, reach up and pull it off."

Suddenly understanding, Tila tried to swing her free arm up towards Crystal's free hand on the edge of the roof. She gasped as her first attempt missed; her legs swung wildly increasing the strain on Crystal's arm, as she lurched up a second time, trying to pull herself up by the arm held tightly by Crystal. Her hand swung wildly again, and then connected as she strained to reach. She gripped the soft fabric on the back on Crystal's hand, and tried to pull using all of her weight. Crystal strained and gave a loud gasp, as she tried to wriggle her hand inside the glove; she knew she could not hold on much longer.

The glove slipped free, and Tila dropped her arm holding the glove, and her weight increased on Crystal's extended arm as she lay on the edge of the roof. With her hand free she gripped the top of the roof edge and white shot down towards the floor, Tila seeing the pole of ice hit the floor, swung out with her legs and gripped the pole. With one final gasp, Crystal felt her hand strain too far, and her grip slipped away from Tila just in the nick of time. Tila grabbed the pole and slid at speed down towards the floor, and Crystal gave a gasp of relief as her arm relaxed, she rolled onto her back and lay on the roof top breathing heavily, flexing her now free arm.

The ice had been blown away from the front of the building, and it rained down onto Martin and the others. The ground shook so violently that Sapphire and the Sage, were thrown off their feet, and blown backwards by the shock wave that erupted out of the and the doorway.

Captive workers streamed out of the front of the building screaming for their lives, and in amongst them the Cutters from inside ran between them firing at Martin and the others, it was impossible to return fire without hitting their own people, and Dutch gave the signal to hold their fire. Over a hundred armed Cutters in black, quickly surrounded them and it looked like the fight was over; Martin gave a frustrated gasp and lay down in the dirt.

From inside the building, as all the Cutters surrounded Dutch and his men along with Martin, a tall scruffy, dark haired, well built man, walked out wearing a large smile. He walked with his heavy chest out and an air of victory, behind his back hung a large two handed sword.

Martin was dragged roughly up on his feet and held tightly, as the tall man stopped to survey the scene. His dark skinned faced and dark eyes peered across the yard, and broke out into a large smile of yellow coloured teeth. "Well, what have we here, are you not a little far from home General Jarrod, and fighting for the wrong side?"

Martin recognised the voice instantly; he scowled at the large Cutter, with a thick beard and matted tatty hair. "Patterson." He spat on the floor as if his name was filth. Patterson gave a hearty laugh.

"I am surprised you remember me General." Martin scowled at him with hate.

"How could I forget the woodsman that sold all his fellow fighters out to Walters?" Patterson gave a slight chuckle.

"Speaking of selling out, it looks like I am not the only one who switched sides." He walked closer towards Martin as he stared at him with hate.

"Thousands did not die when I walked away; do you know how many were slaughtered in these parts because of your deal with Walters? I walked away quietly; I did not condemn innocent women and children to death." Patterson shrugged.

"Maybe not, but during your time you directed just as many to their deaths in the orders you gave to support the war. The way I see it, we are not much different." Martin shook his head.

"My orders were given to trained soldiers, every one of them had a fighting chance, your betrayal saw the innocent hacked up in their beds and strung from trees. The way I see it you are nothing like me. I may have blood on my hands, but it will wash off, the blood on your hands will stain your soul forever."

Patterson appeared irked; he lifted the pistol in his hand and pointed it right at Martin's head. Martin spat on the floor at Patterson's feet. "Pull the trigger, I have made peace with my life and turned towards good, the evil you have done will never be undone, so go on kill me, unlike you I will die with a clear enough conscience."

Martin saw the anger in his eyes; he also saw the green clad figure stood behind Patterson and his men. Patterson gave a wild smile and his finger tensed on the trigger, everyone all around them was watching the scene unravel, no one was paying too much attention to their surroundings. Patterson's finger twitched, and a green tipped arrow came out of nowhere, and hit straight in the knuckle of his trigger finger. Patterson screamed in pain, as his hand jerked up and the gun went off, hitting one of the men holding onto Martin in the face.

Martin wasted no time and with the speed of a lightning bolt, he brought up his fist and punched Patterson straight in the face. There was a resounding crunch, and he sprawled backwards, and before anyone knew what was happening, Martin had his knife out, leapt on him, pushing him down onto his back, and held his knife at the throat of Patterson. He was cradling his bloody hand as he lay on the floor. No one really knew what to do, and just for a frozen moment of surprise they all faltered, it was enough for the Sage to take the initiative and he yelled at the top of his voice.

"DROP YOUR WEAPONS OR YOUR LEADER IS DEAD!"

It was a strange scenario, the Cutters were so shocked at seeing their leader defeated that they were momentarily stunned, several looked round to see Tila aiming from the side of the building at them. Crystal was on the roof aiming down, and Sapphire walked out into the centre of the square. Behind her a large mass of people led by Runestone came into view, walking a line of bound and tied Cutters. It was clear that to continue the fight would be futile. Crystal, Tila, and Sapphire stood pointing their loaded bows at over a hundred Cutters armed with rifles.

From behind the building even more captives appeared holding loaded rifles and pointing at the group, it was clear Rune was surrounded by a much larger group of armed workers. The Sage stood rigid his bow trained on the head of Patterson, as he lay on the floor in pain with Martin sat on his chest holding a knife to his throat.

It was almost completely silent, until one gun fell and clattered onto the concrete, then another, and another, and then more. Dutch and his group lifted their rifles and began to shepherd the Cutters together and check them for more weapons, and those workers who had no weapons scrambled to collect them as they were dropped. Martin looked over towards Tila and smiled. "Nice shot." She gave a smile and nodded back towards him.

Ester ran from the back of the group towards her father, who was holding a rifle on the men being checked, she slowed as she moved in front of the Sage and gave him a wide smile. "I am sorry I doubted you, you were right, it is amazing what a small group can achieve, everyone is free." The Sage winked, and she moved onwards to stand beside her father.

As Runestone walked towards them, Martin released Patterson and dragged him to his feet. Rune slowed and stood before him as he stared at her with indifference. "You are the Woodsman Patterson?" He scowled.

"What of it?" Rune pulled on her hood and lifted it over her head. "This was a land of peace and woodland loving people until you sold them out, you broke the oath you swore to the Woodland Realm of my husband, what have you to say of yourself, for as the Lady of this realm it is I who will judge you?" He smirked.

"Your realm, what right do you have to choose this place as yours, by who's authority do you judge me, your time is over witch, Knox controls this land and will command all of it soon." The Sage stepped forward to speak, but Rune lifted her palm to stop him.

"These lands were created by my lord and grandfather, the Lord of the Green Realm, and know this Cutter, for you are no member of my husband's realm. I will have no need to judge you, for that will be done by those whose lives you sold to Mason Knox." Her eyes flickered violet with her rising anger, and she saw the fear start to grow in his eyes.

Martin held him firmly before Runestone as she lifted her pale hands, and placed them either side of his temples. Her eyes exploded in bright light. "Feel their pain Cutter."

His screams were loud, and filled with a terror like no one had ever heard before, Martin let go of Patterson and he sunk to his knees screaming still held firmly by Rune. He shook on his knees and screamed out for death. Everyone around them took many steps back out of fear as Rune became engulfed in violet light and screamed at him.

"YOU WILL DIE ONLY WHEN I ALLOW IT, BEFORE THAT FEEL THE TRUTH OF WHAT YOU HAVE DONE, FEEL THEIR FEAR AND PAIN AND KNOW WHEN I ALLOW DEATH; YOU WILL GO TO A PLACE FAR WORSE THAN YOUR CURRENT PAIN!"

His screams intensified as his eyes, nose, and ears started to bleed, as he shook with terror, and the surrounding people hid their faces, and quaked with fear as the true power of the Lady of the Woods exploded out before them. "Feel them, all of them, innocent and isolated and unarmed, feel their fear and understand the evil of your foul life here..."

The Sage stepped forward into the bright violet light and placed his hand on Rune's shoulder. His voice was quiet and filled with care. "Enough Rune, this is not who you are, you are far better than this."

The violet light instantly went out, as Rune stood up straight. Patterson lay on a bed of violets on the floor his eyes streaming with blood, and white convulsed froth pouring from his mouth. Rune turned to face the Sage, and he saw the tears that flowed tinged with violet down her cheeks beneath her hood. He smiled a sad smile. "He has suffered, let him live with what you gave him, for that is by far the worst punishment, trust me I know it well." She gave a weak nod, and he took her arm gently. "Come with me."

The Sage walked slowly back to the old building softly speaking to Rune as the others all stared at the shaking body of Patterson on the floor. Understanding he was free, he crawled across the floor weeping and speaking gibberish, many jumped back out of his way as he passed, for fear they may catch whatever torment he had. Tila looked at Sapphire.

"We have a flower on Florae called the Death Hood, it is probably the most beautiful of all the blooms in Florae, but if you touch it, you will receive a sting that will grow and grow in intensity, until it is so painful you will beg for death for there is no cure. From this day I will call it Rune's flower, for what I just saw is the living embodiment of that flower."

It was over an hour later, when all the Cutters had been rounded up and placed under a close watch back inside the building, and Rune walked with the Sage across the concrete towards the melting wall of ice. Rune slowed and looked at him. "Thank you, I went too far." He shook his head.

"No you didn't, he deserved to understand what he did, but as I said, to live with those memories is a far greater punishment than death, and I meant it." She understood.

"You need to give yourself a break, you have done so much to help Robbie, and one day he will know of your deeds, I will assure it." He smiled and she turned and looked back at the groups of people organising. "You have the makings of your command now; I believe my grandfather gave you instruction on how to use them?" He looked back.

"Some of them are old and worn out, but it's a start. The green lord told me to head for Canterbury and then London, he told me to gather the fruits and use the seeds, and so that will be my next move if I convince this lot to follow me." Rune looked round at the place.

"There is little here for them, it is your job to inspire them to believe they can get back what they lost, believe me you were raised by Jake and Robert." Rune looked round at the tall trees that grew all around the area. "You have good wood here, and not enough rifles for everyone, I see Oak and Yew and a few other trees, I know you have the skills, so organise and use the woodland to arm yourself, I feel the life of a great many animals to feed and supply your needs. You have what it takes, just believe in yourself and in what you were trained to do, and it will all fall into place. Trust yourself Billy, you grew up in Loxley at the side of Robbie, so I know you have the right training, and never forget, you will have aid when it is needed, I shall watch from afar and ensure it."

He gave a weak smile. "Thanks Rune, I will do the best I can." She gave a smile.

"Sounds like a plan to me Billy." He gave a chuckle.

"It does indeed."

CHAPTER TWELVE

THE POWER OF FAMILY

It was a dull damp morning around Loxley, as Robbie walked through the main street between the shops. He had slept very little the previous night, and had stepped out of his office in the Village Hall to take in some fresh air. He smiled as Anne and Alice waved from the bread shop, and even Ruben gave him a respectful nod as he passed him on the other side of the road, heading towards his shop with new leather.

Alice came out of the butchers, as he walked slowly lost in thought towards her, she smiled, she had seen that face many times in her life. "Lost in a dream world again I see." He looked up from the cobbles.

"What... Oh, hi Alice."

"You look like the whole weight of the world is on your shoulders." He nodded.

"Today it feels like it is." She moved her woven basket to her other arm, and slipped her free arm through his to walk at his side.

"Fancy some company? It's been ages since we took a stroll together." It felt like a good idea, lost in his thoughts he found it hard to get any perspective. "So where are you heading?" He shrugged.

"Nowhere really, I just needed some air and a little space to think." She gave his arm a squeeze.

"It is a lot to take in isn't it? What with a huge wall round us, and the threat of an instant attack, it must be hard on you?" He gave a long sigh.

"Honestly at times my mind gets so filled with all the details, I feel like there is just not enough space left in my head to think clearly. I have to do what is right for everyone; you have no idea how hard it is Alice, if I make one wrong move everyone could suffer."

Alice listened patiently as Robbie let all his thoughts out of his head. "Not only do I have to deal with everything here, I have to deal with crowning Will if he lives, and then deal with the Dark One, and I have no idea how the hell I am going to pull that off."

His eyes had dark patches below them, and his face looked drawn and thin. "You need a break, and by the look of you some decent sleep." He gave another long sigh.

"Well that is not going to happen any time soon." He looked round at the rows of houses in the distance, and the market to his right, where all the traders were busy doing their best to sell whatever they could before the fight began in earnest. "I have to stay focused and on my toes."

Alice frowned. "That may be so, but a few hours break, and a little relaxed time won't hurt you Robbie." He shook his head.

"I don't have a few hours at the moment, I have to ensure we are prepared and ready at a moment's notice." Alice turned and looked him in the eye.

"I don't agree with you." He stopped and frowned at her.

"Why not?" She gave a giggle.

"Look Robbie, we are as prepared as we can be, we have spent two years in preparation for this, and I mean seriously what else do you honestly think we need to do?" He shrugged. "Exactly, so why not just give yourself a little break. Look grandad built this place for the very reason we find ourselves in now. I have no idea how he knew or even worked out what would happen, but he did it, and this place will take a little more than a crazy psychopath like Mason Knox banging on the gates to end it all. Remember the tapestry above his desk in your front room? It read 'Freedom is the possession of those who have the courage to defend it, and it was right, seriously just take a long look round." He stopped and looked at her.

"What are you saying Alice?" She rolled her eyes at him.

"Seriously Robbie you need more sleep, I mean just look." She lifted her hand, and cast it round in a wide circle. "Honestly Robbie at times you can be so blind, here you are walking around all doom and gloom, and carrying all the weight and responsibility of everything, and yet you miss the most important thing that is right in front of you."

Robbie looked round again, everywhere he looked he saw people attending to their tasks, all under the watchful eyes of what had become a massive Woodland Army. Alice smiled. "See... Whatever thoughts you may have, you are not alone in this, all these people came here because they own their own freedom, and every one of them is prepared to lay down their life to defend it, Pericles was smarter than he has ever been credited for." Robbie looked confused.

"Who?" She rolled her eyes at him again, and softly shook her head.

"Seriously Robbie, take some time out and read a book or two." He looked offended.

"I do, I read all the time." She gave a soft giggle.

"I mean a real book; you know some classics, not Rune's journals." He smiled.

"She writes some lovely things."

"Hmm, I know what she writes, try reading something that isn't about you." He gave a smile and had to concede.

"I hear you." Alice gave his arm a squeeze and started to walk on.

"I tell you what, why don't you and Rune bring the kids to the house tonight, come have a meal with us, it's been forever since we all sat round the table in the farm, why don't we just relax and let others handle things for just one evening?" He gave a nod.

"Yeah, that would be nice." She gave a broad smile.

"I have not cooked for you in ages, and I have some fresh steak here, so I will knock us all up something to boost our morale, and give us the strength to move onward together." He gave a nod.

"I would love that, just like old times, yeah, you know what, that would really make a difference."

"We are family Rob, I think at times you forget you are not alone; you actually have a lot of people behind you just begging to help out."

Back at the Mere, Rune sat with Sapphire and Steph at her table below the house, and once again watched Sapphire's conversation in the chamber of the Whispering Falls. They had spent all morning at the table and watched Opal's vision from the moth, of Mason and Ursula, followed by her conversation with the Sage on the beach. Rune sat back the violet in her eyes fading away as she viewed the frozen picture of Ena in the Cathedral, which still hovered in the air above her table. Steph noticed her gaze.

"I don't know sweetheart, if this woman who serves the Dark One is truly this Ariel's granddaughter, then this Ena must be her mother. Considering her hatred of Morgan, she is not going to be happy to find her daughter is working with her." Rune gave a nod as she thought.

"I find it hard to understand, I mean why would you serve a family that imprisoned your grandmother, and is the reason your mother has been in hiding for years, it makes little sense to me?" Sapphire shrugged.

"Maybe Ursula does not know her mother is still alive." Rune and Steph turned to her and she shrugged. "What...? Maybe they never told her... I don't know it's only a guess." Steph gave her a shrewd look.

"Is it though, after all you are now the seer to the Fae, maybe it is intuition or something?" Sapphire looked at Rune.

"I thought any predictions I have come through dreams?" Rune smiled as she saw the worried look on her face, and Steph gave a smile behind her.

"Well, you are the centre of the table of sight; I would say your instincts are just as important as your dreams." Rune's eyes moved to Steph. "What about the stars, have you any idea, after all you have been up there with the White Lord, what do you think, your gut instincts are just as valid?"

Steph sat back in her seat and gave it some thought. "Honestly I know nothing of them, like you I think it is some deep Fae secret, and you know what they are like? Maybe Saff should go back and ask the water, after all she is the only one they let in there, it is not like you or I could go ask."

The door above the steps opened, and the clatter of cups could be heard as they rattled on a tray, Rune looked at Steph. "I think I have a quicker solution." Filomena appeared with a tray of drinks and fresh baked scones; Rune watched as she placed the tray down on the small side table and served them. Each time she approached the large stone table, she glanced up at the frozen picture hanging in the air above it. Steph thanked her as she handed her cup to her, and then turned to leave, Rune spoke.

"Filomena, would you ask Isolde to join us with yourself, there is something I wish to discuss with you both?" Filomena turned and looked a little uncomfortable.

"With us... I am not sure there is anything we could say that would help you?" Again, she glanced at the frozen image above the table, Rune kept up her gaze on her.

"Never the less, I would like you both down here where we can talk." Filomena gave a nod.

"Yes Runestone." She turned sharply and scurried up the stairs, Rune sat back and lifted her cup to her lips, and Sapphire looked at Rune.

"Wow that made her nervous, did you feel it too?" Rune gave a nod.

"They know something I can feel it, it angers me that they try to hide it from us. There are way too many secrets in the Fae world, and I aim to find out what it is they know. It is time some of the Fae realised that some of their secrets are the reason we are struggling, and they need to help out and open up a little and share some of their secret past."

It was ten minutes later when Isolde appeared closely followed by Filomena. Isolde gave a small curtsy. "Lady Crystal and Lady Tila are attending to the children Mistress." Rune gave a nod and waved her hand towards the seats around the table. She noticed how Isolde looked at the frozen picture of Ena above the table. Rune watched her carefully. Isolde remained stationary, with Filomena slightly back from her, both appeared afraid of her table.

"I shall remain standing if that is alright Mistress?" Again, she glanced at the picture of Ena.

"Do you know this woman Isolde?" Isolde shook her head.

"No Mistress." Rune could feel her discomfort and apprehension.

"Then why do you keep looking at her?" Isolde kept her composure straight as she looked Rune in the eye.

"I was asked if I had heard of a Fae member called Ena, I assumed that was her, as it is clear to me, she is of Fae, but I do not know of her." Rune sensed she was being honest, she leaned forward in her seat as Steph and Sapphire sat silently watching. Rune swept her hand across the table's surface and a picture of an old member of the Fae appeared besides the picture of Ena.

The old man with long grey hair walked slowly up the steps in front of the House of Scribes at Florae, and Isolde and Filomena gave a slight intake of breath, Rune watched their reactions carefully. "Tell me what you know of this man?" Filomena looked visibly afraid, yet Isolde stood frozen and stared at Rune.

"It is Master Elgin of the Fae Elders." Rune gave a slight nod.

"Is that all, can you not tell me more." Isolde gave a slight shake of her head.

"I am sorry but that is all I know." Her hazel eyes looked almost black, her pupils had dilated so much, and Rune noted it, Rune looked to Filomena and spoke softly.

"What about you Filomena?" Filomena looked terrified, her face had gone very pale as she glanced to Isolde, but her sister was frozen and facing forward her eyes fixed on Rune. She looked back to Rune.

"Please Mistress I do not wish to be in trouble, all I want is to be beside the children, I know nothing of the things you ask." Rune's eyes gave a flicker of violet, and Filomena shrunk back slightly from Isolde. Rune slid her hand across the table.

"So neither of you can tell me anymore about this elder of your race?" She watched as Filomena shook her head and Isolde calmly responded.

"No Mistress." Rune gave a nod.

"Ok then... What do you know of a Fae of Earth named Ariel?" It was clear that both of them had heard the name before, Isolde looked Rune straight in the eyes.

"She was the architect of the House of Scribes, and a leading scribe of our history Mistress." Rune gave a nod of acceptance as she already knew from her conversation with Tila that was true.

Rune gave her wrist another flick, and a picture rose out of her table showing the adult Iona stood at her table, both of them looked astounded, and visibly shaken. "Tell me of the stars of life and death."

For the first time Isolde looked afraid, her faced began to pale slightly. "I have no knowledge of such things Mistress." Her words were soft and very carefully spoken, and Rune could see she was lying.

Rune suddenly stood up and her eyes blazed with violet, she clenched her fists and pounded down on the stone table, both Steph and Sapphire jumped in their seats. The table flashed like lightning, and violet streaks jumped out of the table and hit the walls, cascading sparks across the room.

Filomena screamed with fear and Isolde staggered backwards, Rune's voice boomed out into the room. "DO NOT LIE TO ME, DO YOU KNOW WHO YOU ADDRESS FAIRY?"

Isolde recovered her stance looking terrified, as the bright violet star on the surface of the table went out of focus, and violet flowed around its surface sending sparks in every direction. Outside the thunder suddenly roared into the air with a deafening crash, and the lights in the room went out, and then flickered back to life. Sapphire pulled her feet off the floor, as a shower of sparks fell from the table, and curled up in her seat, as violet light swirled around Rune hiding her from view.

"IN MY REALM WHEN I ASK, YOU ANSWER WITH THE TRUTH!"

Even Steph recoiled at the sheer volume of her daughter's voice, and for a moment she thought of the Lord Hearne. The light around Rune began to clear and the image on the table swirled back into a twenty pointed violet star. Filomena was on the floor shrieking with fear and hanging on to Isolde's leg, as she appeared to flicker, as if she was trying to turn into the tiny bright orb the Fae were known for, yet being restrained, as Isolde leant against the wall for support. The violet flickered around Rune's eyes as she stared at Isolde, and the light lessoned enough for her to be seen again, as she calmed down. Rune stood with her fists on the table facing the two Fae staff and her power could be felt in every molecule in the air, it was as electric as was normally known around the presence of Hearne. Rune's voice became calmer.

"Know this Isolde, granddaughter of Elgin Elder of Florae, in my house you will know your place and understand who I truly am, before provoking my wrath." Rune waved her hand across the table and pictures rose of Elgin stood on the walkway before the House of Scribes, with the young Isolde and Filomena, as he introduced them to a slender female member of the Fae with long brown hair and soft grey eyes. Filomena gave a shriek of fear and screamed out.

"Please Mistress we cannot tell, you are not Fae, and we are bound to our oath as Fae to protect our queen." Isolde looked down in anger.

"Be quiet Filomena, it is forbidden." Rune gave a nod.

"Both of you, pack your things and leave my home, return to Florae and enter my realm no more." Isolde shook her head, a look of horror on her face.

"You cannot do this, we are bound to the new queen, it is our sworn duty, we shall be shamed for all time."

For the first time Isolde lost all of her composure and looked terrified, her tone was immediate and panicked. "Please Mistress Runestone you have no idea of what you do, please I beg of you do not shame us like this, it will threaten everything in Florae." Rune sat down in her chair.

"Your land has no queen; I will never allow a daughter of mine to leave this realm." Filomena gave out a desperate wail.

"No... No you cannot do this you have no right."

The lights flickered and Steph pulled her feet up on the chair. "Oh shit."

The room flooded with violet light as Runestone exploded into another temper, her voice was even louder, and outside all over Loxley lightning exploded out of the sky, and people ran for the their lives in fear. The rumbles exploded into the sky deafening everyone.

In a mass of bright violet light, Isolde and Filomena screamed in fear as they huddled together on the floor clinging to each other in fear for their lives. Sparks bounced all over the place, and Sapphire put her head down to shield her eyes from the penetrating violet light, as Rune's voice roared across the room.

"NO RIGHT... WHO ARE YOU TO TELL ME WHAT RIGHTS I HAVE? I AM RUNESTONE SAPPHIRE, LIFE OF ALL THE REALMS INCLUDING YOURS, HOW DARE YOU ADDRESS ME WITH SUCH DISRESPECT!"

It was impossible to see anything in the room as the violet light engulfed it, and Filomena and Isolde screamed louder with fear. Steph stood up and reached into the light, and found the arm of Rune, she softly squeezed.

"Enough Runestone, you have made your point."

The light went out and the room returned instantly to normal, the violet flickered in her eyes as she calmed down, Steph walked over to the two cowering members of the Fae and gently separated them, and lifted them up onto their feet. Filomena was distraught and weeping bitterly, as Steph guided her into a seat, she turned and took Isolde by the arm and guided her round to the seat next to her sister.

"Sit and don't piss her off any more." Rune sat down and looked across the table at the two Fae, she took a deep breath and let it flow slowly out of her lungs.

"All the realms are threatened, and they are my responsibility, you have information I need to save them, so place your hands on my table and start talking, and if you lie, my table will know and you will not leave this room alive." Filomena did not hesitate, she placed both her palms firmly on the cool surface of the table, Isolde fought her fear and tried to avoid going anywhere near the table. Steph gave a sigh.

"Stubborn bloody fairies." She leaned forward, grabbed Isolde's hands, and lifted them up and placed them flat on the table's surface where they stuck, Rune gave a nod.

"Ok now talk." Filomena was not taking the risk.

"Elgin is our grandfather; he did know Ariel and he protected her when Rhiannon tried to blame her for bringing the Merle into Avalon. My grandfather knew that as the daughter of Enaria, it was impossible for Ariel to have anything to do with the darkness of the Merle, because it was her mother who died trying to rid Ofmoon of the infection by it. The stars of Enaria are the wisdom of the Fae of Earth; they are the tools of life and death that are wielded by all the queens of our line. Please mistress you must believe me, we are sworn to secrecy in order to protect our future lines, we did not want to hide the truth, but we have to protect our people so Morgan cannot hurt any more of us." She burst into tears and wept as Isolde looked heartbroken.

The table knew it to be the truth and Rune swiped her hand across the table and their hands became unstuck, Rune looked at Isolde.

"Take your sister to her room and let her rest, then return to us and we shall continue with the truth." Isolde gave a sharp nod, still looking fearful for her life, she pulled Filomena into her arms and gently lifted the sobbing Fae member, and then carefully, she guided her to the stairs. Sapphire watched and turned to Rune.

"Holy shit Runestone that was terrifying." Rune smiled at Saff.

"Not really it was all smoke and mirrors." Sapphire looked confused.

"What... Are you telling me that was all staged for their benefit?" Steph gave a chuckle.

"We were talking all the way through it to each other; the flickering lights were my idea." Sapphire looked shocked and she pointed behind her.

"But... But the thunder and lightning and everything outside, I don't understand." Rune gave a giggle.

"Jade." Sapphire suddenly understood the elaborate ruse that Rune had played; she rolled her eyes and shook her head.

"I should have known better." She gave a slight chuckle. "You know you scared the crap out of me right?" Rune gave a giggle and Steph patted Sapphire's arm.

"We are sorry Saff, but you have to understand, your reaction had to be genuine as it was vital, think about it, you are the Seer to the Fae and you did not see it coming, it had to convince them it was a genuine outburst of Rune's. They have important information that will help us and the sooner we find out, the better it will be for everyone." Sapphire gave a nod, and then came the sound of footsteps on the steps, and they readied themselves for the return of Isolde.

Isolde reached the bottom step and walked slowly into the room; she turned to Rune and gave a small curtsy. "My sister is resting, she will be fine, she is very upset and frightened." Rune gave a nod and waved her towards the seat she had previously been sitting in. Isolde hesitated. "Please Mistress I need to say something more." She stood nervously wringing her hands together, Rune saw how upset and frightened she was.

"Take a seat and then say what you feel you need to say."

Isolde gave a slight shake of her head. "I must say this first, as we have dishonoured your household, and as the eldest Fae, it is my responsibility to undo what we have done. I am the older and therefore responsible under our customs, it is my place to apologise and beg forgiveness for my sister who acted under my instruction. There is no need for our future queen to suffer, I will leave in disgrace and humbly beg you keep my sister, for she has had the highest level of training for this task, and disagreed with me often. She did encourage me many times to come forward, she is blameless in this matter and it should be known."

She looked wretched and Steph felt a little sorry for her. Isolde walked to the chair and sat down; she lifted her arms and placed both of her hands on the cool surface of the table, and took a large breath.

"I will answer your questions honestly should you ask." Rune gave a nod.

"Please understand me Isolde, you have been welcomed into this house and treated as one of us, I think we can say that we do not treat you as inferiors, we try to make you feel like one of us, and so as part of that, we expect your loyalty and your honesty, we ask nothing more in these times of great need." Isolde put her head down, and two tears dripped onto the table.

"I am so sorry Mistress, please do not think we have not enjoyed our time with you, for both of us it has been the happiest time of our lives." Rune felt a pang in the pit of her stomach, seeing and hearing the pain within a person who had been invaluable to her and Robbie was difficult to bear.

"What is done is done, I think we understand each other far better now, and from a personal perspective, neither Robbie nor myself would wish to lose either of you." Her voice softened.

"Isolde listen to me, Morgan le Fey wishes to destroy everything we have built here, and when she has done so, no realm will be safe, especially Florae. Do not forget the way in which she treated your queen Gwendolyn, and how she has corrupted your people to create her hideous monsters. It is vitally important that at this time we support each other, all the races need to work together to rid all of us of her and her vile son. I know you have important information that may help us in destroying her, but the secrets of your people are protecting her, they are not helping us." Isolde lifted her head.

"We hate her, we would never protect her." Steph gave a nod understanding Rune's approach, she watched as Rune leant forward onto her table.

"Then help us by sharing what you know of the stars of life and death and Ariel." Isolde gave a nod and straightened up in her chair. She slipped a small handkerchief out of her sleeve and dried her eyes.

"I cannot answer everything, because I was young when Ariel was brought back to Florae, but I remember a few of the discussions my grandfather had with my father." She took a deep breath and looked Rune in the eyes. "The stars of life and death were created by Ariel's father, and her mother cast powerful incantations over them. She wore them as a belt, and they were very powerful objects in the mystical realms. It is said that even the high white lord admired the skill and power of them. On her death bed she requested they go to her best friend, Queen Bridget Violet, to be kept until Ariel was old enough and powerful enough to wield them. My grandfather told my father that when Ariel came of age they would unlock her true mystical powers, and that she would become greater than her mother, which is a great feat, as Enaria was seen as the greatest Fae mystic of all time. After the disappearance of Ariel, and just before the new Queen Iona Violet was born, Lord Bade suggested to the Elders that it was likely Ariel was dead, and therefore they should be gifted to the new queen on the day of her crowning, he felt they would serve all of Fae well if wielded by her." Rune understood.

"It explains why when you saw a picture of my daughter in the future; you looked so shocked, because you saw the twelve stars." Isolde shook her head.

"I was surprised to see the red star was not there, you see there are fourteen stars, twelve white, or golden in the sunlight, one red, and the black star. My queen has only the stars of life, the star of darkness was not there, and I always thought it would be." Sapphire understood some of what was being said.

"The red star is Gwendolyn's table at Carnac, I have seen it and felt the power contained within it." Isolde looked surprised.

"I was not aware the Elders had given it to her, but it does explain her great power."

Rune placed her elbows onto the table and rested her chin on her hands, her mind wandered a little, and she stared into her table for a moment, and then looked up, her blue eyes flashed bright and sparkling.

"Your sister mentioned something about Enaria visiting Tideguyde, and then dying on her return, can you tell me about that?" Isolde could see that Rune was considering her every word.

"This took place long before I was born and few know the real story, it is something seldom mentioned, even amongst the elders. The story says Enaria had a bad feeling or sensed something was wrong after the sacred moon goddess left, so she travelled up to the moon realm; this was shortly before Rhiannon took up her seat. At that time the Fae were living as two tribes within the Forrest of Time, shortly before my people travelled to the Isle of Erin. No one really knows what happened, but shortly after her return she became very weak, she begged Queen Bridget Violet to take her daughter away from her and protect her. It all appeared to be very odd that she would not allow her daughter near her side at the end. No one really knows what she told the queen, but whatever it was the queen wasted no time in removing Ariel. Enaria died shortly after, and then within the month of her death her husband died in the same manner. It was rumoured that she created a special charm of protection and placed it in the moon realm. Shortly after her death, the queen insisted every home built had one placed above the door." Rune was intrigued.

"Do you know what this charm is?" Isolde gave a nod.

"It is a red star within a white circle, you will find one under the future queen and her brothers' bed, it is a tradition in our culture to protect all children with Enaria's star of protection."

Sapphire gave a gasp. "Enaria created the star on Gwendolyn's table, no wonder the Dark One had so much trouble tapping her essence, she had been protected by the most powerful mystic of our time." Isolde gave a nod.

"Queen Gwendolyn was very powerful and very talented; she saved many in her time, and protected our people in ways none will ever learn." Rune understood a lot more now and she pondered the new material in her mind, but it still did not explain the link to the line of Morgan.

"Tell me of Ariel, you met her did you not?" Isolde gave a nod.

"Yes I did. There really is little to tell, she was a scribe of great talent, it was Ariel that started the records of the history of our people back in Erin. When we came via the Violet Isle to Florae, it was Ariel that designed the house of scribes as the first store of the scrolls. Shortly before it was complete Queen Bridget Violet asked her to become the ambassador to Avalon, and when construction started, she was despatched to report on its progress. My grandfather told me she lived on the outskirts with a Fae Ofmoon named Branna, and she fell deeply in love." Rune frowned.

"Why was she sent if her task was in the House of Scribes, especially considering it was almost complete, that makes little sense?" Isolde looked a little nervous.

"You must promise never to mention this or my family will be slaughtered. Please Mistress I should not say a word, for this is a secret bigger than all of us and is known only to my family. My grandfather was a very close friend to Queen Bridget Violet, and he often advised her." Rune gave a nod of understanding; Isolde lowered her voice to a whisper and both Sapphire and Steph leaned forward in their seats to hear.

"The reason why Avalon was given to Rhiannon was due to the fact that Queen Bridget accused Rhiannon of being selective in her favourites. She told her that she showed affection only to those of golden hair and abused those of other colours, especially black hair. It caused a huge row, and the lines split for many years until the White Lord himself intervened, and he demanded they repair the riff between them and bring back harmony. Both agreed, and as a show of good will, Lord Hearne invited Rhiannon to set up Avalon, so there was a place on the Earth Realm where both of the Fae lines could cooperate together. Queen Bridget made a pact of peace, but my grandfather told me she never trusted Rhiannon again, she called her arrogant and fool hardy." Rune sat back in her seat a little confused.

"That is really interesting, I know little of Bridget, but from what I have heard she was seen as kind and fair, so if she had a problem with Rhiannon, it must have been for good reason. So what happened in Avalon that Ariel had to report on?" Isolde licked her lips.

"This is the part that still makes little sense to me. Rhiannon accused her of drawing down the Merle to corrupt Avalon, and she was expelled from Avalon. I was young at the time, but I remember the trouble it caused for my grandfather. Ariel returned to Florae as a prisoner and stood trial before the Elders, she was eventually pronounced innocent, after all how could she be guilty? You see she was Enaria's daughter and had been highly protected by her mother, no real evil could harm her." Rune was enthralled.

"So what happened to her?" Isolde gave a slight shrug.

"She lived for many years in Florae separated from her beloved Branna, she isolated herself and worked alone on her journals and parts of the history of the Fae, and then one night she disappeared without a trace, and to this date no one knows where to. Search parties were sent out, but she had gone without a trace, it makes no sense at all." Steph looked confused.

"Did she run back to this Branna, I would assume he was waiting for her to return?" Isolde gave a giggle.

"Branna was a girl... No one really knows, you see Branna disappeared too, Rhiannon had Luminaria searching for her for years, but neither of them have been seen since." Sapphire realised there was more to the story, but she understood that Isolde did not know the whole truth, the Whispering Falls had told her that Ariel had ended up as a servant for Otto, the grandfather of Morgan, and he had raped her, and she stabbed him during her fight with him. But it made no sense to her as to how she could have disappeared; surely the falls would have known her whole story. Sapphire could see that Rune was puzzling things out. Isolde looked across the table at Rune.

"That is everything I know, and it is the truth." Rune gave a nod.

"I know it is, had you held back my table would have known. Thank you, Isolde, you have helped me a great deal, there is much to understand, but I feel I have moved forward. Go and check on your sister, there will be no need for you to leave, but remember, here you are seen as one of the household, and there are no secrets between us." Isolde stood up.

"Once again I am very sorry, it was not my intention to mislead, but I have to protect my family." Rune understood.

"No one will hear of this, it will remain in this room only, go and ensure your sister is recovered and thank you." Isolde left the room and Steph sat forward in her seat.

"It makes some sense don't you think?" Rune gave a sigh.

"More than you realise mum, you see that is not the first time I have heard the name Branna." Sapphire looked surprised, so did Steph, Rune gave another long sigh.

"The night Raven Merle was born, if you remember Morgan delivered the baby, and we all thought she was going to kill Dana Knox, but when Dana told her they were going to name the child Raven Merle, she appeared to change her whole manner around Dana, and it seemed to be odd to me at the time." Steph gave her a nod of agreement.

"I remember it, but I must be missing something here because I don't see how that relates to Ariel." Rune smiled.

"Oh but it does, you see it bothered me, and I have watched that moment many times since, and what you all missed was as she left, she opened her wings, and smiled a bit of a ghastly kind of smile, and she spoke quietly to herself." Steph shook her head.

"I don't remember that part, what did she say?" Rune looked straight into her mother's green eyes.

"Goodnight Branna Merle."

"NO WAY!" Sapphire gasped out a little louder than she had meant to. Rune turned to her and gave a solemn nod.

"Branna means Raven in the old tongue."

CHAPTER THIRTEEN

NOTES FROM THE PAST

It had felt like an age since Robbie, Rune and the children had visited the farm for a meal, and as they sat in the buggy to make the short journey along the Sacred Wood Road, he felt happy and relaxed, which was odd considering the circumstances they all faced at the moment.

The journey took little time, and as Rune took the children inside, Robbie unhitched the horses and led them into the barn for shelter, and a feed out of the rain. He wiped them down and filled the trough with oats, and was about to join the family in the main living room of the farm when the barn opened. Jess stood by the door clutching a large leather bound book.

"I am almost done Mum; I won't be long." She stepped inside, and pulled the door too behind her.

"I wanted to talk to you alone." He looked up at her. "You see I found this, and I think you should read it Rob, it's your grandfather's journal."

Robbie wiped his hands on his jacket and walked over to look at it. "I did not know he wrote one, I mean I have all his notes from running this place; I never thought he would write about himself." It looked old and dusty. "Where did you find this?"

"I was cleaning out the attic, mum has some stuff that she needs storing, and I thought whilst I had a few moments, because Alice is cooking with Beth in our kitchen, I would clear some space for tonight. I found it in an old toy box of all things. Rob your grandfather wrote all about his life, I have not had time to read all of it, but it goes back until 1970, and in 1971 he talks of being alone at the Mere and meeting a woman... Rob this is going to sound crazy, but the woman he met fits the description of Rune." Robbie furrowed his brow.

"What?" Jess gave a sigh.

"I know it sounds bonkers, but here look for yourself." Jess handed the large heavily bound book over, one of the pages was marked with a folded piece of card to keep the right spot. Robbie looked at the hand writing, it was very neat considering he was only nine when he wrote it. Robbie read the passage and suddenly everything his mum had said made perfect sense, he looked up from the dusty old book at his mum and smiled.

"This is not Rune, this is her grandmother Opal, she looked exactly like her when she was younger." Jess gave a sigh of relief.

"Thank Hearne for that, for a moment I had this crazy idea Rune was hundreds of years old." Robbie gave a giggle.

"No Mum, I can assure you she is still younger than I am." Jess looked really relieved and gave a small laugh.

"I have had some odd ideas since reading that. Look Rob, I know you have a lot of Jake's notes and writing, but this journal from what I can gather talks about the wall and why he felt it should be built. I know it's a long shot, but he had such belief in what he was doing, I thought that maybe in here is the reason why and what he planned to do if attacked. It might not help, but I knew him so well and maybe there is something here that might help you, I suppose it won't hurt to look." She gave a soft smile. "Him and your dad often fell out over the reasons for building the wall, but the thing is, he knew long before we heard anything about forces building in the south, and your dad never quite understood how, I think this journal may answer that. I know it sounds strange but he doted on you from the day you were born, he always called you special, in a really odd way, I think he hid it in the toy box in hope that one day we would give those toys to you, and so I feel it's right you have it now."

Robbie understood and gave a nod as she spoke; he agreed it was worth having a look. "Yeah, thanks Mum, you never know there may be something here to help, thanks I will read through it and see what I find." Jess smiled.

"We better get inside; Alice and Beth are pulling out all the stops on your behalf."

Robbie slipped the book under the seat of the buggy out of the rain, and walked with his mum back towards the house for their evening's entertainment. Just outside the kitchen door Jess stopped and turned to him, he could see the concern in her eyes.

"You are alright aren't you; I mean if you are feeling the pressure, you know I am here for you." Robbie smiled.

"It's a lot to handle, but honestly Mum I am doing fine, I have you and the whole family around me, and it helps." She gave a nod and lifted her hand to his cheek.

"You have had so much to handle; it does not seem fair that all of this is on your shoulders." He lifted his hand to hers.

"Fair has nothing to do with it, this is Mason and his sick families doing, together we will stop them, and then maybe things can get back to normal."

"Alright Robbie I understand, but never forget that I am a mother, and it never switches off, I will always worry." He smiled.

"I never expected less of you Mum; it's one of the things in life I count on." She smiled and together they walked into the kitchen and the sudden noise of a large family gathering.

The rest of the evening was spent relaxed and happy, as Harry with Maggs, Blades and Todd arrived to add to the group of Rowan and Jade, with Beth and John Lox. The star of the evening was Sandra Whitmore, mother to Jess, who entertained all by correcting Harry's English and giving odd looks at Maggs, while disapproving of Blades haircut, which she commented was more boy like than female.

On the way back to the Mere later that night Robbie told Rowan, Jade and Rune of the book written by Jake. It was far too dark to read it in the buggy, but he explained his conversation and his mother's misconception which amused Jade and Rune. It was clear to Rune that Robbie felt some hope might lay within the covers of the book, she knew more than most how much he respected and admired his grandfather Jake. For a long time, Robbie had made it clear that Jake knew far more than he had ever spoken about, and as she watched him talk to Rowan and Jade, she hoped that some of the secrets were inside the book, because she knew how much it would mean to him, knowing he understood his grandfather better than anyone else.

That night as she headed to their room having said goodnight to the children she slowed at the door as she heard the sound of a page turn. She smiled and walked into the bedroom to find Robbie sat in bed reading the book. Rune rolled her eyes and walked round the bed as she removed her pants and top, he looked at her.

"What?" She gave a giggle.

"You are hopeless you know that?" He shrugged.

"Why, I am relaxing in bed and reading." She shook her head as she slipped under the sheets.

"This is the first early night you have had in ages, and I thought maybe you wanted to do something a little more interesting than read." She gave another little giggle, as she slipped up beside him and slid her warm arms across his chest, and he gave a smile. Robbie closed the book and placed it on the floor at the side of the bed.

"So Mrs Loxley, it's early." Rune giggled.

"I know." He leaned forward and kissed her. He pulled back and gave her a shrewd look.

"Why do I suddenly think you and Alice conspired tonight?" Rune gave a laugh.

"I am the one who knows stuff, not you." She gave a shriek as he tickled her side and wriggled; Robbie leaned over to the side of the bed and blew out the candle.

Sapphire sat at her table under her kitchen, in the cellar below the small house at Callanish, when above her she heard a bumping sound. She froze and looked up at the floor boards that were her kitchen floor, her senses searching all around her for any sign of a person. Slowly she stood up trying to make no sound, she was miles away from anyone who could help and alone, and the thought of anyone in her house, especially considering the door was locked was frightening. She strained to listen for any signs, was that a soft footstep?

The trapdoor was closed, and so she tried to think of how the hell she could find out who it was without giving herself away. Slowly she crept towards the steps trying her hardest not to make a single sound. As she reached the bottom of the steps, and looked up, a hand tapped her on the shoulder.

Her scream was louder than even she thought possible, as she almost fainted with fright, she spun round quick, and a bright blue flash exploded out of her right hand. As she fell back onto the bottom step of the stairway, all she could hear was her rapidly beating heart and the laughter of Gwendolyn. Sapphire breathed deep trying to catch her breath. "You scared the hell outta me, don't you know how to knock?"

Gwendolyn smiled. "Sorry I could not resist, I felt you down here, and I thought I would pop down to meet you, when I saw you creeping about, it was just too tempting, and I could not resist." She gave another giggle. Gwendolyn looked exactly as she always had, except she wore a blue dress with a white sash, compared to the last time Sapphire had seen her.

Sapphire stood up. "You know I am not sure you know this but dead people are supposed to stay dead." Gwendolyn smiled.

"Not me I got a reprieve." Sapphire could feel her heart still beating rapidly in her chest, as she watched the solid figure of the last Queen of the Fae of Earth walk around her cellar.

"How did you come back, Una said you were watching the realms out of reach of all of us?" Gwendolyn gave a nod as she looked round the room, and took a great deal of interest in the Table of Sight, her voice was quite casual.

"The Green Lord came to see me, he asked me to help out, so I have been having a good look round to see what I could find to help the red stone in her quest." Sapphire understood.

"Can you help us?" Gwendolyn gave a sigh.

"You are Fae, so I can help you." Sapphire did not quite understand.

"Rune is the centre of everything, why me and not her?" Gwendolyn ran her hand across the Table of Sight, and soft blue sparks jumped into her fingers.

"You have done a nice job here and used your gifts well." She turned to face Sapphire. "Only Fae can see me, I am dead remember? Also, a lot of what I can tell you, must stay only for the ears of a Fae queen, and seeing as I was the one who chose you to educate the next queen, I thought it better we talk in here out of ear shot of everyone, I assume this is a place Opal won't be able to peer into easily?" Sapphire shrugged.

"You know Opal." Gwendolyn gave a giggle.

"Oh do I... even without her powers she still finds out more than most others, which is why I have made your veil stronger. A seer to the queen should have stronger protections and you are using a similar one to the Green Circle, trust me when I tell you the Fae have far more superior ones. I have added that knowledge to your table, you will benefit from it in future days." Sapphire had no idea about Fae magic, or the difference between those Rune used. Gwendolyn pointed to her seat at the side of the table.

"Sit and listen, I have gained what you know from touching your table, and you have done well, but there is more you should know." Sapphire sat down and watched as Gwendolyn paced the room. "I knew Enaria when I was a very young girl, and I was a close friend of Ariel, we grew up together, so I think I knew her better than most, and I can tell you outright that Ariel had nothing to do with the Merle, it would have been impossible for her to be near it such was the power of protection placed on her by her mother. My grandmother argued this with Luminaria who was constantly sent to her by Rhiannon, until eventually Ariel was cleared. As for this Ena, if she truly is Ariel's daughter then you have a big problem, because she will be very powerful." Sapphire nodded as she understood.

"Is it really possible to hide from everyone as she has?" Gwendolyn stopped pacing for a moment and thought. She considered it deeply and then began to pace round the cellar again.

"Your problem is Ariel, I cannot believe the Raven could kill her, and so I think you should assume Ariel still lives, because with the rights of the passage of power Ena would be more powerful than the Raven is currently, and she would have killed her by now, and she has not, so I think it's safe to say Ariel is still alive somewhere." Sapphire shook her head.

"In the Cathedral I was connected to Rune and Ena was crazy angry, she believes her mother and daughter are dead." Gwendolyn looked at her.

"She is alive trust me on that, I lived long beyond my time in the Raven's lair; Ariel would have the same if not better ability to resist. I have spent a life tracking the Raven and I know most of her powers, I think it is safe to say she has not learned enough to kill a daughter of Enaria."

Sapphire gave a nod of acceptance. "Ok so if she lives, we can assume this Ena is unaware, but that does pose the question where is she, even the Whispering

Waters think she disappeared and does not know where?" Gwendolyn smiled.

"You are starting to think like Fae, it's a good point, and all I can think of is that somewhere there is a place that has many protections on it that prevents Fae of Earth power from penetrating. I have to admit that really bothers me, because the only other place that can do that is the crystal castle of the moon realm." Sapphire did not understand.

"Why does that bother you, the veil can hide everything." Gwendolyn shook her head.

"Not from the Whispering Waters, the power in that cave is the most powerful force of the Fae of Earth, so if there is a place hidden from it, then we are dealing with something very powerful."

"What like the Star of the Merle?"

"I would say more powerful than that little rock." Sapphire gave a gasp.

"That cannot be possible... Can it?" Gwendolyn shrugged.

"I think to be honest that is the problem, we simply do not know. I have tried to contact Albanlin as I know he would have knowledge of such things, but so far he is as always being elusive, but you may be right, we may be dealing with something connected to the Merle, just not the star, which is well away from any hands in the safe keep of Eve." Sapphire thought for a second.

"I know it may sound mad, but Rhiannon accused Ariel of bringing down the Merle, what if it was someone else? Rune has thought that, but it just does not seem possible, she said it would be too much power for someone to handle." Gwendolyn stopped and gave it some thought; Sapphire felt that maybe Gwendolyn had already considered that. Gwendolyn gave a long sigh.

"There is a theory, and I cannot say this is true, and you must keep this very quiet, but the theory is that maybe there is a chance that the garment of Tideguyde may have been infected by the Merle. Now if that is true, and I caution you to keep that quiet, there could be some Fae who have an ability to absorb some of the Merle, which in theory, and it is grasping at straws a little, that person could draw down the Merle. Before you go off with wild theories, let me just say this, if it is true, and I am not saying it is, then it would be a member of Fae Ofmoon, all Earth Fae are free of it." Sapphire frowned.

"You know that for sure." Gwendolyn scoffed.

"Trust me I was their queen for a long time, if anyone in Florae had been infected, I would have found out."

"Does Rhiannon know?" Gwendolyn sat down on the bottom step of the stairs.

"That Sapphire is the most dangerous question you have ever asked, and it is not one you should ask anyone else. The Queen of the Moon is very powerful, and she would not take kindly to even be aware you have thought that, and if for one second she thought you had, her actions against you would be swift and deadly."

"So if there is Merle in a line of Fae, does that mean there is a line of Merle in

Morgan? If it was brought to these realms by a Fae who is related to her, it would have to be from the moon line. So how do we find out for sure, would Amethyst know?" Gwendolyn bit her lip.

"Amethyst has certainly made changes her grandmother does not like, but the problem is she is family, and the bonds of family within all Fae run very deep, I think you saw that with Runestone and her Fae servants. I suppose the question is who would be best placed to know, and would Rhiannon entrust this information to Amethyst?" Gwendolyn stood up suddenly. "This cannot be your task, it is far too dangerous, leave it with me, I have a few ideas, keep looking for Ena, I will look into this, after all there is little they can do to me, as I am already dead."

Sapphire felt a little relieved. "Ok what will I have to do if I find something out?"

Gwendolyn turned on the steps. "Put your hand on the table and think of me, you must only do it from here, as here you are completely shielded from everything. If I need to talk I will visit you here." Sapphire understood.

"Ok I will look forward to it, and thanks." There was a popping sound and she was gone, and Sapphire gave a shiver, Gwendolyn was obviously worried and that really worried her. She sat at the table alone on a deserted island, thinking of all she had learned, and suddenly she was not sure who was the real danger, was it Morgan, or was it Rhiannon?

CHAPTER FOURTEEN

LIGHT ON THE TRUTH

The dark damp air lingered under the leaves of the Forest of Time. Above the canopy the stars shone brightly across the dark moonless sky, and the grass felt soft and cool on the path, as Gwendolyn walked briskly towards the cabin. Somewhere above her an owl gave a solitary hoot, almost as if ensuring that everything in the forest was aware of a visitor.

As Gwendolyn walked into the glade containing the long wooden house, she saw the large figure of the Keeper stood waiting almost as if she was expected. She gave a regal bow and approached Fagan. "My Lord Fagan, I would seek your guidance if you would permit it. I am aware that I am not the most welcome visitor these days considering I spoke out against your sister during her time at Florae." His large white brows appeared to lift, and even in the darkness they appeared to illuminate his face.

"Did ye speak with a true heart?" Gwendolyn stopped at the bottom of the wooden steps and looked up at him.

"I believed Ariel was innocent and that has not changed to this date, and as her queen's heir at that time, I defended the honour of the legacy left to her by her mother, who as you know instructed your mother." Fagan gave a nod and pushed the door, and it swung open revealing his old wooden kitchen table and two chairs.

"Me mother always said the truth of the heart is the most precious gift we hold, and I feel ye has a true heart, I always did. Come tell me what ye seek this late in the night, for if it has brought the last queen of the Earth Fae here, and back from her rest, then I feel it must be of importance to our lady of the woods." Gwendolyn gave a nod.

"It is My Lord." He gave a nod as she passed, and then followed her inside. Gwendolyn was surprised to notice a steaming pot of freshly made tea on the table, sat with a large plate of barley crackers, and fresh cheese with two cups. "Are you expecting company?"

He turned and smiled, and just for a second, she thought his ears gave a wiggle behind his thick wide sideburns. "I was, but now ye are here, we can sit and talk as was your intended purpose."

Gwendolyn gave a soft chuckle, as she sat in the chair by the table, and loosened her cloak, as she watched Fagan pour out the tea. He sat down and lifted a cracker onto which he broke some cheese. He looked up and their eyes met, and she could see the bright light of life that burned within him.

"I know what the Runestone seeks and what she intends to do, as does ye, and I see from all your jumping around, ye has been in touch with your lady of eyes on the rock north, so tell me, what brings ye here after avoiding the forest for so long?"

Gwendolyn lifted her cup to her lips and took a sip of the Camomile and Ginger tea. Her bright eyes watched the old man carefully as he slipped the cracker into his mouth and began to chew. "I feel you already know, there can be only one reason I came back here, for you know of my time here and the loss I suffered, sadly for myself this place no longer holds the wonder it did, it is a reminder of painful times." He gave a nod.

"Luminaria." Gwendolyn leaned forward onto the table.

"She was relentless in her belief that Ariel was guilty, and it was as strong as mine of her innocence, and I never understood why. Lord Fagan she is your sister, and on the moon realm she is out of my reach."

"So ye thought I was the next best thing?" Gwendolyn gave a sigh.

"You know her better than any, she was a loyal and very dedicated marshal here who's service to her queen was beyond reproach, and yet she was exiled back to the moon before Rhiannon left, I guess what I want to know is why?" Fagan's face was unreadable, and Gwendolyn felt more than a little apprehensive.

He sat back in his chair and scratched his thick white bushy hair, which made it stand out more than it had when she arrived, his eyes stayed locked on hers all the time, and yet she felt he was also considering her question and remembering times long gone past.

"Ye are a queen, and if any other was to ask such a thing of me, I would let them talk to the scythe. Ye were a fair queen, ye ruled with love and compassion for all ye folks, and if I may say so, ye saved many from a fate worse than death by sealing ye realm and protecting ye people. I admired ye for that, for if little dark eyes had got em, well their fate would have been far worse than a roll in the briar of the south meadows, and that is sayin much."

He leaned forward on the table and stared right intro her eyes. "Ye is asking me to take a side against my queen or my sister, I know ye knows that." Gwendolyn nodded.

"Your Queen is now Amethyst." He gave a soft chuckle.

"Tis a point only another queen would make." He sat and leaned back in his chair and gave a long pause before speaking. "Lumi bless her, never for one moment believed it was Ariel." Gwendolyn could not believe what she was hearing, and gasped.

"WHAT!! How can that be, she badgered my grandmother for years?" He lifted his cup and gave a wink and smiled.

"Well, that hit ye faster than a hornet from a busted nest." He took a deep breath and he sat back and scratched at his thick white tufted hair. "She always believed it was the other one, she just knew that ye Ariel would crack before her lover did, so she pressured ye queen to get Ariel back here alone, so she could crack her like a walnut and get the real truth."

It was a huge surprise to Gwendolyn; she remembered the heated debates that Luminaria had with her grandmother over taking Ariel back to Avalon. In a way she felt angry, Ariel had suffered being on house arrest in Florae for a great length of time, and prevented from being involved with her greatest dream to build the House of Scribes. It was clear that in many ways Fagan had given her the answer she needed to confirm without actually telling her, it was now clear that a Fae Ofmoon had indeed pulled down the Merle to the realm. He watched her carefully understand what he was really saying, and she gave a gentle nod of understanding.

"I thank you Lord Fagan, for you have given me the answer to my question, and it will aid the Red Stone greatly." Gwendolyn slid back her chair, stood up, and bowed. "Your heart is true, and the woodland here is better for it." He smiled.

"Then we is done my fair Queen."

"We are indeed Lord Fagan." She turned and walked out of the door, and Fagan sat and watched as she shrank into a small orb, and swept through the trees. He leaned back in his chair as Brooke flew down to the window and poked his head inside and gave a hoot. "Aye I know, and thanks again for the warning my old friend."

Fagan got up and walked to the door, for a moment he stood and watched the trees sway, then closed the door and headed back to his rocking chair. He slipped off his boots and lifted his feet to rest against the chimney breast wall, and took his pipe out of his pocket and sat back. Lighting the pipe, he pushed with his left foot, and the chair began to gently rock back and forth, he blew a large plume of pure white smoke into the air and relaxed as his mind drifted.

His life had been long, and so much had happened since he had come down to the realm of Avalon with his mother and sister. He had been the Maker, the man charged with the crafting of fine things for the queen, but his skills had been such that before long he earned a reputation for fixing just about anything. He had constant contact with the people, and through his conversations there had been little he had not learned of the ways in which his queen ruled.

He had not agreed with everything the queen did, but he was a loyal servant who kept himself to himself, and with the daily contact with his mother who was seer to the queen, Fagan learned far more than he probably should have. When the announcement came that Rhiannon was to leave Avalon after the death of her daughter Eleanor, he knew he could not return to the moon realm, and so petitioned the queen to stay, and take on a new role as Keeper to the Forest, a job that also entailed keeping Avalon in pristine condition in the absence of the Fae.

The years had passed in solitude, something he preferred, and alone in his hand built home, he spent nights reflecting on his life and the life of those around him. Tonight was no different from any other night, apart from the fact that Gwendolyn had visited, and yet as he sat smoking his pipe, once again memories of so long ago floated into his head, especially the one of that night Luminaria came to see him.

It had been hot that summer and he had taken to sitting out by the back door of his house connected to his makers shop, in the cooler evening air of Avalonia. He had never expected Luminaria to ride up, after all she had not visited him for several years due to her command and duties. She arrived at speed and her horse slipped on the smooth white stone road, and she twisted sliding off the saddle, jumping down to the floor. Her long mane of golden hair wafted up as she hit the floor, her sword glinting in the evening light. She was tall for a woman, and slender from her exercise of combat, her uniform was the deepest blue of a commander with golden bars on her shoulder. She looked worried. "Greetings Brother."

He gave a nod. "Tis been a while since ye sort out my home, ye look like the cat that returned to find no cream, what ails ye?" She walked briskly towards him.

"I need your advice on a matter of great importance." He gave a nod.

"Looking at ye face, maybe we should retire out of sight, come the walls have many ears out here." He got up and walked towards the door, but Luminaria beat him, and was inside before he had a chance to move. Fagan walked in, where she paced up and down the small kitchen. "Ye look like a willow with root rot; maybe ye should sit a while and let the calmness of the evening wash over ye."

She shook her head and continued to pace. "Brother I am in trouble, I have argued with the Queen of Fae and it has not gone well, and I am at a loss as to what to make of everything."

Fagan walked over to her and gripped her shoulders and held her still. "Ye are more skittish than ants on a sugar pile, whatever has ye so riled up? Come sit and take the air and then tell me all about it." She gave a long sigh and her eyes filled with tears. Fagan pulled her close. "I feel ye insides churning like butter, Lumi, come calm yeself and we shall talk."

She wiped her eyes, and Fagan walked her to the table and sat her down. "I think ye needs something with a little more buzz of the bee than tea." He opened the bottom cupboard and took up an earth coloured bottle, and lifted two glasses, he turned back to the table, and sat down and pulled on the cork. "Tell me what has ye so spinning like the wind ribbons?"

He poured the dark liquor into the glasses and slid one across the table towards her; she lifted it and took a long swig. "Whoa Lumi, this stuff will take rust off cart wheels, go lightly with it." She looked at him, her face pale and her eyes sparkling from her damp tears.

"I have made a grave mistake." He gave a nod.

"The Ambassador, I figured as much, ye understand why she is innocent; does ye now, see how fruitless your actions were?" She gave a soft nod.

"She is the daughter of mother's teacher Enaria, I honestly had no idea. The queen told me it was her who was guilty, and I simply believed her, so I went to see Queen Bridget, they told me she was sick and not to be disturbed, but I barged my way and we had such a row." She shook her head. "How could I be so foolish, she was so angry, and when she told me who this Ariel is, I could not believe it, what am I to do?" Fagan took a swig of the drink.

"I warned ye did I not? Caught between two queens, ye always did have a way of doing things big." She looked at him.

"It's not funny, Bridget thinks I deliberately targeted Ariel, and Rhiannon wants me to arrest and imprison her here, whatever I do is going to cause another rift like last time. Oh brother, help I don't want to be the one who splits the two Fae apart again, those two have only just repaired their rift." It was an awkward place to be, and Fagan could feel the fear inside of her.

"The way I see it is this, the only thing that matters is the facts and ye feelings, so does ye truly believe this Ariel called the Merle down to Avalon?" She shook her head.

"No it had to be the other one, Branna." Fagan understood.

"Ye wanted to lean on her, to get her to tell ye about the Branna girl?" Luminaria took another large swig of her drink.

"From what I have found out Branna was unhappy with the queen, calling her the golden queen, you know the gripes of the workers. Apparently, she had put in many requests to see the queen to present her work on the darkness, and had been rejected every time. There are reports of her voicing her dissatisfaction, and she was known to complain about the queen, stating she favoured those of golden hair, it was clear to me she was not the type to admit anything. I knew that Ariel was a soft hearted and gentle person, foolishly I thought to get to the truth I had to crack her, so I tried, but overdid it." He gave a soft smile.

"Well, ye never did much by halves did ye?" He shifted in his chair and leaned onto the table. "Ye know what Mother would say don't ye?" Luminaria gave a nod.

"Speak up and speak honest, even if everyone disagrees with you." He gave a nod.

"So ye thinks this girl is innocent, and that the other one did it?" She gave a nod. "I do yes."

"Then ye know what to do, tell the queen ye are going after the one called Branna." Luminaria gave a long sigh.

"That's the problem; I was instructed to prove its Ariel no matter what." She looked at Fagan and he could see her pain. "Brother she is innocent; I cannot do as my queen asks, it is wrong." He reached across the table and took her hand in both of his.

"It is right to speak up and speak honest, no matter what the queen thinks, ye have to be true to ye, if not, how can ye live as ye? I says go after this Branna and bring her back to face her crime, tis the only way I see ye proving yeself." Her head softly nodded.

"Being me is not so easy at the moment, but you are right, I will go and see her and tell her what I know. I do have scouts out looking for signs of Branna." He patted her hand.

"Ye has always been stronger than most, and ye has always walked the line of truth, and no matter what, I loves ye." She smiled.

"I love you too, you are a good brother, thanks." He gave a nod and knew she understood and would be true to herself.

He knew his love for his family could at times cloud his thoughts, but he watched her face the queen and then set off to look for Branna. For years he saw her suffer as she tried in vain to find the runaway much to the annoyance of the queen. Eventually the queen demoted her and sent her in shame to serve in the prisons of the Moon Realm, something Fagan always felt was unjust.

He came out of his thoughts, and took another long puff on his pipe, the wind stirred in the trees outside and he turned to look out of the window. "Tis time the truth came to light, and yes ye are right, what was done will be known, it's time Lumi walked free again."

It was a new day in Loxley, and although the rain had ceased it was still overcast and cloudy, with the threat of yet more rain to come. Sapphire was sat in the living room speaking quietly with Rune as Robbie came down the stair, scratching his head, he yawned. "Morning." They did not notice him they were so involved with their conversation; he shrugged and headed for the kitchen where Tila and Crystal were washing the pots.

"Morning Robbie." He gave a nod and Tila smiled at him. "The pot is still hot; would you like the beans in it?" He frowned, and Crystal laughed.

"It's called coffee." She gave a smile. "We have many rituals here she does not have in Florae."

"Sorry... Would you like the Coffee?" Robbie gave a nod and headed for the table as he yawned again, Tila walked over with the cup and he took it and lifted it to his lips. "You should sleep more after good sex, it helps builds the stamina back."

Robbie jerked and slurped his coffee onto the table; Crystal gave a chuckle and turned to Tila. "People here are not quite as straight forward about their sexual behaviour as they are on Florae; they tend to not mention it." She gave an understanding nod.

"Oh right, sorry Robbie, you look tired and should sleep more." She looked at Crystal, "Is that better?" Crystal gave another chuckle.

"Much better, why do I think you and Jett will hit it off right away?" Robbie smiled.

In the Living room Rune sat back for a moment and thought. "The thing I do not understand is if this Ariel is still alive, why did the Whispering Waters not tell you, surely it must know?" Sapphire shrugged.

"According to Gwendolyn there must be a place that has a very powerful veil over it preventing anything from seeing what goes on within, it sounds almost like wherever they are is inside some sort of protective bubble." Rune gave it some thought.

"But that would imply very strong magic, and we know that Morgan uses potions and powders for her magic, and it makes me wonder why if she can wield that sort of power. To be honest it does not make much sense." Sapphire sat back into the soft cushions.

"Although it might explain Gwendolyn's theory that a Fae Ofmoon was the one who drew down the Merle. I mean let's be honest none of us really understand its true power."

Rune agreed. "It makes more sense that Ena could hide though, considering her family line, we must find her Saff, time is not on our side, Robbie found out yesterday there is a very large force heading our way from the south. I still think this Ena has the answers we need, we must find her, time will run out quicker than we expect, we need to locate her as quickly as possible before it is too late. Have you heard from Cal yet?" Sapphire shook her head, and looked a little worried.

"Not yet, but if anyone is going to find her it is him, as a dream spirit there is no place he cannot locate and enter unnoticed, I just hope its sooner rather than later."

CHAPTER FIFTEEN

UNSEEN FRIENDS

Within the dark room, lit from the fine shafts of light from the windows high above, and by the glow of the fire, crackling in the fire place, faint muttering came from within the enclosure of tables, stacked with bottles and potions. The door at the end of the hall gave a long whining creak, and a voice thundered up the hall from behind the tables.

"WHAT NOW?"

Two deep red eyes peered through the glass bottles, as Ursula slipped into the room carrying a bundle of papers. "Oh it's you; I thought it was that blithering fool you brought in to help Hesketh. The man is a cringing whipping fool, never tell me where you found him, I may be tempted to send him back in a box." Ursula gave a slight smirk.

"Your son recommended him Mistress." She gave a snort.

"I might have known, the man is an idiot, he probably drove Mason as mad as he is me, so he thought he would foist the fool on me for revenge, either that or he hoped I would experiment on him." Morgan peered at her as she walked down the hall towards her. "What do you have there?"

"It's more papers Mistress from your son and his general."

"MORE!! I have done as he asked, he has his wall and all his little new pets enclosed, what the hell does he want now?"

Ursula walked round to the only open space between the encircled tables, where there was a clear surface, and placed the papers down. "I do not know Mistress; I was instructed to bring them to your attention urgently." Morgan gave an exasperated gasp and stopped what she was doing, and snatched the papers up to look at them, her red eyes flicking from left to right as she examined them.

"More of his ridiculous plans, he has half the country to fight for him and surround that old pile of logs, and yet he whines and pleads for more and more, honestly back in the day it took one man to rally the country behind him, and slay everyone who disagreed with him, there are days I wonder if we will ever see true men again."

"Yes Mistress." Ursula turned to walk back to her table and her mistress gave a tut as she read Masons latest plans for Loxley, and then let out a long sigh.

"He does not need anything yet, it's obviously nowhere near as important as he makes out, it is probably that other idiot he brought in. That Dale, heaven knows why he picked him, the man is only capable of picking out a good shirt, he has no real talent at warfare."

Morgan tossed the papers back onto the table and turned back to her potions and bottles, and Ursula sat down and lifted her quill, dipped in the ink pot and began to continue with her translations from old Fae to Modern English, as she studied a large and very old black book.

Deep below the island of Florae, within the tunnel leading from the stairs up to the House of Scribes, and to the entrance of the Whispering Falls, there was a faint pop! Just for a second the walls of the tunnel illuminated with a soft blue light, and then returned to the thick darkness of seconds earlier. Almost as if a soft breeze blew down the tunnel through the darkness the air stirred, and the pouring, thundering, water of the falls parted. Inside the silent round chamber, two soft wet footprints appeared on the floor, and slowly more appeared as if walking across the chamber, the faint image of Gwendolyn appeared and solidified into her human form, as she walked softly towards the seat in the centre of the large room, where she turned and sat down.

A voice whispered from within the water. "Hello old friend."

Gwendolyn smiled. "Hello Enaria, I have little time, but have been granted a return to my old familiar seat."

From within the flowing water a figure of a woman formed, and stepped out of the flow and onto the white stone, she looked like she was made of clear crystal. Enaria smiled, her long glass like hair flowed to the floor, her robes glinted like crystal in the sunlight, and round her waist she wore a belt made of stars that shone like ice in the sunlight. "I am pleased to see you child, it is funny, as the last time you sat in that seat and told me of your vision of death, but I knew it would not be our last time together."

"Many years have passed since that time, but I find myself in great need, and so have returned to speak to the only source of pure truth I know of." Enaria walked closer.

"You always were cleverer than most, you appeared to have such innocence and naivety as a young child, and yet behind those bright blue eyes, which so many were fooled by, I could see the spark of Bridget burning so brightly. You are wise to seek me out, for my words are only for a queen of this realm, even your choice for the future teacher of the next queen has limited access to my knowledge." Gwendolyn gave a chuckle.

"The new queen has not been crowned yet, so under Fae law I am still the rightful queen of this realm." Enaria gave a nod.

"A queen it appears that even death cannot withhold from a sacred vault, you again have outsmarted many in your own realm, and considering the status of Iona Violet, you are indeed correct, you are still queen of this realm, and therefore I am placed at your service."

Gwendolyn rose from her seat. "I know you know of things related to the death of my grandmother, and I know you know the truth of what you found on the Moon Realm after Tideguyde left, and if I am right, you are aware of what happened in Avalon with your daughter, and at this time all the realms are in great danger, and the new Lady of Life has come to claim the red stone, and it is my duty to aid her to rid this evil that infests all the realms." She paused for a moment... "I have important questions about Ariel and my grandmother."

Enaria shimmered as she gave a nod of understanding. "You also know I am forbidden by the High White Lord from speaking of these matters with any living soul." Gwendolyn gave another bright smile.

"Then it is a good job I am no longer living, and like you am here in spirit form."

Enaria smiled and lifted her finger and wagged it at her. "Only you could find a loop hole to outsmart the White Lord." Gwendolyn shrugged.

"It is not a loop hole, it is a fact." Enaria stared at her with joy in her eyes.

"I have missed you so much, I miss the conversation and intellect, you should have taken more care and protected yourself more." She gave a sigh. "Again, I am bested by you, ask me your questions and I will answer what I know is possible, for no other reason than I always admired how you saved our people and protected my daughter whilst she resided here."

"She was my friend and deeply loved by all of us, you told Sapphire you had no idea of her whereabouts, but I know you of old, I know you must have some idea of where I can find her?"

Enaria looked saddened. "I did not lie to your teacher, for I cannot see her actual location."

"But you know an area where I may find her." Enaria looked deeply into Gwendolyn's eyes.

"You assume she is alive?"

"She is isn't she? For had she died her daughter Ena would be far more powerful and would have defeated the Raven. The fact she has not tells me your daughter lives, and I would bring her aid should I know where to look." Enaria gave another small chuckle.

"As always you do not disappoint me with your deductions... It is true that she does live, for Ena has not gained the power destined for her, although I think there is a darkness in her that blinds her from the truth, I feel hate driven by hate, and should my daughter die, I feel Ena would be in danger of being seduced by the forces that live in the darkness, something we cannot allow, as Ariel's gift is far too precious to give to the enemy."

"Where is your daughter my friend, for I will aid her and return her to this land of her line?"

Enaria gave a nod. "She entered a land once known as Sachsen, and disappeared; all I can tell you is that she was heading up into the high regions when I lost her." Gwendolyn frowned.

"How could you lose sight of your own blood, it makes so little sense, you two were bonded so deeply?"

Enaria shook her head. "I have no knowledge of what became of her, all I can say is a circle of darkness engulfed her, and then she was gone, and I have neither seen or felt her since... I will say this to you in hope you pass on my concerns. She followed the trail of the one she loved named Branna, and the last time I felt her she was with Branna, but Branna was no longer just Fae, she has within her a strange dark and powerful force. They were together for a short amount of time before they both disappeared, but I felt great fear for my daughter in those brief moments, if you are to help the lady of the red stone, warn her that whatever creates this circle of darkness feeds off life."

"Thank you, my old friend, I will pass on your warning. Can I ask one more thing, for my time here is short?"

"Once again I cannot give you what you seek, I gave my word to your grandmother her secret would go with her to the grave." Gwendolyn gave a nod of disappointment.

"I am aware of the sacred vow you swore with each other, but I will ask this of you. On your return from the Moon Realm you told my grandmother that your suspicion had been proven right, seeing as it is not part of the sacred vow, can you tell me what your suspicion was that made you visit the Moon Realm?" Enaria smiled.

"Again, you find a way round the promises of old. I will tell you this only. I felt a presence on the moon around the remains of the garment left by Eve when she collected most of the garment, and so I went to recover the scraps, and the presence I felt was not one of light or any of the realms created by the lady or lord of the first forest, what you believe may have happened did. I can say no more to you my old friend." Gwendolyn understood.

"I am grateful to you, for my suspicion has now been confirmed, and I can use it to aid all the peoples of all the realms and I will ensure Ariel returns to this land so you may once more speak with her. Just out of interest, what became of the scraps you collected?"

She gave a smile. "Only you would ask such a question, and the answer is simple, I placed them in the last star my husband made, it was white, until I sealed the pure evil from the shards within it."

Gwendolyn understood instantly. "The Star of the Merle, I always thought you were the creator not my mother, something so harmless to look at, and yet deadly to use could only have been created by your hand. I see now the power it must have taken, and now I truly understand why you became so weakened and eventually begged for Ariel to be taken to safety. You feared the strength of magic it took to combat the merle inside yourself would kill her. I am sorry to know that such an act of protection brought about your demise. I shall ask no more of you my old friend."

"Then we have honoured the pledges we made the day you became queen of this realm, and now I will leave your service and prepare for the new queen. Go in peace my friend, and take the light into the darkness, and defeat it for all of us and the future queen of this realm."

The figure of Enaria broke into a million tiny droplets of water and flowed back into the fast flowing water, and Gwendolyn stood for a moment in silence, and then she too faded away and the soft breeze flowed through the water, and out into the tunnel, where in the darkness there came a faint popping sound.

Big John was sweating as he and Jaz lifted a huge steel plate onto a cart outside the barn of Loxley Farm, John Lox stood in the doorway looking at the papers in his hand, as Una and Maddy walked up.

"What on earth are you guys up to now?" Big John smiled at Una.

"It is for the gates." Maddy frowned.

"The gates, are we having new gates?" Jaz shook his head.

"No Miss Maddy, we have built a twenty foot wall in front of the gates across from the entrance square, we are going to bolt these plates to it so if they shoot guns or cannons at it, the metal should protect it." Una looked at Maddy.

"It sort of makes sense, and I suppose it will also protect the gates, and make it harder for them to force them open." Maddy gave a nod.

"I suppose it does." John Lox looked over his papers.

"Having trees either side of the main gates hides most of the wall, but the gate area is very exposed to cannon fire, our Robbie wants it more protected, but also the wall will hide us taking stuff out into the trees. He wants a few things sneaking out of the gates, and we would prefer Mason doesn't see us, so we built a wall, and now we are making it harder for him to knock it down, he is a bright boy our Robbie, I would never have thought of it."

Maddy and Una understood and gave a nod of recognition, they stepped back as Jaz gripped the steel plate hard, and then pushed with his stomach, to help slide it fully onto the cart, as Big John heaved it from the other side.

Harry came down the road at the side of the barn wearing his favourite black hat; he lifted his fingers in a salute to the brim. "Hey ladies."

In his other hand he held a tatty old grey looking sack, he turned towards his brother. "Hey man look I found it." He lifted the sack and took out a large silver pulley.

Big John gave a gasp as he leaned on the side of the cart sweating. "Bloody hell Harry, you went looking for that three hours ago, we thought you had lost it for good, so me and Jaz, man handled this heavy bugger on to the cart." Harry shrugged.

"Hey man, it was in the loft, it's like totally crowded up there at the moment, it took a while, you know, you got to like check every corner you know?" Jaz gave a titter as he looked at the sweating Big John.

"Doesn't he mean every barrel?" John Smiled.

"Aye, it amazes me his ceiling has not fallen in by now with all the barrels he has up there."

Harry tried to look like he had no idea what they were talking about. "Hey a man has to protect his inheritance you know." Jaz laughed.

"Who from, Joe?" Big John gave a loud laugh.

"Aye, I bet Joe has bequeathed gallons." Harry looked nervous and looked around.

"Hey man chill, don't let Jess hear you, she is seizing everything for rations, have you seen what she thinks we should have?" He stood up straight and shook his head. "It ain't cosmic what she thinks a man should drink, my grass cutter gets more juice in a week than she allows."

John Lox gave a titter and patted Harry on the shoulder. "It's Ok Harry your secret is safe with us... Well as long as you cut us in it is." Harry scowled.

"Man, I never thought family would take advantage of me, wow you dudes ain't too cosmic at the moment."

John shook his head and walked back into the barn; Big John rubbed his belly as he looked at Harry laughing. "I reckon this is thirsty work, I will have a good thirst by evening, what you say Harry are you up for some company later?" Jaz gave a loud laugh at Harry's disgruntled looking face.

"You are less cosmic than them two John dude... But hey man, I reckon I could like squeeze a glass out, as long as Jess ain't about." He looked nervously round the farm, and saw her walking down the greenhouse path. "Bugger it's split time man, I'm off."

Harry turned and scuttled quickly up behind the barn, and back to the cottage to ensure the doors were locked and he was well out of sight, and John and Jaz started to giggle.

South on the coast, where the long causeway of rock had grown out of the sea to create a harbour, the Northwinds bobbed in the water tied to a large steel bar embedded in the rock, as other boats came in beside it to dock and tie up. Just out to sea, Captain Val Andre on board the Avenger trained his cannon onto the beach. High above him on the mast, the black pirate flag flapped in the brisk breeze. Toby walked along the long dock towards Silas, he gave a broad smile as he greeted him. "It is good to see you are well prepared Commander."

Silas took his hand and shook it. "With the extra hands you brought us, the operation has grown and is far more organised, Markus has a knack for organising, and every helper we have had has been put to work at their best." Toby looked back at the large fleet anchored or docked at sea.

"It is good to see things flowing, every moment we are here we are at risk, I have three boats with more helpers for you, the slicker we get this end, the safer it will be for all of us." Silas gave a nod and slipped a packet out of his jacket.

"Here we found a stash of tobacco, I know how you like your pipe, this is far better than that muck you smoke." Toby smiled and took the packet slipping it into his own pocket.

"What are we carrying today?" Silas looked at the long line of men carrying boxes towards the docked boats. "We coloured coded everything, found a stash of paint so we thought we would make your life easier with it. The red spotted boxes go to Phillip; there is food medicine and some weapons. You guys at the Cove get the blue boxes; there is a good mix of stuff we think will help the community including food and boots. The greens get split between Loxley and Carlisle. Handle those with care, we found more explosives and detonators. That pile on its own over there is rifles and bullets, I figured they would be best served on your boats, at least if spotted or attacked you can fight back, there are not so many, but if you divide them up a couple for each boat, Markus figured it would be better than being defenceless." Toby looked at the large box filled with the weapons.

"That is good of you, and yes we could use a little more protection, especially on some of the inland waterways we run up, a couple of boats got ambushed last week." Silas shrugged.

"Wish we had more, but until each container is opened, we have no idea what we have here."

"What about your safety?" Silas gave a chuckle.

"Well we have kept some of the more pristine stuff back for ourselves; don't worry about us we have plenty to stand our ground here with." Toby patted his shoulder.

"It's good to know, you and Markus have done a wonderful thing here, you have no idea of the lives you have saved with your supplies, we get gratitude wherever we dock." Silas smiled.

"As much as I would love to claim the credit, it was the Master Sage who brought us here, it was his plan, I just took over when he moved on to bigger things."

"You built it up to this, and the credit is due to both you and Markus, it's a good thing you are doing."

Silas watched, as the first loaded boats pulled out from the dock to allow some of the others in to take the goods, from the long line of men waiting to hand their cargo over. "I hope Loxley knows what he is doing and takes care of Mason once and for all, although how the hell he will do that with a wall round the place, none of us know." Toby gave a nod.

"You heard then?" Silas smiled.

"Yesterday's boats brought lots of news, it's amazing how much we hear in such a desolate spot as this, I even got a copy of that Tribune paper printed near Loxley, word travels fast these days."

Behind him the horn of the Northwinds sounded, Toby turned to the loaded boat. "That's me full." He took Silas by the hand and patted his wrist as he shook it. "Keep safe, I will be back in three days around mid morn." Silas smiled and patted his shoulder.

"Stay safe out there, and see you soon."

Silas watched Toby walk back down the long dock towards his vessel, other boats were untying and moving off the dock as the steady stream of boxes continued down the dock, and new boats lined up to be loaded. Just out to sea, the Avenger watched as the group of boats it guarded, slowly made their way into the group around it, to wait until the other boats were loaded and ready to sail as one fleet. Silas pulled on his collar to keep the wind off his neck, and gave a chuckle. "Bloody Pirates, how the hell did I end up running their operation?"

CHAPTER SIXTEEN

OLD NEWS

August 15th 2016.

It has been the most remarkable of days, and I find myself with a very confused sense of mind.

I took a trip to the Mere today, just to check on things, it's been some time since my last visit. The grass is very long and needs some attention, I think a few weeks of sheep will bring it down and more under control. Whilst I was on the track heading for the meadow, I wandered almost as if reliving my memory of childhood, towards the ancient oak in the heart of the woodland.

There's been so many times in my life when I thought of that day in my ninth summer, when I met that strange girl in white, and today as I walked between the beech and hawthorn toward the centre, I must admit my mind wandered again back to those days. I have always found it curious that she told me that the old oak was the first tree ever planted here, and was planted by her father, and looking up old records of this land in my great grandfather's time, it is true that it is recorded as being a lonesome oak of great standing. I was fascinated to find that it is exactly in the centre of the land we own as a family, so it really is the centre of the Lox Farm Estate, I am still unclear how such a young woman would know such a thing forty three years ago, when it took me twenty years to find out.

In the clearing just outside the trees, next to the large beech, I saw her again; I must admit I thought for a second, she was my imagination playing tricks on me at first. I could not believe my eyes to find her sat with her eyes closed, and yet she greeted me and called me by name. I am struggling to understand things I must confess, as she has not aged a day since that day when I was but nine. It was a surprise I was not prepared for, and even though I have remembered the tales she told me back then, even to the point where I wrote them down in this journal all those years ago, I think a part of me simply considered them to be fairy tales, but looking at her compared to my aged face and silver hairs, I cannot deny I am prone to believe that this woman has some form of magic, and is telling me the truth.

I sat in the meadow with her for over two hours and spoke with her, she has great wisdom, and yet I cannot believe she is above 22 years of age she looks so young; it is without doubt the most curious thing. I would say it was her granddaughter, if it was not for her very specific memories of that day in my ninth summer. I would not mind, but that was not the strangest part, she talked of a woman named the Countess Le Fey, who she told me was actually a witch or sorceress of dark power, and that one day she would covert this land for her own, and that the road we were thinking of building to make the farm more accessible should not be built, and the greatest protection we would have, would be the fact that this farm is not the easiest of places to find.

She instructed me to build a wall and enclose the farm, not a fence, she was very specific, and told me the resin of the pine and fir contained elements that can resist great dark power, she was quite insistent about it, and I felt the seriousness of her concerns for this land, as she told me many would seek refuge here and it must be encouraged. It felt a little chilling to hear her words, and I cannot say it did not bother me somewhat.

Shortly before we separated and I returned home, she told me a man by the name of Rimmer would reach out to me for aid, and I was to offer this man and his family my protection. She also told me to be wary of a man called Mason, for he was in league with the countess and not to be trusted. I must confess as I sit here this eve in thought and write my thinking down here, I have found it all quite peculiar, but such was the urgency of her words I must say she appears quite credible and believable, because she spoke of things no man but myself would know.

Recently I have contemplated the land of the mere, as I have considered leaving it in the care of my grandchildren. My three lads will have the farm one day, but that place is special to me, as special as all my family is, and she knew. I have no idea how, but she told me to name it Robbie's Mere because one day I shall have a grandson named Robbie, and it will be where he builds his home. It felt so weird; I honestly thought she was reading my own thoughts. She told me one day a boy of high value would come here and offer to our Robbie a lion of silver, for it will mark Robbie for great things, as his destiny is written and he must be based in the centre of everything close to the Oak Tree planted by her grandfather. She was quite passionate in the way she told me, and I must confess looking into her clear bright blue eyes, I could do nothing but assure her it would be his land if he was born, with or without a lion.

I am a little lost in my thoughts tonight, because the strangeness of the day is *overwhelming. The strangest thing in all of this is just like last time, I completely forgot to ask her what her name was, can you imagine that, all that time talking and I never asked, she knew who I was and called me by name so I never got around to asking, it is most peculiar.*

Robbie closed the book and looked at Rune. "So...What do you think?" She smiled a sweet smile.

"You know Gran, she does get around, and to be honest Robbie without reading this book you always knew Jake had more than just an instinct, how many times have you said it was Le Fey who was the biggest danger, well it does look like you are right." He slid his feet off the desk and sat up in his chair.

"It probably sounds daft, but you don't think your gran sort of manipulated him to make sure you would end up here?" He shook his head. "That's sounds bad, it's not what I meant."

Rune leant over the table and took his hand in hers. "Robbie, do you know how long I sat at my window and waited for you to call, honestly there were days when I gave up hope of you ever asking me out, are you telling me that my gran manipulated you as well, to get you to ask me out?" He gave a smile.

"Well, no of course not, I was nervous.... It was your fault you know, you always looked so pretty with your big blue eyes and all that long red hair. I was terrified you would not see me as good enough." Rune giggled at him.

"Seriously Robbie, I thought you were a brave Woodsman?" He looked stern.

"I am... well you know fighting and stuff is pretty easy, I mean it's not like, you know actually asking a you out, hell I am glad you said yes, but honestly fighting Cutters is a lot easier." Rune gave another giggle, and her eyes sparkled with happiness, she squeezed his hands.

"You are funny at times, and trust me I was just as scared, I cannot tell you how my heart pounded every time you went near that retched cheese shop. If you had walked out with Melissa, I swear I would have cursed her into old age within a year." Robbie gave a laugh.

"Really, would turn her old and grey just to put me off, how did you know I was not into older women?" He laughed out loud and she smiled.

"Well you never went near Agatha." He shuddered and she laughed at him. "Scary thought eh Robbie?"

"Yikes! Trust me if that was my only option, I would still be in Lincoln fighting Cutters." She gave a deep laugh and slid off her chair on to his knee, and curled around him.

"Glad you finally found your courage." He kissed her forehead.

"Yeah, me too." She snuggled into him, and he gave a sigh.

"I wish we could take the day off, but it is almost time, the others will be arriving soon, we better get ready." She snuggled up into his neck.

"Just a few more minutes." He relaxed for a second and felt the warmth of her body flowing into him, and the smell of Honeysuckle in her hair, it had been so busy, and just for a moment, like Rune, he wanted to take a moment just for them. He wrapped his arms round her and held her tight, as his eyes focused on the journal on the table.

His grandfather had documented everything, and things in his mind were so much clearer, Jake had been more aware than even he had realised, and for the first time in a long time he understood that Opal had seen all of this coming and had done what she could to try and create a secure place for everyone. But why him? Why did all of this come down to him, his grandfather would have handled this so much better than he had. His mind drifted, and his thoughts slipped out through his lips as he stared at the book. "Why us two?" Rune stirred and moved, and her face appeared in front of his.

"How do you mean, why us?" He looked at her bright sapphire blue eyes and pale soft skin painted with the faintest of freckles.

"Why us... You know, why did we get chosen, my dad or my granddad would have handled this so much better, come to think of it your gran has done a pretty good job on her own. I was just thinking, why us, why do we have to be the ones to deal with all of this, I mean your gran talked to my granddad when he was nine, why not then?" She sat up straight.

"It's our destiny, it was written on the stone that it would be my task, I suppose destiny brought me to you because it felt you are the man to match me, and together we could end this, to be honest Rob I have been so busy doing it, I have not really had the time to think about why."

He thought about it for a second. "I think it is odd that at some point at the start of time you and I got labelled the ones to do it, I have no idea what tomorrow will bring, and yet looking at my granddads journal, your grandmother was working things out and seeing the future years ago. I got to tell you Rune, walking through walls is pretty strange, but hell seeing all this decades before it happened is a bit creepy." She chuckled.

"Not for my lot, it's a bit of a family trait. I don't think you should dwell on it too much; I mean it's here and it's happening and whether we want it or not, we are the ones stuck in the middle of it all." He gave a sigh, and she slipped off his knee, and stood up to straighten her pants.

"I suppose so, I suppose we better get on with it then, come on we have yet another meeting, everyone will be arriving soon."

Rune took his hand and headed for the stairs down from the loft to the middle landing, as they passed the children's room he asked. "Is that what it is like for Saff, you know seeing everything years before it happens?" She squeezed his hand.

"Not yet, but as she matures and her sight increases, then yes it will be her job to see things and try and plan for what is to come." They reached the top landing and the top step.

"Poor girl, it cannot be easy for her, watch over her for me Rune." She smiled.

"Have no fear I do."

"Good."

They walked down the stairs and there was already noise coming from the kitchen to announce that Jade and Jett had already arrived.

Sapphire was getting ready at her home in Callanish in her bedroom, when behind her in the kitchen there was a blinding flash of lightening and the roaring sound of thunder crashing, Sapphire gave a jumped and gasped. "What the hell...?" She spun round gripping her sword to see a smiling Gwendolyn. "Gwendolyn what the hell you scared the life out of me." She chuckled.

"There is no pleasing some people; you said you wanted a warning to let you know I was here, so I made it clear." She chuckled as Sapphire gave a sigh.

"Why do I feel that your sudden rebirth has given you the new delights of life, and I am your chosen experiment of mirth?" She gave a cheeky smile.

"I must admit it is rather fun, and let's be honest." She looked round the room. "In a creepy old cottage like this alone, well you are an easy target." Sapphire shook her head.

"I take it you have news, which is good because I am off to meet Rune shortly." She stepped out of the way to let Sapphire head out of her room.

"I do, as I said some news is easier for me to obtain." She slid a chair out from the table and sat down. "We were right, Tideguyde was infected with the Merle, and it was this Branna who managed to connect to it and bring it down into Avalon. It appears Ariel was just a pawn, because she was in love with Branna, and I do think Rhiannon was trying to use Ariel to get her own back at my grandmother."

Sapphire leaned on the door frame. "Am I in great danger?" Gwendolyn smiled.

"Not yet Sapphire, but again I will warn you about who hears this news, I think Runestone is safe enough, but warn her she must be very careful in how she deals with this. I have been thinking a lot about this, oh you have no idea how much this bothers me, because in an odd way it does sort of explain why she reacted so badly when my grandmother accused her of treating certain members of her people differently." Sapphire frowned.

"Sorry I don't quite follow?" Gwendolyn took a deep breath.

"Sapphire if my grandmother was right, and to be honest I think she was, that could mean that Rhiannon was aware that certain members of the Fae Ofmoon were infected, which could be why she segregated her people. Think about it, what if all those with golden hair are free of the Merle?" Sapphire suddenly understood.

"Those of dark hair could possibly be infected, wow that is pretty serious." Gwendolyn nodded.

"It's a little more than serious, because that could mean that rather than deal with it, she enslaved those most likely to have it, and that is a very dangerous thought, one I would suggest for now you keep secret." Sapphire gave a nod.

"I am not in a hurry to piss off a Fae queen, trust me."

"Yes, me neither and I am already dead. Anyhow on to other things, as long as we are quiet for now we are safe so let's focus on the task for Runestone. You can tell her it is pretty much a certainty that Ariel lives, I cannot tell you how I know, just trust me on this one." Sapphire nodded; Gwendolyn smiled. "I have it on the very best authority that when Ariel disappeared, she was on the slopes of the high ground in a place called Sachsen. It was there she just disappeared and has not been seen since, my source says it was like she was surrounded by a circle of darkness, and then she was gone..."

"If that is true, how do we know she is definitely alive? It's funny you know, I have heard that phrase before, Rune used it. So how can she appear gone if she is alive?"

"I would say crystal."

"Crystal... You mean like a container?" Gwendolyn gave a nod.

"We know the Raven can use them, I spent quite a bit of time encased in one with my children, and we know it is the Raven favourite choice of holding magical guests, so we must assume that Ariel is encased in some form of crystal container." It made sense to Sapphire and she knew that Rune had used them, and so she would understand better how they worked.

"I am not sure if it is the same place but Morgan was born in Saxony, in Germany, I have no idea what the place is like, I kind of always thought it would be a gloomy depressing place considering she came from there."

"Hmmm, yet it makes sense, names have changed a great deal over my life time and certainly the way words are spoken, and it does sound similar, so I would hazard a guess that they are the same place." Gwendolyn stood up. "Ok I will keep looking into things to see what I can find." She crossed the room and turned at the door.

"Have you been to Ariel's house?"

Sapphire shrugged. "I did not know she still had one." Gwendolyn gave a nod.

"She had one in Avalon which they say was sealed after she left and has never been opened since, and she also had one in Florae, which has been locked up by Bade since she left, poor fellow he was rather sweet on her, and I am sure she never noticed."

"Do you think looking at them will help?"

"Sapphire she was scribe, all scribes ever do is write even when they finish for the day, trust me I grew up around them, they journal everything, and if her places have been sealed, they may contain her personal writings. I would say check them out, anything that helps us find them is worth looking at, although remember, choose your words carefully in Avalon." Sapphire agreed.

"Okay I will look into them and see if I can get anything more on her." Gwendolyn smiled.

"We must find her Sapphire, she was one of my best friends as a girl, and she was also as kind as her mother, if she is trapped, we must free her."

"We will, I promise." Gwendolyn gave a smile.

"Our next queen is very lucky to have you as a teacher, I was right in my choice of you, you have done our race proud already, and she will learn much from you." There was a pop, and right in front of Sapphire, Gwendolyn shrunk in a flash and was gone leaving her alone in her house again. Sapphire looked round at the old building.

"It's not that creepy, although maybe some paint would cheer it up... hell if I live through this, I am gonna paint this place a hell of a lot brighter." Her window opened in front of her in a flash of bright blue and she stepped through into Loxley.

CHAPTER SEVENTEEN

THE FINAL GATHERING

The kitchen was filled with bowls of food and stacks of plates, in order for everyone to grab what they wanted, two kegs of ale were tapped and flagons provided, and the group slowly assembled in a host of small conversations. Outside in the Mere it was still raining, but the humidity of August hung in every room, and Rune instructed that all the doors and windows were kept wide open to catch what little breeze there was.

The Specialists arrived in small groups, closely followed by most of the Lox family, and last to arrive was Louisa, who had convinced Ox it was time he made an appearance inside the house, she assured Rune he had actually taken a bath and sorted out some new clean clothes. He did look sort of odd with his hair and beard combed and fresh lines pressed in his clothes. Rune felt very honoured, and did everything she could to make him feel at home, although he chose to stand in the doorway, half out and half in, which Louisa considered great progress.

Hornet and Gaynor were absent, which was understandable, as they had not left Wills side since he had left the cathedral. The last to arrive was Fuse, who carried a large bundle of papers, some which included the sketches done by Steph, with Mel's help. New to the meeting in the house was Rayne and Gwynne, which made Sapphire more than a little nervous, as she had fully informed Rune of her conversation with Gwendolyn. Rune had three extra chairs placed across the stairs in front of the whole room, where Robbie and Fuse were to be seated beside her, everyone else found places sitting on the furniture, or on pillows on the floor, on spare kitchen chairs, or simply stood around the outer edges of the room. As Rune sat in her seat, the house had never felt as full as it did that evening.

Robbie stood up and clapped his hands loudly, the noise suddenly lowered, as conversations ended sharply and everyone turned their attention towards him, he sat down and looked round the room. "I am glad to see you all looking a little better rested, we face uncertain times, so be aware before we begin, tonight is not about planning the next few days, it is about understanding our position." Heads around the room began to nod softly. "The people who have sought safety here, and even the Woodland Soldiers, look to all of us for guidance, and so tonight we will let our opinions be known, and see if we can find a better way to lift morale, because at some point it will be needed more than ever before."

A low hum filled the room as everyone understood and agreed with him. Robbie looked to Fuse, who was arranging his papers on the floor in some sort of order.

"Fuse would you like to start?" He gave a sharp nod and lifted a group of papers off the floor, and then shuffling them around in his hand, he cleared his throat.

"Good evening all. I want to start by simply saying, I am only going to deal with facts tonight, there is far too much wild speculation going around the place, and so I feel it is important that we only look at what we know."

"We are surrounded by a bloody great wall, wow that was a short meeting." Jett smirked.

Fuse looked at her. "That Lady Jett Amber is why I am here, because that is the negative thinking going all around this place, and the reason I am going to set the record straight with facts." She gave a nod.

"Sorry Fuse." He gave a small smile.

"I understand how all of you must feel, including you Lady Jett, so all I ask is hear me out." She gave a nod but kept silent.

"We have found ourselves in a situation we predicted, this is by no means a surprise, so it may bring you some comfort to know we have been planning for this for some time now. It is clear from our observations that no one is getting in or out, and so we have imposed rationing and Woodsman Law for the time being, or until such time as the conflict is over. This is not a panic measure, but a well planned and well executed coordinated effort from all the staff based within this community. Posters will be going up around the place, and if some of you are available tomorrow, we could gladly use the extra help." A few gave hand signals to show they would play their part, and Rune gave smiles of gratitude to each of them. Fuse continued.

"Right the wall. Most of you will not be aware but we have eyes everywhere, some behind the wall, but also some on the other side of the wall, for which I would like to thank Harry and Katie, because it was their efforts some time ago that managed to repair and service some very old radio communicators. They are not the best, but they have worked reasonably well so far. We have also had eyes in the air, thanks to Lady Melanie, and as a result we have drawn up some very detailed plans of Mason's wall."

It was clear that quite a few of them were surprised by what they heard, Fuse continued.

"The wall which you are all aware of is fifty feet and six inches in height, and the walls are actually two feet thick. The inside is hollow and we assume providing barracks and stores for the soldiers of Mason. The top of the walk way is fifty two feet across, so there is plenty of room for troops if we try a head on attack to scale the walls, which for the moment we have ruled out. As has been pointed out, the wall completely surrounds Loxley Farm Estate, and is actually rectangular; it is further from the back stockade wall, than from the front gates. This we have put down to the fact that we expect Mason does not want a big fight in woodland, which would indeed give us a bigger advantage." He lifted some more papers from the floor.

"One flaw we spotted instantly is that he did not take the contours of the land into consideration before he built the wall, which we have speculated is a creation of his mother. The weakest point in his wall is on the escarpment side, because it is vastly lower, and so has provided us with the opportunity to look down on his comings and goings. We have stationed the Night Strikers there to help rest them up and also to provide detailed information, and we will evaluate that situation to see if we can exploit any weakness's they may have there." Smokes looked round to Harry.

"It's been a while since I was over there; I take it that it is too high for bikes?" Harry nodded.

"Most definitely, man that drop would need like birdie stuff, and that ain't cosmic dude."

Crystal stepped forward. "I might be able to provide a means of sliding down to the wall if it would help." Robbie smiled, as did Fuse.

"Thank you, Lady Crystal, I am sure that we would have good use of your gifts as we have in the past, and we will factor that into any plans we may make. As many of you have seen we have built a new wall outside the gates on the edge of the embankment, which has been lined with steel plate. That is not only a protection for the gates, but has also served to allow us to move several catapults out of the Stockade to the escarpment, we have in mind dropping them some calling cards." Bear and Big John looked at each other and grinned, and a few appeared to fully approve of any tactic that helped unnerve the enemy.

"Last but not least, the most unusual aspect of this wall is that for now it only has one gate, which is directly opposite our own main gates. We must understand that this wall is a creation of the Dark One, and so we cannot rule other gates opening when the battle commences, and so for that reason all the walls have been manned with full forces, as has the surrounding area. We have deployed troops from many areas all around Loxley's vast woodland estates, and we have at the moment ten thousand troops stationed outside Loxley's wooden walls, with far more stationed within the stockade, we also have reserved forces at Caerleon, Leeds and Carlisle, as well as a substantial force at Lincoln. We also have a large outdoor force stationed in the large vale at Dove Dale, which was arranged earlier this year by General Rowan of Loxley, where the additional training of twenty thousand men has been taking place. We are hoping to get word of enemy forces coming from the south midlands, and we may have a chance of waylaying them, which is currently under planning as to whether or not it is possible, and some of you may see some action in that play."

Fuse sat up straight and lifted a glass of water from the small table beside him, he took a drink and looked at the assembled group, he gave a sigh. "Look people, this is not ideal, but it has been thrust upon us by a man determined to enslave all of us. The way I see it we have little choice but to rise to the occasion and deny him his goal, but let us be honest here this night, none of us really expected to get this far against him, and yet here we are. Do not lose hope my friends, and stay alert, and maybe just maybe we could win this day." Robbie nodded his head.

"Thank you Fuse, that has helped us a great deal, and yes we may be out numbered, but those have been the odds on everything so far and we have scraped through." Rune stood up and looked to Fuse.

"We are so very grateful to you Fuse, you have worked tirelessly, and we all owe a great debt of gratitude. Alright everyone, I think whilst we all let that set in, we will freshen our drinks before the next bit." The hum of conversations began again as the assembled group slowly moved around talking and headed towards the kitchen. Rowan came up at the side of Robbie and Fuse.

"I think that went fine, if I am honest, I expected more questions from them." Robbie agreed.

"I have never seen them so attentive and quiet; it's not like them to be so reserved." Fuse smiled.

"They understand how serious a situation this is, and I am sure there will be many discussions and questions over the coming days." Rowan looked across the room at Bear, John, and Hawk talking.

"It is a lot to take in, and I think they know we are doing our best to protect everyone, never forget, these guys have friends and relatives here, we know when the moment comes every one of them will rise to the occasion and fight for all they are worth, I felt it at Lincoln, they fought harder than I have ever seen them before."

The group moved around for half an hour, Melanie and Una helped out in the kitchen, Tila filled Ox's glass with ale, to which she got a cheerful thanks, and she noticed the rest of the Outlaws were sat outside on the lawn, so she organised drinks and food with Crystal and Blades for all of them. Rune could see that even though they did not want to enter, they could hear all that was being said, and it also explained why Ox had stayed close to the doorway, he was ensuring it stayed open.

Once it appeared everyone had been taken care of, Rune called them all back to her attention, and they all made their way back to their places and waited for Rune to address them. She sat straight and gave the matter some thought before she spoke.

"Most of you were at the cathedral where Will was injured, and so most of you know the story, but for those of you absent let me fill you in. Inside we found what we mistook for a nun of the Christian Church, as it turned out her name was Ena, and she was of Fae origin, and she attempted to kill Will in order to stop Morgan le Fey, the Dark One from getting him. No one has ever heard of Ena before that night, and she is still very much a mystery to us, but one thing we did learn, is she knows far more about the family line of Morgan than any of us do." Treen gave a cough.

"I do not see what it matters where she eez from or who the relatives of this vile women eez, to kill her is all I am in the caring about, can you have the ways in which we do it?" A lot of the others looked around at Treen and gave nods of approval and agreement. Rune understood.

"Trust me Treen, no one wants her dead more than we do, but none of you understand the complicated magic she has used to live this long. Understanding her family and her true roots are the key to killing her, and for that reason it is very important we try to learn who this Ena is, and how she knows so much about the Dark One." Treen shrugged.

"I ave not been in the meeting of much that did not die with a blade in the insides of them." Sapphire who was a few feet from Treen and opposite Rayne turned.

"Her life has been extended by Fae magic; killing her is not as easy as it looks, if it was up to us, we would have done it already." Rayne stood up straight, and looked right Sapphire.

"You are part Fae of Earth, so you have no understanding of the true complexity of Fae magic, but are you aware of what you just implied Saff?" Gwynne looked very uncomfortable next to Rayne, Rune turned to him.

"Sapphire is only echoing information I have received from a well known and strong Fae source Rayne." He shook his head.

"Rune this is dangerous to talk about so openly, you are aware of the implications of this I know." She gave a nod as the others looked on not quite understanding what was happening.

"I understand Rayne, and I am not thrilled to say this, but I am the Lady of Life and Woodland, all life is my domain, and when I confronted Morgan in the cave of the Mirrored Lake, I should have killed her, but could not pull her life force from her, and you alone will understand that I know."

He looked startled, and she noticed how Gwynne gripped his hand and tried to pull it back as if to say just listen, but Rayne was physically shaken by the revelation. Rune was defiant and faced Rayne with her eyes bright blue, it was a look Robbie knew well, and he knew better than to interfere, it was Jade who broke the tension between them.

"What's going on guys?" Rayne looked to Jade then back to Rune, his discomfort was visible.

"Rune if what you say it true and provable, I beg you please talk to me alone first." She gave a nod.

"Come join me at my table."

Rayne gave a nod, let go of Gwynne's hand, and moved straight away to follow Rune, as she led him round the stairs to the door that led below, and the room of the Table of Runestone. As she walked ahead down the stairs Rayne appeared to soften a little.

"Rune I am not your enemy, I want to help, hell I have done all I can, but this news is grave for my people, do you understand that?" Rune turned at the bottom of the stairs.

"I have fought in frustration and watched people I love die, I am well aware of what my words imply, but I will say this to you as my family and my friend Rayne. I will leave no stone unturned to rid this world of Morgan le Fey, and I am more than aware of what the consequences will be. If the people I love live, then I will face whatever comes from my actions." He held up his hands.

"You caught me off guard, again I am not your enemy, but if what Sapphire said is really true, you know that spell can only be used by the Fae Ofmoon, and that is my concern on this earth, and I may add is the concern of a Queen of Fae at Avalon." Rune showed him a seat close to hers.

"Please Rayne sit." She moved to her seat and placed her palms on the table. "Morgan le Fey is a direct descendant we think of a Fae named Branna." As soon as she said the name she saw his face change. "You have heard that name before I see?" He nodded.

"I once argued for a girl I cared for called Luminaria, I still feel she was unjustly treated by my mother. She was set a task of bringing Branna's lover to court, and failed as the girl in question was a ward of Queen Bridget. I was very young at the time and not as aware of the facts as I am today, I often visited Luminaria in the prison complex at home." Rune understood and smiled.

"So, Fagan's sister told you who Ariel really was, and in doing so you understood the politics of your mother?" He gave a long sigh and shook his head.

"I have told her so many times this would haunt her in the end, I took the side of a Marshal above my mother and queen, and as a result was punished, and taken home away from my wife and children."

"Does Gwynne know?" He nodded his head.

"I thought so, I felt her emotions rise when Sapphire mentioned it. I am sorry Rayne, I really am, but if I have to take on your mother and defeat her first to get to the root of Morgan, I will do, I have no choice if I want to save the realms built by my Lord and Grandfather the Green Lord." He lifted his head and met her stare.

"I would do the same, I am not against you Rune, I just need a little time to try and smooth things out, Amethyst is my daughter, I cannot risk losing her again." Rune understood the difficult position he was in.

"What do you need me to do?" He rubbed his chin and took a long breath.

"I need to go to Avalon, and speak with her, you will have the protection of a Fae Queen in this, and she has grown very powerful." Rune felt sorry for him, but she felt the pureness of his heart.

"If it is any consolation Rayne, I can sense the Merle since I received the red stone, and I can assure you, Crystal, Amethyst, Gwynne, and yourself are not tainted by it."

"I already know." Rune was surprised.

"How do you know?" He looked at her and placed a hand on her table and it flashed bright yellow.

"Bridget Violet told me. I was the one who secretly sought an answer to the argument between my mother and Bridget." Rune was stunned.

"You actually spoke to her and she told you?" He nodded.

"Watch." Rune turned to her table where an image rose out of it and into the air above it.

Bridget Violet looked worn and sick, her violet eyes shone, but below them black rings lined her cheeks and her skin was pale. Rune looked at the young version of Rayne sat with her. Bridget turned to him.

"Both our people are infected, I have taken all of it from this line in Florae, and as far as I know none of my people are now at risk, I have found a way with Enaria's star to take it with me, but you must convince your mother that not everyone has this sickness. Rayne if she takes it from them all, she will not live, but all the Fae will be safe from it forever, you must be ready to take control until you have children of your own."

The picture faded and Rune sat back in the seat. "I take it she refused?"

"She did, she was so sure she could breed it out by working certain parts of our people to death. Many have accused her of favouring those of golden hair over others, and they are not wrong, but you must understand Runestone, she is a political animal and has great power, and has never been afraid to use it. You have no idea of the danger you have put yourself in, she favours you, but trust me, that favour will be removed very quickly if she even suspects you know any of this."

Rune thought about her situation for a moment before turning to Rayne. "If I ask, will you tell me your answer honestly?" He gave a nod.

"Yes."

"Do you think your mother is tainted by the Merle?" Rayne slumped back in his seat.

"There is no way to answer that question and win. If I say yes then I must remove her and replace her with Amethyst, if I say no and she even knows I have doubted her, she will kill me just for this conversation." Rune understood.

"Then do not answer, it is not your place to judge her, I will be the one to do that when the time comes. For now, go to your daughter and look at what options there are for finding out more of this Branna and her location, for I believe that Ariel is still alive, and this Ena is her daughter, and I must find at least one of them to reveal the whole truth and defeat Morgan le Fey." Rayne lifted his hand from the table, and stood up.

"Thanks Runestone for giving me this time, I swear to you I will help make this right and bring aid where I can."

"I am sorry Rayne, you have been good to my people and you defended my daughter in her hour of need at her weakest on the Violet Isle, I will never forget the debt I owe you for that, but I would ask one thing of you?" He turned and looked down at her.

"What can I do?"

"Protect Sapphire." He smiled.

"It will be my honour to ensure her continued health, and you owe me no debt Runestone, you have shown great wisdom, something I cannot say of my mother, any debt you feel you owed me, will be paid in the protection of Amethyst." She took a long deep breath.

"Go and be swift, time is not on our side, so go with speed and good luck."

Rayne came up from the stairs and walked across the room as everyone watched. Gwynne tried to move towards him, but Crystal took her arm and held her back. "Let him go mum, this is dad's task." Rayne lifted his cloak off the rack and walked past Ox through the open door, and within a few seconds a bright yellow flashed across the doorway.

As Rune returned, she met a white looking Sapphire. "I have filled them in on just the basics of Saxony and our hunt for Ariel and Ena. Is everything ok, he looked like the world around him has collapsed?" Rune gave a weak smile.

"He has a big responsibility to his people, it is his task to sort this out for us, fear not you are well protected Sapphire."

Rune looked across the room to Gwynne who looked as scared as Sapphire, her eyes were fixed on the door where Rayne had passed moments earlier. The rest of the group were in intense debate, as each of them shared their thoughts with each other and Robbie.

Stood beside Sapphire at the foot of the stairs to her home, all Rune could do was hope that Rayne could find an answer to the long riddle of the missing Fae member Branna and her whereabouts, and hope that between all of them, some answer would show her the path to bring all this to an end. She gave a long sigh and noticed Sapphire looking at her.

"What?" She gave a small smile.

"I could not handle the problems you have, honestly I have no idea how you do all this Rune... I am just really glad that you do."

CHAPTER EIGHTEEN

WISPS IN A JAR

At a time when the world of men was still young, and the tribes fought each other for land and resources, in the mountains of on the edge of Bohemia, under a veil cast by Branna of the Fae, a small caravan sat in a clearing surrounded by trees.

It had been over a week since Branna had conducted her ritual, and joined Berengar to herself and the Merle. She had risen the following day filled with great energy, and had hitched up the horses and travelled north to the high areas that led back to the trail to Sachsen territory.

The raven that had been inhabited by the first merle she had drawn down in Avalon, who referred to itself as Roack, had realised that Branna had used her Fae powers to slowly mix with the merle inside her, and as a result she had been able to manipulate and control most of her own will, and had fooled the Merle into thinking it was in control.

Roack was unhappy and had stayed high in a large tree away from the caravan unable to work out what was to happen next. It was clear Branna was in control and had a plan, and Roack was curious as it looked down on her washing out a large glass bottle and then cutting a wooden bung for the top of it. Roack whispered inside its mind. "What is she doing, what does she want from us, will she kill us, will she use us, can we fight her?"

Branna continued to work as Berengar, who had been drained of his strength during the ritual was still recovering, and resting inside the caravan.

When Branna was happy the bung fitted with an air tight seal, she lifted the jar and walked off into the trees heading in the direction of the river, Roack had to know what was happening, and decided to leave the safety of the tree and fly quietly behind her, muttering inside its head all the time asking question after question.

It took Branna an hour to find her spot, high up the path next to a tall waterfall, where there was a wide smooth, flat ledge. Placing the large jar down, she looked out on a clear view of the horizon. Roack swooped in silently behind her and landed higher up the rock face, and looked down on her. Branna stood still watching as the sun began to lower towards the horizon, and smiled.

"I know you are there Roack, I feel you like I never have before since the ritual. Whisper all you like to yourself, or the others, or whatever you are, the oneness of Merle, you cannot undo my powers and control me as your puppet as you thought you were. I control everything now, and it is time you understood that, you serve me, or else I shall release you back into the blackness of that empty place in which you exist, and you can seek another to try and control."

Roack's head bobbed; in her mind she felt the feelings of rage in the bird. "You cheated us; it was not what we agreed." Branna gave a chuckle.

"Sulk all you like, our agreement was not that you controlled me, we agreed to share the power and exist together, and I have not broken that pact we swore, indeed it is why we are here as the sun falls. I have a request of you." The bird flapped its wings.

"We does not do deals with those who wish to control us." Branna turned and looked up at the bird high up on the rock.

"Neither do I. Roack you communicate through thought, what would you say if I told you my people have a way of bonding with animals, a way which allows you a voice, and a way that would allow you the freedom to think for yourself? I can take your mass and divide it amongst many, and so more and more of you can live a free life and experience the human life style, only this ritual will also give the vehicle you use, be it bird, fox or human, a life ten times longer than any in this realm. The bird you live in will soon die and you will be cast out of that shell, let me make it live again and again to keep you here as you are now." Roack flew down to the rock floor and walked about in front of her feet.

"We can be many?"

"Yes, and you will live for far longer than everything else." The bird bobbed around on the floor.

"We would want that, we would have wanted that, but we are one, we cannot be split into many." Branna looked at the bird, her dark eyes glistening in the last of the sunlight.

"I know how I can take parts of you and make you live as one, I can bind your life to mine, and show others how to bind their lives to those we will take for our community. Roack you can be a single entity within all of the Merle."

Branna knelt down in front of the bird. "Roack you will be free and share my life, think of what that would be like, one Roack, just one, a darkened free spirit who chooses the life she lives." The bird stopped moving and stared at her with dark eyes.

"We would want that."

"Then tie your life to mine, and bind with me as Berengar has, and fulfil the pact we swore to each other in Avalon." The bird tapped its feet on the floor, and then turned and pecked the large glass jar. In her mind Branna felt the distrust of Roack.

"What is this thing for, and why do you want it here? We will not go in another like we did before."

Branna gave a smile and remembered that first night in Avalon when she managed to capture the black mist that entered the bird that became Roack.

"It is not for you; I want it for your friends."

"We has no friends, we are one." Branna nodded.

"At the moment yes, I want you to join with me, and then we shall draw down more of you and divide it into portions like you did the night you came to me. I will need to store them in this until we reach the place that your kind will inhabit, there will be souls a plenty for you to guide your friends into I promise."

The bird shook its wings, and then pecked at the jar again. "This will not hold us; we can pass through all in this realm." Branna agreed, she had seen with her own eyes how Roack had slipped through his glass container.

"That is why I need you; you must let the others know to remain inside this until I can take t you to the place where you will all be free to choose your vessels. Roack trust me, this is the only way your kind can live in this realm, I am trying to help you all. Join with me and let your kind be free and join with others, be Roack the raven, free of the rest to live as one."

"We agree with you Branna the Raven." Branna gave a smile.

"Good, the night is drawing near and I must prepare."

In a flash a brilliant yellow light, Rayne landed on the long bridge leading into the Crystal Castle below Avalon, surrounded by the calm cool Mirrored Waters. He landed without missing a beat to his stride, and walked up to the steps before the large open doors.

Amethyst was sat at her table watching the activities within the realm; James was sat on a long relaxer chair behind her reading a book. There was a tap at the door and it opened, and Altman stepped in.

"Sorry for the interruption my Queen, but your father has arrived on urgent business and wants an audience with you." Amethyst gave a broad smile.

"My dad is here?" James looked up from his book. Rayne walked in right past Altman, a serious look on his face, and as Amethyst rose to happily greet her father, Rayne walked right up to her and took her by the arm.

"I have no time to explain, I need to talk and now, but not here." Amethyst looked shocked and confused, and then there was a brilliant flash, and both of them were gone, leaving Altman and James alarmed and shocked.

"What the frig..." Altman looked as confused.

"My Lord?"

Across the vast Forest of Time, on the edge of the Shrouded Lake, just in front of the small cottage, the air was still and calm, there was a brilliant flash and Amethyst and Rayne appeared. Amethyst was not happy and tried to pull free of her father. "Dad what the hell is going on? I am the bloody queen here; you don't just pop in and kidnap me."

Rayne carried on walking, half dragging her onto the small wooden jetty, where a small boat bobbed on the water. "Just do as I ask, I cannot say anything until we are both safe."

"Dad you are hurting my arm!" They arrived at the boat and he twisted and let go of her arm, and clasped her face with both of his hands.

"Amethyst I love you; I would give my life to protect you, do you believe me?" She felt a little afraid.

"Dad you are scaring me, you know I love you, what is going on please I beg you tell me?" Rayne lowered his voice.

"Amy honey, just get in the boat, I will explain everything, but only once we are safe out of the views of eyes and ears of this realm, please I beg you trust me." Tears had welled in her eyes, and she gave a slight nod.

"Ok Dad, but please hurry because I have never seen you like this, and I am filling with fear." He pulled the boat close and held it firm so she could board.

"Good...Fear at this moment may save our lives." He lifted out a huge coil of rope from the boat and tied one end to the stern, and then the other to the small jetty, as Amethyst climbed into the boat and sat down at the bow, where Una had once sat.

"What is this place anyhow, I have never seen it before?" He shook the rope free of tangles and then climbed in at the stern and sat down. Leaning back, he gave the jetty a huge push, and the momentum set the boat in motion across the water, as he slowly fed the rope out.

"This is the Shrouded Lake, it's not a place to be adrift, but it is impossible for anything to be seen or heard in here, and at the moment we need complete secrecy."

As the small boat drifted out, held only by the long length of rope attached to the jetty, the mists rolled in, and the cottage and the jetty disappeared from view behind a veil of white.

After several weeks of long boring days and nights of travelling, Berengar had grown in strength and power. His body had been weak before the ritual, as he had not recovered fully from his wounds, but over the last weeks he felt more powerful and stronger than he had ever done before. With his rapidly gaining strength, and the knowledge that he was heading back towards his home, his mood had changed from quiet and sultry, to one of optimism, and a rapidly growing thirst for revenge.

Branna pressed on the brake and Roack flew down and landed on the roof of the caravan, she turned to Berengar. "Is this the pass?"

He gave a stern nod from under his black hooded cloak, and turned to look at the familiar sight of the track leading away from the high cliff towards his home settlement. "It is a little further on; the path will open wide and reveal the plains that my home is built within. We must be wary, for it will be well guarded, they will already be aware we are here."

Branna spurred the horse on, and the caravan gave a slight jerk, and rolled on the dry stone road. "Remember not to reveal yourself until I say so, as far as they are concerned, we are traders looking to trade goods for meat." He grunted.

"I trust you, but I am in need of the swing of a sword, the time for reckoning is upon them so do not fail me Branna, I have placed a belief in you, and if it is a bad judgement we will die this day."

"As you will soon see, my magic will not fail you, and before the sun falls, you will have an army to stand beside you, and a loyalty you have never known from fighting men to support you. Swing at only those who betrayed you, and leave the rest to me, for today your kinsmen will feel the cold fingers of the Raven inside their souls, and you will finally rule as you should have done."

In the settlement the word had spread of a mysterious wagon on the trail. By the time Branna and her cloaked companion rolled into view, all around the large circular settlement Varisci warriors had taken up their positions with longbows and swords. In the centre of the circle was the large long house that was now the house of Vulgan, the leader of the tribe and Berengar's father. Vulgan watched from the top of the five steps that led into the long house, as the cart slowly trundled towards the centre of the large settlement. Elric, the head warrior and defender of Vulgan walked out into the centre of the circle to meet them, Branna applied the wooden brake, and the caravan slowed to a halt, she smiled at the scarred and shaggy haired fighter in front of her.

"Greetings friend." Elric looked back to Vulgan, who gave a nod; he turned with a stern face to Branna.

"Who are you, and what is your business here?"

Branna stayed sat in her seat, her dark eyes glinting, her long black shaggy hair blowing gently in the soft mountain breeze. She eyed the man before her, and then cast a glance at all the heavily armed men that surrounded the outer buildings of the village, in her estimation there were at least four hundred men, heavily armed and waiting for an order to kill, and deep inside she felt calm, as she sensed the silence around her.

She smiled again. "I am Raven." She poked a finger towards Berengar. "This is my demon, and that up there is Roack. We are traders looking to trade with the Varisci, we were told you are devils in men's skins, but wealthy, and I have a fondness for wealthy devils, they make me richer." She gave a laugh, and Roack above her gave a screech. Elric looked unsure and glanced back to Vulgan, who gave him another nod, he turned back to Branna.

"What is in the cart?" She rose from her seat, and dropped down onto the dusty floor.

"I have goods to trade, herbal cures, and many items of fine things to attract the eyes of the ladies; I seek trade for food and supplies for my long journey back to the lands of Hispanica. Come I will show you."

Elric was nervous as he viewed the hooded and cloaked figure, she had called her demon. "Bring them and let me see."

Branna shrugged. "If you wish."

She calmly walked to the back of the caravan and looked around at the warriors all brandishing their weapons and looking fierce, at the windows she could see women and children, all trying their best to view the scene. At the back of the caravan, she calmly folded down the steps, stepped up onto them and undid the latch of the door. The door swung inward revealing the large glass jar with a wooden bung, and filled with hundreds of what looked like swirling shapes of black smoke.

She gave a heave, and pulled the large bottle towards her. It had a net bag of rope around its base, and slipping her fingers into it she lifted the bottle and lifted it out of the caravan.

Elric eyed the raven sat on the roof with suspicion; he could feel the hairs on his arms bristle as it stared into his eyes. Branna gave a grunt and carried the large bottle round from the back of the caravan, and placed it gently on the floor in front of Elric, who looked at it with a very confused look.

All around, the warriors moved from side to side curious as to what was in the bottle, Elric could not understand what it was he was looking at, and he lifted his head to the smiling Branna with a stern stare.

"What is this trickery?" Vulgan who could not really see what was happening limped onto the steps, and bumped down them to the floor. "What is it?"

Elric turned to face him. "She has a jar of smoke."

"Wisps!" Branna corrected him; she turned to look at Vulgan. "They are Wisps."

Vulgan limped a little closer. "What do they do, we have never heard of these things before, and what use are they to us?" Branna shrugged.

"I hear many rumours on the road, and if what I hear is true, that the devils in skirts kill their own kin, then all of you need Wisps, for they purify the soul, it is the reason I made such a hazardous journey, for the souls of the Varisci it seems need to be cleansed."

Elric scowled at the jar, the others in the settlement fidgeted as they watched, and Vulgan grew angry. "What is this madness? You have a nerve girl to walk into here with your half truths and lies about the honour of this tribe; I should kill you where you stand." Branna looked at Vulgan with a blank expression.

"You cannot do that, my demon will not allow it, he rose from the depths of the dark places he was sent to, in order to protect me, it was he who suggested I bring the Wisps to you, for he alone knows of the treachery that rots all of your souls."

Vulgan's temper rapidly rose. "TREACHERY!! WHAT IS THIS TREACHERY YOUR DEMON SPEAKS OF? SHOW ME THIS DEMON THAT CANNOT DIE, AND I WILL SHOW YOU A MAN IN A CLOAK THAT BLEEDS RED LIKE ALL MORTALS!"

Berengar stood up from his seat and cast off his cloak, he jumped down from the wagon and in one swift sweep of his sword, he stepped towards Elric as the silence was broken with gasps, and brought his gleaming blade out of its sheath and high into the air. He strode with great strides towards Elric who was far too shocked to react quick enough, and with a thunderous sweep of his blade, the head of Elric who had betrayed and stabbed him, flew into the air before the shocked tribe, and fell with a splat on the floor and rolled towards Vulgan.

Roack gave a mighty screech, and the wisps of dark smoke flowed out of the jar through the glass by the hundreds in the direction of every warrior accept Vulgan, who stood staring and lost for words at his son. Having never seen anything like this before, the warriors froze unable to understand the scene, as wisps of dark smoke flowed towards them and then expanded and stretched before each warrior, forming a perfect copy of each of them. The warriors stared with horror as the smoky forms floated towards them, and the stretched out their arms to embrace them.

As the smoky figures embraced the first of the men, and slipped within their skin, disappearing inside them, the men shuddered and began to scream with horror, and fell to the floor clasping at their heads and convulsing violently. Other men seeing what was happening, panicked and dropped their weapons, as they tried to get away from the icy cold wisps of smoke that had formed into the replicas of them, and floated towards them with their arms outstretched.

It was chaos as Berengar walked slowly towards his father. "YOU BETRAYED ME; I WAS LOYAL TO THIS TRIBE!"

Vulgan stood his ground, his wife ran out of the house at the sight of her son, and watched with horror as the tribe were slowly being absorbed and screaming for mercy by the Wisps. Vulgan did not blink.

"You were loyal to Grembald, you protected him as others suffered, I did what was right for our people." Berengar lifted his sword and pointed all around him.

"They are my people now, see what you brought on your own people because of your own greed, you never forgave me for being ambushed, you never forgave me because you got wounded saving me, when it was you who forced me to go out on that hunt for your meat. All this time you have punished me for your mistake, and it cost you the head of the tribe. It was you who took the road of dishonour, and arranged an assassin to slay me when my guard was down. Well today father, you will pay for your crimes, and I will take this tribe back down into the under realms of darkness with me to suffer for eternity.

Berengar walked up to his father, and plunged his sword into his heart, and pushed it through to the other side, and it appeared out of Vulgan's back with a gush of blood. Berengar looked into the eyes of his father as he held his sword fast. "I will meet you in hell when I am done."

With that he pulled back on the sword and it came slipping out, dragging with it bone and tissue. Vulgan collapsed with a horrified look set on his face, and hit the dusty floor dead.

Berengar stood upright in the centre of the settlement, and wailed out the Varisci war cry. Branna stood calmly and watched as the writhing men on the floor grew still, and then slowly rose back to their feet. She watched as Berengar turned to her.

"You are true to your word; I am yours forever and bound to you as your demon and protector." She smiled and walked slowly towards him.

"No, I am your queen and you are my king, for this is the centre of the empire we shall build together, look around you Berengar, look at the men who rise as my raven did, they are your men, your army, yours to rule for eternity at my side. Look my lover, these are your ravens, all of them, for they are your Ravens of Berengar."

CHAPTER NINETEEN

FAMILY MATTERS

The rope to the jetty was taught, the little boat was out in the water surround by a thick dense layer of mist. Rayne sat at the stern, leaning forward towards Amethyst, as she leaned into him and spoke quietly to her, whilst the boat gently rocked.

"Now do you understand why I could not talk in the halls of your realm?" She was lost for words, unable to comprehend what he was telling her.

"I really do not know what I should think or feel, Dad you are talking about Grandmother, she has been a massive aid to me here in this role, I have talked to her in ways I have never talked to you and mum." Rayne understood, he remembered when he had first found out and questioned her, and then Bridget, it had felt like a family member had been slain before him, such was the pain in his heart.

"I understand your feelings, I too felt the same when I found out, but the fact is Amy, she is in love with the power, and our people have suffered because of it. There have been so many acts of injustice to our people, why do you think those here have embraced you warmly with such love? Amy you are nothing like her, you have been fair and just, everyone says how loving a queen you are, hell half your staff have brown hair." Amethyst smirked.

"Yeah, Gran does not approve of that, she has told me often not to trust them and replace them."

"See it is there if you look hard enough." Amethyst shook her head.

"Why are you even telling me all this? She is Rhiannon, the most powerful Fae queen, and the wisest advisor to all, knowing the truth now is pointless it's too late Dad." He shook his head.

"Amy you are a queen, you are nowhere near as powerless as you think. The line of Le Fey is a direct result of my mother; do you not see that it is our place to undo this?" Amethyst shook her head.

"Is it though? Dad it changes nothing, will Eleanor rise from the dead, will Eve come back, can Enaria be saved? Nothing changes no matter what we do." He reached forward and took her hands in his.

"Knowing is not enough Amy, this has to stop, and I am the only person who can stop it, but I really need you to understand and support this, you are my daughter and I love you, I care not that you are a queen, honestly if you and James had slipped off into the trees and lived in the wild, I still would love you as I do, and I need you to understand that as your father I have to do this, with or without your support." Amethyst gave a long sigh.

"Dad how could you even think I would not? Of course I am going to support you, but you have to understand, this is not going to be easy for anyone. If the Fae are infected, we must cleanse them as Bridget did." He gave a nod and smiled.

"Yes, we must do, Amy we have to make the Fae pure again I am just not sure how."

"Bring them to Avalon, I will cleanse them." Rayne shook his head.

"No I cannot allow that, Amy this is her responsibility, and it is up to me to persuade her to admit her mistake, and make a mends. You are far too precious, and if you want my opinion, I think you rule with a fairer hand, and in that you must be the future for the survival of our people."

"She has the experience I lack, there is no queen in the Fae of Earth, it will be another seventeen years before Iona takes the throne." He could not accept that.

"Amy she learned the same way you have, through experience, and one day you too will be admired and respected as she is, but you would have earned it honestly, and not from exploiting our people. I care not what happens to me, but you must live and take the line of Fae forward."

"Dad she will die." He agreed.

"She may suffer the same fate as Bridget, I honestly do not know, I just know that she has lived a long life and had her own way for far too long, this is something she has to face, and she has to make amends and cleanse our people, and then free them back into the world as was meant for them."

His face was resolute and Amethyst could see that he had set his mind on this, and she would not change it. She moved forward and on to her knees, and pulled him close.

"I lost you to her once, I fear I will lose you again, and this time it will be forever, please I beg you, find a way to do this and live."

He pulled her close and enjoyed the feeling of holding her, for so many years he had yearned for moments like this, she meant everything to him, and in the back of his mind he knew this could well be his last ever moments with her. He felt her shake, and knew that she had started to cry, which made this so much tougher as she squeezed him even harder.

"I love you Dad." He felt the choke rise in his throat and fought with all his might to hold it back.

"I love you too, never forget that, no matter how tough it gets." He held her for what felt like an age before he found he could finally let her go. "I have to take you back; James will be worried about you."

Slowly he released his hold on her, and she slipped back, and wiped her eyes. He smiled and lifted her sad face to look at her. "Amethyst Diamond, my queen of the stars, go and rule in a way that will make me proud to be your father, and never forget, that no matter how hard things get, you have a mother and sister who love you as much as I do."

Her violet eyes sparkled with her tears. "Just live, no matter what, please live for us all and come back to me." He leaned forward and kissed her head softly.

Rayne pulled on the rope and coiled it in the bottom of the small boat, as it drifted back towards the tiny jetty. The mists thinned and it appeared as a dark outline that sharpened as they drew closer. Once on the jetty he took her hand and led her to the front of the cottage, there was a brilliant flash of yellow light and Amethyst felt her feet touch the steps of the crystal castle, set in the centre of the Mirrored Lake. She turned to say her final goodbye, but her father was not there. "No!"

Amethyst ran up the steps and into the corridor in the direction of her table, members of staff who had obviously been alarmed, tried to stop her to find out what had happened, but she ran past them. James came out of the library and saw her sprinting down the corridor towards him. "Amy where the he..!" She flew past him and shouted.

"NOT NOW!"

He spun on the spot as his eyes followed her, and he simply froze just watching her as she slid on the polished floor to brake for the room of her table, into which she disappeared. Altman came out of the room behind him.

"She is back and safe, see I told you her father would return her soon; he was this unpredictable as a boy as well." James was still looking at the door where Amethyst had disappeared, his voice was calm, yet noted his concern.

"Something is very wrong Altman." Altman looked down the corridor.

"Then I would say My Lord, we should be beside her." James agreed.

The two men walked down the long corridor, and in through the door of Amethyst's Table of the Moon, she was already stood over it as pictures flooded to the surface and muttering to herself.

"Where are you daddy?"

Robbie yawned as he sat at the table in his office, behind the main operations in the Village Hall. He had been up until quite late with the Specialists talking, as he tried to gauge their reaction and listen to their thoughts on how to fend off the army of Mason. He had been woken early by Rune with the children, she had taken to bringing them into their room early in the morning to have alone time with them, and her laughs and giggles had woken him. He found himself after a hurried breakfast sat in his chair with his legs up on the desk, enjoying the peace as he sipped coffee and gathered his thoughts.

It was quiet and peaceful and he was relaxed in the chair, drifting in his own thoughts, and trying to piece together all of the suggestions from the Specialists from the previous night. Just for a second his eyelids fluttered as he breathed out and relaxed more.

BANG! "WHAT!"

The door swung open and hit the wall, Robbie jumped, and his feet slipped off the table, making him jerk forward in his chair, sloshing coffee all over his legs and the floor. He blinked his eyes awake to be confronted with a somewhat enraged Alice leaning over the desk at him.

"JUST WHAT THE HELL DO YOU THINK YOU ARE DOING?" He shook himself, trying to come to his senses and sharpen his thoughts, whilst brushing the wet coffee off his pants, which was not going to work as it was liquid.

"What the hell Alice?" He turned to her. "Actually, what the hell are you going on about?"

Alice looked really angry, and Robbie thought she had more than a little bit of Beth in her, her face was quite red and he noted her fists were clenched. "What's this about... Seriously? You plan to strike at York with Jacques in command and send him off to his death, and you ask what is it about, what the hell were you thinking?"

Finally, his brain kicked into gear, as he remembered the conversations from the previous night. He pointed to the chair.

"Sit down Alice and just calm yourself, nothing is written in stone." She gave a deep gasp and then flopped down on the seat.

"You know how much he wants York back, Brett is half blind and almost crippled, the fact he is alive is a miracle, and with Sebastian dead, he is the only intact member of that family left, how could you allow him to risk his life alone without me at his side? Robbie York fell barely a month ago, and Mason has been filling it up with troops since, do you seriously think we have the slightest hope of winning it back?"

Robbie looked at his half empty cup and took a swig. "Alice we have decided nothing, yes Bear came to us last night with his plan for a diversion, he thinks Mason has stored a lot of weapons and explosives there. We did not discuss an attack, just a hit and run strike to cause chaos and a diversion if Mason tries a full frontal attack, none of this is planned or even approved yet, it was just one of several ideas put to Rowan and myself last night." She looked suspiciously at him.

"So you have not agreed any of this?" Robbie shook his head.

"No not yet, I hate to point out logic here Alice, but as yet we have no real idea of what we are facing, or from which direction it will come from, as I said, nothing is set in stone." She appeared to mellow.

"So you won't attack York?" Robbie sat back in his chair and saw her almost hopeful and pleading look, he gave a long sigh.

"Alice there is a very high chance we will be invaded; I want to make sure I have my best here. In regards to York, I know how much Bear wants to right the wrongs of Mason, in that respect we are very much alike, but I will not send a man to his death needlessly, especially one who is family."

She wiped her eye with her hand, as a single tear ran down her cheek. "I cannot lose him Robbie, I lost Billy, and I could not handle losing another person I love so much." He understood.

"Alice we have little time, make the most of it, and of this I will make you a promise, whatever happens, I will ensure you remain at his side throughout all of it." She tried her best to smile.

"Thank you, Robbie." She stood up, and wiped her eyes before walking to the door, he sat back and watched her leave, feeling yet more pressure sit on his shoulders, and gave a long sigh as he looked down into his empty cup.

"I was really enjoying that, it was the best I have had in ages."

In the days long since passed, the settlement of the Varisci had been shaken to its core by Branna and Berengar. That night they had lodged in the long house, whilst Roack sat on the roof of the house feeling amazed that Branna had been able to successfully separate the Merle, and blend them with humans to create a whole army of separate entities. It was a strange experience to realise each of these people had a part of themselves within them, it was even stranger that since the ritual where Branna had joined their lives together for eternity, Roack had felt individual, and had even started referring to what she always called us, as "Her."

As the sun rose, Branna left the house, and Roack flew down to her shoulder, as she walked through the trees to the edge of what was a high drop off. She looked across the wide gap and saw that the canyon or valley was almost a perfect round circle, with a huge column in the centre, which was topped in a flat wide circular plateaux.

She smiled as she looked on it. "Roack this is perfect, this is where we will build an empire."

The Raven took to the sky, and crossed the wide gap and landed on the smooth flat surface, and Branna could see how smooth the stone was, it was perfect. She watched as Roack walked round pecking at snails. "This will be our new home, this will be where we will grow and plan, and I will one day see my revenge for all of those who suffered. This is where the golden queen will fall, but first I will hide everything within a circle of darkness, and she will never know of the enemy growing right in front of her eyes and under her precious moon."

Roack lifted into the air and flew back to her shoulder. She landed softly and spoke in her new croaky voice, which she was still getting used to. "This place has no name, and is unseen to most but this tribe." Branna smiled.

"I will name it and one day people will quake when they hear it, for here will be the Castle of Berengar, and from here I will create an army of little ravens, who will grow and spread, and undo all of the work the Fae has done. They dream of a world of peace, I will bring chaos, pain and destruction to everything they touch and all of it from here unseen. Roack it is perfect, we will be happy here, Berengar has his army of slave soldiers, and I have the mind to create a world fit only for us, soon more of the Merle will flow to me, and from here out into the world."

She turned and walked towards the trees. "Come let us go and gather what we need, I have an empire to build for my future husband."

Turning points in history are rarely noticed, but as Branna walked back to the long house whilst she planned her new future, the fate of everything shifted. Out of sight and in her own small circle of her veil of the Merle, she would build her empire from the foundations of a crude castle decorated with roughly shaped ravens of dark rock. Her and Berengar would build up a huge army, which would slowly take over the whole of the country and lead to the invasion of many lands.

Branna and Berengar would be joined by his brothers Vladimir and Otto, who had been spared the death of living Merle, due mainly to the fact that they had been kept in chains for opposing their father, and going looking for the body of their brother. Branna would have seven children of which her third born would be a crude and disfigured vile female, who would eventually marry her Uncle Otto, who would grow into a sadistic and equally as vile brutal killer.

Maud's first son would be slaughtered in battle against the Celt army led by Uther, her second son Victor who in many ways was not unlike Berengar, would be a wiser and more accomplished warrior, who would invade the lands of Celts using his wit and skills as a warlord to overcome the population. Once established, he would build a castle that would become the focal point of many stories in Tintagel Cornwall, England.

Victor would, through cunning and brute force, win the hand of a Celt Queen, and from their union would rise another raven of even greater cunning, and her name would become far more recognised than that of Branna's, for she would walk the land known as the darkest of all women, feared and referred to as the Dark One.

The error of Rhiannon would go unknown for many years, but like all truths and the best plans of Branna, the day would come when the name of Morgana of Berengar, would reveal all the lies and injustice of the past.

CHAPTER TWENTY

THE WAY TO THE TRUTH

It had been a long morning, but several coffees later, and some quiet time alone in the office reading reports, had managed to bring Robbie from his drowsiness to his usual alert self. Rune dropped in around twelve with some baked pies that Beth had cooked. They sat together quietly talking about the reports, and Robbie filled her in a little more on the night previous with the Specialists. Rune slipped an old map out from under his pile of papers.

"What is this?" Robbie looked down from his latest drink.

"It's a map of the area behind his wall, it is a little out of date, but I wanted to try and get a better look at the land over there, it will help to understand where he may set up camps, and which would be the best route in for his troops." Rune looked at the pencil marks where Robbie had tried to work out Mason's plans.

"This is not accurate Robbie; things have changed since this map was made." She turned it over inspecting it. "When was this thing printed the 1950's?" He shrugged.

"Not sure but it is all we have, it's sort of odd, this place has maps of just about everywhere except here." Rune looked at him.

"Your dad knew this place like the back of his hand, he knew every short cut and market route off by heart, I suppose it makes sense, this is the one place he would never get lost." She gave a fond sort of smile as she remembered him.

"The thing is Rob, when Mum and Mel joined me the other day, we were not that far from some of these places you have marked, and they are a lot different now." She pointed at the map. "For starters there is a road here now, Mason has cleared it, so I would say that will be one way in for his men. When we were sat somewhere around here, I think." She drew a little cross on the map. "We could hear his machines working somewhere over here, so I think it is clear he is looking at that direction to bring men in."

Robbie leaned over the desk and took a closer look at where she was pointing. "That is in the direction of what was Ashbourne." He thought for a second. "That actually makes a lot of sense if he is bringing men from the Birmingham area, because he won't be able to use the old motorway like we did, as we still have patrols on it."

She saw how he studied each area of the map carefully. "You know Rob it would be better if you could get this updated and more accurate than it currently is." He gave a slight laugh.

"Well yes... All I need to do is find an old shop that is about forty years old, and not succumb to damp and I can just grab one." She smirked.

"I didn't mean buy one, Rob why don't we just go over the wall, and plot the new details you need on this map by actually looking at the actual area?" He looked up from the map.

"Can we do that?" She looked at him baffled.

"How do you think Mum and Mel got out there with me?" He smiled.

"Oh yeah I forgot, we are not trapped as you can make archways." He scratched the back of his head. "Sorry my mind is a little cloudy after last night, there was a lot to think about." She gave a giggle and shook her head.

"You are so funny at times, but seriously Rob, let's get a small group together, and then go and have a look at what he is doing on that side. We can land a ways out, and walk in this direction, and get the lay of the land over that way. Be honest it will put your mind at ease knowing you have the information you need."

"We will need a few, possibly in a few groups." She got up from her seat.

"I will round them up, get your kit and bring the map and some extra sheets of paper for notes." He gave a smile as she walked towards the door.

"Meet me outside when you are ready."

Rhiannon was in her garden of crystal, admiring her latest creation, a rose of rose quarts, when her aide announced "Lord Rayne, my Queen." She flicked her wrist in a motion of allowance, and the aide stepped back behind the gate. Moments later Rayne walked through and the gate closed behind him, giving the Moon Queen and her son privacy. He walked towards her as she examined the flower paying him little attention.

"You have been busy, bouncing from Loxley to the Mirrored Waters, and then surprisingly the Misty Lake, and now here, I wonder what mischief you are bringing to my door now?" Rayne smirked.

"Your spies have been busy Mother, yet it does not surprise me." She turned.

"Nothing you do surprises me at all, although a dead Fae queen wandering around our new seer, who just happens to be in Loxley at the same time as you, makes me interested. Tell me what plans are you cooking up to save the green realm this time?"

"The same ones that got me banished from Avalon, and held here against my will last time." Rhiannon stopped tending her flower and shot a cold look at him.

"I thought you understood last time. I was quite clear as I remember, that has been dealt with, and you are to stay well out of it." He looked at her with equal determination.

"The truth always comes out eventually Mother, and at this moment in time things are being revealed. I am here because Runestone has given me a chance to talk with you first, but she is on the trail of Ariel and Branna, and you know where that will lead to?" He could see her expression change and it was not good, her anger showed a little.

"What does Rune know; I hope you have kept your mouth shut? It is old news Rayne, and you should know better than to interfere and stir the pot." He stepped back as small flashes appeared around the rose coloured flower.

"Mother it's not old news, it is unresolved business, and I may add something I told you a long time ago you had to face and deal with." Her face angered.

"I told you then and I am saying it again, do not involve yourself in things you do not understand."

Rayne gave a long sigh as he watched her anger smouldering. "I am not a young inexperienced youth anymore; I am fully grown and matured, and I think I understand this better than you realise, but there again, I am not the one clinging to power for the sake of glory."

Rhiannon twisted and turned towards him, her hand came up and white light erupted from it like a bolt of lightning. "HOW DARE YOU!"

Rayne was blasted back thirty yards and went smashing through a crystal statue, which exploded in a million fragments, and he landed heavily with a thump on the white stone path behind it, and slid another four feet until he hit a low wall. "You dare to lecture me on my position, you ungrateful brat, I am the one who has held all the realms together single handed. I built Avalon; no one would be here if it was not from my efforts."

Rayne looked up as a small trickle of blood ran down the side of his face, and he laughed. "You built Avalon, don't you mean your infected dark haired slaves, I did not see you chipping stone in the early years, you were far too busy, fitting your new garments and planning a coronation to rival anything ever seen before."

She lifted her hand again. "If you were any other person I would..."

"WHAT MOTHER.....KILL ME, OR IMPRISON ME LIKE YOU DID LUMI TO SHUT HER UP?"

Rhiannon stepped forward aggressively, her hand was raised ready to strike, when there was a burst of bright blue light, and as Rhiannon unleashed her spell, firing a bolt of light at Rayne, the blue intensified and her spell bounced, with a deafening explosion, shattering crystal into a fine shimmering dust all around for forty feet.

As the dust started to settle in an array of rainbow coloured sparkles, Rhiannon saw a figure in front of her son crouching over him, its arm raised up behind them to defend against her spell. She was momentarily lost for words as the figure slowly stood up and turned to face her, Rhiannon was in complete shock, as her words fell out from her mouth.

"Amethyst?"

"This is enough, both of you will stop this now, he is your son, and you are a queen, think of your position and responsibilities." Amethyst gripped the collar of Rayne, and in another flash of blue, she was gone with him, Rhiannon stood lost for words as Fae guards flooded into the garden.

"Save the queen, protect the queen, defend the queen!" The guards covered every pathway in a panic looking for the cause of what they perceived was an attack of their queen. They gathered in a circle to try and hustle her out of the area, which just enraged Rhiannon more.

"ENOUGH!" Guards scattered in every direction as her powerful burst of energy sent them falling head over heels, she pushed her aide in the chest. "GET OUT OF MY WAY!" And stormed passed him heading out of the garden.

Altman did his best to mop the head wound of Rayne, as Amethyst paced angrily round the room. "What the hell were you thinking? After all the lessons you gave me for years on diplomacy, and you just barge in there like a Marsh Hound with a blood lust, seriously Dad are you insane, she is the Queen of Fae for Hearne's sake?"

He winced as Altman dabbed and tried to push his hand away as he watched Amethyst pace. "It has to be done Amy, trust me there was no other way." She stopped and stared at him with a fixed angry stare.

"How, by dying? If I had been just one second later, she would have killed you, I told you to be careful why did you not listen? You are no good to any of us dead." Rayne smiled.

"By the way Angel, that was one hell of a brilliant defence spell, I didn't know you could do it, actually I had no idea you could transport to the castle, how long have you been doing that?" She looked angry.

"Stop trying to charm me, I am as mad as a Houlen at you." She gave a little smirk and her voice softened. "That was my first time; Altman told me how to do it seconds before I did." Rayne looked very impressed.

"Wow that took me months to master, well done Altman, you served your queen well." Altman gave a proud smile.

"I will always do my best for her highness."

"Do you both mind, this is serious." Altman shied back and lifted the cloth back to Rayne's head, Rayne winced again.

"Ouch!" The room erupted with violet light, and Rune's archway appeared, and she walked through it.

"Sorry to arrive unannounced, I was about to leave on a fact finding trip, when my table felt the power waves and alerted me, is everyone alright?" Amethyst walked up to Rune and threw her arms around her.

"Oh Rune, I am in so much trouble, I used my powers against my grandmother." Rune smiled.

"I know, I saw it, and frankly Amy I was impressed." Rayne gave Rune a cheeky grin.

"She was good, wasn't she?" Amethyst groaned into Rune.

"Please tell him to stop." Rune gave a small giggle and pulled on Amethyst's arms to pull her out of the embrace, and looked at her straight in the eyes.

"You swore an oath to protect your people, well your dad is also your people, you did nothing wrong Amy."

"Oh Rune, I attacked my grandmother, I used magic against her." Rune shrugged.

"It was magic, but it was not an attack spell, it was defensive to protect one of your own, if I am right under Fae law you did nothing wrong." Altman straightened up.

"You are right My Lady, the use of defensive magic before the queen is an accepted practice, you did not attack and so therefore you were protecting her." Amethyst turned to look at Altman.

"Who from?" Altman shrugged.

"Well, I would say herself, you broke no rule from what I could see." Rune looked at Amethyst.

"See, you are fine, you acted like a true Queen of Fae should, and you protected everyone."

James appeared in the doorway with a healer to look at Rayne's injuries; he spotted Rune and gave a big smile. "Rune!" She turned and smiled.

"Hello James." He came over and embraced her.

"It is wonderful seeing you, how is everyone, we have heard what is happening, can we help?"

"We are fine at the moment, as you know we are planning and preparing for Mason to make his move. Robbie is out and about with Mum and Specialists having a look at what Mason is up to on the other side of the wall at the moment, you know Robbie, he likes to scout everything out to see what he has available. We are well prepared." He appeared like he wanted to say more, but he could see Amethyst waiting and decided it was better he stepped out.

"I realise you are busy, but come see me before you are done, I would love a quick chat." She smiled.

"I will." James stepped back giving Amethyst the time she needed, and he excused himself with Altman leaving the three alone with the healer who was busy applying a thick paste to the cuts on Rayne's head. Rune took Amethyst by the arm and walked her to the other side of the large room. She lowered the tone of her voice.

"I know this is frightening, but if I am honest, it is long overdue." Amethyst was surprised.

"Overdue...Rune I stepped in between her and my father and used magic to block her attack spell." Rune agreed.

"Yes, and in doing so you executed your authority as the Queen of Avalon, and protected one of its subjects. Amethyst this is your realm; you control everything here, and from each moment since you took over you have been becoming stronger. Listen I know Rhiannon, and even though you stood against her, she will admire you also for standing your ground. You showed her today you are quite prepared to act when necessary, in a strange way you have reassured her she made the right choice." Amethyst was unsure.

"She was very angry, I could see her face when she realised what I had done, which is why I came back here straight away, and did not hang around." Rune gave a slight chuckle.

"That was probably the most prudent action, but she has not retaliated, and I think that is a good thing, to be honest I was not sure, which is why I came straight here just in case, but it appears to me she has stood down to think about this. Amethyst never forget that she rules with a political motive, I think you will find that Rhiannon thinks long and hard before she acts, and even then, she will be cautious."

"I hope so; I do not want a war between us." Rune smiled.

"As I said it was bound to happen, I would say sit back and see what she does next, that will give you a far better idea of what you can do. For now, Rhiannon is aware that the truth of the infected Fae is coming out, she is no fool, she will think long and hard about it." Amethyst was unsure.

"Will she though? Think about it Rune, since the demise of Gwendolyn, she has been the only queen of Fae, she has been the one everyone went to for advice, and even Bade of the Earth Fae has consulted her on many occasions on how to maintain the royal household until the coming of Iona. That is the main reason Crystal was made an ambassador there, it opened a channel into the Fae of Earth for her. She has a lot of power Rune, and as my dad has said, she will not want to give that up without a fight." Rune looked her straight in the eyes.

"I am Life, she has no dominion over me, and I will not let her wriggle free of her responsibilities so easily." She gently took Amethysts hands in hers. "Trust me, I am aware of more than you think and I am watching, your responsibility is to the Fae in Avalon, and if she threatens them, it will be your place to prevent it, anything else she does, let me handle it." Amethyst gave a gentle nod.

"Ok Rune I will."

Rune stayed for several more hours just to ensure all would be fine, she talked more to Rayne and convinced him he had made his point, and should not return to the Realm of the Moon, to which he agreed and said he would return to Loxley with her. James joined them and was eager to come back to Loxley, but Rune told him it was better if for now he stayed close to Amethyst, as she needed his support more. He was disappointed but understood. Eventually the time came and Rune opened her window and returned to Loxley, Gwynne was nervously waiting and she snatched Rayne into her arms, Rune felt it best to head home and wait for Robbie's return. She returned to her table and watched the events with Rhiannon again, and then she started to go through everything she had discovered for the hundredth time, in hope she would spot something obvious that had been overlooked. The pressure felt like it was building, and deep down inside, she was nervous that she would not be able to help solve the riddle of Ena before Mason attacked.

The Sage sat quietly by the fire with Ben and Ester. They had a large pile of freshly peeled willow sticks, and were holding them over the flames, to bend out the kinks and set them as straight as possible for arrow making. Martin had gone with Dutch to talk to the community and hopefully convince them that they should leave this place, as it was unsafe and a known destination for more Cutters. Dutch was hoping they would follow the lead of the Sage and join him, but many had hidden during the fight to free them, and so with Martin's assistance, he hoped to convince them to join the fight for the freedom of everyone. They had been away for four hours, and so the Sage could do little but pass the time helping out the few who had already decided they were going to help him.

The minutes appeared to drag by, and he gave a sigh as he tossed the straightened stick onto the done pile and reached back for another. Ben looked at him. "They are taking their time." He gave a smile.

"It is a very important decision, we cannot rush them, it will take time Ben." Ester lifted another stick from the pile.

"It's not that big a decision; it took me all of three minutes to make my mind up. If we all stay here the Cutters will come back and let's be honest, when they find out what has happened, they will slaughter everyone. I am going with you, I will take my chance out there and fight if I have to, staying here is certain death, if my life is going to end, it will be with a sword or bow in my hand."

Ben gave an encouraging nod. "Me too." He looked up from the willow twig and stopped, then pointed. "Look it's Martin."

The Sage turned to look back at the old factory building, and saw Martin on his way over towards them. He dropped the willow stick and stood up; Martin walked over and gave a nod of a greeting. Ester looked at him with Ben, and he smiled. "You have about 80% of them, they realise the Cutters will be back, and they would rather stand with you and face them than face them alone."

The Sage gave a relieved smile. "That would be about four hundred, it's a good start, but we will need more." Martin agreed and lifted his hand and gripped his shoulder.

"There are a lot who know about London on the route, they have heard all the stories of you, Dutch will send men ahead to spread the word. Trust me the closer we get, the bigger we will be, this is a good start, we have more than enough to take on any raiding parties we meet, and by the time you reach his cities, they will have grown in number, trust me you have the start of your green army."

CHAPTER TWENTY ONE

THE WRONG AUTHORITY

Rune was sat at her table with pictures flowing across the surface, and hanging in the air above it, when Robbie arrived home and came down the steps. Rune leaned back and smiled. "Good trip?"

He smiled as he slid into a seat close to her. "Yeah, I am glad we did it, you were right the map was far too old, but the good news is I have a better idea of some of his plans now." Rune flicked a frozen picture on her table and it rose into the air.

"He has been busy with his earth movers; there were some nice old trees up there. That is a big site Rob with a lot of soldiers already, look how many tents they are setting up, he has bigger plans than we thought." Robbie looked at the pictures carefully.

"Yes he does, but he still has to get them through that door in his wall, down the valley side, over the river, and then back up this side to get at us. He knows half his men will die before they ever step on Loxley land, which is why he has taken his time to build up such a big force, this is not such an easy place to storm into." She watched as he studied the detail of the camp.

"What about direction, do you have a better idea now of which way they will come?" He was focused on still looking at the pictures Rune had on her table, she noticed how he studied every single detail, and his eyes did not leave them as he spoke.

"I did think Ashbourne, but it looks like his earth movers are building a bigger road across the moor to Bakewell. The last people to build a decent road on that moor were the Romans when they built the Ashbourne road. There is some pretty soft ground up there, it won't be easy." He sat back in his seat and gave a sigh.

"The good news is he looks to be avoiding Dove Dale, we have a lot of stores and troops in the valley there at the moment, so we may be able to set up a rear guard strike. He won't expect us to come at him from behind, it might help us sandwich him and force his hand, a few errors on his part could be what decides this." Rune brought another picture up.

"What are these for?" Robbie looked at the tall crude looking towers he had seen all along what would be the new road.

"I think he will use them as look outs and possibly beacons to light the way at night, I got a good look at one they have finished through my scope, it looks like they have some sort of steel pans up there, which I think are to contain fire, they are pretty big so they must be for beacons. Rafe thought it would be good to blow them up at the base and watch them topple fire onto his troops; I think he fancies having a try." Rune smiled.

"Well you know our wolf, he is all about making a statement, you should look at it." Rune looked at him and her eyes flashed with the small amount of violet light in them from using her table. "You do know Robbie roads means wheels." He gave a nod.

"Carts of weapons and carts of men."

"Cannons have wheels too." He looked down for a second, and then back up at her.

"I know...Be honest Rune we are too far in, he aims to blow this place into ashes, and as hard as it is, I am the one who has to find a way to stop him; honestly the pressure is just..." She got up out of her seat and leaned down and kissed him. He relaxed and felt the warmth of her radiate all around him; she pulled slightly apart; her forehead still pressed against his.

"We will do this Robbie, you don't have to say the words, just trust in Jake, Opal, and us, and you will make it through all of this." She lowered her face and kissed him again softly. "Trust in me also, I am trying as hard as you are...never forget we are together, and no one can face the force that is shared inside us, we will get through this." He lifted his hands to the side of her face and held it just a few inches from his, her bright blue eyes with hints of violet illuminated his dark brown eyes.

"Runestone kill that witch, find her secrets and do whatever you have to, and rid me of her and her vile creations, and I will take the fight to Mason, and he will meet his match in me." She smiled.

"I love you Robbie." He kissed her nose.

"I love you too Runestone Sapphire."

It was pitch black at the small cliff top cottage on Callanish, and even though it had rained that day, it was warm as the wind had dropped. Sapphire sat on her door step with a drink, listening to the sound of the waves crashing below. The light from her kitchen illuminated her path, the gate, and a few windswept hawthorns, but not much more. It was restful and quiet, and she loved to sit out, as she had with her mum many times when she was a young girl. Sat with her knees up, holding her steaming mug of tea to her mouth, she sipped it as her mind wandered through all she had done and heard.

Her mind was on Rhiannon and Amethyst, she had witnessed some of the day's events, and her stomach was unsettled, the last thing they needed at the moment was a war with the Queen of the Moon.

Her mind moved to Cal, she had not heard from him in two days, and she was starting to worry. He had told her he may be a while, but she missed him, and just needed to know he was alright. She knew that few could overcome him as he had the ability to just disappear, but regardless of it she was still worried, and just wished he would pop up and let her know he was fine.

"Where are you Cal? I wish you would hurry up; I am no longer sure we have time. I feel strange, something is coming I can sense it, and I would rather you were here when it does."

It was late, and she suddenly felt the chills run up and down her spine. Sapphire stood up and looked into the darkness as the feeling intensified. "What is this feeling, it's been around me all day?" She decided she would be better off indoors, and turned and walked back into her kitchen, closed the door and slid the heavy bolts across to ensure nothing would enter. As she turned towards the table her mind exploded with pictures and she swayed, almost losing her balance.

The pictures flooded into her mind, she saw the trees, the path, the large wooden house, and it was on fire. Sapphire staggered and found the edge of the table, where she stood and held herself upright, and closed her eyes, as the pictures repeated themselves. "Oh, shit Fagan!"

Her eyes snapped open. "I have to get Rune." Behind her the violet light exploded, and Rune stepped through into the kitchen.

"I am already here; come we have little time."

Fagan sat in his old rocking chair smoking his meerschaum pipe, when the hair on his neck bristled, he turned slightly and listened, his large ears straining. "Well blow me, I bet ye lot will not be wanting barley crackers and tea?"

He slowly stood up as the sound in the trees grew louder, and then walked calmly towards the open door and stood in the frame of it. It was dark in the trees, but he did not need eyes, his trees were already talking, and they did not like the feet of the men in steel hats.

Fagan waited patiently and saw the torches burning as the group trudged along the path towards his cabin. He gave a sniffle and sniffed the air. "Bad oil that burns with soot, not good for the trees is that stuff, no wonder they are talking, so not from Avalon, I cannot say it was not unexpected. So it's time for ye to finally join Lumi is it, ye thinks so old man, she was never going to let things go, she will hit out at ye one by one, tis for sure?"

The light from the torches grew brighter, and very shortly the first of the Royal Guards of Rhiannon arrived, and walked into the open pasture in front of Fagan's house. They trooped in orderly fashion all holding up their torches with one hand and their spears with the other. They came to a halt, and a high ranking official with golden braid across his shoulder stepped forward with a long rolled up parchment. Two of the guards stepped forward to his side and lowered their torches as he unrolled the parchment and then cleared his throat.

"Are you the man known as Fagan Sylvester Hammond, formerly the Maker of Avalonia?" Fagan smiled.

"Ye have that right." The officer peered over the parchment for a moment then dropped his eyes, as Fagan continued to lean on his door frame.

"The queen of the realm has decreed that the rights granted to you by her to maintain a position in the Forest of Time, are to be revoked. Your property is to be confiscated and your dwelling removed, and you are to accompany us back to the realm where you will be charged with the offence of high treason to the queen. What says you on this matter?"

Fagan gave a sniffle, and scratched his snow white scruffy tufted hair. "Which queen?"

The officer looked over his parchment. "Pardon, what did you say?" Fagan leaned off the door frame.

"I asked ye which queen; there is three at this time if ye counts em, so ye gets asked which one?"

The officer looked astounded. "The Queen of Fae of course." Fagan shook his head in disbelief.

"Aye, I get what ye said, ye just has to wonder which one, there is three of em." He scratched behind his ear, and it gave a little wiggle. "Hold up and blow me, nope there is four, so which one of em wants a chat with Old Fagan?" The officer looked even more confused.

"Four what?" Fagan gave a sigh.

"Ye is not as bright as the honey locust is ye? Look it's simple, if ye just focus ye brain. There is four queens of Fae, Amethyst Queen of Avalon and Fae Ofmoon on earth, Iona Violet future Queen of Florae, Gwendolyn White Circle departed Queen of Florae, although she ain't dead or alive, but is still getting around, and then there is Rhiannon Queen of Fae Ofmoon. It's as simple as a buttercup if ye thinks about it, so which one is it as wants Old Fagan for a chat?"

The officer appeared to be getting annoyed. "It is Rhiannon Queen of all Fae, and of the Realm Ofmoon." Fagan gave a nod of understanding.

"Finally, tell her I ain't interested I have trees to tend, she is the queen of the moon realm and this is not her realm." The officer looked puzzled.

"If we have too, we will use force, it's better in the long run if you come with us in a peaceful manner." Fagan gave a chuckle.

"If ye fancies ye chances ye can try force, but ye will talk with the scythe first, ye ain't got enough men to be taking Old Fagan in quietly." Fagan stretched out his right arm and gripped the shaft of Merlin's newly restored scythe, and pulled it towards him.

The officer looked dumbstruck; he rolled up his parchment and slid it into his belt. "I have thirty armed men here."

Fagan gave a sniffle. "Ye knows how to count, and it's not enough." He pointed to a small thick hawthorn growing near the edge of the forest, not far from where they were stood. "Ye see that little hawthorn over yonder, come back with a man for every leaf, and then ye will hear the scythe talk, and ye will see who is right."

The officer looked, and as he did, the whole of the clearing burst into bright violet light, and Rune and Sapphire came walking out of the light and crossed to the bottom of the steps in front of Fagan.

"By what right do you impose yourself on my employee?" The Officer looked confused.

"I am here on the official royal business of the Queen of Fae." Sapphire looked back at Fagan and smiled.

"Which One?" Fagan gave a chuckle.

"Ye should not ask that, ye officer has trouble answerin it." He chuckled some more. Rune looked at the officer.

"You have no jurisdiction here, it is time you left." The officer was losing his patience and snapped.

"Look I have my orders and I aim to take this man, remove his property and clear this place of his house. I think you will find an order of the Queen carries the day here." Sapphire shook her head.

"Oh Dear!" Rune's eyes flickered with violet.

"DO YOU KNOW WHO I AM, GET ON YOUR KNEES WHEN YOU ADDRESS ME SOLDIER." Sapphire sighed.

"Too late." The officer looked stunned, but some of the soldiers stepped back a little. Rune glared at the officer.

"I am Runestone Sapphire, daughter of Opal, granddaughter of Eve and Hearne, Lady of life and owner of the Forest of Time." Her eyes illuminated with violet light. "THIS IS MY LAND, MY CABIN AND THIS MAN IS IN SERVICE TO MYSELF AND THE QUEEN OF FAE IN AVALON, HOW DARE YOU SHOW ME SUCH DISRESPECT."

All the soldiers dropped to their knees; the officer remained standing. "I am ordered not to leave without the prisoner, I am sorry My Lady but I must take him with me."

Rune lifted her hand and a bright ball of violet light erupted from it and shot into the sky. The glade flashed blue, and Amethyst walked out from a wall of light, she crossed the glade to Rune's side and the officer fell to his knees.

Amethyst looked down at him. "You have no rights here Grand Marshal, why do you bother one of my most loyal subjects, and I may add a servant of the Lady of Life?" He looked up at her from his knees.

"My apologies your Royal Highness, but I have been ordered by the Queen of Fae to take this man for the crime of treason to the queen, I cannot leave without him." Amethyst stared at him, Fagan whispered.

"Don't go askin ye which one, it confused the poor blighter." Rune smiled, as Amethyst took a step forward.

"I am the Queen of Fae and I have issued no such order, I will remind you Grand Marshal, that this land is administered by the Keeper of the forest on behalf of the Lady of Life, and under the protection of the Queen of Avalon, as agreed in a pact made by Albanlin the White Lord, Eve the Lady of Life and Rhiannon the then Queen of Avalon. That pact still stands, but her Highness Rhiannon has given all rights to that pact to the new Queen of Avalon, namely myself. The queen you serve has no legitimate rights here, and so I am ordering you as Queen of this territory to leave."

He faced the floor in utter frustration. "Please Your Highness, don't do this, I beg you to listen to me..." Amethyst raised her hand.

"NO!" With a flick of her wrist, the whole troop turned to light and shot like shooting stars into the sky. "I will be obeyed in my own realm." Fagan winked at Sapphire.

"More impressive than a sugar maple in the sunset of autumn she is." She gave a broad smile as Amethyst turned to Runestone.

"Avalon will be sealed to all without my consent from this moment onward." She looked back at Fagan who dropped to one knee and bowed. "Your house and life are safe here Master Keeper, I will protect all my subjects with great care." He looked up at her.

"I am honoured by ye gesture and serve ye with all I is, and if ye would not mind, I would be more tickled than a buttercup if ye would grace my humble abode and take a barley cracker and some jasmine tea with me self." Rune gave her a smile and she turned fully to Fagan.

"I would be honoured to be invited into such a famous abode, and the idea of crackers is very tempting as I am eating for two now." Fagan looked delighted and jumped to his feet, and gave a long sweeping gesture of entrance to his house, he then rushed inside and lifted his best copper kettle off the rack and filled it to boil. Amethyst led the way followed by Rune and Sapphire, as they reached the top of the steps Sapphire leaned into Rune and whispered.

"Jade is right you know; his ears do wiggle when he is excited." Rune gave a giggle and followed Amethyst through the door for tea and barley crackers.

CHAPTER TWENTY TWO

LOST WORDS

Rhiannon paced up and down the room cursing, Pwhyll sat patiently reading, his eyes lifting occasionally to watch her, before returning the pages. She turned again for the hundredth time.

"He has no right to spread rumours." She stopped and looked at him. "He is your son too, why are you not doing more?"

He put his book down, and stroked his long white beard, as he thought about the situation. "I have to confess, all of this is even new to me, you have hidden far more than I realised." He leaned forward in his chair. "Our boy is not wrong though is he? If as he says the truth is going to come out, then you must act, not by attacking our child, but by setting things right. I cannot see your meeting with the White Lord being comforting when he returns, you know how he feels about the Merle."

She glared at him. "You are not helping; you are supposed to be on my side."

Pwhyll stroked his long white hair back over his shoulder. "This is not about sides my darling; it is about what is right and what is wrong. You made a mistake and hid something you should have dealt with, be honest, you should have listened to Bridget instead of flying off the handle. As the figure our people look up to, it is your task now to make amends and rectify the problem."

Rhiannon started to pace again. "It cost Bridget her life force, is that what you want, me dead in a tomb like hers, for our people to place flowers on and weep over?" He gave a long frustrated sigh.

"You are supposed to be the wisest of all the Fae, there must be a way other than the one Bridget used to solve this. Come on who knows more of the magic of old than you? Go to your books instead of wearing out the floor, there must be a cure, go and find out, and correct this problem. I am surprised I have to tell you, I remember a time when you would have done that without thinking, you most certainly would never of attacked our boy."

"FINE!" She spun on the spot and stormed out slamming the door. Pwhyll sat back and lifted his book, and started to read where he had left off.

It was early morning and Rune looked tired as she stood on the grass with Sapphire and Crystal, as Tila talked Sapphire through her procedure again.

"This is fun; I am the teacher of the teacher." She gave another little titter. "Look it's simple, focus your mind as you always do with your window, and then think of the exact location in Florae you wish to land, then open the window and step through." Sapphire gave a nod.

"So it really is no different from any other window?" Tila smiled.

"No...Well accept it is the home of our people, but apart from that it is the same as any other time."

Sapphire gave a nod and then focused her thoughts, as she tried to remember exactly what the steps to the House of Scribes had looked like. It all felt like a bit of a blur, as last time she had tried hard to take it all in, but there had been too much. The window opened and she carefully stepped through to find all was well, and she had landed exactly where she had meant to. Tila came through with a huge smile and walked onto the first steps and straight into Bade.

She stepped back quickly and apologised, he looked at the blue window through which Sapphire had arrived followed by Crystal.

"Back so soon?" Sapphire looked up.

"We have something important to discuss." The window closed behind the group, Bade looked puzzled.

"In what context exactly?" Tila gave a huge glowing smile.

"Enaria and Ariel." His face dropped and his voice lowered.

"That is forbidden for house scribes." Tila looked at Sapphire at her side.

"Not for the teacher and her guest it's not." Bade gave a superior frown.

"Guest?" Crystal side stepped revealing Runestone, who gave a courteous bow. "I am..."

"I am fully aware of who you are." He came down the steps and gave a regal bow, and then held out his hand. "I am honoured to know you have paid us such a special visit; please come I shall alert the council of your presence this instant." Tila sniggered, and he cast her a sharp look, she leaned into Sapphire and whispered.

"See I told you."

Bade almost whisked Rune up the steps, as she tried to explain. "It is not really an official visit, we really do not have much time, but there is a matter I would greatly like to discuss with Master Elgin if he is available."

He was positively filled with excitement, something Tila had never seen; even

Sapphire noted the difference between his curt manner with her, and his attitude towards Runestone. Bade led the way constantly talking and praising Rune for providing such an honour to the house, leaving Sapphire, Crystal and Tila stood where they had arrived. Sapphire suddenly realised and hurried up the steps to catch up closely followed by the other two.

The size and scale of the inside of the house was impressive, as was the intricate carvings on all the pillars holding up the huge triangular structure. Floor upon floor rose to the high pent of the roof, with many landings, all containing stacks of parchments, and old bound dusty books on orderly shelves. Rune marvelled at the wonder of the building, as Bade showed her to a set of comfy seats, and asked if she would kindly wait, whilst he called for Master Elgin the head of the Fae council of Elders.

It took some time before Bade returned; he gave a sharp bow to Runestone. "Lady Runestone, Master Elgin is in his day room, and he would be very happy to meet with you and your party, if you would come this way, I shall take you to him." Rune stood and thanked Bade, then followed him towards the back of the House of Scribes, where there was a series of doors leading to side rooms. Bade opened the door and announced the arrival of the party, and escorted them inside.

Master Elgin stood before a luxuriously upholstered leather chair, leaning on an elaborately carved walking stick. He was a short man of great age; his long snow white hair was combed back over his head, behind his ears, and flowed down his back. He had a small very neatly trimmed goatee, and eyes of the deepest green, that sparkled with great life from his pale wrinkled face. His smile was wide and very welcoming, as Rune walked up to him and he greeted her with great respect.

"My Lady of Life, I am indeed honoured to meet you in person... I apologise for my age, and my need to be seated, my legs yearn for youth, but sadly they have been deprived of it." He signalled to a seat opposite. "Please would you join me and be seated." Rune smiled.

"Master Elgin it is indeed a pleasure to meet with you, I have heard much of your work here, and as much as I would love to spend a great deal of time debating with you, I am afraid my visit is shorter than I would wish for." She sat in the seat opposite, as the others found seats around the room.

Like all things in the House of Scribes, the room was decked out in the highest grade of old timber. To the side of Elgin was a large fireplace where logs burned and cracked. Around the room were many ancient volumes of Fae writings, which Tila eyed with envy, she had heard much of this room, but had never been granted the chance to see it.

Elgin sat down slowly resting his stick beside the arm of the chair, and straightening his deep red ceremonial robes, that was the customary attire of all the council in the house. He leaned back in the chair and appeared very relaxed. "Tell me My Lady, how are my granddaughters doing, are they living up to the expectations we placed upon them to aid our future queen?"

It was not an unexpected question for Rune, and she smiled warmly. "My husband and myself are more than pleased with the care and attention they have placed on our children. They are to say the least, very thorough and attentive to their tasks." He gave a satisfied nod.

"I am pleased, we demand only the highest service for our future queen, and it pleases me to know they have attained such good standards in your service."

The door opened and two Fae staff entered with trays of food and drinks followed closely by Bade. They both waited as he slipped two tables from the side and carried them over, and then the maids placed the trays down and took two steps back. Elgin gave a respectful nod to Bade.

"That will be all; I am sure a talented scribe such as Lady Tila will be capable of attending to our needs Bade."

He looked disappointed, but dismissed the two waiting staff, who turned and headed for the door, and he reluctantly followed closing the door behind me. Tila looked a little pink in the cheeks as she approached the table.

"My Lord I was not aware you knew me." Elgin looked at Rune.

"I know every scribe in the house by sight and reputation, they are not aware of it of course, but I notice everything, even if it does not appear so, and I always spot talent." He gave a smile as Tila lifted the pot and poured out the tea into cups, and her face reddened more.

He took his cup and took a small sip. "So, my Lady, I am old enough and wise enough to pay attention to this realm and others, I assume you are here on what would be considered sensitive matters for this realm?"

Rune placed her cup on the table at her side and placed her hands onto her lap, her ring flashed blue as it glinted in the large windows illuminating the room. "I feel Master Elgin this subject may be sensitive in any realm I visit at the moment, but I do have important questions to have answers to." He gave a nod as he lifted his cup.

"Ariel?" Rune smiled.

"You are well informed." He gave a small titter of a laugh.

"Not as well informed as you may think, it appears the household of Loxley has many secrets, so much so even an elderly relative is unable to learn much... I deducted from your recent visits with Queen Amethyst and her father's rather rapid departure from the Realm Ofmoon that once again the subject of one of my brightest scribes had arisen again. It is not unexpected, this matter has been unresolved for too long now, and maybe I feel it is time this matter was brought to a close once and for all. I cannot say I have the answers you need, but if you ask, I will answer truthfully what I can."

Rune did not waste time. "You knew her? I am informed it was you who protected her when she was expelled from Avalon. I have heard the rest of the council wanted to hand her over to Luminaria, but you convinced them she should remain here." He gave a surprised smile.

"You are better informed than I realised Lady Runestone, but yes, you are indeed correct, I took sole responsibility for her during her confinement. I will also add that I knew she was wrongly accused and this was yet another political manoeuvre by the Queen Ofmoon, to undermine Queen Bridget who was ill at the time. I have no tolerance for politics at the expense of the people, so I fought her case and won."

"I believe she was confined here in the house, and her rooms have been sealed since the night she left?" He gave a nod.

"That is true, her rooms were given to her by Queen Bridget herself, and they were sealed by Bade. He was somewhat protective of her, it was nothing to do with the queen or council, he chose to seal the rooms, and they have been that way since. I must confess I have no idea why, but we have a great deal of space, and she was very instrumental in the design of this house, so no one has ever objected." Rune appeared pleased.

"Would it surprise you to be informed that it is my soul purpose for this visit? I have come to ask for permission to enter the room and investigate, as I feel there may be items of interest that could uncover the identity of the real culprit for the drawing down of the Merle into Avalon." He gave a cheeky smile.

"You want to prove it was Branna, I must admit I always thought it was, but honestly I really do believe after many conversations with Ariel alone, if it was Branna, Ariel had absolutely no knowledge of it."

Rune understood him perfectly. "I believe you may be right Master Elgin."

"I have no objection to you looking into her personal effects; if it reveals the truth of this matter. I would certainly be glad for the resolution; it's been many years and at times an old man likes to know he was right and did the right thing. I must confess Lady Runestone, you have rekindled my interest in this affair. I shall ensure you get entrance to her rooms." He pushed his stick into the floor, and with his free arm levered himself to his feet. "I have been delighted to have had this private moment, and look forward to many more in future days."

Rune stood up and he shook her hand, he then turned to the table and lifted a small silver bell, he gave it two sharp swipes, and the door instantly opened and Bade entered.

"Bade, could you escort Lady Runestone and her party to the rooms of Ariel please, I have given them consent to look at her personal effects." He looked astounded and his colour whitened a little.

"Master Elgin is that prudent?"

"I have given my consent, and my word is my bond. Do as requested Bade." He gave a somewhat disappointed look, and gestured to Rune.

"If you would care to follow me." He turned sharply and left the room.

Elgin held Rune by the hand. "I hope it helps, the task you have is not an easy one for anyone, but I do wish you all the success in your quest, and we are all here and support your struggle against such darkness. Go with peace My Lady of Life, for all lives rest on your shoulders." Rune gave a bright smile and shook his hand.

"I am indebted to you Master Elgin; I will not forget the support of your people in this hour of need." Elgin smiled and then looked at Sapphire.

"I would care to meet with you on your return Teacher, we have much to discuss about the future." She smiled as she shook his hand.

"I will be back as soon as we have dealt with this matter, but I am looking forward greatly to spending more time here." Crystal and Tila paid their respects, and Elgin held on to Tila's hand a little longer than normal. His bright green eyes locked into her hazel eyes, and he lowered his voice.

"You protect her, no matter what it requires, she is the life in all of us, lose yours if that is the price of her protection." Tila gave a frightened nod.

"I will on my families honour Master." He smiled.

"Try not to die; I have no tolerance for teaching more scribes to your ability." He winked and she gave a big smile.

"I will try." He patted her cheek softly.

"Good, now go with her, and stay close to her."

It was clear Bade was not at all happy, his bright and rather suffocating disposition had quickly vanished, and the more normal and a little aloof character of Bade returned, much to the relief of Rune. Tila found it very funny and smiled even more than normal, which was quite something, and Crystal understanding more of Tila's working relationship could not help but smirk a little with her.

Bade strode at a quicker pace than normal, out of the main doors and turned left. Runestone and the others followed as he walked along the wide railed deck in the front of the House of Scribes, which consisted of two huge triangular buildings of wood, which had a row of small apartments built in between the two. The last door was where Bade stopped and faced the group, as they tried to catch up. Rune looked at the small single window, and the varnished wooden door that bore a small wooden painted plaque of the Star of Enaria.

Bade slipped his hand inside his robes, and pulled out and old and very ornamental highly polished brass key. "This is her apartment, it was sealed when she left, and has not been used since."

Rune smiled and held out her hand for the key. "I am grateful for your assistance and hospitality; we will return the key when we are done."

Bade looked very uncomfortable, as Tila stepped up at the side of Rune. "We may be some time Bade, and I have informed Lady Rune of how busy and such a huge asset you are to the house, so I will return the key when we leave." It was clear he was reluctant to hand the key over, Rune understood, and as she placed her hand on the key, she lifted her other hand to his shoulder.

"I feel the love you hold for Ariel within you, and I think it is not against any rules to say that we have it on a very trusted authority that she is still alive." He looked like he was going to faint, the colour ran from his face so quick. Rune smiled as he gasped for air and was barely able to utter his words.

"What... That must not be possible?" Tila gave him a wide smile as she saw a tear well into his eye.

"Bade we think she is held captive and has been for a very long time, but for now that is a big secret." He just stared at her unable to speak, as the tear ran down his cheek. Rune squeezed his shoulder.

"Her possessions are quite safe, no one here is going to tarnish her memory, if anything we aim to prove without doubt she was innocent, and if possible we wish to return her to her rightful home." She held him firm, as his legs gave a tremble. "Go and rest, and recover your composure and trust in me, for I seek her truth, and I hope the answer to where we can find her lies within." He swallowed hard and tried to gain some composure.

"I do not believe you will find anything, I have looked a thousand times, if there was any hope, I would have found it." Rune gave him a smile.

"I do not just use my eyes; I have other ways of sensing where the truth lies. Trust me Bade, we will come to you when we are done." He gave a nod, and Rune took the key and handed it to Tila, who slipped it into the lock, and turned it until she heard the door click. Bade gave a regal bow, and took two steps back to let the others pass him.

Tila entered first, followed by Runestone, Crystal and then Sapphire came last. Sapphire turned and closed the door as Bade stood frozen outside still in slight shock, and very emotional. The door closed and she leaned on it. "I actually feel really sorry him, did you see how quick he unravelled, it must be awful for him, all this time without her and loving her that much. Poor sod it must have been terrible knowing he will never see her again, and not even knowing if she is alive or dead." Tila nodded as she scanned round what was actually a plain and boring room, apart from the walls which were filled with hand drawn pictures.

"I did not know he could feel, I felt a little sorry for him too... Wow Ariel is good, have you seen this picture of him?"

Rune was focused on the main wall, which was covered with pictures of a scruffy haired happy smiling woman, with dark hair and grey eyes. Sapphire came up to her side.

"I assume this is Branna?" Rune gave a silent nod, as she took in every detail of the pictures.

The room was small with two wooden chairs and a small table, on which was a small ink pot and neatly trimmed set of quills. Under the table was an open wooden crate filled with fresh new parchment. Tila crouched down and looked at Crystal.

"Look familiar?" She grinned and shook her head.

"You scribes are all the same, more paper than clothing." Tila smiled back.

"Yeah but I was right, look at the book case behind you."

They all turned to see a row of neatly bound books; she stood up straight and walked across to them, and slid the first volume out and opened it and began to read the first inscription. "Wow these should not be here, these are her journals of the Fae in Erin after they left the Forest of Time with Bridget, before the travels to Iona, these should be in the main reference library, this is of great historical importance, they actually journal how she planned this place years before Florae was even thought of."

Rune smiled at Crystal. "I think those books are Tila's idea of utopia." She gave a chuckle.

"You have no idea, we better make sure we lock this place up good, otherwise she will sneak back and sit reading until she starves to death." Tila turned and smiled.

"I wouldn't, I would sneak a book out and read while cooking at home."

Sapphire had gone through the doorway into the room at the back unnoticed. She looked at the bed and the cupboard, and saw a small wooden bench with a wash basin and three beautifully laced towels hanging beside it. She looked back through the doorway as she opened the cupboard to find a few garments of clothing hanging but little else.

"This room is as sparse as that one, I am not sure we are going to find much more Rune." Tila scoffed and came into the room.

"She is a Scribe; you are looking in all the wrong places." Crystal came through the door and was about to speak, as she had a good idea of what Tila meant, when she saw her drop to her knees and look under the bed. "See I told you, scribes are so predictable." Crystal laughed.

"Says the obsessed scribe."

Tila reached below the bed, grabbed something and tugged; a large wooden lock box came out from under the bed. She looked at Sapphire and smiled. "Under the basin." Sapphire frowned.

"What is?" Tila chuckled and pointed to the lock.

"The spare key silly." Rune stood in the doorway and giggled, as Sapphire rolled her eyes and turned to the basin and lifted it up. There underneath was a small cloth, and in the centre, which had been hollowed a little within the folds was a small key. She picked it up and handed it to Tila, who was looking far too excited for what was not the most adventurous task they had ever had.

The lock gave a click and Tila slipped it out of the loops and pulled on the lid of the box. It swung open revealing piles of parchments and some small precious objects. Rune moved in closer with the others as Tila examined the contents.

"More pictures of Branna and these must be the house they shared. Wow this one of Branna sleeping naked is really good, although I can see why she locked it away." She gave a very cheeky smile. "There are a lot of writings about day to day stuff, but nothing too revealing."

She lifted a large wad of parchment out and began looking through them, some of which were sketches and some notes on her day in Florae, and there was a lot of love poems.

Rune looked at the bottom of the box. "What is that?" Tila looked down and her eyes lit up with excitement, as she moved some soft cloth and revealed another book. She carefully lifted it out and held it up to look at it, and then opened it and read the first line. She gave a gasp and looked at Rune.

"Oh wow, this is her personal journal of her time with Branna in Avalon." She looked back at the box. "Well it is at least one of them." Rune took the book out of her hand and opened it up, as Tila looked in the bottom of the box for another, but it was not there. Sapphire was curious.

"One of them?" Tila gave a nod as she continued to look at the other things in the box.

"Yeah, that is the second volume, I would have thought the first one would be here, but it is not."

Sapphire turned at looked at Rune who had the book open and was reading it; she leaned in and saw the page filled with strange looking runes. "Can you read that?"

Rune blinked. "Yes why?" Tila appeared at her side.

"Rune is the stone all has been written on, this is really old Fae, there are few who could read it, but she will see it as ordinary writing because it is one of her gifts, Eve could do it too, it was what Bridget loved the most about writing to her, because she did not need to translate it, Eve could read every language easily." Rune gave a smile and Tila shrugged.

"Sorry I get carried away, too much information, right?" Rune giggled.

"It's fine Tila, I can see why this would be exciting for you, I too like old works to read." Tila leaned in and tried to see the page.

"Can we use it, will it help us?" Rune closed the book.

"I think it will, the problem is we cannot take it out of here."

Tila took the book and winked as she slipped it up the back of her shirt and slipped it into the waistband of her pants, then pulled her top over it, and then gave a huge smile.

"We do this all the time around Bade, he never notices. Give him his key and let's get back to your place, I am dying to read this."

Ten minutes later, the room was left as it was and tidy, the place was locked up and Runestone was again in front of a seated Elgin. "I hope your search was fruitful?"

"It was, we have an idea of what Branna looks like, some details of the house in Avalon, and a few other things." He smiled.

"I take it Bade did not see you slip it out?" Tila put her head down, and he smiled. "If it helps use it, and Tila can return it when you are done, I shall handle Bade if any problems arise." Runestone smiled.

"I am very grateful for your help; it could be the vital thing we are looking for." Elgin gave an understanding nod.

"We will play our part as I am sure many will to rid all the realms of the darkness that threatens us, go with speed and with our blessings for a victorious outcome." Sapphire's window opened behind Rune, and she turned and walked into it followed by Crystal, then Sapphire and as Tila turned to follow, Elgin gave a nod to her.

"Remember, at all costs." Tila gave a nod back and walked through the window and it closed behind her. Elgin sat and gave a heavy sigh. "Such brave young souls, I would give anything to be out there with them."

CHAPTER TWENTY THREE

DARKNESS AND THE LIGHT

Whilst Rune was off in Florae, Robbie spent his time back at the office behind the operations room of the Village Hall. The trip out to observe Mason's set up had inspired all the Specialist's, and he found as the day wore on towards noon, they had made their way to his office to talk about what they had seen. By noon most of the Specialists were gathered and crammed into his office surrounding Rowan and Robbie. It was clear that being stuck in Loxley with the large wall looming on the horizon was getting to them, as they felt they should be doing something useful.

Robbie explained that just their presence inside the Stockade was doing a lot of good, and had given everyone reassurance and hope, but they were restless and wanted to do something more than train on targets of straw. Robbie sat back and looked at Rowan.

"Seriously what can we do with a huge wall all around us?"

Rowan leaned forward onto the desk; his grey eyes focused on Robbie. "We have never sat back; I think what they are saying is that we have always been the ones to do something to mess with his plans. Admit it Robbie, we are all sat here going through the motions, and all of us are waiting for those bells to ring, and none of us know what will come." Robbie sighed.

"It is no different for me; I am sat here while Rune bounces all over looking for this Ena or her mother in hope one of them can lead us to a clue of her family origins. All of what she is doing is based on the slightest hope that maybe there is a place that will give us what we need to kill Morgan. I am just as restless as all of you, but just what can we do?"

"I seem to remember stories of stealing carts and burning fields, I was part of attacking a castle and blowing it up, not to mention blowing up an ammunition factory, it seems to me Robbie we are the ones that have always struck where least expected, and then disappeared creating fear on the other side." Big John looked at Jett and then back to Robbie.

"Aye, she is right, the last time we really scared the hell out of this lot was Dunnottar with them violet feathers." Jett Looked at Robbie.

"If we lose our edge, what use are we to everyone?" He fully understood what both Jett and John were saying, but it did not seem that easy these days.

"Back then we were winging it, this is different, and it's bigger and far more dangerous now." Rowan shrugged.

"Is it though?" Robbie shook his head

"There is more to it than back then guys; it's just not that simple." Steph leaned forward in her seat from behind Rowan.

"I really I am not sure I agree with you Robbie, maybe we have all just got a little too used to sitting behind desks or consulting and organising training sessions. Our skills got a little sharper at Lincoln, but that was eleven days ago, maybe some sort of exercise like yesterday would help get us in battle mode a lot quicker." Robbie sat back in his seat.

"Not you too, I thought you were the voice of reason in this group?" Smokes sniggered and she looked at him.

"What? We agreed when we got married that I was irresponsible and you were the grown up, and most reasonable." He hunched his shoulders. "It's worked well enough so far."

Rafe gave a smirk, he turned to Robbie.

"Mother is right, maybe we do need a little target practice to get back on the ball more, I have had plenty of sword action recently, maybe a little time with a few arrows will benefit us all, after all if they come running at us, our longbows will be the first weapon we reach for." Robbie listened and thought.

"Target practice, like what?" Jett gave a wide grin.

"Well to be honest Robbie we know where there is one hell of a camping spot, how about a little night shoot?" The rest of the Specialists all gave a beaming smile; just the thought appeared to physically raise their spirits. Robbie looked at Rowan, he gave a grin.

"It would be better than sitting here waiting." Big John nodded.

"Aye and a hell of lot more fun than sitting on the walls watching their torches burn all night."

Robbie slowly looked at all their faces; he could see how badly they needed this. He gave a smile.

"Ok we will work something out, prepare your kit, and load up extra arrows, we will meet at the main door of the hall around eight tonight." All of them looked instantly happy and all started to smile, they turned and headed for the door, and for the first time in many days Robbie heard the familiar hum of laughing and joking Specialists. Steph lifted her chair and moved it to the side of Rowan's.

"Ok I can take us out, and put us anywhere you need us, so what are we going to do?" Robbie unrolled his map.

"Ok if we are doing this, we do it right. This is the camp with all the tents, half at least have occupants, and this looks like some sort of stores, so I say we take a little more than arrows." Smokes leaned over and looked down.

"You know what you need don't you?" Robbie looked up and shook his head.

"No, what Smokes?" He gave a wide grin.

"You need one Jay, one Dove, and a bloody big Rigger." Rowan gave a laugh, and Robbie's face broke into a huge smile.

To the South West of the central city of Florae, half way up the lonely mountain of Mount Bridge there was a deep cave. It was one of the deepest on all the nine islands that made up the realm of Florae. At its deepest point, in a wide cave with walls of crystal and seamed with rich veins of amethyst, lay the sealed stone resting place of Bridget Violet, queen and saviour of her people.

The marble box that held her last mortal remains was large and decorated with some of the finest masonry work ever seen in the lands of Fae. The tomb of Bridget was surrounded by a huge ring of fresh flowers, for such was the love of her people, they all made a regular pilgrimage from their homes below the mountain, to lay flowers and pay their respects.

The air of the cave was filled with the scents and fragrances of many flowers, some of which have never grown in any other realm. On the opposite side of the cave, were the equally ornate, yet lesser in stature tombs of Malcolm her husband, Ninian her son and his wife Erin, and also Filomena the wife of Gwynfor. In the centre of the ceiling, high above, was a small flower of white crystal that had been charmed by Gwendolyn, which shone casting a gentle light across the whole cave.

In front of Bridget's tomb stood the tall black tattered robed figure of Albanlin. He looked at the tomb and laid a bunch of white flowers on the centre of it. "Such a waste, they would benefit greatly from you now my friend."

A soft blue light cast across the walls behind him and he straightened up as he felt the new presence arrive in the cave. "I wondered when you would appear, it seems I cannot sneak into a realm these days without finding company arrives shortly after."

"You made me the watcher of the realms, are you surprised I would sense you and come to you?" He turned to face Gwendolyn as she walked through the cave with flowers in her hand.

"I often visit her, she was a good friend, we did not always agree, but I liked that about her, she did not bow and scrape and was not afraid to argue with me. I respected her a great deal, she was honest and true to herself and her people, as were you I might add, she taught you well, and I see you have placed a great deal of that wisdom into Sapphire's table for her to teach the next queen."

Gwendolyn bowed to her grandmother's tomb, and carefully placed the flowers next to Albanlin's. She turned and stepped over the flowers on the floor so as not to disturb them, and walked to the side of her White Lord and stood facing the tomb. "I miss her, I have always been sorry she chose not to return, there was so much I wanted to say to her. I admired her more than any other living soul; she was the greatest influence of my life, for she taught me to be simply a member of the Fae race, long before she taught me to be a queen." His hood twitched as if he had given a nod of respect to the comment.

"I watched Malcom and Ninian build this realm, I watched Uther rise to power, and Arthur unite the land of men, I have seen so many since the creation struggle with their lives and face such great odds, but to me there is no other braver or a more courageous person that has graced the realms we have built, she truly was a glowing example, not just to Fae and men, but also to me."

Gwendolyn turned her head to him. "Is Rhiannon not on your list, for she has done great things?" Albanlin gave a slight titter.

"Rhiannon is wise and has done many things she should be praised for, but her undoing has always been the treatment of her people, she has never understood that each person has value. She has been preoccupied with her own ambition and her own adoration of her mythology, and because of that she has always failed to recognise her flaws." Gwendolyn was slightly surprised to hear his words.

"You know the truth, don't you?" Albanlin turned to her, and he slid an almost transparent hand from his robes and took her by the arm.

"Walk with me White Circle." Gwendolyn allowed him to lead, and slowly the White Lord made his way back up the long tunnel that headed back towards the outside of the cave, and he spoke quietly.

"I have to confess that I am now fully aware of the full tale, much of it thanks to yourself and the Red Stone. It is not easy to admit that all of the ruling council became so preoccupied with their tasks, they failed to see what was right under our noses, and it has brought chaos and pain to everything." Ahead of them the entrance of the cave was lit as the sun set behind Mount Bridge, but illuminated the two other peaks of Florae with a deep orangey red. Gwendolyn looked out of the tunnel end in the distance.

"So if you know the truth, why not change things?"

"I am not certain you will understand, but it is the imperfections in everything that provide the most pleasure. I understand that perfect is in itself a flaw, because without the imperfections you lose the depth of something. We made mistakes at the start, but you have to understand that we were all new to the things we did. Even for us with our powers that appear so superior to all the races, we struggled with our limitations and our understanding of the things we created. Eve was amazing in the way she simplified everything, and I have always admired how she helped us all understand what we had done, and what we could do in the time to come. We are no different than all of you, we too have made mistakes."

Gwendolyn understood. "But you have the authority of the universe, why have you not stepped in and called Rhiannon out for her behaviour?" He slowed his pace.

"Listen carefully White Circle, there are some who see us as gods, there are those who think they are gods, and those who yearn to be gods. I feel the thing they all miss is a god is a made up thing, it is an idea, a theory, a story to tell, but they are not real. Yes they provide hope and understanding, but people do not understand that it is their own self they understand, not the gods." She stopped and looked at him.

"I do not understand, I see you, I have grown up around all of you, you have immense powers and could change the course of everything with just a snap of your fingers, how can gods not be real?" He gave a chuckle.

"Yes, I have powers, I am from a different world, but you fail to notice that in my world I was just an ordinary being, everyone was like me, so am I still a god?"

"Here in these realms yes. It was your work and that of your sister that gave life to everything." His hood gave a twitch.

"We gave you what was considered normal in our world, so does that make us gods? White Circle you are missing my point, think deeper on the words I use." She tried to consider everything he had said.

"If what you say is true, then you consider all are like gods." His hood twitched.

"Almost...Look in my world I am a simple being, in this world you were a queen, and worshipped like a god, and yet you did not act like one, neither did Eve, she lived a simple naked life and took great joy in all she did, is that not what Bridget Violet taught you?" She felt confused, but thought she understood.

"Well yes, I was an ordinary Fae long before I was a queen."

"So when you were an ordinary Fae, what changed that made you a queen, or a god like entity?" She shook her head.

"Nothing changed."

"I disagree."

"You do...Why?" He chuckled again.

"White Circle you stayed true to who you are, but once the crown touched your head, you had to face the responsibility of your position. You could have abused it, yet you chose to remain a simple Fae, and so therefore understood your people. Your rule will never be forgotten, but not because you were god like, quite the opposite, you will be remembered for the love and care you showed to your people, for showing them you were at heart simply one of them." Gwendolyn suddenly understood.

"Rhiannon lost her way, and as a result half her people will remember her with distrust and anger."

"She could have followed the example of your grandmother who sacrificed herself for her people, not unlike yourself, but she chose not to, because she believed she was god like, and in doing so she lost her connection to her people." Now she truly understood him.

"What will you do with her?" He started to walk again.

"For now I will do nothing, the imperfection of everything at the moment interests me, and I wish to see the outcome of all of this." It suddenly hit her and she gasped.

"You have been around all the time, you have not been away on your travels as we all thought, you have been watching Runestone Sapphire, and Robbie to see how they will handle Rhiannon."

"You are wise Gwendolyn White Circle, wiser I would say than the guardian of the moon at this time. I will sit and watch and see what happens, I live in the hope that Rhiannon will gain wisdom from this, and so I will rest a while and wait for the outcome." It amused her to think that all along he had been there on watch as always.

"Opal always called you an old fraud; I think I am starting to understand more of her now." Albanlin gave a small laugh.

"I have a great fondness for my niece, she is the simplest of all of us, and yet at times wiser than most of us."

As they reached the mouth of the cave they stopped and watched as the sun slowly slipped to meet the horizon, and the shadow of the mount cast a dark veil over the realm of Florae. Albanlin turned to her.

"The darkness always feels at its worst at this time, and yet it gives me great hope, for when it is this dark, it is clear the light will once again flow and everything will take on a different perspective."

Gwendolyn stood beside her White Lord and smiled, she knew for now he would not interfere even if she felt he should, but somehow as the darkness surrounded her, she felt a strong sense of relief, just knowing he was there in the shadows watching. For a moment her mind slipped into thought and the hood of Albanlin twitched.

"You are wise to question that." She turned slightly to look at him.

"You sense my thoughts?" The hood twitched again.

"The Merle is powerful, and the question is very much, did Branna draw it down, or did it come of its own accord, and I think you show great wisdom to question whether or not something that has existed for longer than the span of our own time here, can indeed be destroyed easily."

She gave a slight chuckle, and nodded in response. "I just thought about its power and how much it has corrupted."

"And therefore, if it can corrupt the lines of Fae, can you defeat it?"

"Yes, I realised my grandmother died in that task, as did Enaria, and you are the only person I can ask...Can we kill it, or destroy it?"

"Your question is more complex than you realise White Circle, but in the simplest of terms my answer is short. No you cannot."

Gwendolyn gave a gasp. "Then why allow Runestone to pursue a task that may destroy her?"

"It is why I watch and wait White Circle. Runestone is life captured and held within a human like form, she is the purest form of what the Merle feeds off. I will tell you this, she will bring about a great change, but when the final moment comes, Runestone knows she will not be able to destroy that part of the Merle within her enemy, without allowing it to be free in this world, for to kill Morgan, the Merle trapped within her will be set free." Gwendolyn could not believe what she was hearing.

"Then you must go to her and tell her not to try."

"I cannot and will not do that, this task was set to her and I will await the outcome, but rest assured White Circle, when the moment arrives, I alone shall take the Merle from this world back into the realm in which it belongs." Gwendolyn gave a sigh of relief.

"Thank the heavens, for a moment then I was worried all of this was to be in vain."

"To show the people you care for, you will stand up for them, and stand beside them in times of need is never in vain White Circle, you of all people should know that."

O n the open land on the far side of Mason's wall, Robbie lay in the long grass with his telescope to his eye. He watched the rows of carts, and the black vested men as they unloaded boxes, and walked into the wall via a small door. "What do you think, could that be the stores?"

Rigger lay at his side with a pair of old battered binoculars, chewing on a long strand of dried grass.

"Well it could be anything, but considering they are unloading into it, I reckon it might be worth a pop, what you say Dove?" She lay at his side with half a set of binoculars; the other half was with OX. His pair had been snapped in half in a fight, and she had claimed half for jumping in and helping him, now she used it as a make shift telescope.

"It's bloody busy there, it's close to the wall, but look at all the tents and troops, it's taking a big risk to try and pop it." Rigger turned to her.

"You busy tonight?"

"Well, I was going to stay in and wash my hair, but if it's your party I may be interested." Rigger smiled and turned to Robbie.

"Make em look the other way, and we will get the party started, lend me Jay though, she is fast with a fuse." Dove poked him.

"What and I am not?" He giggled.

"Girl you are one of the best, but for this party we are going to need a threesome." She shook her head.

"You're a kinky bugger, but oddly enough, I like it."

Robbie slipped back through the grass to where Steph and Rowan were crouched down in a small group of windswept hawthorns. He looked round. "Where is Maddy, I am going to need a light show?"

CHAPTER TWENTY FOUR

RELIVING OLD TIMES

It took about forty minutes to organise, but as Robbie saw it, there was no real rush as the darker it got the better, and also Rigger with Dove and Jay would need plenty of time to prepare. The group spread out in a semi-circle around the far end of the largest group of tents, it was far enough away from the main action around the gates, and they held a position in wild overgrown scrub, so as to be kept well out of sight of anyone passing.

Robbie briefed them as quickly as he could. "Take out tents, carts, piles of boxes, anything that will lower their morale and weaken their abilities. Avoid the carts round the doorway over there; Rigger is working in that location, so draw all eyes away from him." Jade and Jett smiled and they lifted their bows.

"Finally, it's party time girls."

"Keep it down Sting, and hold the steel, tonight is a rain of arrows, I want no heroics, I want all of you back in base alive and well tonight. Right we strike hard and fast and do as much damage as possible, if they organise and come at us, the large Oak behind us is the rallying point, and Mother will get us all back safe. OK Specialists we go on Maddy's arrow, let's wake this lot up and let them taste some Loxley hospitality." The group all gave a smile and moved slowly and silently into their positions.

Maddy knelt in the grass with Robbie. "What is the target?" He gave her a big smile.

"It appears we have no view of the camp from Loxley, tell me Maddy, how much fire will it take to light up the main gates?" She looked at her arrows and gave a devilish grin, as she slipped one out of its holder.

"I would say this one Robbie, it's a little special, but I have not had the chance to test it." Rowan looked at what was to him just an ordinary arrow.

"Would it not be wiser to test one first before using it in action?" Maddy placed the arrow on the string, and brought her bow up to her sights, her voice was calm and collected.

"The problem Rowan is that when it comes to testing these things we make, it's not always possible to find a safe site to do it on, especially in Loxley."

She pulled back the string to full tension, corrected her aim and then released it. The arrow left her bow like a missile, Rowan lifted his head slightly to watch. It whizzed across the landscape at a tremendous speed, heading straight for the centre of the main gates above all the tents and carts, and hit with a splintering crack.

Rowan lifted his head a little higher in the darkness. "Is it a dud?"

"Just wait a moment."

Suddenly the darkness vanished, throwing them into almost day light, Rowan slammed himself into the floor. "HOLY SHIT MADDY!!!!"

A ball of fire the height of a skyscraper erupted out of the gates, and flames engulfed two hundred yards of the camp in a wide semi-circle from the wall. All the Specialists hit the floor fearing they too would be consumed in the fire ball, as even this far back, the heat was insane. Robbie gave a loud laugh, as he watched Rowan push his face into the dirt; Una chuckled as the fireball raged across the whole camp.

"We may have over done that one." Rowan turned to Una and pulled his face out of the grass.

"Overdone it... seriously? I am surprised we still have eyebrows and we are at five hundred yards away." Jett and Jade sniggered to his left.

Robbie gave the signal as the camp sounded the alarm and chaos ensued. Across the valley, David Williams smiled next to Henry, as they watched what was a dark area, where the gates stood, suddenly illuminate. He lifted his binoculars to his eyes, and could see right through where the gates had stood, and watched the chaos on the other side of the wall through the gap.

"It looks like our boys are busy Henry?" Henry gave a satisfied smirk.

"It is about time, they have been a bit slow to the games this time around...Still it's good to see em enjoying themselves."

B ells rang out everywhere, half dressed men ran around, soldiers on duty screamed and hollered at each other whilst running in every direction. Men grabbed sheets and tried to put the fires on the carts out by hitting them. Soldiers looked for an unseen enemy, and in all of it, out of the darkness from every direction came a hail of arrows.

Jett, Jade and Blades, stood in a line aiming. "Red shirt mine." Jett smiled at Blades as she sighted her arrow.

"Ooh black vest, that's mine, man with a bucket!"

Jade aimed. "I got it." Arrows whistled, and far across the way in the camp three men fell.

Out of the darkness Rigger appeared with Jay and Dove running, they skirted the group and came sliding up behind Robbie, Rigger gave a gasp.

"Bloody good diversion, you guys, seriously scared the shit out of me. You know I hate to point this out, but when your guys are in the midst of everything with five bags of dynamite, it may help to limit the amount of fire you use. I thought I was gonna be barbecued for sure." Dove gave a giggle crouched behind him.

"I reckon you will be needing clean underwear too when we get back Rig." Robbie turned to Rigger.

"How long?" Rigger thought for a moment.

"I lost count in all the excitement, but it cannot be much longer." Bear came up from the side.

"They are pulling carts together for a barricade; we have done as much as we are going to." Robbie gave a nod.

"Hold for a few more moments Bear, we are waiting for the finale."

BOOM!...BOOM!...BOOM!...BOOM!

The earth shook as each large explosive went off. Massive clouds of dust erupted from the wall, and stone was flung into the air. Each blast blew the soldiers of Mason over, or tossed them over tents and boxes, screams and wails echoed between each blast. BOOM!

Rigger patted Robbie's shoulder. "That's the lot." Robbie turned to Rowan.

"Ok let's take them back."

Rowan gave the nod to Bear, and he headed back down the line, Robbie stood trying to work out what damage had been done through the clouds of swirling dust in the fire light. It was hard to really estimate the damage, but it was clear there were five very large holes in the wall, and from what he could make out, he could see several floors inside the walls, outlining what he thought were once rooms and supply stores. It felt good to know that her wall was not impregnable; it gave him hope that even though it had been built with magic, he now knew it could also be destroyed by hand.

At the tree Steph made sure everyone was present, Jaz and Bear watched the rear just in case they had anyone on their trail, as Steph opened up a long wide tunnel, the Specialist's quickly moved into it, and came out before the gates of the Stockade. As they walked out and the gate swung open, all the bowmen that lined the walls raised their longbows in the air, and shook them as they cheered as loud as they could. The Specialists all walked with pride through the gates, where other woodsmen patted their shoulders and welcomed them like heroes. Steph walked out last with Robbie.

"They need this Rob; they did good and struck the first blow. The talk tomorrow will be just what they need, hell it will be what everyone needs, I would imagine there will be a few sight seers out here tomorrow, looking at the lack of gates on the wall, the fact you can see through them, will make a massive difference to everyone here, you did good tonight."

He said little, but it did feel good to know they had at least shown Mason they would not go down without a fight. Rowan stood at the gates looking out across the valley, where the outline of the gateway was still clearly visible, silhouetted by the flames, he patted Robbie's shoulder, and he turned to look back across the valley. Both of them stood side by side as they took in the view, Rowan gave a happy sigh. "It felt just like reliving old times again tonight."

Robbie smiled. "Yeah it did a bit; it's good to make a statement that everyone can see." Rowan chuckled.

"That was one hell of an arrow; I understand now why she did not test it here, hell with all the wood we have here, she would have burnt the bloody place down." Robbie chuckled and lifted his hand to his face, just to check he still had eyebrows.

As Robbie sat in the darkness and waited for the attack on the wall, deep below the ground, in the cellar of the house at Robbie's Mere, Rune sat at her table with Tila and Sapphire. Rune looked at the book in Tila's hand. "Tell me of this book, you have read far more of it than I have."

Tila looked at the pages. "It journals everything of Ariel's visit to Avalon, and her life with Branna, it's pretty interesting, she really notes down every aspect of the Fae life, but also her relationship with Branna, and to be honest Rune she really loves Branna, and I would say Branna really loves her too."

Rune slid her hands across her table. "How does the book make you feel Tila?" Tila looked confused.

"I like it, I like her story, I suppose I feel I know Ariel a little better." Sapphire sat silently, but she thought Rune's question was odd.

"Why how she feels?" Rune smiled.

"Can you sense it?" Sapphire thought for a second.

"I sense something, but it is something I have never felt before, and it is a faint sort of background feeling, why what is it?" Rune swiped her hand across the table and images of Ariel appeared with Branna, Tila looked surprised.

"How did you do that? I have just read that part of the journal." Rune gave a small chuckle.

"Some books talk, all you need to listen is a table, the runes are charmed." Sapphire blinked and looked at the pictures.

"Charmed, in what way?"

"OH ON NINIAN'S TOES!" Tila looked almost as if she was about to explode, she held the book out at arm's length and looked at it as if she was fit to burst. "IT'S TALKING RUNES!" Sapphire frowned.

"It's what?" The excitement exploded out of Tila as she bounced on her seat, Rune could do nothing but giggle, as Tila exploded with an explanation and her somewhat geeky side of books showed right through her.

"Sapphire it's a talking book, I have heard so much about them, hell I read loads of scripts about them, but I have never ever ever held one." She took a deep breath. "They are a really special kind of charmed rune, they are strictly Fae of Earth only, you see what you do is you take your memories and go into a trance like state, and then as you think you write. The special runes are charmed so as to not just write your words, they actually take the memories from your head and hide them inside the writing. They are incredible and I have read loads of stuff on them, but I have never encountered any until now." She gasped another large breath. "They were invented by Enaria to allow you to actually preserve memories, so the owner can literally relive every detail of their lives in their head, and feel all the same feelings and stuff, they are some of the coolest ever scribe magic, but they are really hard to do, and it takes years or huge power to be able to do them. A queen can also place your book on a table and it will read the book for them and play it back in pictures and sound. It's like it is actually happening all over again, I am telling you Sapphire if you can, you really need to learn how to do them, I have tried but I have not done it yet." She flopped back on her seat with a massive happy smile still holding the book and looking with glee at its cover.

Sapphire just stared at Tila as she talked at high speed nodding her head as if she understood a word of what she was garbling about. Rune giggled.

"Tila likes the book, because it has pictures." Which was her best translation of everything Tila had just said, Sapphire just nodded.

"I can see that, but what does that mean, we can actually watch Ariel's life?" Tila nodded happily and Rune swept her hand across the table.

"It would take hours to watch everything, but earlier I placed the book on my table and let the table absorb its contents, it showed me this and I think it is important, which is why I lifted it up for you both to see." All the other images on the table faded apart from one which hung in the air, Rune sat back in her chair and relaxed. "Play."

The pictures began to move and Tila slid forward and leaned her face on the edge of the table with excitement, Sapphire sat back in her seat to watch.

All over Avalon the heavens opened, and the rain thundered down with force, Ariel tossed and turned in her bed, her mind filled with images that flashed with the pictures of a screeching bird.

Ariel sat up in her bed and shivered with the coldness flowing through her.

The air outside exploded and lightening streaked down hitting a tree close to the house. It flashed with white light and then split down its trunk as flames erupted. "BRANNA!"

Without thinking, she jumped out of bed and grabbed her dress. As she crossed the house, she fumbled awkwardly into it. She raced out of the door and into the pouring rain, and ran for the path that led up the side of the steep rock towards where Branna had gone.

Her heart pounded in her chest as the rain pelted into her eyes, and she gasped for breath, her legs running for all they were worth. It felt like the hardest fight of her life, as she forced her slender body forward against the pressure of the driving rain. Half blinded by the water and gasping for air, she staggered to the top of the path and onto the flat summit, trying her best in the total darkness; she shielded her eyes with her hand, to hold back the rain from her pale grey eyes. "BRANNA... BRANNA WHERE ARE YOU?" She screamed for all she was worth.

The lightening flashed high above her. For the briefest moment she thought she saw a slumped figure on the floor below her shelter. Ariel ran in the general direction hoping the lightening would guide her to the right place, it did, and she realised she had almost stepped on her. Ariel fell to her knees below the broken shelter at the side of Branna, as her ears exploded with the noise of the crack of thunder. She dragged the soaked limp body of Branna into her arms and held her tight as she wailed with fear, hoping she was not dead. Branna was ice cold, and she pulled her as close as she could to let her own warmth flow into her, and leaned forward to shield her face from the driving rain. The skies lit up again, but Ariel was too busy looking down at the pale face of the woman she loved, to see the huge figure of a black bird outlined in the clouds above her.

"Stop." The picture hovered above the table, and Tila and Sapphire saw the large outline of a bird in the sky. Sapphire gave a gasp and leaned forward.

"It's a raven." Rune gave a nod.

"Hold that thought and watch...Play."

Branna moved and gave a slight moan, and Ariel's tears exploded from her eyes with relief as she snuggled into her and held her close. All she could do for the moment was hold her tight and cradle her and protect her with her love, Branna's cold white hand came up to her face. "Ariel?"

Her voice sounded weak, and Ariel squeezed her as hard as she could and wept. "I am here my love, I have you, you are safe."

Ariel felt a ripple shudder through Branna, as if somewhere in the distance of Branna's mind a voice croaked in a vile tone, and her eyes snapped wide open. "Get rid of her, she needs to leave."

For a moment Branna felt dazed, but then her mind cleared and she twisted on the floor, and lifted herself up and was instantly snatched back into Ariel's embrace.

Branna slipped her arms around the weeping figure in the darkness. "Ariel it is not safe here, we need to leave." Ariel just hung on tight and wept. "We must go Ariel it is not safe for us here."

Branna struggled free and tried to stand, her legs felt weak and she wobbled, Ariel was up in a flash, and grabbed her and pulled her close. She pulled Branna's arm around her shoulder, and then taking her weight she lifted her slightly. "I thought I had lost you, never scare me like that again." Branna could feel the fear in Ariel's shaking body, and pulled her tighter.

"I am sorry, I never expected this."

Together in the driving rain they began to slowly make their way towards the path that would take them down the side of the rock. The lightening continued, and the thunder roared, as they staggered down the path towards their home.

As they approached the doorway Branna noticed the plaque, and suddenly she felt a huge wave of fear pass through her. Ariel staggered for a moment, and Branna tried to stop and not pass under the door, the fear coursed through her body, but she was just too weak, and the strength of Ariel had appeared to increase as she approached the door. Her body began to shake and spasm, but she could not prevent Ariel dragging her over the threshold and into the house.

"Stop." Rune looked at both of them. "What do you see or feel?" Sapphire shuddered.

"I know it might sound odd, but I felt fear." Rune pointed to the pictures where Branna held by Ariel were just about to cross the door threshold.

"What do you see?" Tila moved forward and stared at the picture.

"On the lords of all realms look at the star, it's glowing." Sapphire leaned in at the side of Tila, and there it was above the door, Enaria's Star was glowing faintly with a blueish coloured light. Rune looked happy.

"The star is the protection from evil, and it has reacted to one of them." Tila nodded.

"That was its purpose; it is why we have one on every house in Florae, it renders the evil powerless in that home. Bridget insisted every house had to have one, which is pretty much why it comes as standard on all new buildings." Rune felt satisfied and looked back at the table.

"Play." The pictures began to move again.

Ariel and Branna collapsed through the doorway, and fell sprawling onto the wooden floor, and they felt a wave of peace flow through them. Branna lay still for a moment feeling a little strength seeping into her body, she had not realised that she was gasping for air, and as she breathed in deeply, her head turned to see the soaked form of Ariel lay on her back at her side gasping for air. She watched as

Ariel lifted her left foot and kicked out at the door, and it swung at speed into the frame and banged closed. Ariel turned her head to see Branna watching, and she felt a huge wave of relief wash over her, she took a long breath in, and let her lungs fill with oxygen. "Please tell me you did not cause that Bran?"

The pictures faded and Rune looked at them both sat staring at her. "So tell me, what did you make of that, was it as enlightening for you as it was for me?" Both of them looked confused, Tila frowned and tried to figure it out.

"Well Branna was obviously weakened by whatever it was she was doing, and it is clear the star did something, because Branna appeared to recover a little as soon as she was inside the house. I am not sure about the bird though, although I think it is significant it was a Raven." Sapphire nodded and agreed, she too thought that. Rune sat back in her seat.

"It was a little more than significant, you see I have been through the Merle, I had a brief moment with Eve inside it before I received my final gifts, and as a result I see the Merle as it really is, and you two do not see it because it is hidden to you." She swept her hand across the table and then placed her palm flat on its cool surface and closed her eyes. "This is how I see it." A new picture rose from the table of the raven in the clouds as the lightning struck, Sapphire and Tila gasped as they saw what looked like black smoke surrounding the bird. Sapphire turned to Rune.

"Is that what the Merle looks like, a smoky mass?" Rune gave a nod.

"Yes, or at least that is how it appears through my eyes." Tila spotted the obvious.

"Hang up, why is the bird filled with the Merle, I thought it was Branna?" Rune smiled a huge smile.

"Exactly...I wondered when you would realise. At this point in time Branna was not in control of the Merle, which does explain how she could be close to Ariel and not detected. Luminaria was so busy looking for Branna, when what she should have been doing was looking for the bird."

Sapphire gasped. "And Morgan tied her life to a raven, what if..."

"It was the same Raven? Exactly Sapphire, we have been looking at this all wrong, we thought Branna had absorbed the Merle or had the Merle within her, which she may have I am not at the moment sure. I have been thinking since I first saw this earlier, what if the members of the Fae have just a tiny little part of the Merle within them, and it is that which attracts the Merle? I think it becomes a connecting point between the Fae member and the Merle?" Tila suddenly understood where Rune was going with this.

"And the Merle needs a means of connecting to the Fae in order to fully take control, it's the bird, the bird is the connector. Oh on Ninian's toes, I understand when you join with the bird, it gives the Merle access to the body of the Fae, in this case Branna, the raven allows the Merle to flow through it into Branna, we need to remove the raven to kill Morgan."

Rune smiled and relaxed in her chair. "There is a place somewhere that has a raven in it, and where ever it is we have to find it, and then we need to get that raven and kill it, and I think if we do, then Morgan's empire will topple as her life drains away, I have thought it for a while, but this confirms it, we need to find that bird." Sapphire gave a nod.

"It has to be in her family home in Sachsen, the problem is Rune it's been hidden by a very powerful veil, we could walk right up to it and not see it." She agreed.

"I have not figured that out yet, but I will."

CHAPTER TWENTY FIVE

CRINA

On this hill surrounded by woodland, next to the large stone rock with a flat top you see, is a cottage stood alone. Around it is a small garden wall of white stone, and a wooden gate of oak. Behind the wall is a garden filled with fruit trees, which protected the small cottage with its thatched roof, and a small plaque above the door that depicts a red star, set within a white circle.

The cottage was once home to two members of the Fae a very long time ago, one Fae Ofmoon, and one Fae of Earth. Both of them were young women, one short, slender with long brown hair and soft grey eyes, named Ariel, the other tall, stocky, with short rough tatty black hair, dark eyes, and a snow white complexion, and her name was Branna.

Together they lived here as lovers, and together they brought a curse to the realm of Avalon that has infected this site since. All are forbidden from entering this site by Rhiannon Queen of all Fae. To enter and live, will bring instant arrest, followed by sentence of death.

Administered by Luminaria, High Marshal of Fae.

Gwendolyn read the sign and smiled. "Seriously did they honestly think that would work?" She looked round in the darkness. "Why do I sense something is not right here, why am I drawn here?" The gate that barred the road to the cottage was locked with chains, chains that had rusted over the years. Gwendolyn could only smile as she walked round it through the gap, which was at least two persons wide at the side of it.

She walked slowly up the steep road, which was weed covered from lack of use, and she made her way in the blackness of the night, until the silhouette of the cottage, just visible through the thick trees came into view. Gwendolyn stopped and watched for a second, she sensed a presence, and as she stared into the darkness she saw movement. "Clever girl, only a queen would sense that little soul, your table has taught you much Sapphire."

Gwendolyn saw the small faint figure of Cal, as he stood flat against the gate peering through the slats, she moved even slower so as not to startle him, but she was aware he would sense her long before she was too close to him. She was right, when she was fifty yards away; he turned and looked at her, rather than startle him, she smiled and waved softly, Cal blinked, and she knew it was safe to continue.

Gwendolyn moved closer, crouching down to him as she came almost up beside him, she whispered very quietly. "Have you found what your mistress seeks?" His eyes blinked rapidly and she smiled.

"You clever boy...You must go to your mistress now and bring her to me, we have to tread lightly on this property." Cal blinked, and with a pop he was gone, Gwendolyn stayed low and peered through the slats of the gate.

The cottage was in darkness, apart from a very faint flicker of light in what looked like the back of the house, someone was inside, and it was pretty clear who. She watched and she waited, her mind fixed on what was inside.

"I must admit, that is clever, living in the one place no one would bother to look, your own mother's house. Clever indeed, it even fooled me for a while."

Rune sat at her table with Sapphire and Tila, as they looked at the frozen picture of the black raven in the clouds above the flat stone rock on which Branna had done her experiments, as they discussed their theories of how the Merle was passed through the conduit that was the raven, and the connection to Branna. Tila was convinced that considering Branna was Fae Ofmoon, she would have the power and ability of mind to control the flow of the Merle, which interested Sapphire and Rune a great deal. She sat with the book on her lap smiling as she spoke.

"Yeah, don't forget, Fae have great power of mind, we have the ability to control a lot of what we think and feel, which is why we are all natural negotiators. The gifts of fellowship and earth are remarkable gifts if you think about it, we really do have mind over matters." She stopped and thought for a second. "Which is why I find it odd; Rhiannon has allowed her thoughts to slip from her role of balance into judgement, it is quite extraordinary for any Fae member."

Rune noticed a little movement, and she leaned to one side to look past Tila and Sapphire and smiled. Noticing her sudden change of posture, Tila and Sapphire turned, Rune gave a little wave. "It is fine here you are safe, come on to your mistress."

Tila gave a squeak. "Oh wow you have a dream spirit...Oh he is so cute." Sapphire stood up and went to Cal who had come silently down the steps to Rune's table and now stepped into view, Sapphire went down on her knees feeling huge joy.

"Cal where have you been I have been so worried about you, are you alright, you are not hurt are you?" His little eyes blinked rapidly and she gave a sigh of relief. "That's good...Did you find anything?"

Cal again blinked his eyes, and Sapphire stood up and turned to the others. "He has found something; I have to go."

Tila moved to get up, but Sapphire's blue window appeared and she grabbed Cal's hand and walked right into it and the window closed, Tila turned back to Rune looking disappointed. "Are we not going?"

Rune winked and swept her hand across the table and images started to flow to its surface.

Sapphire stood in the front of the sign in the darkness and looked at it. "Such bullshit." She looked at Cal. "Where is she?"

There was a faint flow of a breeze across her face, and Sapphire saw what looked like a translucent mist, flow down the road towards her, it swept up in front of her and formed into the shape of Gwendolyn who winked and smiled.

"I hope that was less dramatic?" She laughed and turned and pointed up the path. "I cannot be fully sure, but someone is in the cottage and trying to hide their presence, I would say it is our girl considering the energy I get from the house. I must admit it's clever, no one would look there it's been shut down for years." Sapphire gave a nod as she looked up the track.

"She is tricky, we will have to be extra careful." Gwendolyn gave an agreeable nod.

"She can change form and leave if we are not quick enough, but if I am fast enough, I may be able to get a trace on her, she is after all half Fae of Earth, and I am her queen." Sapphire frowned.

"Can you do that dead?" Gwendolyn gave a giggle.

"I may not be fully solid, but my powers are intact, well at least up until Iona takes the crown and the throne." Sapphire nodded.

"Ok how are we going to do this?" Gwendolyn shrugged.

"Not sure yet, the house is old so it will be creaky, probably a bit like yours." She gave another giggle, and Sapphire shook her head.

"Well let's hope it's not as creepy." Gwendolyn gave a smile.

Ena sat on the bed with her back to the window, her small candle flickering as she ate her sparse meal of one apple and a slice of cheese. The door to the main room was open slightly, giving a limited view of the kitchen come living space. She was sleepy as she had been busy that day foraging outside the realm of Avalon, in the town of men forty miles from the border of the realm, and she had taken to walking instead of using her Fae skills. The town's folk thought she was an ordinary human who lived in the wild, they had no idea of her real name or identity, to them she was a healer named "Crina," who came to town to trade herbs and medicines.

She sat chewing, her eyes flickering from her sleepiness and was not quite as aware as normal, when just for an instant a faint pale blue flickered as her eyes closed and she jumped awake. There before her was the translucent figure of Gwendolyn. Startled, Ena jumped to her feet and turned quickly for the window, there was a flash of violet and a violet figure of Rune appeared, and with a flick of her wrist, a golden fiery coil erupted from her hand.

The glowing coil shot through the window pane and grabbed Ena by the wrist, it separated into two pieces and wrapped the other part round her other wrist, where both of them glowed violet and turned into bracelets of polished violet crystal, and Ena realising what was happening, fell to her knees and screamed out. "NOOOOOO!" Rune gave a satisfied smile as Sapphire entered the room.

"Got you at last."

Ena pushed her face into the floor, and wailed, both her wrists were bound together; Rune looked through the window at Sapphire and gave a nod. "Good work Saff, bring her to me at Loxley, do not fear I have bound her powers, she cannot escape you." Sapphire understood her and gave a nod.

"We will be there shortly Rune." Rune faded away, and Sapphire looked down at the sobbing figure.

"Why cry, we have no intentions of harming you, all we wanted to do was talk, no one was ever going to hurt you?" Ena shook her head and she wept.

"You do not understand, if I am found by either side I will be killed." Sapphire shook her head.

"Not on my watch." She leaned down and grabbed her shoulder. "Come on, we can protect you, no one will harm you with us." A blue window opened, and she lifted Ena from the floor. "You will be safer in Loxley than anywhere else."

Mark Richard Dale walked round the smouldering and burnt out remains of the camp, next to the massive area of collapsed wall, and screamed at the soldiers who were still dazed and confused after the sudden short lived attack. His temper was flaring as he lifted chunks of stone and hurled it at some of the soldiers. "TEN THOUSAND MEN, AND YOU CANNOT STOP A HANDFUL OF HEATHENS BLOWING THE HELL OUT OF EVERYTHING, WHAT ARE WE EVEN PAYING YOU FOR?"

The stone hit a man in the back and he wailed in pain, Dale kicked at the splintered wood on the floor from one of the burnt out carts, and it careered into the air, and the men in front of him ducked as they moved out of its way. Mason walked through the devastation with Dana towards Dale. Mason smiled as he saw him pick up and other piece of stone and throw it at a man.

"WHERE THE HELL WERE YOU, AREN'T YOU SUPPOSED TO BE GUARDING THIS PLACE?" Mason shook his head as he got closer, and Dale noticed him. His eyes were wild and his face red, as he looked at Mason, but Mason just shook his head.

"Mark I told you what they are like, come on old fellow, this is nothing, we have men and supplies arriving any minute, seriously don't take it so personally, we locked them out of their home, what did you think they would do?" Dale gave a long sigh and tried to recover some of his composure.

"I didn't think they would do this; I mean yes you said they were good at stealth, but how the hell did they get inside?" Mason laughed.

"It's what they do; trust me I have been asking myself that for a year." Dale shook his head.

"I am going to kill that bastard and hang him on his own wall, I mean it Mason, I will hang every last one of those woodland heathens up in the sun and let the birds eat them." Mason continued to chuckle as Dana walked towards Mark and gripped his arm.

"Mark darling, do not get yourself so worked up, it's almost our time, relax a little, come on join me in the dining room and have a drink, you will feel much better after, I promise. Mason is heading back to York tonight, so relax for a while, and let the men clean this place up, after all it's why they are here." Mark Richard Dale gave a long sigh and nodded.

"You are right Dana, yes a drink about now would be nice, I could certainly use one after dealing with these cretins." She gave a warm smile and slipped her arm in his.

"Mason we are having drinks are you joining us?"

He was looking around with a smile on his face, as he looked at the burning carts and burned out tents. "He has nerve, but I like that, oh what we could have done had William only have seen things my way, now that would have been a fight worth having." He turned to Dana and Mark. "I always have time for a good scotch, and then I really must be going." She smiled as she walked towards him.

"Good, we shall make it our first of many to toast the start of their imminent destruction."

Ena sat sobbing in Rune's living room with her head down, she looked worn out and tired, Tila stood watching over her, admiring the bracelets that bound Ena's power rendering her useless as a Fae. It was a pitiful sight to see, as Rune stood across the room looking at Isolde stood in the kitchen doorway, looking horrified to see a member of the Fae in such a poor state. Rune turned to her.

"Prepare a room for her, she will also need a good meal and some clean clothes, I wish to talk to her, and then run her a bath and let her wash." Isolde gave a nod.

"I will mistress."

Rune walked over to Ena and stood before her. "Look at me." Ena lifted her head and Rune could see the fear behind the tears in her pale blue eyes. "You have no fear here Ena, we have no intention of harming you, but we do need you to talk to us so that we fully understand what you have been doing." Ena shook her head.

"I am finished, when they find me, and they will here, they will kill me." Sapphire gave a shrug.

"That is all she will say, but she will not say who." Rune understood.

"She is afraid, I feel it, never the less if we are to defeat Le Fey, we need her." Just the mention of her name made Ena flinch. Rune bent over and gently took Ena by the arm.

"Come with me, I need to talk with you privately, no harm will come to you, and I will have food brought to you, you look like you have not eaten properly in days."

Ena stood up, and Rune took her slowly towards the steps that led down to her table of power in the basement, leaving Sapphire and Tila upstairs. Ena walked slowly down the steps still sobbing quietly until she reached the bottom step, and the lights blazed on revealing the Table of Runestone. For a moment she hesitated as she saw the image of her mother rise out of the table and hover in the air above it.

"What are you going to do with me?" Rune smiled as she guided her towards a seat.

"As I said simply talk, I want you to see this table; I know you are aware of such things and the power they hold. It is important you see that this is the most powerful table today, and also that you understand that this table is also what will protect you here." Rune looked at the chain round Ena's neck.

"That trinket you wear round your neck is a crude and outdated seeing table, did you make it or did your mother give it to you?" Ena sat down and lifted her hand to her neck.

"It is all I have left of her. She made it in our camp and then handed it me before they took her." Rune could see that she was starting to calm down a little, as she understood she was not going to be killed or harmed in any way. Ena looked round the room and at the large powerful table, and the image of her mother floating above it.

"Why are you being nice to me, after all I killed your heir, surely you will want revenge?" Rune shook her head.

"You failed to kill him, he lives, he is not good, but he is alive and recovering slowly." She looked shocked.

"He must die, she must not get him, if she does, she will rule for another thousand years, and all of us will die. You must believe me you have no idea of what the Berengar family can do." Rune understood but sat resolute.

"The new heir will survive, and she will die, mark my words." Ena shook her head.

"No...You are wrong, killing his line is the only way, there is no other way to kill her and her family, you do not understand these things, how can you be so stupid as to think you can defeat them?"

Rune gave a smile. "I will defeat them, because you are going to help me." Ena looked stunned.

"Are you insane? You have no idea how to even get into their territory." Rune sat back in her chair.

"No...But you do." Ena shook her head.

"You are wrong, I have tried, once you get out there is no going back, the raven knows all that pass the circle of darkness, and it is the raven who allows passage into or out of the realm, it will never allow anyone who threatens it inside."

"We will see then, won't we?"

Upstairs in the kitchen Sapphire sat with a drink in her hand, leaning on the table. Tila sat opposite eating a slice of bread with a chunk of cheese, she looked at Sapphire. "You know, considering you have not been raised on Florae, I am really impressed at your level of skills. You have done a lot for Rune, you are so much better than you think you are, I think you should be more confident."

She rested her cup on the table. "I feel like I am winging it most of the time, and I know so little of Florae, I feel under pressure when people talk of things I have never heard of." Tila gave a happy nod.

"We are all winging it Sapphire, none of us have encountered the things we do today or the events that we face. You know considering everything that's happening, I think you have set a high bar for the rest of us." Sapphire gave a slight frown.

"How so?" Tila shrugged.

"I live in a realm with nine islands filled with people, you know the central city is not the only place on the island with a large population, there is also West Bridge Town, it has ten times the people the central city has, and yet here we sit just you and me. We are the only two members of our race, joining in the fight and helping to fight for the freedom of every realm." Sapphire considered her point.

"Well, it's not just us, there is my mum, and our Jaz, and also Una, Treen, and Maddy, and they are all related to Gwendolyn as I am." Tila gave a sigh.

"But out of a million Fae, don't forget not all Fae of Earth are in Florae, there are still a lot scattered in all the realms?" Sapphire stared at her cup lost in thought.

"We fight to defend those who cannot defend themselves, to be honest it is the only thing in all of this that has ever made any sense to me." Tila smiled.

"It is a nice sentiment, who said it?"

"It was Robbie." She gave a slight smile. "The first time I ever heard him say it, I think was the first time in my life I felt a really powerful jolt in my stomach. It made so much sense to me, and I think in a way I was lost, unable to understand my life until that moment, after that it was all that mattered."

Tila sat listening to Sapphire's quiet words with a smile, and she fully understood her, she too had waited years and dreamed of being able to be the one to defend her people, and just as Sapphire explained, she too felt her stomach jolt, and she realised, that the two of them had so much more in common than she had ever guessed.

Downstairs, Rune looked at Ena, who had calmed a great deal. "Tell me why you left the circle of darkness?" Ena fidgeted in her seat.

"Mid Summer, something happened. After I lost my mother, I ran into the forest and ran to the camp of the travelling people I have lived with, as they had given my mother refuge when she had escaped. They had been trapped when the circle was made, and the leader of the group who was called Crina, she gave my mother and me protection. They were like my family, I had been raised with them along with the rest of the community, and the men fought with the guards of the Raven in the large forest to keep our place secret." Rune knew this part of the story from what Sapphire had told her of the Whispering Water.

"Did she tell you who your father was?" Ena shook her head.

"No...I found out after she was captured and I was a little older. Crina told me because I did not understand why they wanted my mother or me so much, I had no idea how they knew about me, they just did and they were relentless in searching for me. All of us were trapped as the circle would not let us out, many tried and failed, many also died trying when the guards found them trying to escape." Rune gave a nod.

"How did you escape?"

"I was twenty summers long when I became involved with Dorin, he was the grandson of Crina. Something happens at Mid Summer that weakens the circle, Dorin thought it was something to do with the brightness of the sun, for several years he would creep close to check and throw things at the edge to see if it went through. I accompanied him one year to see if there was another way, it was my first time with him that far away from camp and it was exciting. We sat in the grass out of sight and watched, and then suddenly there was a deafening scream that echoed all over the region." Rune gave a nod as it made some sense to her; Ena looked at her as if trying to get Rune to fully understand the situation.

"You have to understand that if you are on the outside, you see nothing, but if you are on the inside, it is sort of dark and overcast. As we sat in the grass and we heard the scream, the edge disappeared for a moment and bright sunlight streamed in. Dorin grabbed me, picked me up, and just ran like the wind with me in his arms, and we went through, and he did not stop running until he was out of sight hidden in the trees. I do not know what happened; I just know that we got out." Ena started to cry and tears filled up her eyes. "I tried to go back many years later to help my family after Dorin was killed, but I could not get back in."

Rune leaned forward and held her hands.

"I will get us in Ena, and I will find your family and save them...All of them, including your mother." Ena looked up and her tears stopped.

"My mother is dead." Rune shook her head.

"No Ena...She lives, we know this because her gifts were meant to pass to you in the moment of her passing, and they have not done so. Ena she must still be alive and a prisoner." Ena's eyes widened and she pushed back in her chair.

"Do not try to fool me Runestone Sapphire; there is no way she could have lived." Rune sat back in her seat.

"I do not lie Ena, you are of Fae decent, the granddaughter of Enaria, and if your mother had died, you would have her powers, and would easily have killed Morgan le Fey, and yet you have not...Your mother lives, you must trust me on this, and we have every intention of going into that circle of darkness to get her, and kill whatever lives in that awful place of darkness to defeat Mason and his vile mother." Rune sat and looked deeply into her as she saw the look of hope and desperation on Ena's face.

"The way I see it you have two choices, you either join us and help us, or you sit here and wait for us or Mason to return it's up to you. I want to trust you Ena, but at the moment I am not sure you will run the moment I take those bracelets off, until I know for sure those bracelets that bind your power will stay on. We have a room prepared for you here; you will be protected whilst you decide. No one will know who you are apart from a few individuals, so we will use a different name for now, so what do you want us to call you?"

Ena gave a long sigh. "I want to believe you too Runestone Sapphire and it appears for now I have little choice. When I visit the towns of men, I used the name of Dorin's grandmother, so call me that for now, call me Crina." Rune gave an agreeable nod.

"Ok Crina, for now we rest, we will talk more tomorrow, come I will show you to your room."

After a long talk with Sapphire and Tila, Rune made her way up to check the children before bed, Isolde was sat in a chair watching the children as Rune entered. Isolde looked up at her. "Is that her, the child of Ariel?" Rune gave a tired sigh.

"Does it bother you Isolde?" She shook her head.

"You misunderstand me Mistress, if it is you must protect her, she is a great asset to the line of our people, you must protect her from the Queen Ofmoon." Rune sat on the end of one of the small beds next to the cots.

"Why would Rhiannon want to harm her, she is Fae?"

"Yes she is, but she is also the line of Branna, a dark Fae, Rhiannon will not allow her to live because she will one day inherit the lines of Enaria and become very powerful. Mistress please you must trust me and protect her, for I have the ability to sense others, and there is no Merle in that woman."

Rune gave a nod. "I have felt that too, her power is whiter than any I have seen." Isolde agreed.

"Wait until you find her mother, only then you will see how white the spirit of a Fae can be." Rune smiled.

"You too believe Ariel is alive?" Isolde smiled.

"If she was not, that vile dark woman who's bastard of a child sits at our walls would be dead and him with her."

CHAPTER TWENTY SIX

THE FIRST BOOK OF BRANNA

It was still early when Rune came downstairs, she had slept little and had decided to get up rather than lie in bed over thinking everything. As she walked through the living room, she noticed Ena was sat outside with a drink at the top of the wooden steps to the house. Tila had the door of the kitchen wedged open and was watching her as she ate next to Crystal. "Morning Rune."

"Morning guys, I see our guest is up early?" Tila gave a nod as she slipped a piece of bacon in her mouth, and spoke as she chewed.

"Judging by the sound of pacing in her room last night, I don't think she slept much." Rune poured out a tea.

"I am not sure any of us have slept that much recently, I can understand why she would not, she is afraid she will be attacked anywhere not the house in Avalon." Rune turned and walked back out; she took her cup and sat on the step next to Ena outside the doors.

"How are you feeling today?" Ena looked straight ahead; her pale blue eyes fixed on the Mere.

"This place is beautiful; you are lucky to live here." She turned to Rune. "I am grateful, it may not show but I am, I would not have blamed you for attacking and killing me, after all I have done some terrible things to survive and get my revenge on that family." Rune patted her knee.

"There is no one in this war blameless for acts of violence in the quest for survival, William is alive, but it does bother me you want him dead." Ena lifted her cup.

"It is not personal; it's the only way to stop her." Rune shook her head.

"But why?"

"Roack is hungry, she will need to feed to continue her life cycle, and renew the bonds with the Berengar's. Only the soul and the blood of a king can do that.

Uther did not die by accident, that whole battle was planned by the family, it was a knight of Berengar that killed Uther, Branna was there and used his soul and the blood he spilt for the ceremony to give the bird more life. When Arthur died all hope was lost, until the rumour spread of a child, she has been hunting and killing them since, but she has always just missed out on the next child, and time is slowing. Roack must die, and all the other ravens, it is the only way to end the lines of evil."

"How do you know all this, and who is Roack?" Ena turned back and stared at the Mere.

"You still do not know enough Runestone Sapphire. My mother was a slave there when she refused to join with Branna, she learned a great deal in her time, it was the biggest mistake that family made, they had a relative of Enaria in their midst and knew nothing of the power that would come to her when the stars were revealed. To them she was just an ordinary scribe; they have no idea how stupid they were."

Ena took a swig of her drink and swallowed, her eyes never leaving the Mere. "If you truly want to understand, you have to understand the scribes of Fae. My mother wrote two books, the first book was only half written, the second she wrote in secret in Florae. The first book was the life of Branna, everything she knew about her up until their separation. She chronicled everything Branna told her, including her life on the moon realm with her family. She only had time to write half and left it in Avalon when she returned to Florae, only expecting to be there for a month. She was not aware of the charges against her, and so did not understand she would never return to live with Branna." Rune understood why Tila had only found the second volume.

"What happened to the first book is it still in Avalon?"

"She took it with her when she left, the night she understood where Branna was, she jumped to Avalon under a veil, got the book and then went to Branna. She told me it was always meant to be a gift, a record of her life and the good work she did for the Fae, but once she arrived and overcame the emotion of being reunited, she saw the truth of Branna, and so started to complete the book. That book is a true record of her life with Branna in the castle, to keep it secret she charmed it and hid it out of view. I know you understand the secret of the talking runes; I heard the second book talking through the wall last night, that Fae girl is a scribe is she not?" Rune nodded.

"She is. That is Tila."

"The second book will tell her little, it is the life of my mother and Branna, but there is nothing in those pages that will help you, for a scribe it is a book of historical wonder, but for you it is useless. When she escaped and discovered she could not leave, she hid the book in the camp, and when I was ten summers, she took the book and showed it to me, she then took everything the book contained, and using the blood magic of her line, she made the pendant round my neck. This book only speaks to me, for it communicates with my blood, it is useless to anyone else. Roack is the raven that the Merle first possessed when Branna caught it, and it connected with her mind but could not take over her. From her thoughts it understood that Branna in the old tongue meant raven, so it looked for a raven to inhabit to please Branna. The weird thing is Branna could not catch one, so my mother without realising caught Roack for her."

"So Roack is the raven Morgan is bound to, what happened to Branna?" Ena shook her head.

"My mother never finished the book, her last entry was the night before I was caught, and at that point Branna still lived." Rune was confused.

"So how do you know that the raven connected to Morgan is Roack?" Ena laughed.

"That part is easy, Roack is the part of the Merle that channels parts of itself from the outer Merle, and Branna devised a way to take parts and divided them into single entities to take over others. Roack is the source; if that bird dies every one of the others dies with it. It is easy to see that Morgan wants the heir to keep Roack alive, either because she now controls Roack, or she has another raven linked to Roack, or she understands that the part in her will die if Roack dies."

It made complete sense to Rune; suddenly everything fell into place for the first time in two years. "Ena you have to help me, together we must find a way and kill that bird, can I trust you not to run?"

Ena put her cup down and turned to Rune. She lifted her hands to her neck and undid the pendant, then slid it off her neck. Ena held her palm out containing the necklace. "Swear to me Runestone Sapphire that you will stand beside me and kill that bird, and then take this and hold it for me until we are done. I swear to you on this, the only living part of my mother I know to be alive, that I will stand beside you whatever we face to kill that bird, and if my mother is alive, free her and I will not leave until we have completed our task."

Rune smiled and placed her palm onto Ena's so the necklace was sandwiched between the two of them. "I will stand at your side Ena of Fae until we have destroyed the bird, and the empire of all that family falls, and your mother is free, you have my word it is a sacred bond."

Ena gave a small smile and nodded. She lifted her palm into Rune's, and Rune's fingers closed round the necklace and she took it out of Ena's hand. Ena stood up and held out her hands. "Take these off, I will need to match each of you blow for blow, for we may need a few, tell me of your people and how you use them."

Rune stood and touched each of the violet bracelets, they glowed golden, and disappeared and Ena gave a nod of thanks. Rune smiled and lifted her cup to her lips and took a drink of her tea. "Walk with me and let me show you my home."

Together they walked down the steps and through the gate, and onto the large meadow that led to the water's edge. Tila stood a little way back from the door and looked back at Crystal and Sapphire, she smiled. "I think if I understand the words of the one they call Big John right, he would say, look out girls, shit just got serious. Is that right?"

She gave a smile and Sapphire started to giggle as she looked at Crystal. "Letting Tila hang out with the Specialist's may not have been the wisest of decisions."

Mark Richard Dale lay in his bed deep in sleep, beside him the cover moved and a slender arm containing three solid gold bracelets slid across his back, and the sound of a woman gave a slight moan under the cover. He disturbed from his sleep and opened his eyes, yawned, and took a long deep breath. The figure beside him moved again, and the sheet slid back as Dana Knox moved up onto the back of his shoulder and kissed it with a happy moan. He turned and rolled over, and she slipped her head on top of his chest and looked at him with a smile.

"Don't get up yet, he is away all day." She stretched and kissed him slowly. He wrapped his large arms around her soft white skin, and she gave a naughty giggle and slid the cover back up.

High above them on the top of the wall the look outs spotted the first of the long convoy. Down below on the soot stained ground soldiers ran around as they prepared for the arrival of another large force from the south. The men high on the walls peered out at what looked like a never ending line of black vested soldiers, carts, and cannons. This had been the moment that Mason had waited for, after twelve days of marching his army was finally arriving and it was huge.

Melanie sat on the floor with her back to the wooden wall, with her eyes closed. High above her in the sky the hawk hovered watching the view. Melanie stretched out her hand and gripped the pant leg of David Williams. "Davie, I think you need to send for Robbie and Rowan, they have arrived."

He looked down at her, sat with her eyes firmly closed. "Are you sure?"

"Davie I can see them, and there are thousands of them stretching back for miles." Henry gave a snort

"Miles you say...I never realised there were that many idiots in this bloody land." David Williams looked down at the floor below the high platform on the wall.

"SLATER!!" The soldier looked up from his post.

"Yes sir."

"Get your ass up to the Village Hall and tell them 'the grass is flattening' and we need Lord Loxley and his General here ASAP." The soldier looked a little oddly at David Williams.

"Did you say the grass is flat sir?"

Henry leaned over the edge. "YES, HE BLOODY WELL DID. NOW GET YOUR ASS UP THERE AND TELL THEM."

Slater gave a jump and yelled. "Aye Sarg." He turned and ran as fast as he could, up between the barrack house and the newly built hotel, in the direction of the village hall. Henry turned to see the soldiers looking at him and pointed out across the wall.

"GET THOSE BLOODY EYES THAT WAY. HE IS STILL OVER THERE AND NOT IN HERE YET!" All the troops snapped back round to look out across the valley, in the direction of the giant wall on the horizon, where they now understood a large force was assembling.

Ena looked out across the calm water of the Mere. "I have always loved water, I lived on it once."

Rune understood. "I heard you lived with the boat people?" Ena looked at her.

"Yes I did, I am surprised you know that. When Dorin and I escaped, we crossed the lands of the Sachsen, and made it to the coast; we came across on a large ship to this land where Dorin had family who worked the boats. We got a boat and lived on it; I was so in love with him, I could never love another that way. We spent years travelling up and down taking goods from one place to the next. We married you know?" Rune gave her a smile.

"I heard that too, and I also heard you had a daughter?" She nodded.

"Yes, I lost her too; his men came and killed everyone, no one survived." She shook her head and Rune saw the tears fall to the grass.

"I never should have left, she wanted to go with me but I said no she would be safer with Dorin. I should have died with them; it would have been a blessing." She looked up with her tears running down her face. "There is no greater pain than the death of your child, she was just twelve summers, she had so much to live for, but he came and he killed them. When I returned there was nothing, just burned sunken boats and all my friends and family dead." Rune stepped forward and embraced her.

"Not all is as you think; she was named Ursula was she not?" Ena gave a sniffle and lifted her head.

"How would you know that?"

Rune took a deep breath. Her bright blue eyes locked into Ena's. "She too is alive Ena, but I am not sure you will like what I tell you." Ena stepped back.

"Why are you playing games with me, you swore an oath Runestone?" Rune looked her straight in the eyes.

"Ursula escaped and went looking for you. We think she got lost in the town and she ran into Morgan."

"NO!"

"Morgan did not kill her, she enslaved her Ena, Ursula translates the works of Morgan from the old language to the modern, I have seen her and met her, although at the time I was not aware of whom she was, but I swear this is no game, she is alive and currently in the realm ruled by Morgan." Ena shook her head.

"No daughter of mine would work for that vile woman." Rune gave a sigh.

"Ena, I think she saw her father die, she was afraid and she ran in hope of finding you, hate the idea as much as you want, but the facts remain that she was too young to understand who Morgan was, and as a result Morgan took her in and gave her safety, I can show you on my table, as you know a table of power does not lie." Ena shook her head and walked backwards.

"How could she, she was meant to be the child of light not darkness?"

"I do not know Ena, I have told you all I know, and I do plan to recover her when Morgan is dead, my grandmother is in that realm and she is watching out for her."

Ena stared at Rune with horror in her wide eyes. "I know you do not lie, but I cannot accept a daughter of mine would do such a vile task."

Rune walked slowly towards her. "She was twelve, and Morgan is very powerful, Ena think of what Morgan has done to the Fae. Think of her monsters the Houlen, or those vile dark creatures the Darkmares, she created those from members of the Fae. Your daughter is not one of them, she is intact, and yes she will be freed and you will have her back, Ursula, You and Ariel are bound together as the line of Enaria, she must have those gifts within her, she must be able to resist the darkness, trust in your blood, and with hope she will return to you and all that has been done to her can be taken out of her and she can be saved."

Ena shook her head. "I am not convinced Runestone, I have seen what they can do, and if my child has been turned, even you with all your powers could not turn her back." Rune looked at her with a serious expression.

"Do not give up on her Ena, let me try, let me save her and return her to you and your mother."

"You can try, but honestly, there are few who could come back from that level of darkness."

"Then help me find a way, and together we shall bring her back into the light where she belongs."

"You ask much Runestone, none of this is easy, you still have no idea of what you are up against. That castle is not easily won over, it sits on a rock in the centre of a huge wide crater, thousands of feet above the valley floor, there is one bridge from the land to the gate, and it is heavily defended. This will be no day trip; it will take skills and power that challenge every one of us. Below that castle cut into the rock is a labyrinth of caves, and at the centre there is a darkness that will even challenge your light."

Rune took her hand in hers. "We have an army approaching the walls that surround us, beyond that is a wall of stone of her device, and beyond that is a land that yearns to be free. Those of us within these four wooden walls are all that can stop her vile family from turning this land as dark as hers, it is our task to stop them and stop them we will. My only question is, will you honour your vow, and stand beside me, rise or fall, Ena of the Fae, and will you stay true to your family and fight for the light?"

Ena took a deep breath but smiled. "I have dedicated my whole life to destroying that vile and corrupt family, and I have no intentions of stopping now. Rise or fall Runestone Sapphire, I will not leave your side." Rune gave a nod.

"Then we shall do this, come, we have a lot of planning to do, I shall call those who will lend us their powers in this task."

Across the plains of Derbyshire, on the outskirts of Dove Dale, Peter Darwin ran as fast as he could into camp and skidded to a halt gasping for air. "Lenny where the hell is the Commander?" Lenny pointed towards the tents at the side of the river below the caves. "Cheers mate!"

He turned and ran for all his life, skipping across the boulders sticking out from the fast running water of the river to the other side. Gasping and hardly able to breathe, he ran the last twenty yards towards the group of officers consulting the maps. He came up at speed and slid to a halt on the damp grass. "....Sir....Sir... Message from...The observation posts...They are here Sir...Thousands of the buggers..." Panting he held up a note neatly folded and sealed with a wax stamp. Darwin looked round the group of officers as Commander Millington opened the message to read. Darwin shook his head as he breathed in new air. "Thousands of the buggers...Carts.... Cannons... the whole frigging shebang there is, and it goes back for miles... all of em heading for Bakewell"

Commander Millington read the note quickly and passed it to his second. "Get this to Williams as fast as you can, use the radio thing, send a pigeon also just to be sure, and use the strongest, as they will need to see this as soon as possible." His second gave a nod, took the message and hurried as fast as he could over to the Radio/Pigeon station. Darwin sat on the grass recovering, as the sweat ran down his face, he fanned himself with his hand.

"I am not used to running this much, I think I am more suited to standing still and bashing stuff."

CHAPTER TWENTY SEVEN

SEPARATION

Martin stopped and looked back behind him, as the tall shape of the cathedral bell tower rose up from in amongst the thick dense woodland in the distance. "We have made good time." The Sage was stood on the crumbled wall of whatever building this had once been, and was looking out over the vast canopy across what he thought was the start of the estuary that marked the River Thames.

"If I am right, we are not far from Graves End, although the speed this woodland has spread, I really do not recognise any landmarks at all. If we are where I think, we will cross soon into the desolate areas, we should find stragglers there, but I doubt any communities, this close to London I would think few have remained."

"We have grown since leaving, we must have at least a thousand now, I say keep moving and see how many join as we move."

Since the moment the group of charcoal workers had decided to join with the Sage, Dutch had sent out five riders on the only horses they had, to spread the word that they were moving to London and taking the fight to Mason. The Sage had not been over confident they would gather many more, but as they worked their way to Canterbury, small isolated groups appeared and joined the march.

Whilst they stopped at the old cathedral and collected as many bags of seed as they could for the time of year, more and more appeared and asked to join, and in the last few hours the group had more than doubled as they marched through the woodlands in the direction of London.

The Green Lord had been true to his word, his green oasis around the Cathedral had indeed spread, and buildings and walls had been smashed down and crushed, as the green world had expanded at ten times the normal growing rate. The Sage was starting to wonder if the woodland was growing at high speed ahead, to simply give him the cover he needed to get his group to the central city.

Any old outposts they found they looted for spare weapons and equipment, and the rag tag group now sported all kinds of weapons from swords to spades and pitchforks. On board the only spare cart they had, two carpenters worked on long branches of rowan, oak and yew, as they carved new long bows which they strapped to the sides of the carts on racks to dry properly in the sun and breeze. Children sat on some of the carts up front with their parents, fitting flights and points to the long wooden prepared lengths of willows for arrows. It had become one long moving caravan of preparation to help join the fight for freedom.

Robbie stood on the rampart of the wall with Rowan at his side and looked down his telescope. David Williams handed his binoculars to Rowan. Robbie watched through the gap created by blowing the gates off the wall in the distance. "It is not easy seeing much is it? I find it amusing they have placed carts in the gap to replace the gates, do they not remember our lighting strikes and what we do to carts?" Rowan gave a chuckle as he adjusted his view.

"There is a lot of dust and movement, but this far out it is hard to say how many." David leaned on the wooden ridge bar looking out over the wall.

"Mel was pretty certain it was thousands, she had a birds eye view, and said it stretched back miles, what do you think Robbie, will they come at us soon?"

Robbie lowered his scope. "That is the question we all want answering. I would say watch the walls, if they fill up with thousands of men along the top battlements, we will know the time is soon, if he keeps them all in camp, then I would say that will give us a little more time, as he will be getting ready for the final stage. What is the date today?" David frowned.

"What you don't know?" Rowan smiled.

"It is August 12th, why is that relevant?" Robbie smiled.

"An August attack it is then, we will fight in the summer, it should be hot and bloody." Henry gave a smile.

"I was hoping for something a little more specific." Robbie shrugged.

"It could be tomorrow or in a week, all I know is this August we will finally fight for our freedom." David Williams gave a sigh and nodded.

"We are as ready are we are ever going to be." Robbie patted his shoulder.

"Keep them alert Davie, he really could come anytime now, be it day or night."

"Fear not we are on it."

Rowan and Robbie climbed down the ladder to the dusty floor, and walked towards the barrack house. Rowan looked at Robbie and he noticed. "What?"

"You appear pretty relaxed about all this." Robbie shrugged.

"How else should I be? I have been preparing for this for well over a year, to be honest by September we will either be dead or building a new world." He considered the point.

"So this will not last a month?" Robbie looked out across the training field where yet more practice was ongoing.

"If we hold out it could last months, we are certainly prepared for at least a siege of a year, or it will go fast and furious with Mason throwing everything he has at us at once, and by the end of the month only one of us will live. Rowan this is the one time where we know what will happen to a degree, but sadly the outcome could go either way." Rowan curled his lip and thought for a moment.

"Considering that point, I suppose you are right, we just defend against whatever comes at us and hope we whittle it down enough to finally wear him down. How is Rune doing with the Fae woman?"

"I am not sure, she said last night she wanted to convince this Ena to join us and help us. She certainly has knowledge we need, and if Rune can convince her, we can look at that as another part of this fight, killing whatever secrets Morgan has will greatly weaken Mason. I just hope Rune has what it takes to get wherever this place is, and we can take it down before Mason strikes. Time most certainly is not on our side."

"We...Does that mean we will be leaving here to fight elsewhere?" Robbie shook his head.

"I am not leaving Loxley at this vital moment, Rune thinks she should deal with Morgan's side, and I concentrate on Mason." Rowan gave a long breath.

"Good, for a moment the thought of leaving all these without you worried me, I will sit out Morgan too, she is all spells and voodoo and stuff, I need a sword and bow to make my mark, and that will be better served here." Robbie patted his shoulder.

"Good to hear it, I offered her Fox and Blades, they are better at close quarters fighting, and if Rune gets into trouble those two work well together, I told her to take Jaz as well, that guy is like a building falling on you when it comes to brute force, so again if they need muscle he has the power, as well as his ghost talking stuff, somehow I wondered if talking to the dead would be more in Rune's field than ours."

"Who else will you send?" Robbie shook his head.

"Rune will choose based on ability, I think she will need more specific members of the Specialist's based on their gifts, the rest will stay here and help defend." Rowan gave a nod as he looked to the Village Hall doors.

"I hope she leaves Jett, Jade will stay with me, at the moment with the thoughts of the baby and everything, she will not leave my side, Jett will keep her stable, and Rafe is always handy. " Robbie smirked.

"The thought of Jett keeping anyone stable boggles the mind." He chuckled. "We will be keeping Steph here too, she was involved in the planning with Scarlet, and she can help move troops fast." Rowan looked round the training field.

"Actually, Robbie where is she, I have not seen her for two days?" Robbie smiled.

"She is in Scotland today, she met with Ian in Carlisle yesterday, and we will have forces on hand should we need them. Treen will work form the hall in contact with all the family, and she will pass orders quicker and faster by thought than we can. Steph will be ready to grab troops if we need them from any of our other forces across the nation." Rowan felt a little relieved.

"We might use every free fighter in this country before the end if Mel is right about his numbers." Robbie patted his shoulder as he pulled open the door to the hall.

"We might, but don't let numbers scare you, think about this, how many of them are really interested in this fight. We are fighting for our lives and our freedom; they only fight out of fear of what Mason will do to them. If we can make it look like we have the edge, how long will their will to fight last?" They entered the hall and the hum of talk and movement rose to a deafening pitch, as all around the large hall people focused on their duties and the planning and executing of a defence of Loxley.

Rune sat upstairs in the loft with Sapphire, Ena, Tila and Crystal. "Una has powers of great protection; we will need her." Ena understood and agreed, the others all gave a nod to Rune, and she looked at her pad.

"Robbie has given me Blades, Fox and Jaz, they are good in a fight, and I have asked to take Jay, she has spent a lot of time with Rigger and is talented with explosives, she is also an ace with an arrow." No objections were raised so Rune continued. "I also have considered Maddy, her fire arrows could be very useful if we encounter a large force or anything dead, I know you can freeze things Crystal, but in the past fire and ice have always been a huge advantage." Sapphire gave a frown.

"Is Robbie Ok with that, she is pretty much an all round player, he would have good use of Maddy here, as we saw the other night?"

"I am coming too." Rune turned to see Rayne standing at the top of the stairs. He stepped up and walked down the room. "My mother has shirked her responsibility, and so I feel one member of the family should take a stand to undo the damage, argue all you like Rune, in this matter you will lose, I am going." Rune gave a smile.

"I do not disagree with you, it appears I cannot prevent people walking into my private meeting in my own home, but if you want to be a part of this, I can use you, you have Fae Ofmoon powers, I am sure your knowledge and skills will be more than helpful." Rayne gave a nod.

"Good, I am glad that is sorted." Ena looked up at him.

"Who are you, you look familiar but I cannot place your name?" He held out his hand.

"I am Rayne Ofmoon, son of Rhiannon." Her eyes widened as she took his hand.

"You fought with her?" He smiled and lifted his long golden hair to reveal the red angry sore on his side temple.

"Sadly, I lost."

Rune closed her pad. "So, we are agreed, then get prepared, we will leave tomorrow morning."

Ester leaned over the broken wall and picked a few wild raspberries off the leafy canes in front. She leaned back and handed a few to Ben, and he gave a big smile as he greedily ate them. Dutch watched at the side of the Sage. "When you said an outpost, I expected something bigger." The Sage shook his head.

"No this is here for one reason only, which is why it is kept low profile." Dutch was curious.

"What is that then?" Martin smiled.

"Believe it or not that tiny encampment has a lower floor, and below that are the maintenance tunnels that lead under the river. Basically, it's the fastest route we know to the other side." The Sage added.

"Don't forget it also stores a lot of extra weapons. That Dutch is our equipment store, we should find weapons and food as well as a quick way across, it is the doorway to the secure parts of London." He was impressed.

"So how do we do this?" The Sage gave a smile.

"To begin with, we use hail."

Two hours later, the guards did their regular change, which as always was the same drill, performed for the same sergeant, in the same manner, as every day for the last ten years. Those coming off duty dragged their feet as they turned and walked slowly towards the gates of the compound looking forward to a good meal. The compound was not huge, it comprised of a yard for unloading, and a small two story office block, built out of red bricks. It had been used in the past as a service station and inspection point for the water authority, and was sometimes used by the rail authority for access to the further ends of the underground rail.

Below ground was a much bigger complex that had several large store rooms, which had once held spare parts and inspection equipment, and also led down to the tunnel entrance that dropped below the river. The soldiers took off their hats and loosened their tunics, as they trudged toward the gate; they were bored, uninspired and sick to death of their sergeant.

Ben was a little ways off behind an old factory wall that at some point had partially collapsed; he lifted his bow and fitted his arrow. Somewhere to the side came the low whistle that told him it was time, he turned and looked at the treble rows of men and women, some of which had never fired an arrow in their lives. He spoke quietly, even though at his normal volume, the chances were that the guards would not have heard him he was so far off.

"OK you load the arrow...Lift it up and lean back...Pull the string back like this." He cast his eyes sideways to make sure they all had it right. "And...let go and fire." His bow gave a twang, and the arrow shot high into the air, the others followed and suddenly the sky filled with long deadly arrows all heading skyward. For a moment they hovered, and then they tilted, and rained out of the sky.

As they trudged towards the gates, no one was aware of what was to come. Silently the hail started as in the distance another mass of arrows headed upwards. The first scream came as one of the guards going off duty took a direct hit to the shoulder, before anyone truly understood what was happening, the rest of them felt pain, and saw arrows collide and stick in the floor all around them.

What had been a dull and dreary uneventful day became an instant nightmare. Soldiers fell to their knees in pain, and within seconds screamed out in agony again, as more arrows rained down on them. Some of those who had minor wounds tried to make a dash for the gates, only to find themselves impaled by the next batch of arrows. All around men were screaming and crying out, and they rolled on the floor in agony.

From behind the scrub and trees, on the other side of the clearing, a group of hooded and cloaked men appeared, and took aim and fired at those still standing. The men at the gates grabbed them and tried to hurriedly close them, but the Sage and Martin took aim and hit them, sending them cascading back onto the floor behind the swinging gates.

Dutch led the charge, closely followed by Ester and Taylor, and within seconds they had passed the wounded and dead, and were in the compound giving cover as more hooded men appeared from the trees, and rushed across the open space. The soldiers had no time to react or even comprehend what was happening, before the yard was filled with hooded men, and their compound was no longer under their control.

Most of the soldiers dropped their weapons, and put their hands up and screamed out for compassion. The Sage walked in through the gates with a smile, to see the joy on the faces of all the men, it was their first test and a very successful one. The morale of the rag tag group was at its highest since leaving the charcoal fields, and it was good to see.

Martin winked at Ben as he led his group into the yard. "Nice one Ben, your guys did grand." Ben gave a beaming smile, he was young and small, but today he was a leader of men, and it felt wonderful.

The Sage wasted no time, and within minutes he was below ground with a large hammer smashing the locks off the steel cupboards, as men waited in line to help distribute the new weapons. Swords, knives, and crossbows, were a plenty, and they were very well received, as hunters, farmers, labourers, and fishermen armed themselves to become warriors for the cause of the hooded man.

Just over an hour later as the sun lowered in the sky, the yard was full of the new fighting force of the Sage. Fires were lit and meals were cooked from the well stocked stores of food. Back packs and blankets were used to pack everything, the tunnel meant losing the carts, and Dutch organised the details for carrying everything they had under the river into the new territory of Mason's London.

Back in Loxley in the orchard of Lox Farm, Rayne walked with Gwynne, and she held his hand tight as she gave a sigh. "The decision is made and there is nothing I can say." She turned to face him and slipped her arms round him, he pulled her closer and wrapped his powerful arms around her, and held her as close as he could, she looked up from his chest.

"We have been parted too many times, I hate it when you are off far away, I wish I could come with you."

"Gwynne, it will be dangerous, you are better off here."

"Rayne they are right outside the gates waiting to attack, it will be dangerous here too." He gave a sigh.

"I have to do this, she will not, and someone has to." She nuzzled into him.

"But why you? She should climb down off her high horse and deal with this herself, Rayne this is not your task, even Amethyst agrees with me, she is your queen why do you not listen to her?" He gave a chuckle.

"Never in my life did I think you would tell me to take orders from my own daughter." She looked up and smirked.

"If I thought it would convince you and you would do it, I would demand it." He leaned down and kissed her.

"Look, I will be fine, I am going to be with Chris, and I also want to keep her safe, we will both watch each other's backs." She gave a stifled grunt and rolled her eyes.

"I know...I know, I am a wife and a mother, I worry Rayne, I worry about all of us, we have no idea tonight if we even have a future, and you are off again leaving me behind. Give me this at least." He had to concede; he pulled her close and held her tight.

"I am coming back, I have never lied to you, so believe me now, I am coming back and we shall live the life we were promised years ago, one way or the other, I will return to you, I love you."

CHAPTER TWENTY EIGHT

SACHSEN TERRITORY

The following morning was busy; Rune was up early preparing and going through everything with Isolde and Filomena for the children. Once that was complete, she packed her kit in her bag, checked her bow and filled two slings with arrows. By the time she had slid into her green pants, boots, and top, grabbed her cloak, ate a hurried breakfast, and gathered everything together in the living room, Tila and Crystal were up and busy, Ena was sat out on the deck in the sun meditating, and Jay and Maddy had arrived.

Steph arrived shortly after with a few quiet words alone. Rune walked with her in the meadow, close to the mere as she spoke. "I am not as comfortable with this as you think, please Rune, I won't be there but I will stay in touch, just be careful, from the little we know she is one of a family, so if there are more like her, then keep on your toes, and make sure all the others are alert." Rune understood.

"I will be fine Mum honest, you know I do have some strong gifts from the family, I am not completely defenceless. Watch the children for me?"

"As if you have to ask. Your dad sends his love, so does Jade, but she is sulking as she wants to go but Rowan won't let her." Rune shook her head.

"No Mum, this is not the place for a pregnant woman, I have no idea what forces are there, I just think they would not be good for an unborn child, I want her safe...well as safe as possible, and at Rowan's side that is the best place for her now, he will fight to the death to protect her." Steph looked rattled.

"I hope it does not come to that." Rune turned to see Blades and Fox had arrived with Jaz, Una, and Rayne, and were walking together down the track towards the clearing.

"We better get back up there Mum, all we need is Sapphire and the group is assembled." Steph gave a nod and then pulled her into her arms.

"I love you Runestone, please be careful." Rune held her Mum for a little longer than normal, and squeezed her hard.

"I love you too Mum." She released her and smiled, and Rune could feel the fear inside her mother, but said nothing. Together they turned and began to walk back.

Sapphire grabbed her bag, shouldered her bow, and lifted her arrows off the bed post; she turned and jumped out of her skin. "Will you please stop doing that?" Gwendolyn smiled.

"I am coming with you." Sapphire looked at her with a blank expression. "How?"

"I am dead remember, I can go where I like." Sapphire thought about it.

"Ok come on then." Gwendolyn stared at her.

"What I can come...Just ok, come on then, no objections about being seen, or frightening others, just OK?" Sapphire shrugged.

"You want to come fine, you're a dead queen, you are big enough to make your own decisions, plus a ghost might be useful."

"That was going to be my argument, because I honestly thought you would object." Sapphire shook her head.

"Nope, we can use all the powers we can get." Gwendolyn looked disappointed.

"Oh... I'll meet you there then, I will know when you arrive." Sapphire gave a nod.

"See you there then." She turned walked out of the door, locked it, and then opened her window and jumped through it. Gwendolyn stood in her kitchen looking puzzled.

"I am not sure I like this new found confidence she has." There was a pop, and the house was empty.

Everyone gathered on the grass outside the gate of Rune's house, she had a rough idea of where she was going from looking at the map with Ena, so she focused on the spot and opened her window. Jaz and Fox were first through closely followed by Blades and then the rest. Rune came last and the window closed behind her. Ena appeared very interested in her window, and smiled as it snapped shut.

The terrain was rocky, high up, and thickly wooded, the change in air was noticeable as it felt cleaner than anything they had ever breathed, it was a little cooler than Loxley too. From what little Rune had read on the place, the highest areas were filled with rocky outcrops and high drop offs, below in the lower lands there were deep forests, and valleys with an abundance of streams and rivers. Where they stood the rock was jagged and fissured, and was a pale grey coloured granite like rock. The trees were mixed with birch and oak, interwoven with pine and spruce, and it was hard to really understand where they were, as the trees obscured the view of everything.

The group spread in a wide circle watching every angle to ensure they were alone and safe. Ena had been given a pair of Rune's pants, something she was not used to wearing, new boots, and a top with a long waistcoat like jacket. Around her waist she had a small bag attached to a thick belt, with a dagger and sheath, and across her back she had crossed quivers filled with white tipped arrows, in her hand she carried her bow. She stood still and turned slowly as she sniffed the air and sensed her surrounding, everyone waited until she looked behind her. "It is that way."

Rune watched interested, and trying to understand how Ena sensed her way, she gave a nod to the rest and they fell into a double line, with Rayne and Jaz taking first watch on the rear. Rune walked at the side of Ena, who filled her in.

"I cannot explain it, but once you have been in there you never forget the way it feels, it is a strong feeling, and the closer you get the harsher it becomes, and it can be overbearing. We should be fine here, we have a long walk ahead of us, as we get close, we will encounter guards from the Raven army, they patrol a wide circle on the outside and the inside, it is better to dodge them if we want to get in unnoticed." Rune agreed.

"Surprise is going to be our strongest weapon." She looked back at the others walking behind and watching all around, she had never seen them as alert as they were at that moment. Ena had filled all of them in on the land and what it contained, and it was clear they were taking her seriously. The one thing that had got all of them on edge was when Ena described the royal guards. She told them that they were controlled by the Merle, and if you killed them with a blade, a smoke like apparition would flow out of them and try to take over their bodies and souls. It had completely creeped out a few of them, especially Tila who had made it clear, that she would not be killing any royal guards near her new friends.

Sapphire got the shivers as she understood that what Jade had called Smoggets in Dunnottar, was actually parts of the Merle looking to eat their souls, and inhabit their bodies. Just thinking about it gave her goose bumps, as the memories of her smoky self came back into her thoughts. Ena assured them that light was their biggest fear, and that they should defend at first with light, something Una was very accomplished at. Maddy appeared completely unmoved by it, she had eaten dark things all her life, and felt confident she would have no problems with them.

The land was steep, and after an hour, all of them were slowing, as they wove through the dense trees towards the summit. Jay, who had an extra bag more than the others, was red in the face and sweating; she wiped her face with a cloth and tucked it in her pocket. She looked at Fox who was as red. "This is one hell of a hill." He nodded rather than speak in the thin air, and took in a gasp of oxygen and attempted a response.

"Let's hope we take a break soon." Jay gave a nod back; the backs of her calves were aching. Being home in Loxley on light duties had taken its toll. Una was over ten times their age, and walked along with her long pole, enjoying the journey with hardly a gasp to her breathing.

Ena slowed and held out her arm to Rune. "We are not far now, rest a moment, we could meet guards." Rune signalled back and the group separated to take watches, and crouched down and relaxed. Jay sat with her back to a tree and rubbed the backs of her legs. Like Una, Tila appeared unaffected, and stood looking round whilst eating a slice of cake she had taken from her bag.

Rune looked ahead and could see the trees were thinning out, and grass had grown with ferns and smaller trees. Ena pointed through a gap in the trees. "That is the start of the outer circle, there will be patrols in that clearing. You will not see the edge of the circle, but you will feel it long before you touch it." Rune understood and looked back to Blades just behind her with Tila; they both gave a nod of understanding having heard Ena.

Sapphire stood with her back to a tall pine tree and watched the land as it fell steeply in a tree lined bank. She blinked and a very pale outline of Gwendolyn appeared in front of her and winked. "Look down."

She frowned, and then looked at her boots, and Cal popped into view with another dream spirit. She smiled and Cal blinked. Understanding Sapphire looked back at Gwendolyn. Her voice was low. "What?"

"What is the greatest quality of a dream spirit?" She did not at first understand, and then realised and gave a big smile.

"Thank you." Gwendolyn smiled and faded away; Sapphire looked at Cal with his friend. "Come with me."

Rune and Ena crouched down working out their approach to get to the edge of the circle unnoticed, Sapphire came up beside them. "I was thinking, I have Cal, and he has a friend, I think she is called Leaf, Rune they are dream spirits, they can enter any realm undetected, they can pop us all in one at a time, well in pairs at least." Rune gave a big smile.

"Of course, I never even thought of that." Ena agreed and Sapphire brought the two spirits up to Ena and Rune. Sapphire told Cal and Leaf what she needed, both of them blinked their eyes and Sapphire smiled.

"Ena tell them where you want to land, and they will take you and Rune, and then come back for the rest of you." Blades interjected.

"Wait a moment, you guys are needed, Ena I will go with you and Fox can go with you Rune, that way the first ones in are protected." Ena looked at Rune.

"Makes better sense, although I am not completely defenceless." Blades smiled and pulled one of her long swords out, Ena smiled. "Ok I am convinced, let's go."

Cal and Leaf took the hand of Blades and Ena, there was a pop and they both disappeared, Rune looked ahead but saw nothing. The two dream spirits popped back and grabbed Rune and Fox, and with another pop they were gone.

Rune felt a twist in her stomach, and she was sat in amongst some giant ferns next to Ena. "That was strange."

She looked around and instantly noticed the difference. The day had been warm with scattered clouds, and here she was just 200 yards away, and yet the whole atmosphere had changed. Firstly, it was a lot warmer, but the sky above was overcast and cloudy, and the trees all around her were a greater age and dark and brooding, unlike any woodland she had seen before. There was no denying, the whole place felt depressing, dismal and more than a little bit creepy.

Jay and Tila popped into view, followed shortly by Crystal and Maddy. All of them looked round at the scene, and it was clear that the place had an instant impact on them. Over the next few minutes, the rest of the group popped into view, and Rune looked to Ena for direction.

"Give it a few minutes, you will all feel a little depressed, let it subside and then we will move out."

Ena was right, everything felt oppressed, almost as if the sky was pushing down on them making them feel like they had to force themselves to do anything. All of them felt a strange melancholy deep inside, even Tila who was normally buoyant and happy had a serious look to her. "I don't like this place; it makes me feel sad and away from nature." Ena gave a nod.

"As I told you, you will never feel anything like this place in any of the other realms; I know I have been to most of them. This place pulls at your soul and tugs away your happiness. You will adjust, but the first few minutes in this place will really test your sense of self."

Rune stood up and took a long look round. "I care not what it makes me feel like; I will stay true to me, and will hold my sense of self and purpose strong in my heart with my love for Robbie." Her mind slipped into her last few moments that morning as he held her tight in bed, and she cuddled up close, as he told her of his love and to be careful. Rune felt a warmth radiate out of her and smiled. Tila looked up at her.

"What are you doing?" She looked down and smiled.

"I am thinking of Robbie." Tila gave an understanding nod.

"You do know you are glowing purple right?"

"What?" Rune looked down and saw her arms and legs glowing with an aura like purple light. It was not bright, but it was clearly visible. Tila turned to Crystal.

"You know I love you right?" Crystal smiled and blew a kiss.

"I love you too."

Tila instantly began to glow with a green shimmer, and Crystal radiated a faint white light, Ena smiled, and started to glow with a faint blue haze. Rune looked at her smiled. "Dorin?" Ena gave an almost shy like nod. Rune turned and looked at the others.

"Find the love inside you all, think of those you love the most, it helps relieve the oppressiveness of this place." They sat for a moment and faint shimmers appeared around them, Blades turned and looked at Jay and winked.

"So who is he?" Jay almost turned scarlet as she saw the huge smile of the others, who had all turned to her, she put her head down.

"I am too embarrassed to say." Una gave a big smile.

"We are all friends here, come on no secrets, who is the lucky guy?" Jay went even redder.

"He does not know." Rune gave a giggle, and Ena leaned over and patted her leg.

"Love is a beautiful thing Jay, you should not hide it, especially in times like this, it is our love that binds us and gives us greater strength." She looked round the group with a bashful sort of smile.

"I cannot tell him, but he is wonderful and kind, and really caring, but please if I tell you." She shook her head quickly. "You cannot tell Jett; I will never hear the end of it." Blades gave her a puzzled look.

"Hearne help us it's not Rafe is it?" Jay jumped back in her sitting place and stared with horror at Blades.

"NO!" She looked coyly at them all, and put her head down, and quietly spoke. "It's Rigger!" Tila frowned.

"The huge hairy guy with the beard longer than my arm, that blows stuff up?" Jay nodded, Tila raised her eyebrows. Jay looked round and a smile broke across her face.

"He is so good with dynamite, I watch as he wires the fuses, and his fingers are just so perfect for the job, and so nimble." Crystal gave a smirk, Blades smiled.

"Fuse's eh? I bet he his good at wiring a lot of things, maybe you should let him at your fuse." Chuckles broke out as Jay looked absolutely shocked, and took a huge deep breath, and put her head down. Tila gave a nod and looked at Jay.

"You should have lots of sex with him, and then you will truly know."

"What?" She shook her head rapidly. "I cannot." Tila shrugged looking confused.

"Why? In Florae we find someone we like, and have lots of sex, and if we like it, we stay with them." Crystal gave a chuckle as she looked at the almost purple and terrified looking Jay.

"It's not like that in this world Tila; I have told you, they all have different customs here." She looked round the group.

"Your customs are less fun." She smiled and Rune looked at Ena.

"I think they are feeling better." Ena gave a smirk.

"Let's get going, we have a long walk to the castle, and darkness comes fast here,

I want the safety of the rocks before night fall."

The walk in the heat under the overcast sky made everything around them look eerie. The trees were old and tall, with wide spreading canopies, and the air was so heavy with humidity that all the trees had large dark mosses covering them. The moss hung in large heavy curtains from the branches that obscured the view, and made the whole place feel even more oppressive than it was.

It was not long before the group could feel their strength being sapped, and their spirits fell as they trudged through ferns up to their waists, with hardly a clear pathway in sight. They had been walking for hours, when suddenly Ena and Rune at the same time stiffened, and Ena thrust her hand behind her with a flat palm to tell them all to stop. The group went low and blended into their surroundings, wearing green and in the low light it was easy to disappear. Ena looked wide awake as she tried to peer through the deep undergrowth, everyone around was on high alert, and felt the tension in the air grow.

In the distance a horse gave a pant, and the sound bounced through the trees towards them. Blades sat with her hands already over her shoulders on the long thin black covered leather handles of her swords. Tila and Jay both knelt side by side with their bows loaded and ready. Maddy had her long white bow with an ordinary arrow fitted on the string, and Una was poised ready with her staff. Rune could sense a presence, but it was not one she knew, and there were a few of them. The sound of muffled horses on soft earth grew louder, it was clear a mounted group was slowly approaching with caution. Ena looked to Rune and lowered her voice.

"They will not be royal guards, they never leave the castle, these will be her soldiers, they are her hunting parties, looking for the travelling people, stay low unless they spot us, if we can avoid them we should, if we cannot, none of them can live."

Rune turned to look back, but it was clear the others had heard, they all sat waiting as the tension mounted. Peering through the ferns, Rune felt them getting closer, her eyes strained as she stared through the gloom trying to spot them, all of them held their breath. Through a wide patch of hanging moss, Tila who had keen eyes spotted movement, and pointed her bow at it. Blades noticed and tapped Ena on the shoulder and pointed in the direction Tila was looking, Ena spotted the rider, and the group all trained their weapons that way.

The group of the soldiers from the castle were all seated wearing dark robes, which made them even harder to see in amongst all the shadows of the woodland. They moved at a slow pace, as if inspecting every aspect of the trees and plants. It was clear they were looking for something, Rune was not sure if they were aware of them, she had thought that their arrival had been unnoticed, but was no longer convinced. The riders came into view about 100 yards slightly to their left, Rune tensed.

Ena spotted something and lifted her hand, she was well adapted to this environment, and Rune was surprised at how quickly and easily she had settled in to the surroundings, but it should have been no real surprise, as she had after all lived in these woods for many of her earlier years.

To the far right of the riders, a man stood up in the fern with a crossbow and fired, and then dropped back into the cover. The rider gave a grunt and rolled backwards off his horse. Rune blinked, and another arrow came from another direction, she looked at Ena who was smiling.

Rune turned back and three more had fallen from their horses in an attack that had no sound at all. As she watched five men dressed in tatty shirts rose out of the fern with long poles containing wide blades, they ran with speed through the fern, and the riders who were left drew out their long swords, and the battle commenced. Ena patted Rune's shoulder.

"Stay low but move closer." Rune gave a nod and followed Ena's lead; the whole group followed behind moving closer to the fight between what Rune assumed was Ena's people and the searching soldiers of the castle.

The fight was fierce, the soldiers dismounted and attacked back, and the two groups met and clashed. Rune could see more detail of the soldiers, and the group that attacked them. The fight was brutal and three of the attacking group fell dead instantly, it was clear these soldiers were extremely strong. One man with long grey hair held a giant two handed sword, and thrashed with utter hatred and brutality into the mass, cleaving with power against the soldiers, who defended with great strength. The fight lasted for twenty minutes, and Rune wanted to help, but Ena kept her arm out to Rune.

"Wait...these are very proud people and a little old fashioned, don't distract them from their duty." Rune looked at her.

"Duty?" Ena gave a nod.

"They believe that it is their duty to avenge the deaths of thousands of their people, we only enter if they absolutely need it, I understand the feelings in you. I want to join in too, but let them be a while."

Rune gave a nod and turned back to the fight, which was coming to an end. One rider had tried to grab his horse to return, but had been grabbed by two of the fighters and dragged down, the rest of the group were standing still breathing heavily, and looking at the dead soldiers on the floor. The tallest who was the grey haired leader was stood thirty feet away giving his orders to the group.

A dark clad soldier rose up behind him with a sword, Ena gave a gasp, but before she could react, an arrow came out of nowhere and hit the soldier in the side of the head entering his ear. It shot right through with the tip coming out of the other side, the tall grey haired fighter twisted, he saw the small lone figure of Tila with her bow stood up a few feet away in the tall fern, and he gave a growl, and lifted his sword, as the soldier collapsed dead in front of him.

He took two giant strides raising his huge sword high towards the startled looking Tila. From nowhere, a figure lifted into the sky and bounced over her head, and landed square in front of her, as the huge sword came swiping through the air, and the clash rang out loud in the woodland.

Blades stood, her swords crossed in front of her looking determined, and glaring at the tall fighter, her swords held his up above Tila, who had her eyes closed and screwed up waiting for the impact. The tall fighter stared at Blades holding up his giant sword with her small swords, crossed above her head. It took a moment to really understand what had happened as Ena stood up in the fern. "CEZAR!"

He looked at Blades, staring defiantly at him with her jaw locked as she held back his strong force. A wide smile broke across his face, and he began to laugh as he looked across at Ena stood alone in the fern looking at him with a startled look. It took him a moment for him to fully understand what was happening, and he stepped back and lifted his sword, and stared at Blades and Tila, who compared to him were like children. "What is this? What woman fights this way?" Blades unlocked her swords and stepped back and pushed Tila back.

"A stronger and faster one than you obviously." He gave a huge howl of a laugh, and realised what he had just seen, his head snapped round as he fully understood.

"ENA!" He dropped his sword and bolted into the fern towards her, the others all stood up; he snatched her up like a rag doll, and swung her into the air, and then pulled her close into an embrace. She had tears in her eyes as she looked at him. "Oh Cezar, I have missed you." It was clear that there was a very powerful bond between them as his eyes filled with tears.

"We thought they had got you." She shook her head and gave a big sniffle.

"No...We made it out, we did it, he was right all along." Cezar looked round the group.

"Is he here?" Ena gave a huge sob.

"We lost him." It took a few seconds to understand and he stopped moving and lowered her to the floor. Tears streamed down Ena's face. "They got him on the outside papa." He lowered himself to his knees and she looked at him. "They came for all the boat families, very few of us lived."

The effect on him was obvious, Rune did not fully understand everything, Ena turned to her. "Rune this is Cezar, he is Dorin's grandfather."

Rune suddenly understood as she looked at the large long grey haired old man, and she felt the great sadness in his heart. Ena looked at Cezar. "We have come back to kill all of them." He looked up with sad eyes.

"You should have stayed out, they are far stronger than they were back then, I fear they are not destined for death." Ena shook her head.

"We know a way, and we are going to stop them forever and free this realm, this is Runestone, she has powers beyond my mother's, she can help, Cezar trust me, we know how to do this."

The other members of the fighters group walked up as they spoke, and Cezar rose to his feet and looked back. "It's alright lads, they are on our side." One man stood a few feet away.

"Ena is that really you?" She turned and looked at him, he came forward, and she walked to him with a smile and pulled him into a hug.

"Hello Max." He pulled her close and held her tight.

"We thought we had lost you."

"I got out, but I have returned with help." Cezar looked at Rune.

"You are small, how strong are you?" Rune's bright blue eyes sparkled in the dim light.

"Strong enough." He looked amused.

"Prove it." Rune lifted her palm and a violet grew out of it, he scowled and looked at it.

"How is that powerful?" Rune looked at it in her hand and then held her palm higher.

"Smell its scent." He looked amused but decided to play along, he looked at the rest of his men and gave a superior smile, and then leant in to smell the flower.

There was a blinding violet flash of light, and Cezar gave a wail of complete surprise, as he was launched twenty feet into the air, and tossed across the woodland. He landed with a crash into a rotten and decayed old shrub and demolished it. Maddy and Una both sniggered as the rest of his group watched with their jaws dropped.

Rune walked over towards him and offered her hand to him, as he lay bewildered on the floor. He looked up at her as his eyes came back into focus and looked at her. His face broke into a huge smile and he gave a roar of a laugh, he sat up, and bellowed with laughter. His group saw him and started to smile, Rune looked at him sat in the grass and pieces of broken tree.

"Where I come from, women are not as defenceless as you think." He took her hand still laughing, and lifted himself up.

"I am wise enough to stand corrected, you are right, I should have listened to Ena."

Ena walked over to him and he smiled. "You keep impressive company, come we will head to the camp, it is not where it used to be, you know she will want to see you." Ena shook her head.

"Not yet, we have to do this, the world in which Rune lives is under siege and time is short, we must make the fall off by night fall." He looked concerned.

"You know this place, and you know how dangerous it is to be out here in the dark?" She shook her head.

"We have little time, we must do this as soon as possible, I have news that mother may still live, if she does, I have to get her free of them and out of here." He looked shocked.

"How could she have lived Ena, you know what Maud was capable of, and the Raven will kill her before she lets her go, as she will kill you if she knows you have returned."

"Even so, I must do this. Take my love to her and tell her if I live she will live to see me again." He gave a long sigh.

"You have capable company, even so take Max, he knows of safer caves that way, and keep a fire close in the darkness."

She stepped forward and he gave her another hug and kissed the top of her head. "If you must do this, go with speed the night is not far away." He turned to Max. "Go with them and keep her safe for me." Max gave a smile and lifted his bow off the floor at his feet, he noticed the green feathered arrow of Tila, sticking out of the almost blue white face of the soldier. He gripped it and snapped it off and handed it to Tila.

"No one here uses green feathers; take this with you so as not to alert them to you." She took the arrow and smiled as she slipped it into her sling.

The group assembled, and shortly after Ena had said her goodbyes, they set off as the light faded. Cezar stood for a long time watching as they walked away, then he turned lifted his sword off the floor, and headed away in the opposite direction.

Max led them quickly along trails, weaving through the trees with skill. It took about forty minutes of fast hot heavy work at a fast pace, following the trail as the light faded. Suddenly the trees broke, and they ran out onto a wide ledge and Max came to a halt, he pointed out over the cliff to a wide open chasm, within which was a huge pillar of grey granite that grew up from below in the centre.

It was almost a huge perfectly round pillar of rock set in the middle, almost as if the whole surrounding area had been carved out falling thousands of feet to the bottom. Built on the top in dark stone was a huge and crudely built castle, it was as ugly as it was frightening, and Rune walked to the edge of the high drop off and looked at it. She was surprised, she had expected something similar to Dunnottar or the Hidden Realm, but it was nothing like them. It was rough and crude and disfigured in its construction, but there was one theme she recognised.

Along all of the battlements and crudely built towers, there were statues by the hundreds, and all of them were the cold cruel ravens, just like everything else of theirs she had seen. Max walked up to her side as the others all stood and looked out at it.

"This is a land that has not changed since the start of time. Welcome to Berengar's Castle."

CHAPTER TWENTY NINE

THE RAVEN GATHERING

The cave suggested by Max for safety, was actually down what was a very perilous path, down the side of the drop off. The track was little more than eighteen inches wide, with what looked like a very old woven rope nailed into the side of the wall. The path fell away to a drop of thousands of feet, and for a few of the group, it was quite a challenge making it down without falling off.

The cave was large and went back into the side of the cliff for a good forty feet, before opening into a wide cavern. It looked like it was used on a regular basis, as there were stacks of blankets, four large filled water skins, and two large stores of dry fire wood. Close to the entrance of the tunnel that led to the cavern, there was a ring of stones which were blackened with soot, from many fires.

The group were tired and settled down quickly. Una had dried vegetables and meats, and two of Magg's pans that slid into each other, which Harry had made her, to enable them to cook. Maddy had a small kettle and tin cups, so before long a meal was cooking; Max added some rabbit, to increase the meal size. Tila had many assorted biscuit like cakes, which she handed out ensuring everyone that they were pure gifts of nature, and would increase their stamina.

Rune stood alone at the entrance to the cave looking out at the castle, as the darkness engulfed everything and lights came on all over the battlements, and in all the rooms. It felt strange to her, as for so long she had always thought of Morgan as a single entity, but before her was proof that she was indeed from a family like everyone else, but no one knew anything about them.

Rayne walked up the tunnel and leaned against the wall looking out into the darkness. "You should not stray away from the group alone Rune."

"Sorry, I have a lot on my mind." He looked at the castle with its hundreds of burning torches.

"Max says there is a lot of coming and going there today, his people think it is what everyone calls 'The Gathering.' Apparently, it happens every five years, the whole family comes together to celebrate the first victory of Berengar." He stared into the darkness as his mind drifted; Rune felt his inner feelings and glanced at him.

"You are not responsible for all this, this was your mother's mistake, and you should not carry the weight of that." He smiled.

"You are as bad as Gwynne, your circle reads emotion too easily for my liking, but you are right, I do feel a responsibility for this, I knew long ago about her treatment of others, I should have stood up to her more, and when I tried, I should have been more than I was." Rune understood.

"Not everyone can turn back the clock and make good the mistakes of the past, all of us at some point wish we had done things differently, I once had Morgan almost encased in crystal. I should have reacted quicker, but was too slow and as a result she brought Mason back, and Robbie will have to face him a second time. Every day since, I have thought of that moment, but the truth was at the time I was not experienced enough, and I would say the same to you." He shrugged.

"Maybe...I had her alone the other day, maybe if I had been stronger?" Rune turned and her eyes burned bright blue in the darkness.

"She is queen for a reason Rayne, you had no chance walking in there, and yet you did it. I think that alone says everything, and showed your people the kind of man you have become, and I also think it was the greatest thing you have done for your daughters. Amethyst learned from you that day, so much so she confronted Rhiannon alone, and I may add prevailed. It was one of the most important moments in the history of your people." He looked her and furrowed his brow.

"I am not sure it was that significant." Rune looked surprised.

"Well you should."

"How so?"

"Amethyst rose to match the power of who she really is for the first time as queen, and she won. Rayne your daughter proved that she will be far more powerful than Rhiannon, if you ask me; I would say that moment will mark the decline of Rhiannon's rule. Fae Ofmoon cannot have two queens, there is only room for one, and at the moment your mother has more pressing things to think about, as her successor is ready." He leaned off the wall.

"I am not sure that Amethyst is ready for that Rune, she is still a child in the span of things."

"Most queens are when they come to power, child or not, she matched and successfully controlled the situation, I think that is the mark of a true queen of Fae."

"That is a talk for another day, you should come and eat, in this place I think we cannot depend on regular meals, I also think you should talk with Max, he knows a great deal of what goes on over there, he could help." Rune gave a nod.

"I will shortly, I just want to check a few things out." He gave a smile.

"Ok see you shortly, be careful and keep your guard up."

He walked back down the tunnel into the cavern, and Rune watched the lights continue to go on, but one in particular light interested her, it was not in the castle, but much lower in the tall column, well below the level of the castle. She watched it flicker; something was down there and they were using fire.

When Rune came back, Una handed her a bowl of steaming stew, she moved to the side wall and sat down on some blankets to eat. Most of the group were gathered by the fire listening to Max, Ena appeared to know some of this, she leaned back on the wall as he spoke and listened carefully.

"The gathering is a family thing, a celebration of sorts. Tonight they will arrive, and tomorrow the whole family will come together and celebrate the first battle, where Berengar took over his Varisci tribe and built the castle. There will be a celebration all day tomorrow, and then at midnight they will gather in the central chamber, it is a place few see and live to talk about." Ena interrupted.

"My mother has been in that room." Max was surprised.

"She has?"

Ena gave a nod and sat forward so everyone could see her. "I heard her tell Crina about it one night by the fire when the camp was asleep, I was awake and listened to her. She spoke of a round room lined with seats, in which each family member sits. Those who have died are preserved in their seats and encased in glass like boxes. Above each seat is a perch, and on that sits the raven of the family member who sits below. She told her that Armand, Branna's first son who was killed by Uther is there in his seat, so is Vladimir, Berengar's brother, and Victor son of Maud who was killed by Arthur. Their hatred of the line of Pendragon is fierce, and at each gathering, they swear to destroy the Pendragon line."

Una looked at Maddy, both of them had seen Victor before the final battle in which he died, as he had met with Uther when they swore the alliance between them, before the breakup over Igraine.

Rune sat quietly taking all of it in, as Max picked up where Ena had left off. "Fifty Summers ago, my father witnessed the ceremony from close to the bridge that leads to the castle. It cannot be seen from here, as it is around the other side, but it is the only way to get to the castle. He and a group of our men were thinking of sneaking into the castle whilst the Gathering was happening, in hope they could overpower the guards and destroy them all in one go. He was very badly wounded when he got back to the camp, so badly that he died days later. Before he died, he told Cezar that as they fought, in the sky above the castle a giant silhouette appeared of a raven, and those who saw it cowered in fear, it was that which gave the royal guards a greater advantage, and they were beaten back across the bridge."

Rune sat motionless her spoon still in her hand between the bowl and her mouth, Sapphire noticed and got up and walked over, and sat beside her.

"You thinking what I am?"

"The bird in the clouds at Avalon?" Sapphire nodded.

"What if..."

"That is the moment when the Merle is drawn down?" Sapphire gave a nod.

"Yeah, it does make sense... do you think they need a top up or something?" Rune put her spoon back in the bowl.

"I have no idea, but what I do know now is we need to get in that castle before midnight and find Ariel fast and get out." Sapphire gave a shudder.

"If they are drawing down more of the Merle it must be for them, or they intend to corrupt more." Rune looked at her.

"I was watching tonight and thinking. This place is hidden by a veil, a veil that has some of the Merle in it, and because of that everyone is sealed out, and no one outside can see in. I was wondering if it is possible to somehow seal everything in, after all the whole family will be here." Sapphire looked vague.

"Can we do that?" Rune thought for a second.

"I am not sure as I have no idea of what the true power they use is, my senses are confused in here and I cannot contact mum, so I wondered if there was a way I could use the Violet Lines to seal everything inside, you know like a veil within a veil?" Sapphire shrugged.

"I have no idea if it is possible, I have so much more to learn of the powers of Fae, but I suppose if anyone can do it you can."

For the entire day things around the castle had been hectic. Servants hurried in their duties, and below stairs the kitchen was frantic as foods and wines of the best quality were being prepared. Carts arrived, and family walked into the main entrance, to be greeted by Rosamund, Branna's second daughter, of her seven children. She was tall and thin, and her skin was as white as snow, her eyes were dark and filled with malice, as she pretended to smile, but it was clear she had no liking for any of her family.

Rosamund had never married, but in her wake was a long line of male escorts who had all died suddenly of natural causes, even the twenty two year old Hector. Rosamund had been a disappointment to Branna as she had very little power, whereas her first daughter, and third child Maud, had been exceptionally powerful, even if she was a stunted and hideously deformed child filled with hate for just about everything. Maud had come to an end when she clashed with Morgana, shortly after the birth of Mason.

Morgana had not been given an easy time, Maud had been so wild and vile that no man would touch her, and in a last bid to produce an heir, Branna had agreed for her marriage to Otto, Berengar's brother, who had grown into an equally sadistic and brutal warrior. It had felt like a match made in hell, and had surprised the whole family when Maud gave birth to a healthy strong boy Ivor, who had died at his Uncle Armand's side fighting against Uther. Her second son Victor had disgraced Otto by marrying a Celt queen instead of a Sachsen woman, which had resulted in the birth of Morgana, and as a result Otto was vile to her, resulting in Maud making Morgana's time in the castle particularly harder than it had to be.

The clash between them that was inevitable resulted in Maud's death at the hands of Morgana, who used an unknown curse that severed Maud from her raven, she then claimed Maud's prized raven Rajani as her own, something that shocked the family and gave Morgan far more power in the family than they thought she deserved, and yet Branna was unusually nice to her over it.

Inside the castle, Ulric and his wife Amalina, Maud's third child stood talking with Lothar, the youngest of Berengar's children. Otto was not to be seen, much to the relief of everyone. Merwig, Berengar's other son, was still in his room, and there were still members of the gathering to arrive.

Ulric turned to Lothar, who looked very young considering his age; he too had a long line of mistresses behind him. "What of the Celt, will she be here to enrage the old man?"

Lothar who actually liked Morgana gave a smile.

"I do hope so, although from what I have heard she is busy with that grandson of hers trying to beat that bloody nation into submission again." Ulric rolled his eyes.

"I have no idea why they go to such lengths; we had an uprising about seventy years ago, we did not waste our time building huge armies and infrastructure, we just sent in our ravens, and took their souls, now they are compliant and work hard for us."

Amalina looked bored. "Be honest the woman has always had a chip on her shoulder because that king took her daddy away, and her grandfather did not care for her, it made her impossible, she struts in with poor Rajani on her shoulder, and thinks she runs the family since Maud was killed. I mean the woman has no understanding of loyalty, killed her own son and his wife so she could have a son, it says everything you need to know about her if you ask me." She turned to Ulric. "I am bored; I am going for a drink." He gave a nod and she walked off towards the drinks cabinet. Lothar watched her.

"You should warn her Ulric, Morgana is powerful, she should be careful in her choice of words. Morgana has risen quicker than any of us, one day she will rule this family, you mark my words, that girl has ambition and a point to prove." He gave a nod.

"She will be fine once we are out of here, she hates these things."

Outside more carts arrived with guests for the night and the late members of the family. Tonight, would be the pre gathering ball, and would be held for all those who had risen to power in their regions to help the family. Over two hundred would sit for a meal and celebration of the wealth they had amassed since the Red Death. There would be bishops, cardinals, generals and the really wealthy, even a few ex kings and queens. The hand of the Berengar's had a very long reach, and in a world that had struggled after the Red Death, they had been swift to take power and control in every country that had survivors.

It was late at Loxley as Robbie sat in his office with Rowan, Jade and Steph. Steph looked worried as she shook her head. "I should have gone with her." Jade looked really worried; Robbie gave a sigh.

"She is with this Ena and she knows what she is doing, I talked with her for a long time last night, and she told me that under that veil she may be out of contact. Look Rune said she would find a way to let us know she is safe, we have to trust her, and stay alert. If she can do what she is trying to, then that will make life for all of us easier, we have to believe she will find a way as she always has." Steph sat back in her chair.

"I know...I just hate not feeling her within me, I know she will be fine, hell she is the most powerful of all of us. I am her mother; I will not stop worrying about her." Rowan patted Steph on the shoulder.

"If that wall falls without notice, I am telling you she will get the biggest hug ever from me. Looking at their movements I would say they are close to something. We need to hang in here and hope for the best."

Back within the realm of Sachsen, Rosamund entered the hall, and wove her way through all the people, grabbing a glass of champagne as she passed the servant. She smiled and shook hands with the guests, as she wove her way in the direction of the fireplace, and finally made it to the side of Ulric. He looked as bored as she was, drinking his Scotch, she gave a withered smile. "It's only two days and then you will have the castle all to yourself for a while." He gave a snort and looked round the room.

"See anything you want? Let's be honest the only reason we both tolerate this is because it is rich pickings for the bed chamber." She gave a smile and looked round the room.

"I think De la Roche would be fun, I do like the new ones, and have heard he likes to be rough with his women. I could use a little sport, and he has eliminated that tiresome monk for us, although I won't be the one to tell Morgana. He has rich pickings, you never know if he enjoys the night, I may go and visit him for a while." She gave a crude smile, and Ulric rolled his eyes.

"Can your vault hold any more than it does, I am not sure which you like most, the full vault or the full bed." She gave a chuckle.

"My dear nephew, I like both, you should know that, and speaking of, it's been a while." She gave another cackle of a laugh and looked across the room. "OH Finally! Gundobarld and Dagaric are here, we can get this thing started at last."

High above them on the balcony of the first floor, a neatly dressed if not upset looking maid pushed the wheelchair closer to the rail. The old white haired man sat within it leaned forward to look down, his face set in a permanent grimace of displeasure, his long thin white hair hung lank as he viewed the mass below. "I see the cockroaches have arrived." He turned to look at the maid. "Is that Celt bitch here yet?"

Rune sat up with a start. She looked round to see most of the others were sleeping; the fire was built up and burned brightly, illuminating the whole inside of the cavern. Sapphire looked up from her bed a few feet away. "You not sleeping either?" Rune rubbed her eyes.

"Dreams or visions, I am not sure which, the atmosphere in this place interferes with my senses, although I have been thinking all night." Sapphire sat up in her bed.

"And, have you got any new ideas?" Rune turned and gave her a smile.

"I think I may have found a way into the castle undetected; I won't know until I have spoken to Max tomorrow." Sapphire gave a smile.

"You know, I knew you would. So tell me, what is your idea?"

CHAPTER THIRTY

OVER THE BRIDGE

Rune had finally gotten some sleep, and was the last to rise. By the time she had woken and eaten, most of the others were busy cleaning their equipment, and sharpening their weapons. Rayne was on watch with Fox, and Blades helped Una and Maddy clean up their dishes and pots, ready to pack again. Ena sat alone meditating, although Tila who was intrigued by it, sat a few feet away from her trying to copy.

Rune sat with Max and questioned him. "So, the guests will leave today, leaving only the family?"

"Well in the past according to the staff we had contact with, a few have remained, you have to understand, these people are so powerful they are above all of the rules. If one of them wants to bed your wife, you leave and let them, so there will be a few stragglers." Rune understood.

"So at midnight tonight, they should all be sitting in this round room ready to do whatever it is they do?" He gave a nod.

"Yes why?" She sat back and gave the moment a pause for thought, her blue eyes sparkled as she looked at him.

"That is the time they will be the most preoccupied, so that is when we will strike." He took a depth and exhaled.

"It is not going to be easy, during the ritual the front will be heavily guarded, they will place most of their force watching that bridge." Rune smiled.

"That is exactly what I want, all of them watching the bridge." He did not understand.

"It is the only way in, if they are going to all be watching, how will you be able to get more than ten feet across it?"

"I won't, I will be using a different entrance, one they will not care much to watch." He shook his head.

"There isn't one." She gave another big smile.

"If there is one thing I have learned from my husband and his team, it is there is always a backdoor, and I think I have found it."

It was mid morning, and Morgan le Fey walked up the stone steps with her long cloak of black feathers flapping behind her. The guards that saw her coming stepped quickly out of her way. She arrived on the top, and saw Mason stood with Mark Richard Dale, both looking out from the wall across to Loxley.

"I am here, are we going to get on with this? I have that wretched family thing to do later, and I want to enjoy as much of this as possible before the drudgery of family." Mason smiled as he turned to look at her.

"It is nice to see you so enthusiastic Mother, the troops are ready, and we are eagerly awaiting your arrival." She smirked as she walked towards the edge of the wall and looked out across the valley at Loxley in the distance.

"You have everything prepared?" Mason smiled.

"Of course."

"Good... I shall draw down the powers and get started then."

Morgan stood at the top of the battlements and lifted her arms into the air, and the clouds began to darken, streaks of lightening shot down from the sky. Below her heavy iron windows appeared in the smooth black stone walls. She looked to the floor as lightening came down in a sheet, and the roar of the thunder echoed across the valley.

Henry looked out across the vast wide open area. "I used to love thunder, but since she moved into the neighbourhood, I have learned to hate it." He turned to David. "She has arrived, you better get Robbie, I think we will have company soon." David turned and looked down.

"Slater!" He appeared from under the ramparts.

"Yes sir."

"Go fetch Lord Loxley, we think we may have guests." He looked stunned.

"You are joking?" Henry looked over the edge.

"GET YOUR FRIGGIN ASS IN GEAR BOY, AND GO GET YOUR LORD!"

He nodded rapidly, turned, and ran at full speed towards the Village Hall. David looked up at the observation deck above, as lightening shot down from the sky, and the rumble that followed deafened everyone.

"SOUND THE BELLS, WE ARE UNDER ATTACK!"

The two soldiers above grabbed for the rope and pulled, giving the bell a large swing, they let the slack of the rope go, and the bell gave its first chime, that vibrated the floor of the decking shifting the dust. All around Loxley other bells rang out, and from every direction woodsmen came running. David sounded his orders as he walked along the deck.

"Seal the gates, prepare your weapons, look lively lads the bitch has arrived, and we are in for bad weather, hoods up, eyes clear, and aim straight."

The sound of galloping hooves came down the road, as Robbie, Rowan and the Specialist's rode with speed towards the inner compound of the gate house. Robbie's horse slid on the hard floor, as he let go of it, and jumped clear onto the ladder, and scrambled up to David Williams above him.

"Commander Williams report the situation." Rowan came up right behind him. There was a flash of bright white light and Steph appeared beside Robbie.

"The bitch could not wait a few more days, my god she is impatient."

Rune looked out across the wide valley, as she stood beside Crystal. "I know it is a long way, but what do you think?" Crystal studied the distance.

"I can do it, but it won't be very wide, it will have the strength and hold, but it will push me Rune, I have bridged a few things, but over that space, it's a tall order." Rune understood.

"But if we helped you, then you could probably do it?" Crystal smiled at her.

"I never said it was impossible, and I have grown a lot stronger, all I can say is, I will try." Rune knelt down on the floor.

"Look we do not have to walk it, if it is easier, you could do it like the metal supports they used in the old days. They are sort of triangular, three long poles with supports all along. Hell if we have to sit on them and slide we will, just as long as we get over and fast. I cannot use power until the moment I want to reveal myself, so for now this is the only thing I can think of; once we are in, we can use windows if we need to." Crystal understood, as she watched Rune draw out the shape.

"It's less structure so that will be easier, let me study it and see what I can work out in my mind. Look Rune if you need it, I will find you a way, OK?" She patted her shoulder.

"I believe in you, so do your best."

Robbie looked out across the valley, and there was no mistaking the dark shape of Morgan le Fey, clouds were forming above the wall, and starting to slowly flow in the direction of Loxley, he felt his heart beating in his ears. "It is game on David for sure, I can see her." David smiled.

"I think the dark brooding clouds gave the game away a little so we are not surprised." The floor began to vibrate and shake. "Here we go. BRACE YOURSELVES LADS, AND HOLD ON TIGHT!"

Morgan stood with her arms outstretched and looked to the ground at the base of the gates. In one flowing movement she swept her arms down, and then back up in the air, and as she did, the earth below began to shake and vibrate. The earth parted and a wide plinth of black shining stone, fifty feet wide rose up. It came through the surface and shuddered to a halt level with the gateway.

She pulled her arms close to her chest, and the lightning bounced out of the dark clouds, and struck the centre of the black surface. Morgan gave a gasp, and then screamed out with all her might and the black smooth surface below began to expand.

Her screams echoed loudly across the valley, and Robbie watched as the smooth surface that had risen out of the earth began to extend towards Loxley across the valley. As it extended, archways grew out of the underside of it, and travelled downward to meet the land below, he pulled his glasses away from his eyes and shouted out.

"SHE IS CREATING A BRIDGE, AND IT'S COMING OUR WAY, PREPARE YOUR WEAPONS!"

All along the walls of Loxley, arrows fitted to strings and were tensioned ready. The bridge picked up pace as it grew more stable with the archway building itself underneath, Rowan looked at Steph. "They will storm us, is there anything you can do to stop it?" Steph had white light flashing in her eyes.

"I am doing everything I can." He nodded and lifted his bow ready.

Morgan screamed with joy as the bridge flowed across the valley, and before it had even connected on the Loxley end, Mason had given the orders, and black vested soldiers flowed like ants onto the bridge. All along the wall at Loxley the bowmen prepared, they were greatly outnumbered by the enemy, but they were loaded and ready, knowing they had the longest reach of all the weapons, and their arrows could take out a large number before they were anywhere near the gates. David Williams held up his bow and screamed out loud.

"TAKE AIM!" The black horde swarmed towards them with the bridge, as it hurtled across the valley, and over the river below, and onto the land that rose up towards the steep bank and the gates of Loxley. Rowan gripped the wall, his bow with a fitted arrow in one hand, as the floor began to shake even more, it was like they were at the centre of an earthquake.

It was one hundred yards away, and the soldiers were catching up fast to the moving end, as they all yelled with their swords, ladders and crossbows raised towards Loxley. David Williams hung on to the wall judging the footage of the soldiers; he lifted his hand ready as he waited for the first soldiers of Mason to come into range. The bridge came to within forty feet of the banking that led up to the gates, and suddenly it shuddered to a halt. David Williams dropped his arm and screamed out.

"FIRE!" Thousands of arrows hit the sky like a plague of locus. They rose at great speed as the soldiers of Mason continued on unaware that the bridge had stopped short, the arrows hung in the air for a moment and then tilted. As the soldiers ran towards them, the arrows came out of the sky like a host of bees, and before the soldiers realised, they felt the long white tipped arrows of Loxley bite into their skin. Men tripped and fell in agony, some fell dead and dropped off the sides of the bridge, falling down a hundred feet to their deaths on the wild landscape below, and the rest unable to stop, ploughed on over the dead, as a second hail of arrows came out of the sky.

Morgan le Fey leaned over the battlements and screamed with hate. "NOOOOOO!" Mason turned to her and snapped.

"Why have you stopped it, finish it for god's sake, we are losing men." She turned, her eyes glowing red with hate.

"That bitch has done something." Mark Richard Dale looked very angry, and could not contain his anger.

"FINISH IT OFF, YOU OLD HAG!" She looked even angrier, as her head snapped towards him, her arm shot up from her side, and there was a flash of red light, Dale screamed, and shot backwards away from the wall, and he landed hard and slid twenty feet across the smooth surface of the floor.

"When I want your opinion, which I don't, I will ask you, you witless fool."

Steph jumped with joy on the top of the walkways and laughed. "Oh, you clever girl Runestone, my god my daughter is a genius." Robbie stared at her, as she bounced around not really understanding what had happened, Steph was wearing a massive smile and pointed at the bridge that fell short. "You see it, do you see it Robbie? She is an absolute marvel, my god I am so proud of her."

He had no idea what she was talking about, he looked out to see the short bridge, and the dead piling up under Loxley arrows, he shook his head and lifted his arms in a gesture of confusion.

"WHAT! What did she do, I have no idea what you are talking about?" Steph grabbed him her face all smiles.

"Look at it, remember?" He shook his head.

"No!" Steph let go and did a funny little dance on the spot. Her green eyes filled with flashes of white, were filled with joy, she looked right at him.

"Iona Robbie...Iona...The scatterings, they are protected with some of the oldest Fae magic, she cannot cross them, and neither can her bridge." She jumped towards him and gripped his shoulders. "Runestone scattered them all round Loxley, her bridge is dark magic, and it cannot cross it, my god she is clever, I did not even think of it, but she did, she is insanely clever."

Rune stood behind Crystal and held onto her shoulders. "I am ready when you are." Her eyes began to flash with violet, and Crystal closed her eyes, and held out her ungloved hand, and it started to sparkle. Rune's eyes intensified as she gave Crystal the extra power she would need. Tila watched from the side next to Sapphire.

"Oh Hearne it turns me on when she does this." Sapphire's eyebrows rose.

"OK!" Tila gave what she assumed was a lusty smile.

Crystal's hand looked like it was on fire with ice particles as Rune whispered quietly. "Now."

Crystal bent down and touched the floor at the base of the cave tunnel, as Rune's eyes intensified even more. Ice shot out of Crystals hand, and grew out over the edge above the high drop off; it grew like a long pole outward towards the castle slightly pointing down. Tila leaned out a little more to watch as the pole of ice grew across the massive drop, in the direction of the window, below the ground level of the rough looking castle. Sapphire was amazed as she watched it finally reach the window, and the end spread out securing it in place. Once it was fully attached, side bars grew out at an angle pointing down to recreate the image Rune had drawn out on the floor. Crystal gave a gasp as the ice ran back towards them building a strong structure like a triangular metal frame, which they could use.

The final section connected to the wall of rock below the floor of the tunnel, and Crystal fell to her knees, Tila instantly jumped forward and grabbed her and pulled her close. Crystal opened her eyes and gave her a smile. "I am tired baby." Tila smiled, and kissed her softly on the lips.

"You were amazing, wow I am so aroused right now."

Rune opened her eyes and smiled at Rayne. "Ok get your kit, we are all moving out."

The word went round, and a few moments later as Crystal rested, Rayne took the lead followed by Rune then the others. Each of them was touched with Crystal's snowflake pendant, then climbed onto the ice structure, and sitting backwards on the top pole, they kicked off, and shot at speed sliding down towards the window below the castle.

For some it was great fun, Blades landed with a smile on her face. "That was wicked, we should make one back home."

Others did not enjoy it quite as much, Una gave a squeal, closed her eyes and panicked all the way down. So much so she came through the window at high speed, and hit Blades, Rayne and Jay knocking them flat. Max, Tila, and then Crystal came last giggling as they entered.

Rune and Ena looked around the vast room filled with tables and potions, and for Rune this looked like a very familiar sight, she has seen it at Tintagel and Dunnottar, as well as the hidden realm, Ena looked at the bottles and powders, not truly understanding what it was, she was after all Fae, and used pure magic directed through her limbs. Rune saw her confusion and came close to her.

"This is where they experiment, they make potions to increase their abilities, they are not like us, it does not flow naturally through them." Ena understood things around Rune that she had always questioned, and they were finally starting to make more sense.

Rune walked deeper into what was a huge room; her eyes traced the grey stone walls and ceiling which had all sorts of ancient tools and weapons hanging from it. On the far side was an old double door, and she walked towards it as the others fanned out round the room. Rayne came up at her side.

"Remember, be careful Rune." She nodded as she slowly approached the door.

Rayne crossed to the other side of the door and lifted his bow, as Rune grabbed the black heavy iron ring and slowly turned it. The door moved slightly, she looked at Rayne, and he held up his bow with an arrow on the string, and she gently pulled.

The door creaked open, Rayne leaned out to look and gave a nod, and Rune came round the edge of the door cautiously. The room was empty except for a long cloth covered table that was connected to wires that led up to the roof. A large set of doors connected the roof to the floor above; it was some sort of trap door, but what for?

Slowly and quietly Rune walked into the room, her eyes now fixed on the cloth covered table. She noticed the scrape marks in the dust on the floor towards the table, she looked back and saw a plinth, and suddenly realised what she was looking at, she had seen it in the basement of Dunnottar.

Ena entered the room and watched as Rune rushed over towards the cloth covered table, and lifted the cloth to look below it. Her eyes lifted and Ena's eyes connected with her bright blue, and it was almost as if she understood.

Her heart rose as she rushed towards the table and grabbed the cloth. It fell to the floor revealing a long tube of white crystal, and there inside hardly visible through the rough unpolished stone was a figure, her heart almost exploded, as the word rushed up from her chest, into her throat, and out of her mouth.

"MOTHER!"

Rune looked at her. "We must get her out now, help me."

Bodies were piling up at the end of the bridge, soldiers were starting to realise what was happening, and slow their pace to a halt. Another rain of arrows lifted into the air, and the soldiers looked up and watched them, almost as if mesmerised by them, they tilted and pointed back to earth. The men at the front in range, understanding they would be added to the large pile of dead, turned and began to push against those behind them to get away.

It had the effect of a stampede in reverse, as the men panicked and pushed their way back, creating a backward flowing serge. The arrows rained down hitting those furthest forward in the back. Men fell littering the bridge, and the surge caused pushing against those coming forward, exploded into complete disorder and panic. Men were sent sideways falling off the bridge by the dozen, and fell screaming to their deaths below.

The sight was enough for those at the rear, and they turned and fled back towards the tall black wall. Mark Richard Dale jumped up on the battlement wall and screamed at them.

"What the hell are you doing?" He turned to Mason who was quite aware of the scene and pointed. "They are retreating, what kind of soldiers have you trained?"

He spun round and screamed at the generals, whilst pointing behind him. "Loxley is that way, send them back, send them back now or I will kill every last one of them myself." He was rapidly becoming unhinged at their incompetence and this was just the start of the battle.

Mason turned to the generals and calmly spoke.

"Bring up the cannons and send them onto the bridge." The general saluted, and then grabbed a phone on a box, he lifted the handset, and then wound a handle on the side and it gave off a buzzing noise.

"Bring up the cannons." Morgan le Fey was losing patience, she turned and walked down the wall to above the section filled with metal window covers that kept banging and crashing. Morgan screamed with madness, and light shot from her hands across the valley bouncing off trees and causing them to explode. She leaned over the wall in an absolute rage and screamed at the top of her voice.

"OPEN THE DOORS, AND RELEASE MY CREATURES OF THE NIGHT, COME FORTH MY HOULEN AND DESTROY ALL OF THEM!"

The sky above Loxley suddenly darkened, as all the light from the sun was blocked out completely, and hideous wails echoed across the valley.

CHAPTER THIRTY ONE

THE END OF A DREAM

Ena lay across the crystal tube and wept, as her mother's face looked back with dull eyes from inside. Rune ran her hands along the edges of the tube; she looked at Rayne and Sapphire. "What time is it?"

Max answered. "I would say looking at the sun before we left the cave, it has gone midday." Rune felt for the seam.

"This will take time, make sure we are safe and secure here, I must get her out before they prepare." Sapphire came over to the tube.

"Prepare, how do you mean?" Rune looked up and her eyes flashed violet.

"The ritual starts at midnight; I think it will be right above us." She glanced up, and Sapphire followed her eyes and saw the trap doors. "I think this is to be a part of it, so they will come down to prepare in advance, that gives us less time, we need to crack this open without alerting them and get Ariel out safe." Sapphire understood.

"Ok, what do you need me to do?" Rune looked up from the side of the tube.

"Focus your mind and talk to her."

"What?"

"Sapphire try and connect with her, I need her awake, she can help from inside like my grandfather did."

"Rune it's crystal, it blocks the passage of power." Rune shook her head as she ran her hand along the side towards the end.

"Not this stuff, it's crude and not as sophisticated as Morgan's, I think she will hear us, so try and talk to her, I need her awake Sapphire."

Blades headed over to another set of doors that she assumed led out into a corridor, Fox joined her and both of them pressed their ears to the door, where they could hear voices. She looked at Fox. "This is one of those times when I wish Pebbles was here; this is her area of expertise."

Henry yelled across the gateway. "Light the beacons." The darkness flowed over them casting them into almost twilight. Rowan watched as the men on the bridge surged back, he lifted his binoculars as he saw something glint.

"Crap they have cannons." He watched the darkness ripple around the large stone wall and panned round with his binoculars, and saw the metal windows in the wall start to move. A flash caught his eye and he moved to above the windows and saw the dark clad figure ignite something in her hand, he turned and screamed at Robbie. "INCOMING!"

Morgan made a fist as she gritted her teeth in anger, she leant back and with all her might she thrust her arm forward as her tight fist ignited, and then opened her hand. A ball of fire exploded out of her, and came hurtling like a missile across the valley.

Henry saw it. "HOLD ON TIGHT LADS!" The fire wall widened as it came closer and then at the edge of the bridge it exploded in a deep fiery red explosion that illuminated what looked to Robbie like some invisible barrier like dome. The whole place shook as the fire engulfed the air above them. They felt the heat, but the fire did not penetrate, the old magic of the Fae had held true.

Morgan watched and laughed as she turned to Mason. "It is a dome, bring me those explosives." He clicked his fingers and a soldier ran down the steps, he looked at her shrewdly.

"What are you up to Mother?" She gave a cackle and her eyes sparkled with malice.

"You will see." He gave a big smile as Dale grabbed a phone and wound it up rapidly. The line gave a buzz and he waited as he watched Loxley.

"I am done with this, let's up the stakes, if you want to play Loxley, let's see how you handle this lot." The phone clicked and he looked down. "Open all the doors and send everything in we have."

Morgan gave a gigantic and almost insane laugh. "Now you are talking, it is about time you got serious dim wit, now you are acting like a Knox." Mason watched her delight and found it contagious.

Robbie turned to Steph. "Bring on the valley team, if he is bringing on cannons; let's confuse him on which direction to point them." She gave a nod, clicked her fingers and disappeared in a flash of white.

At Dove Dale Commander Millington was prepared, as his men lined up all along the side of the river. There was a flash of white light and Steph appeared out of the end of a long white tube of light. He gave a nod and turned to his number two. "Send them in and start the rear attack." The second gave a salute and began to move men into the tunnel; Commander Millington gave a bow to Steph. "Lady

Whiteline, how is it going?" Steph smiled,
"It's about to get rough."

Mel turned on the top deck. "Robbie, we have an attack on the moors side, and Gwynne has reported men moving into the woodland on the York side, they are coming at us from all sides apart from the Escarpment." There was a white flash and Steph reappeared.

"Rear guard is in place and will strike shortly." Robbie gave a nod as he looked to Jett who was looking frustrated.

"Say it Jett, don't hold back on me now." She looked him in the eyes, as hers flickered with traces of blue light.

"I swore to you I would die for you and I will, but not up here, this is not my fighting style sitting on logs with a bow, I need to see the whites of their eyes Robbie, it's what I do best." He understood and gripped her shoulder.

"I would die for you too, but if we are going to die Jett, it will be side by side, your moment is coming, please you most of all must trust me in this moment." She gave a nod.

"Ok Robbie, I am with you, but my sword wants truth and it's over there on that wall." He smiled. "That time is close."

Blackness flooded into the air outside the wall of Mason, Rowan was on the ball.

"HOULEN!" Robbie snapped his head round, and looked out across the valley where a dark mass had lifted into the air, he looked at Steph.

"They are part Fae can they breach the protections?" She shook her head.

"Honestly I do not know, but screw this; if they do I am holding a sword." He nodded.

"Bloody good idea." He turned to Jett and the other Specialists. "SWORDS!"

Jett pulled Truth out and it gleamed in the darkness, she turned to face the wall and smiled. "Bout bloody time."

Men in black vests streamed down from the moors with ladders, John Lox walked along his lines and bellowed. "Take the ladder men and then clean the rest!"

Arrows flew into the hoards, and the men tumbled and fell tripping over each other. Deep in the woodland behind Loxley, Gwynne flanked by Louisa and the Outlaws, took cover in the trees and waited. The troops of the black army flooded onto the path, and arrows came from every direction. They hit hard throwing soldiers in every direction, as more dived for cover.

The arrows stopped and all went silent, one soldier lifted his head slightly to look, an arrow whistled through the trees, and hit him in the forehead, and he was thrown backwards back onto the path. The others all pushed themselves lower, for now it was a stalemate.

The Houlen came fast; Robbie pulled Destiny at the side of Rowan with Honour, and waited. The group divided in the air and one group swept to the bridge created by Morgan, they landed and ripped and pushed at the bodies, dropping them off the edge. The other group shot up higher into the air, Robbie pointed his sword and yelled to the Bowmen.

"Aim for the heads, it's the only way to kill them." Arrows shot into the sky as the Houlen screamed out their blood curdling cries. Arrow struck and they thrashed in the air, others fell like stones, hitting the protections of Loxley and instantly ignited into flames.

The Houlen swept up, as if able to see the Fae protections, Rowan watched not understanding their tactic. "What are they holding?" Steph looked up.

"Shit... It's explosives and the Fae magic does not stop them." Robbie turned and screamed at the top of his lungs as the Houlen suddenly dropped in the air and swept towards them.

"COVER!"

The wave of Houlen came in fast, and let go of the objects they were carrying, they dropped like stones towards the front gates, as all the soldiers ducked behind the wooden wall of the deck for protection. Robbie looked up as they swept past high above him.

The whole wall shuddered, and Robbie snatched out at the wall, as the whole place lit up like daylight. The blast with the explosion ripped like a wave across the wall. His legs slipped and he felt himself slide backwards. His ears rang as he shook his head, and saw the flames rip up through the gates, and the splinters fly back into the compound blowing the men off their feet.

He pulled on the wall and gripped the deck with his boots, and dragged himself back up; Rowan was hanging on covered in dust. Specialists were appearing in amongst the other bowmen, he could hardly hear as he looked round slightly dazed.

Below him on the ground the gates lay in tatters, broken and splintered and strewn across the bodies of his dead men of Loxley. He turned to see the damage and a whole section of above the gate had gone, and flames licked the edges. Men were throwing buckets of water and running around below. Teams battled with the fire, and others pulled the injured from under the splintered wood, his eyes stung as the smoke bellowed up towards him, and he staggered back against the wall for balance. He looked down, and saw the bloodied face of David Williams and his heart broke, as a few feet away was Melanie, who had been beside him when the bomb hit.

He felt his legs go weak and he gripped the wall for support, as his ears rang and he fought with all he was to push the rotten rising feeling in his throat down. Someone gripped him and shook him, two large green eyes took up his face space, as Steph said something, and he strained to understand her words. She clasped his ears and her eyes flickered white, and the sound came back to him as she screamed at him.

"ROBBIE THE MERE!!"

No one expected it; Isolde was busy with the washing sorting it out and laying it on Rune's bed. Filomena was in the nursery with the children. Furry Face lay at the bottom of the stairs, he lifted his head and sniffed the air, and his fur bristled as he looked up at the ceiling.

From nowhere, the whole house suddenly shook throwing Isolde over, and knocking the clean washing everywhere. Filomena screamed, and Isolde felt the fear rise inside of her, she dragged herself up and ran for the door. Smoke was bellowing up the stairs, as Furry Face bounded up them towards her. She saw the bright orange eyes of the tiger and could see he understood the situation, he gave an almighty roar, and she understood him instantly. Isolde ran along the landing towards the children's bedroom.

She grabbed the doorframe as another huge explosion went off and the house appeared to lurch. Filomena was holding on to each of the babies cots, with a hand on each, as she tried to stabilise them. Isolde slid on the floor as it moved again, and dragged herself onto the bed and screamed at Filomena. "Take the queen!"

She scrambled across the bed as Filomena lifted Iona from her cot, and wrapped her in blankets. Isolde screamed. "GO...GET OUT NOW!"

Filomena looked terrified, she closed her eyes and there was a loud pop and she was gone.

Isolde grabbed Halbert's cot and dragged it towards her as the house gave another huge shudder, and the bedroom windows exploded outwards. She dragged Halbert into her arms and then pop. She jumped to Filomena who was outside in the trees out of sight shaking with terror. Furry Face bounded across the room, and with an enormous roar, he jumped through the broken window.

Isolde appeared and she gasped with relief, as she turned and saw the house with flames pouring out of the downstairs windows, she turned to Filomena.

"Are you alright, is the queen safe?" Filomena pulled back the blankets were Iona was wide awake, her bright violet eyes locked on the darkened sky. Isolde gave a deep breath as she saw the house burning, they had been very lucky indeed.

Filomena suddenly looked startled, she pushed Iona at her. "The Stones!" Isolde did not quite understand, as Filomena again pushed Iona onto her. "She cannot be crowned without them."

She pushed hard and Isolde opened her free arm and she tucked Iona into it, she shook her head as she saw all the downstairs was now a blaze.

"It's too late Fili, the house is going." She shook her head.

"There is still time now take her." Filomena popped and was gone, as Isolde watched with horror. A white light exploded just outside the house, and Robbie came running out, Isolde screamed to him.

"LORD LOXLEY!"

He turned and saw her with the children; he looked instantly relieved; she felt the panic inside her. "My Lord, my sister she is in there." He looked at the house as it raged with fire, and turned to run towards the doors, but the heat beat him back, somewhere inside the fire there was a terrifying scream and the roof gave away. Robbie stepped back as the frame fell down in front of him, with a whoosh, followed by a deafening cracking and splintering.

Isolde fell to her knees holding the children and wailed into the floor, as the tears streamed from her face. Robbie could do nothing as he stepped further back feeling the devastation of the moment in the heat that blasted onto him, and watching Rune's dream disappear before his eyes in a roaring inferno. Steph gripped his shoulder.

"I am so sorry Robbie." He shook his head and swallowed the feeling inside, he turned round and his eyes burned with a dark fire as he gritted his teeth, as two tears ran down his dirty face.

"She may burn down the wood, but I will die before I allow that bitch to take Rune's dream away."

Steph pulled him close and wrapped her arms round him. "Hold onto that feeling, you are going to need it, go back they need you there. I will be with you shortly." She let him go and held him by the shoulders and looked him deep in the eyes. "Kill that bastard Robbie, take the fight to him and for the love of Hearne kill him for all of us."

Robbie gave a nod and walked back into the tunnel. Steph ran across the grass to Isolde and knelt down in front of her as she wept. Her voice was gentle. "Isolde I am so sorry, but you must protect your queen." Isolde lifted her tear filled eyes and looked at Steph in a daze. Furry Face bounded up to them and gave a whimper of a snort; Steph looked at the large tiger and understood he was ensuring the children were safe.

"Isolde you must protect the children, do you understand?" She gave a blank stare but nodded. Steph smiled. "Go now to Florae, take the queen to her people and protect her till we can get there."

Steph lifted her fingers to Isolde's eyes and gently pushed. There was a loud pop, and Isolde and the children were gone. Steph breathed a sigh of relief as she ran her fingers behind the large tiger's ears. "Ok now I am really pissed off, no one drops shit through the barrier onto my grandkids." She stood up and turned back to her tunnel and looked at Furry Face. "Protect this place; let no one near that house until your mistress returns." The tiger gave another long whine and sat down on watch, as Steph walked into her tunnel of white light, her anger rising.

Rune looked up from the end of the tube. "I got it." She lifted, and the tube separated; Jaz stepped in and took the weight as Rune moved to Ena. "Help her, she is very weak." Rayne came in behind Ena and reached in, he gently lifted her from the bed of silk she was lay on, and pulled her free of the tube.

Rune turned to the group who were waiting. "You all know what to do?" They nodded. She climbed up onto the base of the tube and lay back. "Ok Jaz gently lay it down over me, and don't forget wait for my signal." Sapphire looked worried.

"Be careful Rune, we do not know which ones have powers and which ones don't; I will be there in a flash." Rune smiled.

"I know, you have not let us down yet, and don't worry, before they know it, we will have that bird and be gone." Sapphire gave a worried nod.

"Ok see you soon."

Robbie stood on the wall reassuring Jade and Jett the kids were safe. He had just promoted a teary eyed Henry to the rank of Commander, and given his instructions. Behind him Loxley burned, the Village Hall had some damaged but was reasonably intact, Some of the farm cottages were on fire, and the house at the end of the village was damaged, a lot of windows on the main street had been blown in, and there was glass all over the cheese shop, and the bakery. The worse hit had been the hotel, where the back wall had been completely destroyed, and men ran round it with buckets of water trying to put it out. At the farm, Jess and Beth were a little shaken, one of the greenhouses had taken a near miss, but it had smashed the majority of the panes, exposing the plants to the elements.

As Robbie was talking to Jade, the ground in front of the gates flashed white. He turned to look, and saw Steph as she walked to the edge of the entrance square. She stopped and looked out across the valley as the Houlen regrouped and turned screeching in the air to return.

Like starlings in the autumn, they turned as one in the air and flew round to fly above the black stone wall of Mason on route back to Loxley. Steph stood frozen and stretched out her arms, Robbie stopped talking as he watched, as did everyone else, it felt almost as if time had stopped. White light appeared to flow down the arms of Steph as she stood alone with her long golden hair flapping in the breeze behind her.

As the Houlen cleared Mason's wall and came across the valley, Steph turned her palms to face out with her thumbs up, her bright green eyes flickered and white flooded into them as she watched the swarm of Houlen heading right for her. She looked at them screaming and wailing with joy, and hatred filled her insides.

"You want to hurt my family do you, well we will see about that, taste this you vile bastards."

Robbie watched as Steph brought her hands together as quick as lightening. The slap was deafening and the floor trembled, white light shot out of her in a wide line, and then expanded and moved at high speed towards the flying vermin. They had little time to react, the wall of light hit them and flew past them, they ignited and screamed in pain as they burned white hot, and fell from the sky burning with the brightest white flames Robbie had ever seen. Jett gave a gasp.

"Wow mother got serious with her white light shit!" Robbie gave a nod.

"Tell me about it, I say we never piss her off, and I mean ever." Jett gave a nod back. Steph turned on the spot and looked up at the wall, her eyes were almost white.

"Are you ready to take this across there?" Jett looked at Robbie and she gave a wicked smile. He smiled back and pulled out destiny.

"You ready to work up a sweat Jett Amber?" She gave a big smile.

"Bout friggin time, I thought you would never ask My Lord." Both of them stood smiling.

The wall at the top of the moorland, in front of the old stone circle, had a perfect view of Loxley, and could see the fires burning. The soldiers of Knox gained greater hope and surged even harder, as line after line of more men were allowed through the newly appeared gates and down the steep bank and across the meadows.

John Lox stood with his men watching the bowmen, as they fired into the mass of black swarming their way. The Windmill went up in flames whilst the sails still turned, and black smoke bellowed out of the windows. All over Loxley fires burned and black smoke rose in giant spirals, blown by the wind, mixing in with the ever increasing dark clouds. It was becoming so dark it was hard to tell if it was still day or night. John Lox had little time to think about it, as he saw Skip, Treen, and Woody riding to the gates to join the defence of Loxley.

He gave a smile as Treen appeared at the top of the ladder. "Good to see you, we have our hands full." She gave a sharp look out over the wall; he grabbed her hood and pulled back. "Watch yourself, this lot have rifles." She looked along the wall towards the back of the farm, it was clear that a lot of men had been killed or wounded.

"I ave ordered you more of the men for this section, they will be appearing ere very shortly." Skip came up and looked around.

"What do you need, and where do you need us?" John gave a grunt as another bullet whined through the air and hit the wall, spraying splinters everywhere. He pointed to the North East of the estate. "That area has been hit hard, they need fresh leadership, if that end goes we will lose the top of the farm, I need more men up there they are swamped."

Treen gave a look and turned back. "This is not in a problem; I am on it." As swift as lightening she started to run along the walkway, heading to take command of the point where the two large walls met beyond the orchard. Skip followed with Woody and yelled back.

"I will hold the middle section; more men are coming."

John Lox wiped his mouth and licked his lips. "We need more, this bastard has just too many."

The second large swarm of soldiers appeared, and came running at high speed towards the walls. Another hail of arrows shot into the air and came thundering down, but as the rifles rang out, John watched as more of his men were blown off the wall and fell dead below.

CHAPTER THIRTY TWO

DEATH AND LIFE

Rune lay still inside the crystal tube; she closed her eyes and focused all of her powers inside herself. Sapphire moved to the group who took up their places ready, above her she could hear voices and movement in the room. Her eyes fixed on the trap door, her breath slow and focused ready for her moment.

Ariel slouched in the arms of Ena, as Rayne did what he could to help bring life to her legs, Tila had her hand on her back trying to radiate energy into her, and Ariel was mixed up and confused not really understanding what was happening. Outside the gloom was darkening, evening was fast approaching.

Thick smoke rose from the gates as the men threw bucket after bucket on the burning crackling timbers. Robbie pulled away broken wood and another Bowman was dragged out dead from under the wreckage. The lookout post was slightly tilted above them, and two carpenters were hammering in extra supports to stabilise it, as all around them timber was dragged back to clear the gates.

On the road just outside the compound, one thousand men of Caerleon waited, as Jett Amber gave her orders to the Lieutenants, ready for them to exit through the gate. Steph waited and watched, it was clear the complete destruction of the Houlen had set them back, but Mason had far more men available than Loxley had.

Behind the wall the force from Dove Dale finally arrived having crept up on the waiting soldiers, their problem was that the army of Knox was so vast, even within yards of their camp, the large stone wall was still almost a mile away. They took their positions and launched an attack of arrows. Tents, men, carts, and small wooden buildings, felt the cutting power of a Loxley arrow as they came down like rain, and the noise all over the edges of the camp went from dull to chaotic, with screams and wails.

Using two lines, one firing, one loading, Commander Millington moved forward slowly clearing every soldier in range. It was not the fastest attack, but it was certainly the most effective, and yet compared to the mass that was encamped, it was still only the tiniest steps towards helping in the fight.

Big John and Bear grunted as they lifted another large log aside, and men scrambled to snatch up anything else that had been pinned down by it, they moved slowly to the side and then dropped the tree pole, and it bounced with a large boom. The roadway was clear enough for troops, and Steph breathed a sigh of relief as she saw more men amassing at the opening of Mason's walls, she turned and called back to Robbie. "Their cannons are rolling." He turned to catch a look, but could see little through all the smoke.

Robbie shoved his fingers into his mouth and gave a sharp long whistle; Jett heard the call and turned to her officers. "Move em out."

Rafe stood back and the troops began to walk in rank. Jett turned and walked quickly to get ahead of her men, she flexed her fingers as she walked, her hand yearned for a blade, and this was finally her chance. The Specialist's gathered as the men from Caerleon made their way to the gates, it was becoming so dark with the clouds thickening that Robbie could hardly see the wall in the distance.

Rowan gripped the hood of Jade. "Where do you think you are going?" She turned and looked at him with bright green eyes.

"I will be where you are." She lifted a finger and poked him in his chest. "Do not even say it...I mean it Rowan, if we are walking to our deaths, I am with you. I am just over a month; it is nowhere near enough to stop me." His cool slate grey eyes looked calmly at her.

"If my child lives, it is no matter whether I die or not." Jade made a fist and punched him, as she shook her head.

"Don't you dare say that...I mean it Rowan, just do not speak, I am at your side as I vowed I would always be, and not you, Robbie or Rune will stop me." Rowan said nothing, he pushed out his arms and grabbed her and pulled her close.

"I love you Jade." She flung her arms around him and pushed her face into his chest.

"Please live...Please Rowan don't leave me, I don't want to grow old with not a lot of memories, I want millions more before we die." He squeezed her tighter.

"I promise Jade, if we make it through this, we will treble that, and live to be old happy and fat, just watch yourself and make sure we are together at the end."

Steph looked at the bridge where it had fallen short, it had been cleared by the Houlen who had dragged the dead to the end of it and dropped them off in hope of creating a pile large enough it would span the gap, they were not far off, as hundreds of dead lay just below the level of the road surface. As The Specialist's advanced Steph opened a tunnel, and leading the way Robbie marched in next to Jett and Rafe.

Mark Richard Dale looked out towards Loxley and gave a grunt of disbelief, he turned to Mason. "Is he marching out to meet us, his whole place is burning, is he insane?" Mason gave a satisfied smile.

"I expect nothing less of him, he is a true warrior, and it will be a shame really to kill him." Dale shook his head not understanding what looked like a suicide mission; he turned back to his generals.

"Hold back the cannons and recall the men, tell them we have an army at our door and we aim to meet them."

Otto was wheeled in with a frown. "What is all this, we never start before the sun dies?" Rosamund turned to view his disfigured face.

"It appears Morgana is too busy enjoying herself and will possibly not make it, and that leaves us with a discussion to have, I assumed you would want to be part of it?" He scowled even more.

"Why that Celt bitch has anything to do with this family I have no idea, we are pure Sachsen in our veins, not a half breed like her." Rosamund watched as he was lifted into his seat in the large circular room.

"Never the less Uncle, she is the daughter of Victor, and has the right to a seat; I believe your brother was quite clear on this." His face wrinkled and his scowl widened as he sat in his seat next to Maud, who was seated in her chair and encased in a thin crystal box that looked almost like glass.

The ritual room of Berengar castle was one of the most ornate. The wide circle of golden chairs, were placed evenly so everyone seated could see each other clearly. In many ways it was probably due to the fact that most of them were so two faced, it was the only way of arranging the seats which made it impossible to be attacked unseen.

The floor was grey polished marble, and in the centre of the room was a large round circle, into which was inlaid a star. The star was a deep red outlined seven pointed star on a black background, the edge of the circle was also the deepest of reds. In the centre of the star was the faint outline of the trap doors in the floor, where unbeknown to those in the room, Rune and her group were waiting patiently.

Every member of the family that had passed was sat in their chairs behind sealed crystal, and it was a gruesome sight to behold, but this was the tradition of the family, and even though the ritual was only done every five years, over time all of them had become quite accustomed to the sight.

On the perches above the seats, sat ravens of all sizes, two perches were empty, the one above Maud's seat, Rajani her raven now sat above Morgana's seat, much to the annoyance of Otto. The largest perch of all, which was above the joint seats of Branna and Berengar, belonged to Roack.

Roack would arrive with the family's heads shortly before the ritual.

The room was vast, and a spiral stairway wove its way down from the top of the tower, in which was a skylight of coloured glass depicting a dark black and blue raven. The walls were filled with the shields and weapons of their enemies, from the previous conquests of the past.

Around the room between each chair were treasures of great value stood on ornate stands. Some were gold, some ancient pottery, and even a few golden inlaid weapons of previous kings.

The rest of the family began to arrive, and walked casually down to their seats, it was clear none was in a rush to start. Rosamund who had a decanter on the arm of her seat, poured a drink into a platinum goblet, and relaxed as the others took their time seating themselves. It took well over half an hour before everyone bar Branna and Berengar was sitting in comfort.

Rosamund tapped her fingers impatiently on her chair arm, which annoyed everyone, until the moment came and she smiled. "Are we all quite ready?"

There was several mumbles and grumbles from the family, but she took that as a yes and looked to Lothar to start. He lifted his glass in a salute. "Everyone, well isn't this nice?" Moans and grumbles echoed quietly around the room and he smiled. "We are meeting early, because as you know tonight, we planned to hold Morgana to account, Roack is aging, and it is for us to ensure the survival of the bird, and therefore the founders of this family, our beloved Branna and Berengar." Otto stared at Lothar with loathing.

"That bitch has taken the greatest share of power, why do we even tolerate her, I say kill the bitch and be done with her, you all have enough pure blood to bring forth another, why do you tolerate her?"

"Not this again Father, have we not said a thousand times, it matters not if her mother was Celt, her powers are pure Berengar, and therefore she is to be seated and given the same grace as all of us." Ulric looked round the room.

"She is the closest in power since grandmother, we need to walk carefully, she has great power and has discovered things about our abilities we have all benefitted from, even you Father, if it was not for her potions, you too would be sat in a glass box. Did she not stop the curse that had stolen your legs and plagued you for years? Hate her all you like, but if not for her, we would have one more glass box in the room."

He scowled and hissed through his teeth. Lothar gave a long sigh. "The fact remains that she has accomplished much that can help us since she was last here. Morgana managed to place her first son's spirit into a future relative, it is an amazing fact, and frankly Uncle Otto, I would have thought you would be delighted with her progress, because it has become very apparent to the rest of us, that we could put you in a younger and healthy body." Merwig gave a frightful sort of look.

"Are we sure that would be wise, he is a grumpy old shit at the best of times, put him in a young man's body and what the hell would we be expecting, more pissed off but mobile, I hope not?" Otto hissed through his teeth.

"You would have to be wary boy, you only got so cocky once my legs had been taken." Rosamund looked annoyed.

"Merwig...Can we not go round and round with the insults as we always do, is this whole day not painful enough as it is?" He lifted his glass to Otto and smiled.

Rosamund looked at Gundobarld. "Have you nothing to say, after all you are supposed to be the thinker of the family?" He stirred in his chair.

"She has accomplished much I must agree, but I have no taste for her, yes she brought Mason back from the dead, but I question as to whether or not he was dead, his bird looked quite healthy in the tower. I will withhold my judgement until she can give a full explanation of herself, and obviously read her writings on the matter." Lothar gave a supportive nod of his head.

"So we shall have to wait, and we shall move on. The next matter I wish us to discuss is the matter of the fairy we have locked in our dungeon. Her life force is powerful and protected, but we may have come across a way, thanks again to Morgana, that we can tap that life force to aid our founder family members, and possibly us." Amalina turned in her seat.

"Are you insane? Branna will kill anyone who lays a finger on her?" He looked at her quite unconcerned.

"She sleeps more than she is awake these days, I am sure when she wakes and lasts the year she would be grateful for the gift we gave her." Ulric looked at his wife and then back to Lothar.

"She has a point Lothar, you know how possessive Branna can be, you are taking a huge risk, I know you have no issues with Morgana, but I feel this would be a big mistake." He gave a smile.

"I do find Morgana interesting there is no doubt, but look at how Branna sided with her over the death of Maud, I am sure that Morgana could convince her it was for the best." Merwig gave a laugh and they all looked at him, he shrugged.

"Branna favours no one, she favours herself above all others, and her only concern is who will warm her bed when Berengar gets out. She took the side of Morgana simply because Maud threatened Ariel's life, and let's be honest, no offence Otto but she was bloody horrible. No one here enjoyed her presence; if you asked me, she did all of us a favour, but never ever think Branna will side with Morgana. She is good, but she will never channel the powers the way Branna has."

Lothar sat back and pulled a lever. "So, what do we do with this?"

The floor in the centre of the star fell away as the trap door opened, and the cranks could be heard below ground. The wires that ran through the floor strained, and slowly the crystal tomb below began to rise up towards the floor. Otto was outraged and shook with rage as he scowled at Lothar.

"HOW DARE YOU BRING THE VILE WITCH INTO THIS OUR MOST SACRED SPACE!" His face went almost scarlet such was his rage. Lothar sat looking smug and smiled at him.

Slowly the white crystal tomb of Ariel came into view, and Otto cursed and spat at it. Below the ground the team rushed to their positions and waited for the moment. Merwig leaned forward in his seat and looked at the tomb, as it came to a shudder and stopped in the centre of the star on the floor. He squinted trying to make out the detail of the body within. "Who is that exactly?" Lothar looked puzzled and leaned forward in his chair.

"What do you mean, it is...."

There was a blinding flash of violet light, and all of them felt the pressure rise from the centre of the room, and thrust them back into their seats as they shielded their eyes. Ravens squawked and cried out on their perches, as they flapped their wings violently. Another flash of blue came from within the glowing violet light, and the sound of crystal smashing on the floor rang into their ears.

The light dimmed, and all of them gasped and sat helpless in their seats as a wide circle of unknown faces held swords to their chests, pinning them into their seats. The ravens screamed and squawked even louder, as they thrashed about sensing danger. The light cleared, and they all blinked to see Runestone stood on what had been Ariel's silken bed, her eyes glowing with bright violet light, and at the end of the tomb, Sapphire stood holding her bow, and slowly circling as she aimed at each member of the family. Otto was outraged as he sat pinned by the sword of Jaz, his eyes burned red with his anger.

"How dare you point that thing at me, do you know who I am?" Jaz shook his head.

"Some vile, nasty, old man without working legs?" Lothar looked calmly at Rune.

"What is the meaning of this?" Rune looked up at the skylight, and then back to Lothar.

"I am the one thing you all yearn for more than any treasure, and I am the one who will take my gifts from all of you this day." Lothar frowned.

"Gifts? Correct me if I am wrong young woman, but I am not aware of any gift I have received from you, after all, how would I possibly forget something as deliciously beddable as you?" Rune smiled.

"I AM LIFE." She lifted her arm up in the air, and her eyes went instantly violet. Rune looked up at the skylight and a bright burst of violet light erupted from her eyes, and shot up the tower to the skylight, which exploded into a million fragments, and the light streamed up into the dark sky of the night.

Cezar turned from the fire and looked back, and over the trees he saw the column of violet light shoot like a pillar into the clouds. There was a deafening roar, and the sky exploded with lightening, and as he took a sharp intake of breath, he saw the violet spread out and swirl into the blackness of the night, as if it was mixing and fighting with it. The sky expanded in what looked like a violet and black swirling marble, as around him all the others in the camp stood up and stared with wonder.

Crina leant on her stick at his side. "What is it?" He shook his head.

"I have no idea, all I can think of is those friends of Ena, but as to what is happening, I am lost for words."

The violet fought with the black in what looked like a rough battle, and then out of the sky came a ghastly scream, that wailed down at all of them stood watching. They covered their ears and fell to the earth, as the sound felt like it was devouring their insides.

Deep within the castle in the circular room, the family members shook in their seats, as the wails continued to scream from the sky. Their eyes and noses started to bleed, as shaking they slumped with their heads on their chest and went still. Rune turned to the others.

"Lower your swords and gather the ravens, we have little time, Branna still sleeps, but she will awaken soon and we must find her, for she has the one raven I need most."

High on the wall in Loxley Morgan le Fey screamed with delight, as Robbie and Jett's men met and clashed with the soldiers on the bridge. They smashed together with a clash of swords, and scattered out as men died and fell from the side of the bridge, the start of the most brutal fight in Loxley's history had begun.

Somewhere in the darkness Albanlin turned. "There you are little red stone."

CHAPTER THIRTY THREE

DRAWN SWORDS

The Sage stopped and looked back, before him the large wall of the London City of Mason loomed. Ester looked at it in awe. "How did they make it so big?"

"They use slave labour and machines, like you have probably never seen. They can carry fifty carts worth of stuff, and have a liquid stone that sets hard in a week. Nothing of beauty is built that way, but that is their way of being, they want all the land, and to own everything including us if we do not stop them." She looked at the wall with greater amazement.

The wastelands had not been the waste that the Sage had first thought, many who had fled the Cutters had headed there, and they had encountered two groups, once they had travelled under the river through the tunnel. Each time they stopped, the Sage would scatter some seeds, although he was not completely sure why, maybe it was the strange feeling he had growing inside of him.

Martin crawled up to his side. "This is the weakest point; we will have no problems getting over that wall and in tonight. Although I think we need to rest up, we have been at a fast pace on foot, and they are tired and weary, let them rest a while." He looked back through the thin trees.

"Yeah, I need to work a few things out, this place would be better than any, we will rest here."

Sapphire found the lever and gripped it, all around the chamber the ravens squawked and squealed, as they were untethered from their perches and thrust into sacks. She pulled the lever, and the bed of crystal began to lower back into the chamber below, where Ena waited holding her mother up.

Una held out a sack in front of her, as it bobbed and lurched in her hand. "How the hell are we going to sneak out of here with this lot making such a racket?" Rune looked back, lifted her fingers and snapped them together, all of the sacks fell still, she smiled.

"Does that help?" Maddy gave a chuckle towards Una.

"She is getting cocky, like we did."

With the lever pulled back again, Ariel came up sat on the bed with Ena, she was looking a little more awake and stronger. She looked at Rune and gave a frown. "What are we doing here Eve?"

Rune turned to her and smiled. "You will remember soon, but for now we must make a move and swiftly." Ariel gave a smile.

As Robbie ran along the bridge, his thoughts shifted to the face of David, and Melanie, and those of the dead that had littered the gate compound, the smell of burning was on his clothes, and his mind shifted to the Mere. He felt the anger burning in his throat and chest, as the thought of having to face Rune and tell her the dream that had been so precious, had now gone. His anger burst out of him as he met the first soldier, and with all of his rage he took one vast powerful swipe, and cut the man clean in half, and then smashed into the others as they came at him.

He had felt calm and alert, and his mind had been focused, but as he saw the red dragon on the shirt of the men before him, a power he did not know he had was unleashed, and he powered forward slashing and hacking through anything in front of him, as only one thought stayed focused in his mind. These men before him, they were stopping him from reaching Mason, and that was all he could think of, all he could see, his anger thrust him forward with a great might and power never seen before.

Just behind him to his left, Jett whooped and screamed, as she lunged and cut her way through the soldiers. Finally, she had the fight she had expected, and she was not going to waste her time sitting on a wall with a bow, this was her destiny as the Red Queen to come, and her men stood around her, and beside her, carving a path to freedom.

Malcolm Prosper looked at Joe. "Does it have the range we need?" Joe patted the catapult.

"Aye it does, I built it meself, so you can bet yer last bit, this bugger will hit it spot on." Malcolm turned to the rest of his Night Strikers.

"Well get on with it...load it up and let's see what we can do from here."

The black wall below the high was some distance off, so any thought of ropes and climbing down to it was out. Joe had built a large catapult, and had guaranteed it would hit its mark. Malcom was not convinced, but with troops running along the wall in the direction of the large gate at Loxley's front entrance, they had to try everything.

The men wound up the coil, pulling back the basket, into which they loaded canvass bags filled with explosives made from fertilizer. Joe lit the fuse and gave a nod, and Malcolm pulled the handle. The basket shot up like a rocket, and the canvass bags spun into the air.

Trees parted and grass was flattened, as every member of the Night Strikers found their spot from which to watch, on the edge of the high escarpment.

Along the wide wall below, men in ranks ran at a fast pace heading to the far end of the wall, and their chance to fight in Loxley. They trudged along at a fast pace when suddenly from nowhere a bag came falling out of the sky, and hit one of the running soldiers. He tripped and stumbled snatching hold of the men either side, which caused them to sway off balance and they fell over him.

The pace was fast, and so a domino like effect happened as the men behind tripped and fell over them, and soon soldiers were weaving and twisting trying to avoid the rapidly growing pile of fallen soldiers. The officer noticed and turned back to yell, when there was a blinding flash, and his soldiers, and stone exploded into the air.

High on the ridge, the Night Strikers cheered as they saw the huge hole in the wall, Malcom was fast to act. "Right, you lot change the angle and turn it this way, let's see if we can land one behind them."

Louisa and Gwynne stood side by side aiming and shooting at a rapid pace. Five feet away Rigger crouched in the grass as he fitted his wires to the little box, ready to wind up the charge. Dove sat a few feet away watching nervously. "Get a move on Rig, there are too many and the bowmen are going to be overrun soon." He worked as quickly as he could, attaching the wires and screwing down the nuts.

"Hell girl, give me a break, I am going as fast as I ruddy well can." She looked back at the mass of men running through the trees towards them.

"Rigg they are almost on the spot, come on man." He grabbed the handle and turned it rapidly to build up the charge.

"Right ready." She lifted her head a little and watched the spot.

"Almost...nearly there... NOW!"

The little box gave a whirling noise, and there was a tremendous BOOM! The soldier's, trees, and soil lifted into the air. Dove ducked as bits of wood, man, and tree soil rained down on them. Rigger grabbed the wires and tore them out of the box; he gave the nod to Gwynne who whistled, and bowmen still firing, lifted up out of the grass, and began to move backwards away from the explosion site, and closer to Loxley.

Louisa fired several shots, giving her men time and then turned and ran. They ran at full speed through the trees until they saw Ox. They ran past him as his men took up the new line ready, and Rigger skidded to a halt and began to dig at the soil with his knife. Dove skidded up at his side and started digging a few feet away.

One hundred yards back, Louisa turned with Gwynne and her men, and a new line formed of men with loaded bows.

Dove wiped the sweat off her face with her sleeve. "That last charge was just right, same again?" Rigger pulled at the soil creating a hole, and swung round his bag for new explosives.

"Same again Dove, this time pack the earth a little harder, it will give us more lift." She stabbed the soil and dug like a wild animal as she looked up to see Louisa and Gwynne set and ready in the distance.

"We can't keep this up Rigg, we need ten times more explosives than we have." He gave a nod as he looked at the hole and packed the explosives inside.

"I hear ya girl, we just gotta do the best we can, there is a lot of folks in town depending on us."

Over on the far side of the moorland Treen jumped up onto the wall, and pointed with her bow. "It eez explosive, stop this people before they eez too close."

The bowman turned to spot where she was pointing, John Lox noticed and looked across to his left where he spotted similar men moving in with other attackers, he bellowed at the top of his lungs.

"STOP THOSE MEN, THEY HAVE EXPLOSIVES AND ARE GOING FOR THE WALL!"

Further up where the wall protected the top of the farm orchard, there was a massive explosion, and both Treen and John Lox turned to see the wall shudder and then lift into the sky. Treen snatched her sword and ran past Skip. "They eez in to the tree farm, be fast."

She sprinted at high speed along the long walkway in the direction of the blast, but she knew it was too late, from where she was, she could already see black vested soldiers pouring into the top of the farm, Loxley had been breached and Mason's men were now on the inside of the stockade.

The only way out was up the spiral stairway, Fox and Blades led the way, with three sacks each tied to their belts. Round and round they twisted, until they saw a small metal platform, and a door. Fox arrived first and pressed his ear to the door. He was breathing too fast and it made it impossible to hear anything, he looked at Blades as she arrived. "Cannot hear a thing, wanna risk it?"

She took a long deep breath. "Take a look and see, but be fast." He gripped the handle and slowly turned it until it felt loose in the frame. Carefully he gave it a gentle pull, and slid his eye round the edge to the gap and peered out. The corridor was filled with guards in deep burgundy tunics; he pushed the door shut quietly, and shook his head. Max came up the last step, and Blades turned to him.

"These guards with soul eating spirits in them, what do they look like?" He caught his breath, and leaned forward holding his knees bent over.

"Tall, cold white faces with dark red robes." Blades looked at Fox, and he gave a nod. She looked down and the others were almost with them. Rune came up next.

"Problem?" Fox nodded.

"Them creepy guards, I reckon the whole castle will be on alert after that purple light thing." Rayne squeezed passed them.

"I can deal with this." He looked at Max. "White or bright light?" Max shrugged.

"What is the difference?" Blades looked at him.

"Ask one when it's sucking your soul out, so come on just pick one will you." He looked worried.

"Err! Bright! Yeah, brighter the better." He nodded his head reassuringly.

Rayne turned at the door, swung it open, pushed out his palms, and brilliant yellow light flooded the corridor. The group heard the screams of terror and pain in the corridor, Rayne turned back with a smile.

"Bright it is then."

The group raced out into the corridor and looked both ways, Rayne turned to Rune. "Any ideas?" Her eyes were flickering with violet, as she tried to sense the inside of the castle, looking for the raven. Ariel gave a shudder and turned to Ena and gasped.

"Ena, you came back?" She lifted her hands to her face and held it. "My daughter." Ena smiled.

"Yes Mother, we came back for you; do you know where you are?" Ariel looked round, the floor was littered with dead guards, but she appeared to recognise where she was, she pointed. "Go that way." Ena gave a nod to the others, and they all moved off at a fast pace.

Outside the castle, high above them the violet mixed and swirled in with the blackness of the sky. Large patches of darkness were being pushed back, as the Violet Lines corroded the powers of the Merle. In the woodland beyond the castle, the rebels hiding in their camps could do nothing but watch in wonder, not really understanding what was happening. Cezar had an idea.

Loxley was still burning. Woodsmen flooded onto the farm, and moved quickly through the orchard. Jess and Beth directed them in ranks as they loaded their bows, and moved forward in a long line, at a fast pace to meet the oncoming enemy. From the walls Bowman took aim and fired into the masses trying to pour through the breech in the wall.

Treen was down the ladder with a hundred men, her sword out closely followed by Skip, as they rushed into the masses of the black vested soldiers, and slashed and cut their way towards the breech. Loxley Armsmen, dropped from the walls as another large explosion went off further down, where John Lox bellowed at his men to redirect the bowman's arrows.

Treen grunted and gasped, as she slashed at the enemy. Behind her, carts were being manoeuvred as Treen and her fighters pushed back against the force trying to plough into the narrow gap. From the walls, arrows rained down and the dead were piling up. Skip cut his way through to her side as she thrashed her sword round with anger like he had never seen before.

Groups of men heaved and pushed the carts, crashing into the soldiers of Mason and bulldozing them down as they tried to block the gap. The fighting was frantic, as Treen's men came together forming a crude line that faced the hundreds of men running at them. A wide ring of the dead lay on the floor behind them. as they stepped forward one pace at a time pushing the mass of black with a determination like Mason had never seen from his own men.

In the far end of the orchard Woodsmen fired in long lines, cutting down the black vested raiders, as they surged towards them. Another group of Woodsmen stood ready with their swords, and as the bowmen let fly a volley of arrows, they stepped up and into the fight meeting with a mighty clash. Jess pulled the bowmen back, letting them fire at free will to target single individuals, and protect the woodsmen. It was hard brutal and bloody, and screams and wails rang out through the fruit trees with the clash of swords.

Beth loaded her bow and took aim, one soldier ran towards her and her arrow let fly, hitting him in the head, and sending him reeling back into the masses, who were running in every direction to find a way through to the farm. Outside on the road just past the school, Maggs with Rags fired at the few who had made it through, as more Bowmen came up the road to help. Jimmy Perkins led the way, shouting at the men and telling them where they were needed, he took his place next to Rags and aimed his bow, and together they fired shot after shot, as Jess with her men held back in the orchard.

Rowan gasped and heaved with Jade just behind him, she had his back, and cut and slashed at any who dared to get near him, she felt the power brewing up insider her, and suddenly out of the blue she felt something warm burn through her.

"Rune is that you?"

"I am here and safe, we are after the ravens, how are things are you all safe?"

"Rune they are attacking and the gates blowed up, I am with Rowan and Robbie and there are thousands of them, please hurry."

"I am almost finished, tell them to hang in there I am coming soon."

Robbie lifted his sword and noticed his white bangle glowing, as he thrust and then sliced, and lifted his leg to kick another one out of his way. *"Where are you Rune?"* He cut back next to Rowan, and with a heavy grunt swung back knocking a soldier over the edge of the bridge. Rowan gasped as he sliced through another.

"We are almost at the wall." Robbie could see the giant structure just above the heads of the soldiers, as he slashed his way forward one more step. Behind the Specialists were in top form, as Big John and Bear hacked and cleaved with power, Rafe growled as he thrust out, and then gave a terrifying howl, as his sword came flashing like lightning back round. Jett laughed and screamed with delight as she jumped and skipped, her strikes with her sword were faster than anything any soldier had even seen, she was ruthless and surgical, and with every little whoop and screech, a slice landed on a new target, and they fell to the side to allow her to dance through.

A few feet away Harry sliced with power, he could see Robbie just up in front, and hacked and sliced as he tried to work his way to his side. His soft leather boots that were his pride and joy, squelched in the blood on the floor, and he whimpered, as his feet came free of the mush to move forward another step. "Oh man these boots are ruined." He looked at the Cutter in front of him and yelled. "That ain't cosmic man!" He then brought round his gleaming blade into the Cutter, killing him instantly.

At the rear with some of the other soldiers, Alice, Hawk, and Smokes, walked with arrows on bows, targeting anyone who was remotely close to getting a hit on one of their men. Alice was in fine form loading faster than she ever had before, and taking out any soldier she thought would pose any threats to Bear. Men all around the swords group, would lurch back with a white tipped arrow in their head, and fall either off the bridge, or into the mass of their own men.

The fighting was the most brutal of any fight they had endured, in Robbie's mind this was what everything had led him to, and for too long he watched his friends die, he saw it as pay back, and his determination was such, nothing was going to stand in his way. His eyes burned with anger, many times when a soldier faced him, rather than fight they would just leap off the bridge and take their chances from the fall, rather than face certain death.

The door to the chamber of the Master of the House and Council flew open, and the council man Alder looked at Elgin sat with his granddaughter Isolde as she wept into his arms. "Is it true...The queen is..."

"Quite safe and protected, the children are here in the house with my wife and four maidens of the crown, you have no need to fret Counsellor." Bade ran in behind him and slowed as he saw the sight of Isolde weeping into her grandfather's arms. Elgin looked to him.

"Bade order the guard to stand on duty and ready this minute." The Counsellor looked outraged.

"Now just wait a minute, what gives you the right to overrule a royal decree, and send our people into a war they should not be involved with."

"Right! WHAT GIVES ME THE RIGHT? HOW DARE YOU... IN THE ABSENCE OF OUR MONARCH, I HAVE EVERY RIGHT AS LEADER OF THE HIGH COUNCIL."

Bade stepped back a little. Elgin looked at Alder with anger in his eyes.

"No queen of this line shall ever be an orphan, her father and mother are in need on Fae soil, to attack them is to attack us, have you forgotten the evil done by that woman to our race, is your mind so filled with power that you have forgotten the hideous monsters she created, by perverting the souls of our people? We make a stand for our queen and her land, as one day we shall share both as people in kinship, now order the guard." Bade bowed and walked backward, he turned in the doorway, and then ran for all he was worth down the corridor yelling as loud as he could.

"Order the guard, take up arms, and stand out ready for your queen." Alder gave a bow.

"I apologise and stand corrected Master Elgin." Elgin gave a sigh.

"I too am sorry, one of my grandchildren has been taken from us, I know better than to raise my voice Alder." He looked suddenly sad and tired. "We must make a stand, I do not want a day to come when we face our queen, and have to admit we sat here knowing her parents would die, and did nothing." Alder gave a nod and stepped back.

"You are right my friend; I will assist in their immediate despatch." He gave a weak smile.

"Thank you, Alder."

As the men of Dove Dale backed away slightly, as the black vested troops came at them, a flash of bright white light erupted behind them. Commander Millington glanced back for a second, and saw the long white tunnel of the Lady Whiteline, he gave a sigh of relief, his men were tired and facing an enemy one hundred times too big for them.

Out of the tunnel came a hoard of brown clad fighters, all roaring and screaming as they poured onto the battle field. He noted the symbols on their tunics and thought for a second. "How the hell did the Scottish get here?"

The Scottish fighters flooded onto the field around his men and charged with fresh legs and arms into the battle. Steph walked out of her tunnel with a young woman with long shoulder length black hair, and the brightest blue eyes he had ever seen. Steph smiled as she walked towards him.

"I brought some extra swords, this is Grace, she is the leader of the fighters in

Scotland, we once loaned them a man or two and so she is repaying the favour."
He smiled and held out his hand.

"Commander Millington, Lady Grace, we are very happy to see you." She
smiled and looked at the wall.

"Is Robbie up there yet?" He looked back.

"Well I must say, I really am not sure." She smiled.

"We got here just in time then."

The candle flickered as she hurriedly made notes on a piece of fresh
parchment. "Hiding away with your books again, I seem to remember another
time when you hid in here for months avoiding your friend?" Rhiannon stopped
writing and turned to the voice as she rose slowly.

"My Lord Albanlin." He walked into the room filled with book cases and scrolls.

"Why are you here and not out there helping, this is after all your making is it
not?" Rhiannon stammered.

"My...Making...My Lord I am not sure all of this should be lain at my door." His
blacked tattered hood twitched.

"Are you not? You knew this Branna was gifted, some say more gifted than your
scholars here, and yet you refused her an audience. Bridget warned you did she
not?" Rhiannon's eyes flashed.

"Bridget did not understand." He took a step forward and she backed away.

"Bridget was right, and I know she told you, I was there when she died." Her
eyes opened wide.

"That is not true she died alone." His hood shook from side to side.

"I was there as her last breath was drawn into the black stone, she only knew of
that because it was you who instructed her in the ways to use it." Rhiannon began
to tremble. His figure was as still as a rock.

"You need to repair this, the truth is out there, and My Queen of the Moon, it is
time you faced it, now go." There was a flash of white and she was gone. Albanlin
turned and looked at the papers on her table. He lifted one up and read her notes.
"You are wrong My Queen, this solves nothing, I know how to fix this, and in time
I will."

Rowan smashed his sword down with a scream, and cleaved into the skull of
the huge soldier in front of him. Robbie slashed three feet from him, with Jade a
little back from them both cutting and hitting the one who had got through. Robbie
glanced up and noticed they were under the gateway; he brought his sword up and
cut forward as he breathed out his words to Rowan. "We are...Almost through,
keep pushing."

He lunged forward stabbing the soldier, and then pushed him aside and stepped forward into woodwork. The men in front separated, as Jade came through the centre, to see the waist high barrier that had been erected there. He did not understand and neither did Rowan, as the soldiers in black vests on the other side of the barrier, hurriedly separated and moved to the side leaving them open in full view and under the gateway.

Twenty feet away, Mark Richard Dale stood with both his arms up, yet looked like he had won the prize of the century, as he stood between two long brass cannons. He dropped his arms, and screamed with delight as the Specialists came to a halt under the gateway behind Robbie, Rowan, and Jade. As Dale dropped his arms, and screamed with all his might, it suddenly became apparent they were in a trap, as high above them, the Dark One cackled and laughed with utter delight.

"FIRE!"

Jade screamed, and stretched out her arms to push Rowan and Robbie back behind her.

CHAPTER THIRTY FOUR

WINDOWS, TUNNELS, BRIDGES

Martin lay in the grass with the Sage as he watched the wall. "Dutch is a good fighter and a good soldier." He gave a nod to Martin.

"He is, he will be very useful tonight." The Sage grabbed another handful of seed and threw it onto the waste ground in front of them. "I have no idea why I keep doing this, but something inside says I need to." Martin smiled.

"Something inside says I need to eat." He gave a chuckle as a little pop sound came from his side. He looked, and there was leaf who gave a big blink, he smiled. "Your little friend is back." The Sage turned to her, she was far brighter and more colourful than he had ever seen her, and yet she looked panicked.

"What is it?" She grabbed at his sleeve and tugged it hard, and he felt her fear, he looked at Martin. "Can you handle things here? I think she wants me for something." He gave a nod at him, and then there was a pop, and he was gone.

Treen was slashing like a wild banshee, when Skip grabbed her hood and pulled her back. A row of bowmen stood on the carts and fired at close range, taking those closest to the their people, and Treen was dragged backwards slashing and screaming, up onto one of the carts by a large and burley Woodsmen called Derek. He lifted her up and smiled, as more Bowmen took aim clearing the pathway back for their men.

Treen jumped from the cart gasping and panting, her long red hair hanging wet and lank with sweat and blood. She looked round and saw Skip, as he drew in fresh air and he smiled at her, his face was dirty and he had a small cut to his cheek. Neither of them could talk, as they sucked in more air to breathe, they simply looked at each other and smiled, just knowing each of them was still alive, was enough for now.

Beth battered and stabbed at every soldier running her way; Jess behind her, still had arrows, and fired at each one of the soldiers that came at them. She looked to her hip, and the rapidly emptying sling on her leg. "I am running low on arrows; they are on the path where I left them."

A soldier came out from the Logan Berry lines with his sword up, Beth cut up and swiped her blade across his chest, she took five paces back closer to Jess, as she waited for the next one, who she could hear coming down the fruit line. "Quick, go grab your arrows, Jessie."

Jess turned; she could see them twenty feet away at the end of the path next to the greenhouse. She ran for her life towards them, as the next soldier came hurtling out of the fruit lines. Beth lifted her sword to strike, and he launched himself at her, smashing into her waist and sending her flying backwards.

Beth gritted her teeth and brought round her fist with a crunch. "Oh no you don't not on my patch you scum."

Jess reached her arrows and turned to look back, and saw the Cutter pull out his knife and plunge it down, straight into Beth's heart with a smile from his bloody mouth. Her body froze as he looked up at Jess and gave an evil grin, showing he had lost one of his teeth from Beth's punch. The arrows lay at her feet, but she was frozen in shock and heartbreak.

The Cutter laughed, as he climbed off her lifeless body and stood up, and started to move towards her, he pulled out his sword and then ran at her with speed, and she could do nothing but stand in frozen terror. He came closer and closer, and she wanted to, but she could not move her legs, or even scream as behind him on the grass lay the body of her sister in law, with a knife sticking out of her chest. Time felt frozen, until, Swish...THUD!

She blinked, and the Cutter shot backwards, a long arrow with black and white feathers, sticking out of his forehead. He hit the ground hard, his eyes open and the leer of his mouth frozen to his face.

Her head snapped round to look behind her. A man stood at the far end of the greenhouse path, dressed in a long green coat with a hood over his head. He held his bow in place with another arrow on the string, his face was shaded but also looked bark like, and his eyes which looked down the arrow, were of the most intense pale blue. He fired, and the arrow whizzed past her, and a grunt came from behind her, and she turned and looked to see another Cutter with the same black and white feathered arrow in his forehead.

Jess gave a gasp as reality kicked in, and she turned back to the unknown figure, but he had gone, her word fell quietly from her mouth. "Billy?"

Her eyes dropped to Beth, as she heard the footsteps of more Woodsmen arriving in the farm yard, and running towards the orchard, and her eyes filled, as the tears flowed, she took a step forward and fell to her knees, and sobbed as her shoulders shook, and she stared at the lifeless limp body of her greatest friend and sister.

Jade opened her eyes. Robbie and Rowan stood still with their eyes still closed, Jade looked round, and in front of her, the whole of the gateway shone like a huge green window. Rowan opened one eye not understanding what had happened. "What the...?"

Robbie opened his eyes as Jade spun round and looked at them with a guilty expression. "It wasn't me!"

Jett gave a laugh out loud. "Where the hell did it go?" Robbie looked down at Jade, who was fooling no one with her attempt to look innocent.

"What did you do with it Jade?" She shook her head.

"I am not lying, it wasn't me." Jett thought it was hilarious, as she looked through the green shimmering window at Mark Richard Dale with his jaw dropped staring at them, along with all the soldiers. Jett pointed to Jade and smiled at them all staring with disbelief.

"She did it. You wanna join the cannonballs, step right through." A lot of the soldiers, who looked horror struck, took several paces back away from the strange green light. Realising what had happened, yet not understanding any of it, Mark Richard Dale screamed at his soldiers.

"WHAT THE HELL ARE YOU DOING, KILL THEM!"

The soldiers shook their heads and stepped back a few more paces, they had heard of the Violet Witch, was there a green one as well? His anger was reaching fever pitch once again, he pulled his pistol out of his holster, and started to walk towards them, he aimed and pulled the trigger, Robbie, Jade, and Rowan all blinked and took a step back.

The bullets hit the green window, flashed, and disappeared, his outrage hit fever pitch as he pulled the trigger again...And again...And again...And again, he screamed with rage as each bullet flashed making Jade screw up her face and blink, and then disappeared.

Rowan looked at her. "You must have done something; you are the one who makes green windows." She shook her head.

"Honestly I did nothing." Jett was loving it, she pushed between them to get a better look.

"This is awesome." She pushed her head through the window. A group of soldiers watched with horror as her head disappeared. One fainted, and the other four screamed with terror, dropped their swords, turned, and ran for their lives. Jett pulled her head back and looked at them puzzled.

"I cannot see anything, I have no idea where it's all gone, it's just black look!" Jade stepped forward and pushed her head through with Jett. More soldiers, who had already been unsettled, panicked and turned, and ran screaming away from the wall.

Dale ran back to the cannon and grabbed the ram rod, he pushed it into the cannon end to pack the ball that had already been loaded, and then pulled it out, dropped it, and ran back to the other end of the cannon and fitted a fuse.

He snatched the lighter off the soldier who was simply staring at the green wall in disbelief, and touched it to the fuse. Some of the Woodsmen behind the Specialist's moved backwards. The cannon exploded with the shot, and Robbie saw the red hot ball heading right for him, but this time he kept his eyes open. The cannon ball hit the window with a green flash, and was gone, some of the woodsmen at the back ducked. Jett gave another titter.

"So, what do we do now, everything goes in, and nothing comes out?" Jade shrugged; Rowan turned to Robbie.

"It's going to be dark soon and we have wounded, and no one is coming through here from either side until we work out what she has done." Robbie looked back at the bloodied and wounded men.

"We will take a tactical retreat, move everyone back to the stockade, I will get Steph to alert the men on the fighting fields to pull back to Loxley, and we will regroup." Jett looked disappointed.

Rayne led the way, turning corner after corner, as they followed the direction Ariel had told them to go in. He turned sharply to his right and BANG! Blood sprayed over the wall, as he bounced back into view, Blades was fast as the Royal Guard came round the corner with a mace in its hand. Rayne lay on the floor out cold; the left side of his face was mangled and cut, his eye bled badly. Blades struck like lightening without thinking, and the hand holding the mace hit the floor.

The guard had no reaction, not a sound came from it, as it turned to face her, its face a blueish white, its eyes dull and dead, and reached for its sword with its other hand. The group behind Blades slid to a halt, as Blades went into defence mode, Sapphire realised as Blades took her stance, and then swung.

"NO NOT THAT ONE!" It was too late, her razor sharp Samurai met in the centre, and his head flipped into the air, as the body crumpled to the floor. As the body hit the floor a black swirling mist flowed out of it and into the air, Blades suddenly realised.

"Oh Crap!" She took three steps back, as it spun in the air and then began to stretch and pull itself in several directions. Sapphire felt the chill run through her; she had never in her life wanted to see one of these again. The smoke began to form into a shape, and they all stepped back three more paces. Rune lifted her hand, but as the smoke formed into a copy of Blades, the room lit up with intensely bright white light.

The smoky figure gave a horrendous scream, its face stretching in agony and then exploded into dust and drifted slowly to the floor, Rune looked to her side, where Ariel stood with her arm extended and her palm wide open, she gave a shudder.

"I hate those things." Rune ran to Rayne who lay motionless on the floor, she ran her hand across him and felt his life force; she looked back to the others as Tila came forward and opened her bag.

"I can help him." Jaz looked down at him on the floor and then looked to Rune, who was well aware time was running out at Loxley. "I will carry him Rune." She smiled.

"Thanks Jaz, if he gets too heavy yell out." Tila sprinkled some powder on Rayne's face, and then pulled a green coloured bandage out of her bag. Jaz knelt down and lifted his head, as Tila wrapped up his head to cover the wounded eye. "It will help till we get him back, but I am not sure about his eye, it is pretty badly cut."

Within minutes they were back on track, Jaz carrying Rayne, as Fox and Blades led the way. They came down another corridor and out onto a balcony, Sapphire saw the stairs and pointed as they hurried along. "That way."

The group changed direction and took her lead, and arrived at the stairs and began down at a hurried pace, Rune suddenly realised where they were, as they hit the floor of a wide hall.

"This is the banquet hall." Max understood as it led to the central corridor that was the way out, and he knew Rune was looking for Branna's private quarters. He turned to her as they crossed the room.

"We do not have time; they know we are here and are looking for us."

"Too Late!" Tila reached for her sword, as through four of the doors that led into the hall, Royal Guards and foot soldiers entered, and they were surrounded.

The Bowmen gave cover as they retreated back to the safety of Loxley. They moved back in two groups each taking turns to fire at the men on the high walls. Slowly they made their way back across the blood soaked bridge.

Morgan le Fey was furious, her eyes burned bright red, as she screamed at Mason. "DON'T LET THEM GO BACK, GO AFTER THEM!" He shrugged at her.

"How Mother...how?" She grew even angrier, it had taken years to get to this point and they had him trapped on a bridge, she screwed up her palm, and it ignited with red flames, she looked over the wall to where Robbie was lifting a wounded Bowman from the floor. She put all her anger into her arm, and the ball of fire exploded out of it and shot in the direction of Robbie.

Steph stood just outside the gates of Loxley watching, she saw Morgan strike and her arm shot up.

"Oh no you don't you Bitch!" The white tunnel from the end of the bridge to

Loxley, suddenly expanded covering the whole length of the bridge, the bright red ball of flame hit the tunnel and exploded spraying fire all over the valley below, which ignited, and began to burn rapidly back towards the black stone wall.

Morgan screamed in anger and raised her arm. Steph gave an angry snort. She lifted her arm, and another huge ball of white light erupted from it, as Morgan swung round to send another spell in the direction of the tunnel, the white ball hurtled towards her, and exploded blowing her off her feet, and throwing her back against the opposite wall. She screamed in pain as she hit hard stone, and her anger wailed out of her. Steph gave a satisfied smile. "That will cool you off madam."

The group made a circle with Ariel, Ena, and Jaz holding Rayne, in the centre to be protected. Jay loaded her bow; Una lifted her holly pole. Blades held her swords fast, Max held his sword, Maddy slid an arrow onto her white bow, Fox raised his swords and Tila slung her bow across her back, and pulled out a dagger, and an ornate and highly decorated Fae sword. Crystal slipped off her gloves as Sapphire pulled out her sword.

The guards were uncertain, and moved slowly towards them, slowly surrounding them on all sides. Somewhere in the darkness below, Roack opened her eyes.

Rune made the connection and turned to Sapphire. "I have to go." Sapphire looked at her in disbelief.

"What...Rune no, we need you." She smiled

"Get them out, that way leads to the bridge, I will give you as good a head start as possible, get everyone across that bridge as fast as you can. Sapphire just go, they know I am here, I can use windows now, no matter what get them all to safety. I am the only one who can deal with this, none of you can help now, time is short so please my sister, get out, get Ariel out, and get out fast."

Rune stepped from the circle as the hoard of dark guards moved in closer. She took a deep breath and then closed her eyes for a second. When they opened, bright violet flowed across her pupils. She pushed her hand forward and a window opened on the floor with a bright violet circle around its edge. She flicked her hand up and the light shot up above them like a circle of violet light surrounding the group. Rune breathed slowly, and then raised her hand and placed her second finger and thumb together.

The snap was almost deafening, and the circle expanded fast like a wall of power moving outward, it slammed into the guards and threw them back with force, sending them crashing in every direction, Rune yelled out. "GO...NOW!" And then dropped through the floor.

Sapphire wasted no time and herded the group through the fallen soldiers and guards. Sapphire ran for her life almost dragging Ena who was holding onto Ariel, they made it to the door, and entered the long highly decorative front corridor that led out onto a court yard.

Tila had her bow out and fired at a guard who was stood in the middle of the open archway leading onto the bridge away from the castle, Fox threw a knife at another, Maddy spun with her bow loaded and stopped, she fired one of her arrows back up the corridor, and then turned and ran like the wind to catch the others. Jay loaded a stinger and as she ran for the gate she aimed up and released the arrow.

Behind them the entrance to the castle erupted with fire, they passed under the archway with Maddy just behind as she caught up with Jay. Sapphire was on the bridge and running half dragging the others. Jaz panted as he carried Rayne, and Blades and Fox took a stance to fire back at the high guards before continuing to run.

In the court yard soldiers came from every door, and gave chase with crossbows. The group were puffing and panting and willing their legs onward. Far ahead across the long bridge Sapphire saw movement. Cezar appeared with a large group of men. They moved forward swiftly and lifted their bows. Sapphire gritted her teeth as Ena gasped for air beside her, both of them holding a hand of Ariel.

Blades looked back at Una, Jay and Maddy were some ways off behind them. "We are losing those two." Una turned and looked back, she slowed gasping for air and turned back to watch as Jay and Maddy ran for their lives, closely followed by a group in dark robes, who were shooting arrows from their crossbows as they ran. Una lifted her holly pole and prepared, as they grew closer to her.

Maddy squealed and went down on the floor, as Jay shot past and then skidded to a halt gasping for air. She saw Maddy lay on the floor with an arrow in her hip. Una rushed towards her, as Maddy grabbed her bow and her arrows. She pulled a long silver arrow and then screamed at Una.

"GO...MY LEG IS DEAD, GO." She pushed her bow and quiver with all her might and it slithered at high speed towards Una. "FOR TREEN!"

Maddy rolled onto her back and sat up as the dark soldiers ran towards her, she looked back and smiled. "I love you sister." Una screamed for her life, as Jay grabbed her, and the long white bow and arrows stopped under her foot.

"NO MADDY!"

Maddy sat with her back to them holding a long silver arrow, and smiled at the dark soldiers running towards her. "So boys, what tune does this one play?" She gripped the arrow tight in both hands.

"RUN UNA, RUN AND LIVE FOR ME!"

The soldiers were almost upon her as she sat with dead legs from the infected arrow, holding the arrow in both her hands she smiled. "Alley my precious, I am coming."

She put all her pressure on the arrow as Jay dragged Una screaming away towards the fighters at the end of the bridge with her friends. 'SNAP!!' The arrow broke in two.

A ball of fire the size of the castle erupted in the centre of the bridge, as Jay tugged at Una, who screamed out in pain as tears flooded her eyes. Jay reached Sapphire, and Cezar snatched Una into his arms and lifted her onto his shoulder, and turned and ran down the rest of the bridge with the others, as the fire swept like an inferno, burning everything to dust in its wake. Una stared across the bridge as tears flooded from her eyes, her voice lost in her pain reduced to a whimper.

"You promised...You promised we would not be parted again."

Below the ground in a darkened room, two beds were set side by side, and on a perch between the two sat a huge raven with dark eyes. A circle appeared on the roof in violet, and Rune dropped through into the chamber.

The raven was still sleepy and swayed on its perch. "Your kind is not welcome here." Rune smiled and faced the bird.

"Probably, but I came anyway." She walked towards the raven she knew was Roack. "You look tired; maybe you should sleep a while longer until your mistress awakens." Rune clicked her fingers and the raven swooned. She grabbed it and held it by the feet. With a smile she turned and walked back towards the far wall to open her window and leave.

A hoarse crackling voice spoke behind her, and Rune stopped. "Roack is mine, put her back and I might let you live Eve." She turned to see the dark shape of a woman in the dim light.

"It's Runestone, not Eve, I am glad you are awake Branna."

CHAPTER THIRTY FIVE

QUEEN UNTIL THE END

The dark figure moved forward into the light. "I have never heard of you, you look like Eve."

"I am her granddaughter, and her heir, I am her replacement in this world." Branna came closer.

"Give me my bird, she is mine you have no right to her."

Rune saw her face for the first time, and Ariel's pictures had been immensely accurate. Her hair was longer, but just as unkempt, and her eyes were darker than death. Rune held the raven by its feet, as it hung sleeping; Branna eyed the bird with possessiveness. "Roack is mine, give her back and you may or may not live; I cannot allow you to take her."

Rune glanced down at the raven hanging below her wrist. "It's not midnight, your powers are weak, and I have broken your connection to the bird, you have no mind connection, so you cannot win me Branna, you know what will happen if I kill this bird?" She gave a shudder, and her eyes widened.

"YOU CANNOT TAKE HER, SHE IS MINE!"

She went to move forward, and Rune held up the raven and slid out her silver knife, Branna stopped, looking fearful, she raised her palms. "It's alright, it was just a joke, I shall not harm you, give her back and leave, please I will not harm you." She slowly dropped to her knees and began to cry. "Please you don't understand what she means to me, she is my life, I cannot be without her, she is all I have left."

Rune was unmoved. "And what a life you have lived Branna, you and your family have travelled far, killing and cursing all you met. Wherever your line walks there is death and darkness. I am life and light, and I am here this day to end your reign of terror and decay in this world. Your tears are worthless compared to the pain and suffering your line has caused."

Branna jumped to her feet, and her tears were gone, she looked at Rune with utter hatred. "You know nothing of what my family has had to endure; locked away for no other reason than they did not look like the image of society she wanted in her golden realm, you talk of suffering, well let's talk of suffering in your own realm, and let's look at that golden bitch Rhiannon." Rune did not disagree with her.

"I know of what has happened Branna, and I do not defend her, as I do not agree with you and the things you have done. If I am honest, there have been moments of late, where I see little difference between you both." Branna's eyes instantly burned with rage, and she leaned forward toward Rune, her voice tone changed to anger.

"I am nothing like her; I should kill you just for saying that." She went to move and Rune lifted the bird, Branna stopped and raised her palms, and took two steps back.

"That is what I mean, she too will do the same if she could hear me, as I said, I see no difference, except her time will come soon and yours sooner." The floor of room turned violet as a circle appeared below Rune, and Branna looked at it with shock. She waved her hands in panic and started to whimper.

"No, No, please do not leave, don't take my Roack." The violet circle gave a pulse, and Rune dropped straight through, Branna screamed and dived for Rune, but the circle went out, and she crashed into the floor.

Cezar pushed them onward hard through the trees. "You cannot stop, we must hurry to the safety of our caves, I know you are tired, but we cannot or they will find us."

His group had Sapphire and her party surrounded. One of the fighters carried Rayne, and another carried Ariel. Sapphire glanced up as she ran, and saw the violet mottled sky, that looked like violet marble with dark seems running through it. Her legs ached as she felt her energy wavering. From nowhere into the dark woodland, horrible and terror laden screams whistled through the trees, she looked back and saw nothing but dark trees, her legs found a new energy, as the fear surged up in her, and gave her another burst of strength.

Lightning flashed across the sky, and the trees lit up. The rough bark gave them sinister and frightening faces, her heart missed a beat. Cezar looked back, he was scared she could feel it, which was no comfort, as he had been pretty fearless the first time she met him. Sapphire heard the call behind her. "They are coming!"

Her heart beat even faster, and felt like it was going to burst out of her chest. The temperature felt like it was falling and she began to shiver, as she followed the track weaving in and out of the trees and tall shrubs. "Oh hurry Rune, I don't like this."

A scream behind her told her one of the fighters had been taken, and her anxiety reached fever pitch. "Oh hurry Rune; I don't like this at all." She looked ahead and saw a faint blue shimmer, she felt a little warmth flow back into her, and pushed her legs a little harder, and the shimmer grew in size and she recognised Gwendolyn's ghostly figure, relief flowed back into her as she approached and slowed a little.

"Don't slow down; run like the wind and I will slow them."

She pushed her weary legs, and gave it her last effort, and sprinted past Gwendolyn, and looked back as the others cleared past her, and Gwendolyn spread her arms wide, and her voice echoed in Sapphire's head. *"Runestone is coming, run Sapphire, run to freedom, I cannot stop her men, but I can terrify their horses, they are sensitive to spirits."* Sapphire looked forward, and pushed herself as hard as she could.

Not that far behind the fighters of Cezar, the soldiers on horses galloped at speed, Gwendolyn stood with her arms spread wide, and as the riders came down the track, she started to glow bright blue. She closed her eyes and channelled her power. The horses ran towards her, and when they were five feet away her eyes opened and exploded with intense light. "BOO!"

The horses reared up and brayed with terror, throwing their riders. The soldiers screamed and cried as they hit the floor, and Gwendolyn waved her hands, and screamed with all her might. The horses reared up again, turned, and bolted off in every direction leaving the riders in pain and stranded. She turned back to the path that Sapphire had taken and chuckled to herself.

Not too far away there was a flash of violet and Rune appeared in the trees holding the sleeping Roack by the feet. She turned and sensed the woodland looking for Sapphire. The lightening streaked across the sky, and above her she saw the silhouette of a large raven, against the background of swirling violet.

"You cannot leave here, you may have Roack, but I am not powerless." She spun round and there was the dark outline of Branna stood in the centre of a circle of trees. "This is my land Runestone, this is the centre of everything I built, and you have no real power here."

Rune shrugged and lifted a hand, it flashed, and a bright line of violet shot out of it and hit Branna in the chest, and blew her off her feet.

"It looks pretty powerful to me; I knew you were all talk." Branna jumped to her feet, and lifted her hands ready to strike back; Rune lifted the bird in front of herself. "Be careful Branna, it would be awful if Roack got hurt."

White smoked swirled up out of the floor between them both, and the shape of a woman formed in the centre, Rune sensed the presence and power of Fae. Branna stepped back and gasped as Rhiannon appeared. She turned and looked back at Rune. "Leave, it is not your place to be here, this is between her and me."

Rune stepped back and gave a nod, she spun on the spot and in a flash she was gone. Rhiannon looked at Branna. "This meeting is long overdue Branna of Vinella and Brandle."

The Specialists walked out of the tunnel, and onto the square of clear land outside the gates of Loxley. They were tired, dirty and bloodied, the Woodsmen on the gates, looked down on them with surprise as they trudged silently through the smouldering gap that had once been gates, followed by the bowmen of Caerleon and Loxley. One of the men stood by the gates looked at them and turned to his mate. "Frig they are brave, look at em." He lifted his hands and started to clap. "Well done lads...and lasses, you guys are amazing."

All around the men started to join in and clap, Henry gave a smile as he saw them walk with pride back into their home. Robbie was last carrying a man across his shoulders. Two medics ran to him, and he stopped and let the man slide from his shoulders. They gave him a nod of thanks and took the man. Robbie smiled at them; Steph came up by his side. "The men of Dove Dale and Grace from Scotland are here, we pulled them back to Loxley with you guys."

He was exhausted and gave a long sigh. "Thanks Steph, I will talk to Grace and the other generals in a little while." She looked upset, and he looked at her. "What is it?" She shook her head and pointed.

"You need to speak to your mother." He looked at what was now just a gap, to see her with red eyes looking at him, he moved towards her feeling a biting pain in his chest rising.

"Mum what is it?"

Her tears rolled down her cheeks as he got closer, and she flung her arms around him, and pulled him tight. "Oh Robbie...Oh Robbie." He felt her shake with the pain inside her, he squeezed her tight.

"What is it Mum?" She shook harder as she buried her face in his shoulder.

"I cannot tell her...How can I tell her Robbie?" He did not understand.

"Tell who what mum, you are not making sense?"

She shook and wailed into him, he waited as he squeezed her feeling his own fear rise, she gave a huge sob. "I cannot face her...How can I say the words? Oh Robbie, what do I tell her?" Robbie pulled at her shoulders to gently pull her back; he looked at her tear streaked face.

"Mum I need you to tell me so maybe I can." Jess shook her head. "Mum please tell me who to tell what?" Tears streamed down her face.

"Alice." He looked at her feeling panicked.

"Mum tell Alice what?"

"Her mum has gone Robbie, we lost Beth." He felt a huge wave crash over him and looked up and saw Alice looking at him from the roadway, just inside the gates. Her eyes met his and filled with tears, she turned, dropped her bow, and ran. Robbie tried to let go of his mother.

"ALICE WAIT!" But she was gone.

By the time he got to the farm, Bear was at the door, he gave a nod as Robbie walked up to him. "How is she?" Bear gave a long sigh.

"Not good, she is in there with her, I would give her a little time Robbie." He nodded.

"Yeah." Bear pointed across the yard.

"John is in the barn." Robbie turned and looked at it, he turned and slowly walked over, the door was open a jar, he looked round the door and saw John sat on a sawn off stump. John turned and saw him; he gave him a nod.

"Come in our Robbie."

He stepped inside and walked over to him, John looked up, His face was dirty, and his shirt was torn and he had soot all over him from the fight, his dark brown eyes glistened as he looked Robbie in the eyes, his voice was quiet and trembled.

"If you are going back out there, and you are going after him, I am on the team, you hear me, I am on the team?" Robbie nodded as he felt the surge of pain rise in his chest.

"You will be John, have no worries, if that is what you want, then you will be."

John looked down and shook his head. "I am nowt without her Robbie, that fuckin bastard; I am going to kill him." Robbie saw the tears fall on the floor, and John wiped his nose with the back of his hand. Robbie placed his hand on John's shoulder.

"We will kill him together John, you and me side by side, I promise." John twisted and grabbed Robbie by the waist; he pulled him close, and buried his face in Robbie, and shook as he wailed into him. Robbie held him by the shoulders, as his own tears ran down his face and dripped onto John's back.

Mason stood with Mark Richard Dale and his Mother; they all looked at the gateway that was sealed with a green glowing barrier. "Can you not get rid of it?" Morgan appeared preoccupied.

"What?" Dale gave an exhausted breath of air, as he looked at her.

"He said can you not get rid of it? You're supposed to be the witch here, so get rid of it." She gave him a scowl and her eyes flashed red.

"Something is not right." Dale looked at her astonished.

"No shit, there is a bloody green barrier stopping us passing." She looked at Mason.

"Don't you have a woman he can bed? I am finding him annoying, and you won't let me kill him. I have told you something is not right, something is missing, and it is making me feel strange." Mason looked concerned.

"How do you mean strange?" She gave a gasp.

"If I knew that I would know what it is wouldn't I? All I know is things feel off, and I am not sure why, but something is wrong." He smiled.

"It's been a tough day, you have been hit by magic, and had that spell or charm or whatever it is to deal with, it's a lot of work for one day. You probably just need to rest and recharge, weren't you supposed to be heading home for your family thing?" She gave a frown that made her face look contorted.

"I am trying to forget that, it is much more enjoyable here. I am not sure I could tolerate Otto and that woodchopper, as well as him in the same day." She looked at Dale with hatred, and he looked at her in a similar manner. Mason looked back at the green shimmering wall.

"We cannot go to them and they cannot come to us, I say we take a rest and sleep on it, we will have clearer heads in the morning." Morgan gave a frustrated snort.

"I have other things to do, I have to find out how they did this." Mason shrugged.

"Why not join Dana and Lance with me and rest with us." Morgan glared at him.

"Did you not listen, something is not right... OH do what you wish, I have things more important to deal with." Mason watched as a plume of smoke came out of the floor and shot to a dark cloud above, he gave a sigh as he watched her leave, and then turned back towards the door that led to his private apartments.

The violet flashed and Rune appeared, Sapphire gave a gasp of relief, and threw her arms around her. "Thank the lords you are safe." Rune dropped Roack on the floor, and looked at the others all sat sweating and exhausted; she looked round the entrance to a large cave lined with crystal. Sapphire smiled. "I remember the cave in Scotland, I thought if I was in there you would not find me."

Rune looked at it. "Maybe we should all get inside then." Max lifted Roack up off the floor.

"What do I do with this?" Rune glanced at the sleeping bird.

"Tie it up and put it with the others, I am taking them back with me." Ena looked at her.

"Why, just kill them and have done with them." Rune shook her head.

"It is not that simple; if we kill them we release the Merle into this realm. To be honest, I also want to look her in the eye when I do it, I actually want everyone to see the fear on her face, I owe everyone that." Ena gave an approving nod.

"I knew you had a colder side; I want to be with you when you do it." Rune looked into the cave and saw an old woman with a very lined face, and a tight bun of grey hair, sat on the bed and wipe Ariel's face.

"How is your mother?" Ena looked back and smiled.

"She is fine, I mean she is very weak, but Crina will help her heal, she is good with all the plants of this region." Rune looked at her.

"She belongs back in Florae, that is where her healing will take place."

Tila smiled and looked up at her. "Is Branna dead now?" Rune shook her head.

"As long as the raven lives, she will also, I left Rhiannon dealing with her."

Sapphire looked stunned.

"Are you sure that is the right thing to do Rune, I mean after the last week?" Rune turned to Sapphire.

"All this started with Branna and Rhiannon, and if I am honest, it should end with those two. We have more pressing business back home, all is not well there I sense it, and soon so will Morgan sense the trouble here, and that is why I need to be there when she realises. We will leave at first light, so get some sleep. I am going to sit with Una a while, she has lost a sister."

Amethyst had been feeling strange for an hour; she walked out onto the Queens Road, and smiled as she remembered her time with the Specialist's on their arrival. It was one of many fond memories that she thought about often. She turned into the woodland and followed the path; it had felt like an age since she had been outside in the air, and her thoughts jumbled through her head, and she really was not paying attention to where she was walking. The brightness of the day increased, and she stopped to see where she was, and discovered she had walked into the centre of the large stone circle of Eve. A small figure in white robes stood watching her. "Evening my Queen."

"Opal...What are you doing here?" Opal smiled at her and beckoned her to come forward into the centre of the circle.

"Come my child, the times are changing and the circle of darkness that has surrounded us will soon open, and the truth of everything will be revealed. Stand with me and watch the sky, for tonight it will be the guide to the fates of many." Amethyst walked into the centre of the circle, and looked up.

"What am I looking for?" Opal looked up with a smile.

"Oh, you will know when you see it."

The blast hit Branna head on and blew her off her feet. "You dare to challenge me? I am your queen." Branna scoffed as she lay in the grass.
"YOU ARE NOT MY QUEEN, YOU WERE ONLY EVER THEIR QUEEN!"
Branna sprang to her feet and spun her arm, as a huge blast of red shot out of it, it hit Rhiannon in the chest, lifting her up and slamming her into a tree behind her. The tree shuddered, and moss covered branches snapped and rained to the floor.

Rhiannon gave a wince as she moved and felt the pain, her wrist twisted, and flicked, and Branna was picked up and tossed for ten feet against the tree opposite. The old rotten branches exploded and crashed to the floor as Rhiannon smirked.

"I thought Ravens were supposed to sit in trees, not get buried by them, finally you grovel on your knees before your queen as is fitting for nothing more than a mere worker."

Branna screamed out with anger, and the fallen branches exploded back up into the air. Her face was as white as snow, framed by her long dark shaggy hair, and her eyes burned red with utter hate. "I never have and never will bow or grovel for your approval that was the last act of your daughter, as she begged at my feet for her life."

Rhiannon felt the air taken from her lungs. "What?"

Branna gave a cackle as she saw the effect on the Queen Ofmoon, and she nodded her head as her eyes sparkled with red delight, as she smiled with satisfaction.

"Yes it was me...You were all so sure it was Morgana." Branna shook her head with delight. "Poor little Eleanor, so pretty, so sweet, loved and admired by all. Where do you think the royal blood came from to enhance the life of my ravens?"

Branna threw back her arms as Rhiannon stared at her with hatred, and laughed into the sky. The power of anger and hate flowed up like a volcano into Rhiannon.

From nowhere a mass of white exploded, and Branna was torn from the floor and smashed into another tree with tremendous force, she screamed out in pain, and yet her face still bore a look of joy, knowing she had hurt the queen of the moon far more than any spell could.

The rage of Rhiannon blew through the trees like a whirlwind, tearing the old trees up by the roots and tossing them everywhere, as Branna crashed from trunk to floor, picked up and tossed like a rag doll, Rhiannon's screams of anguish echoed throughout the woodland.

"YOU VILE, WORTHLESS, WHORE OF DARKNESS, I WILL TEAR EVERY PIECE OF THIS LAND APART AND LEVEL IT TO DUST. NOTHING WILL REMAIN, I SHALL DESTROY IT ALL AND YOU WILL BE BUT A SHADOW BEREFT OF EVERYTHING. I WILL LEAVE NOTHING TO SHOW THAT YOU LIVED YOUR PATHETIC WORTHLESS LIFE HERE!"

Branna crashed from tree to tree, her face bloodied and her body racked with pain, and yet deep inside her joy increased, and she defiantly laughed and screamed. Her back shot at speed towards a mighty old Fir tree, and she summoned her powers, and bent back her legs and pushed as they met the trunk. As they hit the tree, she fired a curse of red light back towards Rhiannon, as the white light faded and she looked breathless stood alone in a wide area of devastated woodland.

"This is the land I built, and you have no place here golden queen, this is the land of the raven, you will find no blonde beauties here, this is my domain, try as hard as you will, you cannot beat me here."

Rhiannon blocked her with a ball of light, and spun her finger. It hit Branna in the chest, and she shot back and hit the floor sliding through trees and bushes, ploughing a dark earthen groove in the floor.

Branna laughed. "Is that all you have got, I thought you were a queen, or has your little princess taken all of your power?" She laughed with a hoarse cackle. "Has your little golden wonder taken the best of you? Ha! You are nothing but a watered down version of your former self." Rhiannon looked at her with utter hatred.

"Your bird sleeps in the hands of Life herself; can you not feel her ripping out your spirit and tearing the Merle out of you? You are not a raven; you are just another foul dark haired little monster that belongs in the mines, like your parents, and that feeble minded brother of yours."

Rhiannon saw the effect of her words. "You have no idea of the pleasure I have had playing with them, and listening to them scream in the darkness."

Branna lifted off the floor with an intensified rage, her eyes exploded with red, and she shot off the floor, and punched the air, a wave of black came out of it, and travelled like thunder across the forest. Rhiannon raised her arms to block, but it passed through her arms and gripped at her, and then flung her back against another tree.

She slammed into it and her eyes opened wide, as the air ran out of her lungs. She looked down and saw the long branch poking out of her chest, Branna gave a wail of a laugh and walked towards her.

"Not so high and mighty now are we? The great Queen Rhiannon with her crown pinned to a tree, whereas my crown of darkness has yet to slip."

She walked right up to Rhiannon her red eyes dancing in her pale blood streaked face, taking pleasure, for finally after all of the years, living up to the promise she made to herself the night she left Avalon. Finally, she was watching Rhiannon die, and her happiness flowed up to her face as she leaned into her and smiled.

"How does it feel to know the queen of darkness has defeated you?"

Rhiannon gave a gasp, and blood trickled out of the corner of her mouth. "You have no idea what a queen truly is." Branna laughed and pushed her face up close, her dark eyes, eye to eye with hers.

"Oh really and what is that dying Queen?"

Rhiannon gripped her by the throat, and pulled her even closer, as more blood ran out of her mouth. "Smarter than her subjects."

Branna gave a sudden jerk, and slipped back; she looked down and saw Rhiannon's hand holding the handle of her dagger against her stomach. Rhiannon gave a jerk and the blade rose up sharply, and Branna winced with the pain.

"Some queen, you're nothing but a shadow of what you could have been, dusted in the Merle and blinded by your own stupidity, and they told me you were smart." She coughed out blood and laughed. "Well not smart enough little raven, your queen just clipped your feathers for good."

She thrust her hand forward and Branna fell to the floor, her blood flowing out onto the ground. Rhiannon looked down. "By the time you fix that, your precious raven will be dead, and the Merle will leave and look for another arrogant idiot."

Branna felt the coldness in her body, and she looked up at the pinned figure of Rhiannon, her head slumped to her chest, and long golden hair blowing in the breeze, as the air ran out of her body. She lay back and looked at the sky, and tears ran into her eyes. Her breathing slowed, and she closed her eyes with a smile. "Ariel."

Out of the darkness walked a figure dressed in long black tatty robes. He walked towards the tree, and gently lifted Rhiannon off the branch into his arms. "You were a queen until the end my child of the moon, for you righted the wrongs of your rule before leaving. It is time to take you home."

Rune looked up as the white light lifted into the sky; it shot through the violet mixed with black streaks, punching a hole right through its centre, sending ripples outward as the sky cleared, revealing the thousands of twinkling stars. Rune sat down on the grass, she felt exhausted and spent. Her abilities found it hard in this oppressive atmosphere, and she sat for a second just breathing and gathering her thoughts. Finally, Rune focused her mind.

"Hear me mother...I am coming home, it is almost done, we have one more raven to deal with, and then I am done."

Amethyst watched the sky, and saw the streak of white light lift from well beyond the Forest of Time. It shot like a beacon and touched the moon, behind her on the mount; the bell started to ring, it was a slow rhythm and felt sombre. Opal walked to her side and took her by the hand.

"The Old Queen is no more, long live the New." Amethyst turned and looked at her.

"What do you...!"

From out of the sky, a blast of silvery blue light shot down, and hit her before she could finish her sentence. Within seconds she was consumed by the light, and everyone in Avalon stopped, watched, and knew that Rhiannon was no more, and that Amethyst would rule over both domains. Out in the wider reaches of Avalon a few sat and smiled, knowing that things would change for the better. Opal turned and walked from the Circle of Eve, as Amethyst took on the powers as full Queen to the Fae Ofmoon. She walked into the trees to where a small figure with bright wide eyes waited. Opal looked down at the dream spirit.

"The times are changing my little friend, come we still have much to do."

CHAPTER THIRTY SIX

EMPOWERED AND IN PERIL

Deep within the Hidden Realm, as the darkness crept in, and the trees swayed in the breeze, within the tall black castle, a light burned softly in the high tower. From the outside all looked well and at peace, but inside things were not quite as they always had been.

The doors exploded open and Ursula gave a startled jump. Morgan le Fey stormed in, and marched down the centre of her room; passed the burning fireplace where two red and tatty looking chairs stood, towards her table of power, muttering to herself angrily.

"Have a rest, you are tired, he says, does he understand nothing? I know something is not right, I feel it and I don't like it." She walked up to her table and placed her hands on it and looked deeply into it. "I feel it, show me."

Ursula stood up and walked slowly down the room. "Is everything alright Mistress?" Morgan looked up.

"Oh it's you; I thought you would be riding that boy again seeing as I was not here." She looked a little embarrassed.

"No Mistress, I was transcribing more of your notes." Morgan kept looking into her table.

"Something is changing, I feel it, but that fool of a son, and that blithering idiot, cannot see it." She looked up and her eyes flashed with red. "That violet witch has not been on view all day why does that bother me so much?" Ursula frowned.

"She was not at the fight?" She moved quickly round to the side of her mistress. "She is always there; it is the most annoying aspect of all of this." She looked at the images showing the Hidden Realm, Tintagel, and even Dunnottar. Morgan slid her hand over the surface of the table.

"She is up to something, I burned down her house and yet I saw no sign of her, it is not right, something here makes no sense." The image of the Castle of

Berengar came into view, and the bridge was alight and burning, she gasped and flicked her wrist to bring up more images. Morgan looked at her table as she saw all the family sat slumped in their seats. "What is this?"

Her voice was startled, and Ursula leaned in closer. "Mistress...where are the ravens?"

Morgan looked at her. "What do you mean, they are...." She looked with disbelief and her hands clamped onto the table. "NO!"

Ursula felt the breeze blow her back, as Morgan became a tall swirling column of black smoke, which funnelled up to the ceiling and disappeared. She leaned over the table and watched.

Morgan came into the room like a hurricane of black smoke, her eyes burned deep red in her white face, and her long tatty hair flapped behind her, as she rushed across the room to Otto. She leaned in and looked at him closely, inside she felt angry and also felt panicked. She leaned back and lifting her hand, she swung it at his face. SLAP!

"Wake up you vicious old lizard." He did not move, she turned to Rosamund, and then looked behind her at the others. "What is this, how did this happen?" She spun on the spot and saw the two empty chairs at the head of the circle, her eyes moved up to the empty perch. "THIS IS NOT HAPPENING." Her voice was panicked, as she looked around for clues. "Who did this, was it you Branna?" Her head jerked left and right, and she felt greater panic growing with her anger, and it was then she spotted blood on the floor.

She rushed towards the side of the trap door and went down on her knees. She touched the tiny speck and lifted her finger and smelled it. "FAE!"

Morgan punched the floor and a bright flash of red exploded out of her hand, the trap door fired open and swung violently. She looked down into the gloom, and then with a twist, she dropped down through the floor to the basement below, where the crystal tube lay broken and empty.

"That witch Ariel and her daughter have been through here, I smell their reek." She looked to the double door leading into the side chambers, and walked at speed towards it, she lifted her hand and the doors exploded open. She stormed through into the sacred chamber, where there were two beds and a tall perch. The perch was empty, and so was one of the beds, in the other she saw the sleeping figure of Berengar. She walked up to him and reached down and gripped him by his garments around his neck, and lifted, and pushed him back into the bed repeatedly.

"WAKE UP YOU USELESS EXCUSE FOR A WARRIOR, WHERE IS YOUR WIFE?"

His eyes snapped open and he grabbed her by the wrist, as she pushed him up and down at speed on the bed, and screamed. "WAKE UP!!"

Berengar jolted and sat up and glared at her with anger. "How dare you come in here and touch me." She stepped back unafraid.

"OH REALLY, WHERE IS YOUR WIFE YOU IDIOT, AND WHERE THE HELL IS ROACK?"

He looked up and then to the side of the bed which was empty. She gave a huff of impatience. "Someone has been here, I sense Fae, and the rest of your offspring are sat like dummies in the ritual chamber, which can only mean one thing." She turned at the door. "RHIANNON OR RUNESTONE HAS BEEN HERE, AND IF EITHER OF THEM HAVE, YOU WILL DIE TONIGHT IF WE DON'T FIND THAT BIRD!" He jumped out of bed.

"What are you saying Morgana?" She gave a snort.

"Runestone is life, she is the granddaughter of Eve, Rhiannon is the queen of Fae, and if either of them has Roack, all of us are through, do you understand Berengar, we are through, does that work in that tiny Saxon brain of yours?" She swirled into smoke and disappeared.

Rune sat up on her bed. "I feel her." Sapphire sat bolt upright.

"Who...Le Fey?" Rune turned to Sapphire, her eyes burning with violet light.

"We must leave and leave now. I want those birds where she cannot touch them." Cezar watched as he lay on his blankets. "You are safe here; the crystal will hide all of us." Rune shook her head.

"Not with the birds, Sapphire wake everyone, we have to go now."

Morgan stood at the top of the tallest tower and closed her eyes. She slowly turned sensing every tree leaf and stick within the whole circle of darkness Branna had created. Her senses picked up on a familiar scent. "There you are."

The black smoke erupted out of the floor, and she turned scanning the ground and then stopped and stared in horror. Branna lay covered in blood on the floor, she dropped to her knees and ripped open her top to reveal a long jagged cut. On the ground beside her hand was the long silver dagger of Rhiannon. Morgana could not believe her eyes as she placed her palm onto the wound, and pressed hard.

Branna coughed and blood shot out of her mouth, as she opened her eyes. She gave a smile. "Morgana, you came." Morgan shook her head.

"How did this happen?" Branna gave another cough as blood ran from the side of her mouth.

"Rhiannon, I killed her." Morgan's eyes opened wide.

"You killed her...You killed Rhiannon?" She lay in the grass and gave a nod of her head then smiled.

"I have fulfilled my vow, she is dead." Morgan could not believe what she was hearing. She gripped Branna and yanked her off the floor by the scruff of her neck, and her deep red eyes flashed with rage, as she held her close and yelled at her.

"HOW COULD YOU BE SO RECKLESS, AMETHYST STILL LIVES, YOU JUST MADE HER TEN TIMES MORE POWERFUL, YOU STUPID BLOOD THIRSTY FOOL!?"

"HA HA HA HA." Her head snapped round, and she glared into the darkness of the dark woodland.

"WHO IS THAT?" The shimmering figure of Gwendolyn came into view, as she stood several feet away laughing at her. It was about as much as Morgan could take, she let go of Branna, who flopped to the ground and stood up facing the Ex-Queen of the Fae of Earth.

"AREN'T YOU DEAD?"

Gwendolyn sniggered. "I am, and I had to die to see this, but it was worth every second of life I lost, you have failed Morgan, she has taken your birds, and she has already flown to a place protected where even you, the mighty Dark One, cannot touch her." She leant her head back and laughed with all her might.

The smoke swirled into the sky. "IT IS NOT OVER YET, WATCH ME LITTLE DEAD FAIRY."

Gwendolyn looked at Branna watching her from the floor, she smiled. "Ariel is free, it is time you let her go and let her live again, as she once did when you shared her life in Avalon. Let her be that person again, let go of her Branna, if you love or ever truly loved her, let her go." Tears welled in Branna's eyes.

"She was my light, it got so dark, I needed her light to see again." Gwendolyn gave a smile.

"She always will be, if you do the one thing that bird never allowed you to do... Open your heart Branna, and let the love of Ariel back in, it has been empty for too long." Branna stared at Gwendolyn as she faded away into the darkness, and she lay still, unable to find the power to move, and watched the sky, as the violet swirled slowly away revealing more stars.

Robbie stood alone at the Mere his heart heavy and filled with despair. Furry Face lay in front of the garden gate his ears twitching. The violet window flashed, and the group led by Rune came through. Rune stood still and stared at the smouldering pile that was once her dream of a life with family and her one love. Tears filled her eyes as she shook, Sapphire was still staring at the remains of the house, lost for words. Tila walked up to the side of Rune and took her hand in hers.

"We will rebuild it, my people are the best with timber, do not be hurt My Lady, timbers always grow back stronger." Rune gave a sniffle and squeezed Tila's hand.

"Thank you." She gave another sniffle.

"RUNESTONE!" She turned and saw him, as he ran across the meadow from the Mere towards her, she dropped her bag and opened her arms, and he lunged into her, and wrapped his arms around her.

"I am home Robbie, but it's gone." She burst into tears, and buried her head in his shoulder. Sapphire moved the others on, towards the house steps, which were the only thing not burned.

Robbie pulled her closer. "The children are safe, they are in Florae where they are protected, yes the home we built is gone, but that just means we can build it again together. I moved the timbers and I think your table is safe. You know it's odd, but I am sure it protected itself." She snuggled into him.

"It will, it is half of me, there is little that can destroy that kind of magic."

Jett sat with Jade on the bank that overlooked the bridge from Mason's wall to just off the hill into Loxley. Jett sat up and tensed. "Rune is back." Jade gave a nod.

"I felt her earlier; I knew she would not be long." She looked across to the wall where everything was in darkness apart from the green shimmering archway that was blocked by her window. "How can I do that without thinking about it?"

Jett shrugged and stared at the darkness. "I really do not know, you and Rune have powers I have never had, so I suppose Rune would probably be better to answer. I thought at the time you just thought of protecting all of us, I mean let's be honest, that cannon would have wiped most of us out, maybe there is some safe place inside your window you can put stuff. I don't know Jade, I am just glad you did it, I am not ready to die yet." Jade sat quietly watching the darkness and thinking about the whole day.

"I want to live; I want to see my baby."

Morgan le Fey rushed back into her room where Ursula still stood watching her table. She looked up and watched Morgan filled with panic and rage. "Does she have them; or do the Fae have them?"

Morgan's face was even paler than usual, and Ursula had never before seen her show any kind of fear. She paced up and down and then stopped at Ursula's table and picked up her black book. Ursula watched as she turned to face her, her voice was cooler than ever. "Can I really trust you?" Ursula frowned.

"Mistress, we have been through this, have I not proven myself to you ten times over?" She thought about it for a minute, her red eyes fixed on her servant. She knew she had no real choice; she turned and grabbed her shawl off her chair. Ursula did not understand what was happening. Morgan paced down the room towards her; she thrust the book into Ursula's hands. Her face was filled with urgency.

"You must leave here; you are no longer safe in here." She handed her the shawl. "Go to the cottage ruins near the cave in Avalon, there is a flat stone in front of the old fireplace, under it there is a magical place that will protect this, leave the book there, and then go to Raven Merle and I will send her mother to you, you must protect them, take your soldier with you.”

“But I don’t want to leave you.” Morgan shook her head.

“I must protect this line for the future; now go, if I live, I will find you have no fear.” She gripped her by the shoulder and moved her away from the table. “Go... Go now, use the veil and hide from the Fae.” She pushed her towards the door as Ursula began to cry.

“But I don’t want you to die.” Morgan pushed her again.

“Stop that it shows weakness, and in this world, you must never let them think you are weaker than them, even if you are. Go Ursula, live and be free for a while, Raven will need you.”

Ursula dried her eyes and turned. “I will never forget you.” She ran for the doors and was gone, Morgan turned back to her table.

“Right, it’s either you little Moon Girl or that Flower Girl, so if either of you want to play hard, I will.”

Under the burnt out floor of the house, the room with Rune’s table looked just the same as it always had, apart from some scorch marks on the steps. Rune sat at her seat, and looked into her table as Robbie watched the events of her time in the circle of Branna’s world.

Some of the group watched Rune, others slept; Rayne had been taken to the farm for medical attention. Rune looked up at Robbie. “What do you want though?” He was not sure what she meant, and he shrugged.

“I want this over, what else is there?” Rune gave a nod.

“Ok then I have a plan, are you up for it?”

“What is it?” She looked back her table.

“You will need the Specialists, I will need mum, and Sapphire after she has taken care of her mother, and then this is what we will do.”

Ariel was feeling much better, and was starting to remember everything that had happened as she sat on the grass with Ena. She did not want to visit Rune’s table, as she had spent too long below ground, and feeling the grass on her bare feet was the closest thing she could get to utopia. She took Ena’s hand. “I never wanted this, I did not want you to get caught in the middle the way you have, I am sorry for your child, I would like to say I was foolish and should have never gone to Bran, but in an odd sort of way, if I had not I would never have had you, and that is the goodness of this situation.”

Ena looked at her. “I understand, I too have made foolish mistakes, but my child serves the darkness, how can I forgive her?” Ariel understood.

"Ena she is your daughter, no matter what you think, there is light within her, she has your blood, which is my blood. You must find her, and I must return home. I belong back in my own world, where I can come to terms with all that has happened." Ena gave a sigh.

"We finally found each other again, and yet we must separate." Ariel squeezed her hand tighter.

"It is not like before, this time we will be connected always, and we can join together as often as possible, but before that, I have to find my way home again." Ena looked at the grass in the darkness and tried not to think of Ursula with Morgan le Fey.

Ariel stood up and smiled. "The feeling of real earth between my toes feels like life is back within me." She walked back towards the house that was still smouldering.

Ariel walked up the steps and onto the warm burnt out wood, she stopped and looked down, she bent over and lifted a piece of wood up, and there underneath were the violet stones unharmed. She smiled. "You are going home too; you belong in the home of your queen."

On the high wall across from Loxley above the glowing green window, on the top of the wall, Morgan appeared and looked to Loxley, and Runestone. "I am waiting little flower girl, I will have my bird back, you or that moon fairy think you have outsmarted me, but you have not. As I took the life of Eve, I will take yours also and reclaim back Rajani and Roack. I am here waiting; this is the day where one of us will die, and if it is not you who has my birds, I will not care less over your death and be rid of you, and then I will end the life of that fairy in Avalon."

She walked towards the stairs, and down into the darkness inside her black wall. Minutes later as Dana Knox sat sipping her claret from a crystal glass opposite a relaxed Lance, the doors burst open and Morgan appeared. Lance gave a startled jump as Morgan moved quickly towards Dana who stood up. "What is wrong?"

Morgan eyed her carefully. "You need to leave."

"What?" Lance stood up and looked at her stood face to face with Dana, before he could say a word Morgan lifted her hand to silence him as she stared into Dana's eyes.

"There was a time I considered killing you, I did not see you as good enough for this family, but you surprised me when Raven came along." Dana blinked and looked fearful as she swallowed hard. Morgan continued to stare into her eyes as if trying to read the truth of her.

"I thought you were nothing more than another of the power hungry whores, who flocked to my son for prestige, but you named your child in honour of this family, and I reconsidered my view of you. Since that time, you have stood by my son and my grandson which has won you favour with me, so now it is time to prove your worth.”

Dana swallowed hard; her face whiter than normal. “I love Mason, and I have done my best to be a mother to Lance.” Morgan gave a grunt of derision as she stepped back.

“Warming the bed of his second hardly qualifies for love, it is loyalty that counts in this family, and you have been surprisingly loyal to us, tell me are you willing to test that loyalty now?”

Lance moved towards Dana’s side. “What is this about, you have the wall, and the woodcutter is trapped and surrounded and will soon be wiped away forever, by what right do you question my mother?” Morgan gave a cackle.

“Finally, you show some grit, good you will be needing it if what I fear happens.”

Morgan walked across the room and lifted a glass decanter off the table, she turned and looked at them both stood together. “You are so sure about all of this, and yet none of you have noticed the lack of a certain violet coloured witch.” Dana felt confused.

“Why does that matter, she is as trapped as the rest of them?” Morgan spun round.

“Wrong.” Lance frowned.

“What do you mean, we built a wall all the way round, no one can leave.” Morgan gave another little cackle.

“She is a witch, and like all other witches she has been busy out of sight, have you learned nothing at all from what we have done?”

Dana looked into the eyes of Morgan. “What are you saying, are we in danger?”

Morgan gave a frown. “We could be, which is why both of you must leave, I need to find out if it is that witch and kill her, or we have the Queen of the Moon to deal with, but there is a threat to this family which I need to resolve, and I want Raven Merle and the child of this Nadia protected.” Lance gave a snort.

“What are you saying, have you fouled things up again?” Morgan gave a screech and walked briskly across the room; she grabbed Lance by the throat and lifted him slowly off the ground. Her voice was cold and spoken with quiet anger.

“Don’t you even try to understand the complex matters of this family, and when you address me you do it with respect.” He coughed and spluttered in her grip, and she dropped him to the floor as her eyes burned red with her anger. Lance hit the floor holding his throat and gasped for breath, Morgan looked at Dana.

“He has much to learn about respect for power, teach him.” She gave a nod her eyes wide with fear. Morgan looked down at him. “There is still a threat to this family and we need to work together to ensure its survival. Both of you will leave here, you know where we have gold, use it. Take Nadia and her unborn son as far away as possible.” She turned and looked back at Dana. “Go and get Raven Merle and go with him, they are the future of this family, and it is your task to protect them, my servant will find you and aide you, she will help you teach the child what to do if things go wrong here, do you understand me?" Dana gave a sharp and hurried nod.

"Yes Morgan... I will protect all of them." Morgan gave her a crude smile.

"Good... Now go, and hurry."

Dana helped Lance off the floor, he scowled with hate at Morgan, as Dana pulled him away towards the door, and Morgan gave a titter as she saw him leave.

"Now little Flower Girl, or Moon Fairy, do your worst I am waiting, and let's see just who has the upper hand, this family will survive and we will rule, just you watch and see."

Martin smiled as he saw the happy face of the Sage. "You are cheerful." He gave a nod.

"Yeah, I feel good." Martin smiled and looked at the wall in the darkness.

"Are we ready for this?" The Sage grabbed a handful of seed and turned and scattered it across the soil.

"We are, this day has been a long time coming, is everyone ready to scale the walls and sow the seeds of rebellion?" Martin gave a chuckle, he looked behind him where over a thousand men lay in the grass with long ladders made of the few saplings they had found, he turned back to the Sage and winked.

"We are ready for anything that comes our way." The Sage looked at the wall ahead of them silhouetted in the darkness.

"Right let's do this, tonight we start the real fight for our freedom. Follow me."

Deep within the Forest of Time, in the centre of all things, the Green Lord watched, as the Sage and his followers scaled the walls of the city in the dark. The few guards were overpowered fast, and Martin with Ester and her father slipped down inside the city, and wove their way through the narrow streets following the Sage, and scattering seed as they went.

The Old Lord smiled as he saw the Sage empty the last bag, having scattered it around the walls of the soldier's barracks. On his command, the group divided into units, and in the darkness, guards and soldiers were dragged into alleyways, or shot at from roof tops, as the sections of the city were quietly taken back by the people, and the seeds of a revolution against Mason's oppressive cities began.

Hearne gave a satisfied nod as he watched. "I think now is the time." He rubbed his fingers together, and then lifting both hands and pressing his large lined fingers together, he clicked both at the same time, SNAP! And quietly in the darkness, small shoots grew from the seeds that had been scattered. "It is time the stone understood the true power of green life."

With a swift swipe of his arms, the seeds shot into life and trees grew up to the sky and the darkness, he gave a chuckle. "It will look so much nicer come dawn."

CHAPTER THIRTY SEVEN

IN THE HEART OF LOXLEY

Sapphire created her window and jumped to Captain's Cove, and after a long conversation and some tears, she opened her window and joined her brother Jaz, and her Aunt Una outside the cottage on Callanish. Toby came through her window with her, and helped Jaz prepare the site in the centre of the large stone circle. Shortly before the sun rose, Melanie was buried beside Tor under the stars and a bright moon.

After they all said their words, and shed more tears, they returned to the cottage, and Toby quietly spoke with Una and Sapphire, of his many conversations over the years in that very kitchen with Mel, a woman he loved with all his heart, but knew he would never be with as long as he had the sea.

As dawn approached Sapphire made one more trip up to the stone circle. Her thoughts were fixed on the day ahead and her lack of knowing whether or not she would survive what was to come. As she approached the circle, she saw the faint figure of shimmering blue that was Gwendolyn stood by the grave. The breeze was blowing hard, and yet not a hair on her head moved, whereas Sapphire constantly stroked back her hair to keep her face clear. Stood in the grass and barren wilderness of the stones, she walked up and looked at Gwendolyn. "She loved this place; it is right she rests here."

Gwendolyn gave a nod her eyes not leaving the mass of freshly dug earth. "It is nice to see her reunited with Tor, he loved her deeply, it was a cruel twist created by that witch that separated them, I honestly never thought she would find love again." Sapphire understood.

"David made her very happy, and Robbie did offer to let me bury her beside him in Loxley, but she always told me her spirit belonged here in the stones." Gwendolyn smiled.

"It does, here she will be free to fly with the eagles, it is right she returns here."

Gwendolyn lifted her face and looked directly at Sapphire. "That witch has taken too many of our family, we must dig deep and in these few coming days, we must strike and strike hard whilst she is at her weakest, and rid the world of her evil. Sapphire she does not know who has the bird, she thinks Runestone, but she also thinks Amethyst may have the bird and her life is at threat. Beware, if there is one thing I know about Morgan, it is that she's at her most dangerous when her back is to the wall, watch yourself and do not join more of this family in death."

Sapphire had thought the same. "I am prepared, and I will be very careful, you need not worry." Gwendolyn smiled.

"But I do, I worry about all my family." She walked closer to her. "You have done so well, and I am very proud of you. I think in many ways you remind me of the struggle of my own life at the start of my time as queen." Sapphire was surprised.

"You struggled?" Gwendolyn gave a sigh.

"It was crushing to begin with, my grandmother had taught me so much, and yet I felt the pressure, and for a long time I felt out of my depth, not unsimilar to yourself, trust me when I tell you that it does get easier. Sapphire believe in yourself more, and do not sacrifice your life to an ideal, life is meant to be lived, and you too need to understand that and start to live again." She gave a small chuckle.

"You sound like Opal." Gwendolyn shrugged.

"Opal has out lived us all, I have clashed with her many times, and yet always respected her, she is wise, listen to her Sapphire, for she is a good guide on the road of life."

It made sense to her, she had always listened carefully to Opal and had been guided by her often, she looked at Gwendolyn. "I owe you much and I am thankful, how much longer will you be here for, as I will be sorry to see you leave again?" It was clear that Gwendolyn felt the same.

"My time now is short, I have a place to return to and a task to fulfil, but fear not, I have added things to your table that will aid you with the queen, soon it will be your task to prepare for my replacement, and trust me when I tell you she will rule well because of you. I still have a little time before I return, I am sure we will talk at least once more before this is over." Gwendolyn began to fade into the darkness leaving Sapphire alone with her parents reunited in death.

Mason turned to face his mother. "How many times did I tell you, they could not be trusted, seriously how could you place your trust in Otto, when he has never been anything but vile towards you?"

She turned angrily and her eyes showed the redness of her anger. "You never understood the way the family worked; do you think any of us had a choice?"

"I understood enough to know that they never cared for any of us, and all they really cared about was their precious Saxon blood." She gave an exasperated sigh.

"This is not helping Mason, we need to find out which one has the birds, and get them back."

"Mother if you have not noticed I am working on it. Look they have not killed any of them, so whoever has them knows something of the powers inside them and how dangerous it will be to kill them here. I have brought every man we have here to wipe them off the map, and if we succeed and don't find the birds, then I will help you storm back into Avalon and find them there. Go and see what you can find out, and if you learn their location tell me straight away."

Dawn arrived and the men of Mason's army gathered in ranks outside the wall. Mason appeared with Mark Richard Dale at his side on the top of the wall and looked down. It was an impressive sight to see. Thousands of men, clad in black vests and armed, waited in large blocks in rank. They stretched for as far as his eyes could see, and they looked formidable and overwhelming. Mason smiled as he looked out on them. "See the power Mark, when you have this many men anything is possible, all you have to do is get things right in your thoughts, and then replicate them in real life. This is the final hurdle, after this every man in the country will fall in line behind us."

Mark Richard Dale was impressed, it was an awesome sight, but in his mind, he still could not understand how Mason was going to remove the green window that blocked the gateway.

Rune opened her window and walked through into Loxley, where Rowan waited with the other Specialists behind him. One thousand men stood in a treble rank of men all holding their longbows. Rune looked down the long firing range, and turned to Rowan who was looking more than a little puzzled. "I am not sure what this will achieve Rune, would you like to explain why we have to do this and how this involves Jade?" She gave a cheeky smile and winked at him.

"All will be revealed, you will see, just ask your men to do as I instructed." He gave a shrug and turned to his men.

"Load and aim into the purple light." Jade watched not at all sure why this mattered to her. Rune's violet window opened in a long wide rectangle. Jett walked up to Jade's side as the bowmen took aim and fired a volley into the window of light.

"What is she up to now?" Jade shrugged.

"No idea at all." The bowmen reloaded and fired a second volley, and then a third, Rune appeared pleased and turned to all the Bowmen and thanked them, and then her window closed, Jade looked even more confused. "Where did they go Rune?"

Once again, she gave a cheeky smile and a slight chuckle. "You will see." She turned to Rowan. "Head to the gate with the rest of your men, and prepare with Robbie." Her window opened and she disappeared.

Sapphire stood with the Sage as his men assembled. He had taken the barracks in Area Twelve over night with ease, as most of the men had been shipped to Loxley. His force had now grown even larger as the word was out all over the city that they had been freed by a liberating force. Sapphire looked at the map in her hand with him. "Ok get your first group ready." Her window opened. "This is Area Thirteen, send them in."

A large group swarmed into the window with rifles, and within seconds the sounds of gunfire could be heard on the other side of the window. Sapphire's window snapped shut.

"Next group, Area Six, go." The window opened and another large force ran into it shooting and screaming, as the last man ran through, and the window closed. He smiled as he looked at her looking down at the map.

"You know you are really quite remarkable Sapphire." She gave him a sideways glanced and smiled.

"You have come a long way too; it's been nice working with you." His brow furrowed.

"What are you saying, surely not goodbye?" She smiled and gave a sigh.

"You have not seen Loxley, honestly there is twenty times our number there, we have lost a lot already, none of us can be sure we will make it through, we just have to do our best and hope." He understood and placed his hand on her shoulder.

"Whatever the result, it has been a real pleasure, just keep your head and your wits about you. He has short wave radio, trust me we are already on his network ready to send the word out all over his cities, whatever happens at Loxley, he will not win this day, he will just find he is back to square one. Loxley is a tough place, have more faith, stronger men have fallen there in the past."

The window behind him opened and she smiled. "This is you, Area Fourteen, good luck and keep your head down too."

The Sage smiled and turned to Martin. "Take them through, we have a diversion to create and people to free."

Sapphire watched as the Sage loaded his bow, and then turned and ran into the blue window of light, the long line of men, which was the longest, ran through behind him. She smiled at each man as he went through, and as the last man approached the window she waved and then the window snapped closed. Sapphire gave a sigh and folded the map up and slipped it in to her pocket.

"Hearne help all of them." Her window opened in front of her and she stepped through it and it snapped shut leaving Area Twelve under the control of the people.

Deep in the woodland to the North east of Loxley, Louisa and the Outlaws had played cat and mouse all night in the darkness. Mason's men had been held back, and had gone to ground, and under the supervision of Gwynne they held the long line hidden in the trees. Louisa with the Outlaws crept through the fern and scrub setting yet more traps, and quietly despatching the forward scouts of Mason. The soldiers in black were easy to spot, and as their frustrated officers tried to move forward, arrows would strike from every direction taking down their men; it was starting to feel like an impossible fight, as they were losing men left, right, and centre, and yet to date no one had seen a single woodsman.

It was like crawling through a mine field of traps and snares, where men would suddenly scream out and be dragged into a tree top, and silenced by an arrow. Trip wires were everywhere, and the quietness of the trees would suddenly be broken as a huge explosion went off, and men screamed for their lives as they were impaled by long shards of wood or were crushed under falling trees.

The officers would push their men forward only to see them swallowed in pinto pits and impaled on long sharp spikes. Things dropped from the trees to crush men, nets would swoop up taking five to ten men up in them, and clusters of long sharp spikes, would come out of nowhere and pin men to the trees. Just watching it happen to someone close by had its effects, as the bravery of Mason's soldiers began to ebb away.

Back in Loxley sat at her table, Rune prepared as her hands swept across her table. Round the edge of the room stood a line of long crystal tubes, each one containing a bird, sealed away out of harms reach. Rune looked up at the pictures floating in the air above her table. "Sapphire are you ready? Mother prepare, I am opening the window in Loxley. The Specialists will go first and then the bowmen will follow."

Robbie stood with Rowan as the light of the sun rose in the sky to his left, and the shade across the valley began to lift, showing the black scorched earth along the length of Mason's wall, and highlighting the green of the grass and trees that grew from the river up to his position in front of Loxley. In many ways it appeared a fitting image of that moment, as the world of green had finally come to the point where they would stand against the blackness of their future should Mason win. The violet window opened in front of him and he turned and looked back at his men. They stood in two lines with their hoods up ready, and the tension in the air around them could almost be tasted. Robbie lifted his bow.

"Specialists of Loxley prepare."

They snapped in line ready and as Robbie walked forward, so began the first real attempt to bring down Mason. Henry stood to the side of where the gates once stood, he smiled at the lads as they trouped past and gave each of them a nod.

"Good luck lads. Look lively now, and keep your wits about you."

Jess watched from his shoulder and deep down inside she felt the most frightened she had ever been. The rest of her family were walking to war, and as her heart beat faster in her chest, all she could do was silently pray to the green lord that she would see them again. Agatha and Anne stood a little way back from the road with Alice and waved at the men, their usual smiles replaced with looks of worry and concern. Jonathan Appleton and his wife also stood in the crowd watching, as their three sons were walking to war, and they felt the fear of wondering if they too would ever see them again.

For the first time in a long time the usual hustle and bustle of market day was quiet in Loxley. The stalls sat empty, the training field was deserted, and the only sound was that of marching feet on the dry road, and it beat with the sound of soft boots on earth, and was almost like the heartbeat of the whole community. Those who could not fight stood silently watching, some of them weeping, and some of them looking drawn and tired from their lack of sleep, over the worry of losing their loved ones. The beat of the boots lasted for almost an hour, and then as the last men trudged through, an eerie silence descended, as those left on the walls stood silently waiting for the moment when the enemy would strike. For the first time since the Red Death, Loxley had come to a complete standstill.

Mason wearing a long black cloak rode on a black horse along the line of his army; at his side Mark Richard Dale wearing a long dark blue cloak rode a pure white thoroughbred horse. They reached the centre of the massive line where a group of generals all saluted, as the two riders steadied their horses and faced them.

On each side of them the line stretched for almost the whole length of the wall. Behind them some distance off on the top of the wall Morgan le Fey waited, her mind caught between her duty to her son, and her constant worry about where the sacred birds of her family line were.

Mason prepared and took a deep satisfying breath. "If all goes well, tonight we will dine in Loxley." Dale gave a titter.

"I have pre-ordered barbecue Woodcutter, look at what you have accomplished Mason, this is simply a clean up of the worst of the rabble, you worry too much, everything will go better than well." Mason smirked.

"I admire your confidence Mark, but do not underestimate them, this will not be as simple as you may think, never forget this has always been a guerrilla war, these people are not easily overcome."

Dale laughed. "Look at what we have; we have a hundred for every one of theirs, they think they are not easily overcome because they are fools, I will drive this army through Loxley like a tsunami and sweep them all to their graves. Leave it to me old man, make sure your mother behaves and we will erase Loxley forever and build the seat of your throne here."

Mason gave a nod, and a soldier lifted a large black flag and began to wave it. Morgan le Fey saw the flag and gave a sigh. "About time."

She lifted her arms as her eyes turned blood red, the clouds above her thickened, and lightning flashed across the wall, as the wind rose up around her. Stood with her arms up and her long black robes flapping in the breeze, she gave out an almighty cry, and lightening shot out from her and bounced all along the length of the whole tall black wall.

The ground gave a shudder and as thunder rumbled above her, large openings began to grow and widen all along the wall creating a long series of many new gateways. The sky gave a roaring explosion, as more lightning crashed down on the wall, and as she dropped her arms and the wind died down, the dust settled and Mason gave a wide smile.

Mason gave a laugh, and then looked at his generals. "You know what to do, you have your orders, as soon as I give the signal, send them through." The Generals gave a salute and then halted, uneasiness swept through the standing soldiers as they all stared at Mason, or was it past him?

Behind them on the hill, the three large towers that held the beacons stood highlighted in the early sun, and the ones to the left and right ignited into flames. Mason turned in his saddle to look back and gave a disgruntled grunt. Mark Richard Dale's horse gave an uneasy bray, and shuddered. He pulled on the reins to steady it, and then turned it round to face in the direction of the towers.

"What the hell is that?"

On the very top of the central tower was a lone figure. It was hooded and holding a longbow. Mason gave a nod and chuckled.

"That my dear Mark is the leader of your rabble, that is the Lord of Loxley, and I must say he does not disappoint. As to what the hell he is up to, I have no idea, but my dear friend, I am pretty sure we are about to find out."

Murmurs broke out in the troops who moved uneasily as they all stared at the lone figure standing high as he loaded his bow, pulled back on the string and fired it into the air. Two hundred thousand pairs of eyes, all instantly looked up and followed the arrow in unison, as it flew straight up into the air and then hovered for a just a second. The arrow tipped, and came hurtling down towards the group of soldiers behind Mason, the murmurs in the soldiers ranks began to grow louder as the arrow hurtled to the ground at speed. Panic took over as the arrow whizzed towards them, and the ranks broke as the soldiers scattered, the arrow came fizzing out of the sky and hit the earth. BOOM!!!

Mark Richard Dale clung to his reins as his horses reared up, Mason's horse jumped on the spot almost dismounting him, and soldiers ran in every direction. Dale screamed out in the chaos, and Mason started to laugh, his long white hair flapping behind him as he tried to control his horse.

Robbie watched from the tower with a smile, below the Specialist all giggled and laughed, as they saw the troops scatter, and Dale fight to control his horse. Robbie looked down as he fitted his second arrow to the bow. "Treen, Crystal, on my count."

Below Treen loaded an arrow on to her mother's long white bow, Crystal slipped out a long white arrow and fitted it to the string. They both pulled back on the string, out of sight from Mason's army, and looked up to Robbie as they pointed their arrows skyward.

Robbie lifted his bow and pulled back on the string, he took a long deep breath, and then pointed his arrow skyward. "One...Two...Three!"

He fired, and the arrow shot up into the sky, closely followed by the two other arrows, that headed to the left and right of Mason's position. He watched the arrows as they hovered just for a second.

"You want a war Mason, well here we come." The arrows tipped, and then raced to earth.

CHAPTER THIRTY EIGHT

THE MOMENT OF DESTINY

The three arrows hovered, and then tipped over and fell from the sky in the direction of Mason's troops. No one looked to the hill, as all eyes were fixed on the falling arrows. Men stumbled as they looked up and naturally moved, not seeing each other. The orderly ranks broke into a shambles, as the arrows came with speed towards them, and any hope of order left the men. In the scramble, men pushed and shoved each other, just to be anywhere which was not near the landing spot.

The white arrow of Crystal hit first and dug deep into the floor. There was no explosion like the last arrow, and the men halted to look back at the arrow. It began to send up a plume of what looked like fizzing water, and instantly the floor around it turned white. By the time the men understood what was happening the frost had spread rapidly, and they screamed as they looked down to see the white frost climbing their legs. A circle of over one hundred feet turned white encasing all the men within it in ice.

The second arrow to hit was Treen's from her mother's bow, the result was a little more spontaneous, as a huge cloud of fire exploded from where the arrow hit, engulfing everyone within one hundred yards in fire. Screaming burning figures ran wildly bumping into others, who ignited and screamed in horrendous pain as they were engulfed. The men not affected fled away from the fire not realising one more arrow had not landed yet. Robbie's arrow hit a running soldier in the back, and he continued running with the other men until the arrow ignited blowing men, dirt, and weapons into the air.

Mark Richard Dale, who was still fighting to control his horse, hit the floor hard as the pandemonium surrounding him was too much for his horse and it bolted for the hill, as far away from the noise as possible. Mason controlled his horse, although his anger had risen at the conduct of his men, he swung his horse round to see the hill above him which was devoid of the lord of Loxley. He fought his horse to stabilise it, and as he gained better control, he watched as a bright flash lit up the top of the hill, and a long line of Scottish fighters appeared.

On the top at their side a long line of Loxley bowmen appeared with loaded bows, and unleashed thousands of arrows. He quickly swung his horse round and bolted for the protection of the wall at a gallop through his men, he made it under one of the newly formed gateways just as the arrows rained down pinning his men to the floor. He could do nothing but watch as men were hit, and fell screaming in pain with arrows in their legs, arms and faces. It was utter chaos as they too fled for cover. Across the chaos Dale cowered next to a wall, hugging it as closely as possible.

The hill above flashed white and long lines of the men from Caerleon appeared to join the ever growing line of men defending Loxley. Dale peered over the wall, and then deeming it was safe, he rose to his feet and ran for his life through the screaming wounded and dead men, to the safety of the gateway. He came running into the cover gasping and glared at Mason. "I thought you said they were trapped in Loxley, how the hell did they all get out here with that dam green barrier still in place?"

Mason watched as the hill flashed with violet and an even longer line of men walked out to join the end of the growing line, as the men of Carlisle came to take their positions, and it was clear Mason had greatly overlooked the part of Runestone in all of this.

He turned to Dale and snapped. "It matters not how he got there; did I not tell you he was resourceful? His witch is playing a greater role than we thought, but nothing has changed, we still have the advantage, we have rifles to his bows, now get up on the wall and let's gain back the advantage, let's see how his bows can handle rifles running at them."

Another volley of arrows came hurtling down, and rained onto the soldiers, Mason walked out from under the gateway and snatched a rifle up from the floor, cocked it, and fired it up the hill at the bowmen. He strode across the flattened ground, littered with the dead and wounded, and grabbed a rifle man by the back of his shirt and thrust him forward.

"Shoot at them, it's what you're here for, now do your duty or so help me I will shoot you here and now." He pushed at the soldier and then grabbed another, and thrust him roughly forward as he screamed at the other men. "Get up there now and start killing them."

One of the officers started shouting at the men, and trying to get them back into order and fight back, and Mason continued to push the men together, one man made an attempt to run for it, and Mason lifted his rifled and shot him in the back, then screamed at the others to fight. The men were terrified, but actually who they were the most afraid of, was a question they could not answer, they either ran against the bowman and died, or did nothing and got shot by Mason, and it had the desired effect. The soldiers reformed in long ranks and then took aim, Mason watched screaming in rage, and slowly his army recovered their composure, and the battle finally started properly. He could see that his men had already paid a high price at the hands of the lord of Loxley, but he knew he still had the far greater advantage of numbers and more modern weapons.

Morgan le Fey was screaming from the top of the wall and hurling balls of fire up towards the hill were the Woodland forces fired down on her son's men, when suddenly she felt a strong sense within her and she stopped in her tracks.

"Morgana, hear me I need you, we must save the family, come to me."

Morgan turned, and black smoke erupted from her, and she fired into the sky, Rune leaned forward on her table and smiled, she turned to Sapphire. "Amethyst was right, send in the Night Strikers, it's time, and now is the moment to take the wall."

Steph leaned forward and looked at the images on the table. "How can Branna still be alive with such a bad wound?" Rune smiled.

"Roack is still alive, and as long as she is, then Branna will live, their lives are tied as one, both must die as one in order for them to be conquered, I wondered when this moment would come."

Branna sat in her seat as the head of the family looking at the slumped figures of her offspring; she turned to Berengar, and gave a weak smile. "Get me a raven, I need to live in order to bring them all back, go and gather ravens, one for each of us, we need to renew the ritual."

He nodded as he understood, and ran from the room; Branna gave a gasp as she tried to gather her wits about her. Black smoke funnelled into the room and Morgana appeared, she looked at Branna covered in blood. "You talk of saving this family, but as you know all of the ravens are caught, including Roack, by either that moon fairy or that woodland flower girl, how can you save us without the ravens?"

Branna sat slumped and covered in her own blood, she coughed. "The only way to save us is a renewal ritual, but I am not strong enough, Morgana you must save the family, we lose more than gold and power, we lose everything if you don't."

Morgana looked at the slumped figure of Otto. "I doubt he would agree with you, I have always been a half breed, a Celt bitch, or endless other vile slurs on my abilities, even your own daughter was vile and mistreated me, and now you ask me to save him and all the others that looked down on me?"

Branna understood. "I know the pain you suffered here as a young girl, especially after the death of your father, but it was not I who did that, and it did make you stronger, I would even say stronger than any of the others. Morgana I gave you the black book over my own daughter, does that not show my confidence in your abilities? I was the one who came to you and helped you kill Eve and Eleanor, you owe me, and I am the symbol of this family, and so I ask you now, help save my children and their children."

Morgan looked round the room and at the many who she despised for their cruelty towards her, but she knew that Branna had learned a great deal of Fae Ofmoon magic, more than she ever had a chance to, her pale red eyes looked at Branna. "You know this ritual, and it is possible?"

Branna smiled, "I studied more than the Merle in Avalon, it had an extensive library, and many rights just for a queen, and a queen can renew their life by changing birds. It is only temporary, we may only have a short time, but with the whole family together we have a better chance of getting back Roack and Rajani." Branna gave a slight grunt and her face screwed up as she felt pain, she gasped for air, and her words came through gritted teeth.

"Morgana listen to me, Raven Merle is not tied to this family, but I cannot say for sure she will survive if we all die, if not for us, do it for her, for she is your true heir." Morgana gave it a moment's thought.

"What do I have to do?" Branna smiled.

"Berengar has gone to collect new ravens. We will need the blood of the recently dead, the more recent the better, at least six." Morgana understood and gave a smirk.

"I can do that no problems, it just happens I can get as many as we need."

Rune sat back at her table. "The moment is almost upon us, she has hope again, I want her to believe she can recover, and then I will take the life that is owed to all of us for those we loved and lost, it is time for the Berengar family to understand the true cruelty of Nature. Get the ravens ready."

Sapphire burst out of her blue window as the Specialists sat in the grass. In front of them the vast army of the Woodland forces held their position at the top of the hill, and fired down at the ranks of Mason. She walked towards Robbie, and he turned towards her and smiled. "Rune is almost ready; you guys need to get ready it is almost time for the Specialist to make their move."

John Lox was armed to the teeth with two axes and his sword, as well as a belt full of knives that Jade eyed with envy. He stood at the side of Robbie and nodded. "Bout time, every moment that man lives is a moment too bloody long."

Sapphire could feel the anger in the group at the loss of their family and comrades, Robbie gave her a wink and she smiled.

"The Night Strikers have landed, and are on the wall making their way towards you, watch for my window, as soon as Rune strikes, it will appear, do not hesitate and go, hopefully Morgan will be distracted long enough for you to do what needs to be done." Robbie gave a nod.

"We will be ready, just be careful, you and Rune will need to watch each other's back."

"Have no fear, we will, and remember, her power has its effects on us, and you may end up scattered, as it is hard to see inside those walls." She turned back into her window and it snapped shut.

Rowan watched Loxley in the distance. "Looking at the smoke in the distant forest, it looks like Louisa and the Outlaws are in retreat working their way back towards us, Mason is gaining pace there and here, we cannot stand still much longer Robbie, sooner or later if we do not move we will lose our advantage." Robbie gave a nod and turned to Treen.

"Give Ian control on this side, and tell him to send in the ground forces, we will have to take this fight right to them if we have any hope of surviving long enough to give Rune the time she needs." Treen looked at Claire stood waiting with her red flags.

"Send the signal to Ian; it will be his for the taking of command." Claire lifted her flags and started to signal. Robbie gave a sigh.

"Come on Rune, everything lies on you now." He turned and looked at the Specialist's. "Get ready we go at a moment's notice and it's going to be close quarters and brutal."

Branna sat staring at her family isolated and slumped in their seats, as her mind wandered through her past, from her time in Avalon with her only real love, Ariel. Her first meeting the night she drew down the part of the Merle that would inhabit Roack, to her life on the road in the caravan with her many companions, especially Boris, who she had always felt should live, when Roack insisted he died, and yet she had spared him. Her thought broke as the violet figure of Runestone rose up out of her floor. She blinked and gave a chuckle.

"I thought you would return, what do you want, is it the final moments you wish for?" Rune looked at her without any sympathy.

"I had hoped you would accept your fate, and then leave, but I am not surprised to know that you would try to recover your family. Rhiannon is gone, you got your revenge Branna, why drag it out? You cannot win I am stronger than Eve, but I am glad to hear you admit it was you who planned her death, for that makes this so much easier for me."

Rune looked at her family sat in the large circle. "I wonder which I should take first?"

Branna gave a smile and started to chuckle. "Cut off the heads of the birds for all I care, you will not kill us, the Merle within them will just pass to another host and infect your own realm, you think you are so smart, but really daughter of life, do you know what you are dealing with?" Rune smiled lifted her fingers, and placed her second finger on her thumb.

"I am aware of how to kill them, that is why your sacred birds are sealed in crystal with the guardian of the Whitelines, pure light will kill anything from their world." Branna smiled.

"Merlin has gone, do you seriously think I am a fool, Morgana killed him in Avalon, there is no guardian of the Whitelines anymore." Rune smiled and clicked her fingers. SNAP!!

"He had a daughter who he left his gifts to, your so called credible witch Morgana, forgot to destroy his staff, and it has passed." Gundobarld jerked in his seat and turned to ash. Rune turned and walked towards the end of the room.

"Your family will not live past this day." She clicked her fingers and Rosamund jerked and turned to ash, Branna screamed out.

"NO!!!!!"

Rune faded as Merwig then Lothar, jerked in their seats and then turned to ash. Berengar ran into the room with a large sack and dropped it as he saw Otto Jerk and turn to ash, he fell to his knees and screamed into the air. Branna sat staring at the ash on the floor, she looked at Berengar and two tears ran down her cheeks. "Goodbye."

He looked at her not understanding, as his hands turned to ash, and his eyes widened in fear. The sack on the floor bobbed about as his face hit the floor, and disappeared into the dust of the earth. Frozen and unable to move Branna watched as a crystal tube slid out of the floor and slowly rose up past her face. The black smoke swirled into the room, and six wounded men hit the floor and rolled in agony.

Morgan saw the crystal pass above Branna and the top seal itself, she screamed and ran to the tube and hammered for all her might on the crystal. "TELL ME THE RITUAL!" But it was too late, Rune had sealed her in, and Morgan knew there was no way she could get Branna free in time, the men on the floor behind her moaned in pain, she turned her red eyes blazing with anger and lifted her hand.

"SHUT THE HELL UP!" A ball of red light came out of her hand, and they screamed and then fell silent.

The blue window opened and the Specialists moved with speed, they shot through fast and found themselves inside a large room on the inside of the large wall of Mason. Robbie looked round. "Hawk, Fox check the doors and see what we have to deal with." He understood as he noticed they were not all there; they had been separated.

Up on top of the wall, Mason laughed with delight as he saw the woodland forces run down to meet with his men, the clash was loud, and the fight had begun in earnest. He could see his army was still seven times bigger than Robbie's, and he knew it would only be a matter of time before he had control, and slowly wiped them out. Mark Richard Dale appeared happier now they were making progress.

A despatch clerk ran up to Mason and handed him a note, he opened it and read it and frowned. Dale looked over. "What is it?" Mason looked up from the note.

"Area Twelve has fallen to a rebel force." Dale looked confused.

"How?" Another despatch clerk ran up and handed him a note.

"Area Ten has fallen to rebels." Another despatch clerk appeared and Dale snatched the note out of his hand angrily and read it.

"HOW THE HELL IS THIS POSSIBLE, AREA THIRTEEN HAS FALLEN TO REBELS, WHO THE BLOODY HELL ARE THEY, I THOUGHT THEY WERE ALL HERE?" Another despatch clerk ran up with another note, Dale pulled out his gun and shot him without even reading the note, the rest of the clerks panicked and scattered rather than wait for replies. Dale looked angrily at Mason.

"Are you telling me whilst we are here, our entire operation has been attacked and over run, how is that possible Mason?" Mason shrugged, unable to answer, he felt his temper rising.

"I have no idea how, but that woodland lout has done this, get down there and order every man we have spare to fight back and suppress this rebel gang." Dale gave a nod and sprinted for the steps; Mason slammed his fist down on the wall. "I HATE YOU LOXLEY!"

Down below men ran around grabbing bullets and weapons, and shipping them out to rearm the front lines, where the woodland army clashed with Mason's men in a brutal and bloody fight. Inside the Specialists went to work against the guard. Jett and Blades took their advantage of close quarters, and ran screaming into a mass of guards. Jett spun like a deadly ballerina, as Blades bounced into the air cutting and slashing, as Hawk, Alice and Jade fired arrows. Doors opened and Specialist's entered. Harry ran screaming into a barracks room waving his swords and stopped as he faced two hundred men. He pointed back to the door he had just come through.

"Oh man it's a totally uncosmic Bull man, you better like split dudes, and you don't want the kind of karma conflict he gives off." The men reached for their weapons and he wagged his finger. "Oh dudes you gonna be like so sorry, and like off to a very unhappenin place." The door exploded and John Lox and Jaz entered with Bear. Harry shrugged. "Man like I warned you dudes."

The three Specialists waded in with axes and swords, and Harry sat down on one of the beds as he watched John Lox swing his huge axe at the side of Bear, and Jaz. The soldiers had no chance, John was like a man possessed, as he swung with a raw powerful rage, slicing through men and cutting beds clean in half with one swipe of his axe.

Robbie had destiny in his hand as he fought against four men towards the stairway leading upward, closely followed by Treen and Jay. Rafe growled as he stood beside Una and she held up her pole, confronted by twenty men. She took a step forward and then thought twice and stepped back. Smokes and Big John appeared at the other end of the corridor behind the men, and saw Rafe bearing his teeth. Smokes smiled. "Wolfie time, cool."

Both of them chuckled, and holding their weapons up, ran screaming down the passage towards the men who realised they were caught. Rafe saw his moment, and pounced at the first man biting deep into his nose, as he thrust his sword into the man at his side. Terror instantly ran through the trapped soldiers who had nowhere to run. Big John clashed hard with Smokes behind him, as Una brought her pole round and the men between the two groups panicked and hit out at anything, including their own men.

Skip, Tila, Crystal and Woody fought their way up the back stairwell, Skip led the way as Tila bounced behind him, and Crystal touched the wall with her ungloved hand and instantly froze any who tried to follow. Woody swung his sword with power, nothing like the panicked nervous outlaw he had been in the past.

When Robbie finally made it to the top of the steps, and out onto the top of the wall, he was confronted with a group of officers, five of which instantly fell with knives in their throats care of Jade. Jay took a stance and turned to see the guards behind them. With a lighter in her teeth, she loaded a stinger arrow, aimed, and fired. The guards, thinking it was just an ordinary arrow that could kill only one of them, ran towards them; the arrow hit the first man and then exploded tossing them all off the high wall. The ones behind slid on the floor, turned and ran in the opposite direction as Jay launched another stinger from her bow.

In the distance along the wall, explosions marked the position of the Night Strikers as they worked their way towards Robbie and the Specialists, along the three mile stretch of guard laden wall between them. Jade turned and looked back. "Where is Rowan?"

Panic flooded into her and she turned and ran back towards the steps. Robbie continued on as other Specialist appeared from other stairways. Robbie cut and sliced as he moved towards where he knew Mason would be.

Treen leaned over the top of the wall and un-leashed an arrow, it hit the back lines of the men and fire spread out in a wide circle, taking out a mass of Mason's soldiers.

Big John slipped round the corner of yet another corridor. "I am not sure I like this guys, I am sure we should have taken the other way." Una sniffed the air.

"Urgh, something smells rotten." She turned in the dark. "What are you growling at now Wolfie?" He appeared round the corner.

"It's not me!" Una Frowned and looked at Smokes, who shrugged.

"ARRRRRGH!!!"

They all jumped, as a door down the corridor exploded open and Harry came belting out of it, he turned, slammed the door, and tried to force it shut, as something on the other side hit it hard, he glanced and saw the group looking puzzled. "It's uncosmic beasts dudes, that ain't no wine cellar it's full of her beasties, run for your lives dudes." Smokes gave a titter and looked back.

"Oh bugger, she has Marsh Hounds." The door gave a huge crash, and Harry squealed like a frightened pig, let go of it, turned and ran towards them. Rafe looked stunned and pointed at Harry.

"Not this way you fool, go that way." John turned.

"Oh Bugger." Harry ran past them, and turned into the corridor they had just come down.

"Run dudes the beasties is coming." Una turned and fled with Harry, Smokes looked at Rafe and Big John.

"Good luck guys." The doors down the corridor crashed open, and eight huge hairy hounds came roaring out, John jumped back.

"Shit!" He turned with Rafe and ran after Smokes. They ran for their lives up the long corridor, Rafe turned to Smokes as he caught him up leaving John at the back, Smokes looked at him as he panted.

"We do not tell Steph, OK?" Rafe nodded, and looked back behind him as John caught them up.

"Where the bloody hell is Jade when we need her, doesn't she eat these buggers?" Rafe smirked.

"I thought you did too." He smiled through his gasp.

"Aye I do, I just cannot eat eight, I need help and she has the same appetite." Some distance up the corridor Una saw a door; she grabbed Harry by his sleeve and yanked him in her direction.

"This way."

She grabbed the door handle as Rafe, Big John, and Smokes came skidding up behind her, she pushed the door hard, and it swung open into the blinding daylight, and they shot through it. The door closed as they all slammed it shut behind them, gasping for air, they all leaned back against the door to keep it shut feeling relieved. Gasping and panting they looked ahead of themselves, where a large group of black clad soldiers looked menacingly at them. Una gasped.

"Oh Crap." Rafe pushed her to one side and grabbed the door handle as he pushed her flat to the wall, the door swung open and the eight large Marsh Hounds pounced out into the sunlight.

Harry, Big John, Smokes, Rafe and Una held their breath as the hounds saw the soldiers, and bolted towards them. The soldiers screamed and fled at high speed, and the hounds gave pursuit. As quick as lightning Una grabbed Rafe and dragged him back through the door, closely followed by the others, and Big John pulled the door closed tight, and gave a long sigh of relief and he breathed new air into his lungs. Outside the Marsh Hounds grabbed the soldiers and shook them violently, as they ripped them apart screaming.

Rowan looked into the room and saw a man bent down pushing something into a bag, he stepped in as the man stood up. Mark Richard Dale looked at him, still holding a hand full of coins he had just discovered and decided to keep for himself. He stared at Rowan. "I know you." Rowan gave a nod

"A lot of people do." Dale thought for a second before he fully understood who it was, and he gave a nod.

"You're his number two?" Rowan watched him with cool slate grey eyes, and took another step into the room.

"Looking at your clothes, I would say you are close to Mason, so I would think you are that Dale fellow?" Dale gave a nod and gripped the hilt of his sword.

"Rowan of Loxley, Oh I am so going to enjoy this." He pulled his sword. "I have killed many with this." Rowan was not impressed.

"With a blade that dull, I am surprised to hear it."

He pulled out the Sword of Honour and it shone brightly in his hand. Dale came at him fast, and Rowan reacted with equal speed, and parried his blow easily. Dale kicked a chair out of his way as he made another lunge, and Rowan deflected it, and flicked his blade back. Dale jumped back out of the way as Rowan's sword swiped past his face.

He stepped back, steadied himself and smiled, as he brought his sword up and gripped it with both hands, Rowan prepared as Dale swung with both hands and began his onslaught.

He was more powerful than he looked and fought with skill, but Rowan defended and took the blows as he moved backwards to give himself more space. Dale attacked with rage and power, Rowan had fought equally as hard men, and was used to the pounding of his blade and cut back and sliced back up.

"Your men will die today, why fight something you could never beat, you are a fool to align yourself with Loxley. On our side you would have had power and total respect." Rowan slashed up with his sword, and his blade collided with power against Dale's, they sparked as they met, and Rowan stared in his eyes.

"Mason stands for death, I live for life and freedom, these are things you will never understand whilst you steal from your own. I am happy with the side I chose, and do not write us off so easily, we have only just begun."

He stepped back and hit out as something caught his foot; it was a dead despatch clerk. Rowan lost his centre of balance, as Dale pounded another two heavy blows on him, and he staggered back and slipped on the wet blood that was covering the floor. Rowan fell back and Dale gave a mighty yell of joy as he brought his sword up ready for the final blow, as Rowan sprawled backwards.

There was a deafening scream, a flash of green, and a window opened up right in front of Rowan. A huge cannon ball came rocketing through and hit Dale in the chest. He was lifted off his feet and went flying backwards down the room, five gunshots echoed, and the bullets came whizzing out followed by another large cannon ball, as Jade stood with bright glowing green eyes in the doorway.

Dale hit the two doors at the end of the room and went through them with a crash, his forehead had two clean bullet holes in it as he hung limp, propelled by the force of the ball. The window snapped shut and there was an almighty explosion.

Rowan scrambled to his feet as the floor shifted, and ran for the door, he dived, caught Jade, and went sailing into the corridor, and crashed into the wall as the second explosion went off, and he pulled her close and rolled onto her to shield her. Daylight appeared several feet down the corridor, the wall collapsed and the bricks crashed down into the valley below, rolling towards the river. Rowan lifted his head and looked back and coughed, he turned and looked to Jade as she opened her eyes and sneezed. "Are you alright?" She looked at him and her eyes flickered with green specks.

"No...What the hell were you doing sneaking off alone?" He smiled and rolled off her.

"I wasn't sneaking, I was lost, I got separated and was looking for a way back." She sat up.

"You are staying by me, and no more sneaking, we need to get back to Robbie." Rowan started to chuckle and she turned on him. "What exactly is so funny?" He gave another chuckle.

"When that cannon ball came out of your window, I was waiting for Jett's head to appear." He gave another chuckle and she gave him a huge grin.

"Yeah, me too."

Outside the generals of Mason were becoming more in control, and they pulled back several ranks, and sent them through the gateways under the large black wall, and onto the valley. They grabbed long ladders and ran to the bridge, and then made their way down the long bridge over the valley. Henry sent up the call as several thousand men flooded towards the gap at the end of the bridge.

At the gap they threw the ladders over the open space, and on the wall of Loxley and in the gap where the gates had been, men prepared. A large force of Armsmen drew out their swords, and filled the gap where the gates had been ready for the imminent invasion. Bowmen on the walls loaded and pulled back on the strings, as the first of Mason's fighters appeared at the top of the hill. Behind them more men streamed over the bridge built by Morgan le Fey.

Henry yelled out his orders, and the first volleys of arrows were released, and the first onslaught of men fell, only to be replaced by more, as the generals poured more men under the wall towards Loxley. The Armsmen dug in their heels, and as the first soldiers made it through the rain of arrows, they clashed and a fight for the gates of Loxley began.

Over the other side of the wall, Grace and Mary stood side by side as they cleaved their way through the wall of black vested soldiers with her Scottish fighting force. Around them cloaks from Loxley and Caerleon, fought in the bloody hard brutal battle, and it was starting to feel like they would never see the end of it. High on the hill, Ian of Carlisle viewed the scene, and from his high advantage point it was clear that Mason had him outnumbered, and was slowly surrounding his forces, he wiped his chin as he looked at his General. "We need more, or some miracle."

A huge burst of fire exploded at the back of Mason's men wiping out a large group, as another of Treen's arrows hit from high up on top of the wall, he shook his head. "It's not enough, Mason is just too strong, within the hour the tide will turn, and we will be on the losing end."

No one could discount the bravery of the Woodland force, they had fought with heart and soul, and given everything they had, but after hours of fighting, it was becoming a tough fight. The dead littered the blood soaked floor, where severed limbs, broken bows and hacked up shields lay strewn all over the grass. It looked to Ian of Carlisle that if they were to lose, it would not have been because of lack of spirit, but the reality was that Mason still matched his force man for man, even though he had the highest casualties. Mason's calculations that sheer numbers would overwhelm Loxley, was now looking to be proven correct.

Una, Smokes, Big John, Harry and Rafe, came sprinting up a stairwell and back into the light on the top of the wall. Around them men in black were leaning over and shooting crossbows at the woodland forces. A few turned, and realising they were Specialist's they drew out their swords, dropped their crossbows, and ran at them. Rafe gave a loud growl, and holding his sword ran at them. They had soldiers in front and behind them, and all of them turned and waded into the masses of black vested men.

Rafe cut and sliced, with pure aggression, driven on by the sound of Jett somewhere ahead of him, as she screamed and whooped with delight. Around him the Specialist's fought with every ounce of power they had left. Harry ran along the edge of the wall with his shining swords, cutting and slashing, and hoping his second pair of boots would be spared the blood stains. Big John pushed Una back towards Rafe as he cut and slashed besides Smokes with brutal force, and Una smacked and hit the men around the edges of the fight, with great force, sending them over the wall and screaming to their deaths, as she nervously looked for any signs of Woody. Inch by inch, they moved closer towards Jett, as explosions and screams were now just one mass of deafening noise from the battle all around them.

Rafe cut up and from nowhere an arrow hit the man before him in the back of the head, he pushed the man aggressively aside as he looked up and saw Alice some distance away, standing on the wall edge, with her bow loaded and aiming. A glint of metal let him know that Bear also was not that far ahead, and he slammed into another soldier and slashed up with his sword, to try and cut a path through to the other Specialist. A loud whoop announce Jett was just a few feet in front, and he glanced back to see the others had realised and were following his lead. Rafe growled with all his might, and pushed hard cutting and slicing his way through until he saw Jett spinning in front. She sliced hard through a soldier and spotted him, and she smiled and blew him a kiss, before launching another scathing attack on the soldiers running up the stairway onto the top of the wall.

The two groups merged, and faced soldiers from both sides, they knew Robbie was not that far in front, and so pushed forward side by side, in hope of making it to his side.

Tila looked over the wall and saw the force running across the bridge, she grabbed Crystal's sleeve. "Fae land is being attacked; I have to save it." Crystal turned to see it and gripped Tila by the sleeve.

"Tila you are one against thousands what can you honestly do?" She pulled her sleeve free.

"If I die, they will defend their land, I have got to go, I love you." She climbed up onto the wall; Crystal gripped the waistband of her pants.

"Hang on you are not going alone."

She climbed up onto the wall at the side of Tila, and loaded a long white arrow. Crystal raised her bow to her eye, and aimed at the gates of Loxley in the distance, she gave a sigh. "This is a long shot but I did it at the castle, so here goes nothing."

The arrow shot out of her bow, and shot like a missile as Crystal's eyes turned white, and her mind guided the arrow, as it left a long thread attached to her bowstring. Tila smiled.

"Oh wow, I am so turned on about now, if we had the time..."

The arrow hit the floor just outside the side of the gates; Crystal opened her eyes, and took the fine thread and snapped it off. She placed it on the wall, and gripping her glove in her teeth, she slipped it off and touched the thread with a bare hand. The thread expanded into a gutter of ice, and she turned to Tila, and grabbed her by the tunic, kissed her passionately. "If we live, you are all mine alone for a week." Tila gave a gasp.

"Oh wow, my knees just trembled!" Crystal turned her, and gave her a push as she giggled. Tila slipped on the ice and landed in the gutter, and shot off down towards the gates of Loxley at high speed, Crystal jumped on behind her and slid off at speed. Jett spotted them and was up on the wall.

"Wolfie Heel!!!!"

She jumped onto the ice gutter, and Wolfie came bouncing over the wall and dived on behind her, closely followed by Harry, Fox and Blades. They shot off at high speed towards Loxley, lifting up their weapons, as Jett whooped and screamed with delight. To their right the bridge exploded with fire, as Treen let another of her mother's arrows go, killing half the men on the bridge.

Robbie battled his way forward cutting and slicing his way through the soldiers and guards. Rowan fought his hardest several feet behind him with John Lox as they tried to close the gap between them and Robbie. Jade was up on the wall with her bow next to Alice, shooting into the mass and taking out any soldiers close to Robbie, as Bear and Jaz cleaved with their axe's and swords to protect Alice and Jade along the edge of the wall. Una united with Woody as they hacked and battered everything within a few feet of them.

Up ahead Mason was in clear view on a raised section of the wall, and Robbie gritted his teeth as he gave his every last ounce of strength to make his way closer towards Mason. His eyes burned with hate in his blood soaked face, as his hair hung lank and dirty, and the filth of the fight stuck to his shirt and shoulders, from which the tattered remains of his cloak hung loose. It was an agonising desperate fight, as he moved inch by inch, grunting and gasping with exertion, closer towards his greatest enemy.

He swiped destiny round, which was hardly recognisable from the blood and dirt that stained the blade, he gave a huge grunt, as his sword came up slicing through another of the many he had cut through. He saw the steps that would take him up to Mason, who was too busy looking over the wall at his men invading Loxley.

Robbie gave one final slice, and suddenly his path was clear, he pushed with all his might to get a purchase on the first step, and he looked up at Mason, and screamed with all his might, as he broke free.

"MASON I AM HERE!"

Mason's head snapped round, and gasping for breath Robbie stepped onto the second step, his eyes fixed on Mason Knox, Rowan came slicing through behind him. Robbie took a deep breath. "This is what you want, well here I am, it is time we ended this Mason." Robbie took another step up as Mason calmly turned round and smiled.

"Finally, we meet again."

Robbie gripped the wall and took the last step, as to his right far down below, Grace with Ian of Carlisle, the men of Dove Dale and Caerleon, fought alongside the Bowmen of Loxley.

Face to face across the top of the empty wall they stood, both leaning on the outer walls separated by fifty feet of smooth black blood soaked stone. Robbie took a deep breath, and felt the calmness of the moment wash over him, Mason smiled.

"We have been here before Lord Loxley, but this time you will not be as lucky as to beat me in a sword fight." His face wore a satisfied smirk, he lifted his hand and pointed a pistol right at Robbie. "Tell me, are you fast enough with that blade to stop a bullet?"

CHAPTER THIRTY NINE

MINOR REPRIEVE

Tila hit the dirt running, closely followed by Crystal; Jett came screaming next with the rest of the party. Black vested soldiers swept up the bank towards the gates, a hail of arrows were released high above the head of Tila. She lifted her bow and with great speed and accuracy, she loaded and fired faster than any bowman had ever seen. Her green feathered arrows hit one, then another, and another as she fired an endless barrage of shots, at those leading the charge up the bank towards Loxley, cutting them down quicker than anything Crystal had ever seen.

Her arrows were running low as she walked forward towards the soldiers of Mason. "This is sacred ground of the peoples of Fae, you are not welcome, leave or I will invoke the might of Bridge and bring death to all of you." She reached down to her hip and felt nothing, her arrows had run out.

The men surged up the hill as Loxley arrows hit some, and others broke free, Tila pulled out her ornate sword and took the stance of a Fae warrior. Jett came across the dirt with her sword towards her right flank, as Crystal pulled out a long ornate sword to her left. Blades bounced into the air and the soldiers clashed into them. Tila fought with great skill, dodging and weaving, as the men twice her size tried to cut her down. A line of Armsmen ran from the gate and joined the fight, as Harry came hurtling down the ice slide, and hit the floor fast, and ran screaming into the mass waving his swords, and began a brutal onslaught of the soldiers of Mason.

High above on the wooden wall of Loxley, the Bowmen were given free will to fire and they began picking off anyone surrounding their men. The surge from the bridge up the bank continued to flow like a wave, as more and more men attacked the gates and tried to cut their way through into the town.

Tila was almost lost in the mass when suddenly there was a bright flash at her side and two men of Fae joined the fight, she looked up, and smiled as bright specks flowed down from the sky like snow, she screamed with all her might. "I will live Master Elgin, watch me!"

As the specks hit the floor along the bridge they flashed, and warriors in all green armour appeared and drove into the soldiers in black, the Fae of Earth had arrived to protect the land of their queen.

High on the hill opposite the wall Ian turned to his generals. "We cannot hold them any longer, if we pull back, we may have a hope of creating a standing position, our men are becoming separated we must regroup. Sound the trumpet and retreat at a slow pace to give us time and space."

The bugler lifted the instrument to his lips, as a white horse rode up at his side. He pushed it to his lips and took a deep breath, as a blue clad arm reached down and took the instrument away from his lips. Ian of Carlisle turned and looked as the stranger examined the bugle. "I have always wanted one of these." Ian was confused.

"Who the hell are you?"

"I am Lord James of Avalon, but you can call me Fish." He smiled. "I bring greetings from my wife in Avalon, Amethyst Queen of all Fae Ofmoon. She sends her regards and a few trusty men to aid your cause, as the lord of Loxley once did for hers."

Fish lifted his arm and a wide white window opened behind him, and a ten wide row of riders dressed in blue came galloping out, and headed down towards the battle. Thousands of mounted men followed, and galloped into the fight wearing bright steel armour and blue tunics. They drew their swords and galloped at speed breaking into two long ranks of five that turned left and right to create an outer wall around all the fighting men. They rode until the white window closed, and there were so many it was impossible to count them, suddenly they turned and charge at speed into the masses of black vested soldiers cutting them down as they rode through.

Ian of Carlisle gave a gasp of relief. "Well Lord Fish, never in my life have I seen a better timed entry to a fight." He gave a smile.

"We would have been here sooner, but it takes quite a bit of time to travel from the moon to here." He gave another smile. "Still, we made it in time, Amy will get better, after all, it is technically her first day on the job."

Robbie gave a laugh, and lifted his sleeve to his bloodied face and wiped it. "I am fast there is no doubt, but I have to admit Mason, I have never had the chance to test my fate with a bullet." He lifted his sword and took a stance.

Red flashed on the floor and Morgan le Fey erupted out of the stone, with her arms outstretched between Robbie and Mason, both of them blinked as she screamed on the top of her voice. "STOP THIS!"

Robbie frowned confused, and Mason looked angry as hell. She turned to look at Robbie, her red eyes narrowed in her pallid face, she sneered at the sight of him, Mason looked outraged.

"WHAT THE HELL ARE YOU DOING, GET OUT OF THE WAY I AM GOING TO KILL HIM AND END THIS."

Her head snapped back to him. "Don't be a fool, she has the bird, if you harm one hair on his head she will kill it, and that will be the end of us. We still have hope, there is a ritual." He looked at her in amazement.

"I DON'T CARE ABOUT YOUR BLOODY RITUAL; I WANT HIM DEAD."

Robbie could not believe it was happening. "Haven't you got fairies to torture or something, this needs to be done, now get out of the way you old hag, and let us end this once and for all."

Her head came round with speed. "SHUT IT WOODCHOPPER, YOU WILL DIE HAVE NO FEAR, BUT FOR NOW, YOU HAVE A MINOR REPRIEVE!"

Mason took two steps forward, and pushed his mother out of the way.

"You have no business here Mother; now get out of my way." He side stepped and lifted his gun, there was a flash of violet, and Mason shot back against the wall.

"Be a good boy Mason and listen to your mother, or should I say grandmother?" Rune stood on the opposite side of the wall where behind her the Night Strikers had gathered. She looked at Morgan.

"It is time Morgana of Berengar."

Morgan le Fey scowled at Rune with hate as her fingers twitched. "Where is my bird, show it to me?"

Rune gave a nod and behind her a violet window opened, Steph stepped through with her long staff and a crystal tube. Morgan's eyes widened. "Where did you get that staff?"

Steph smiled. "It was my father's, and now it has passed to me." Morgan gave a sneer.

"He gave it you, the girl who ran off with her boyfriend, seriously do you even know how to wield the Whitelines?" She shrugged, and her green eyes twinkled, Morgan noticed how like her father's they were.

"I know enough to of killed the other ravens, so for now, I think yes." Morgan scoffed.

"They will give anyone a position of a guardian these days, it was once a job of some standing, oh my how the standards of your council have slipped." She gave her middle finger a flick, and Steph was blown off her feet, and crashed down the steps, dropping the crystal tube, which smashed on the floor.

Morgan made a dash for it, and violet flashed blowing her backwards towards the soldiers of Mason, who had come to a standstill. The Specialists stepped out of the way, and she hurtled into the soldiers crashing against them sending them flying, she screamed with hate as she looked across to Runestone, and the empty broken container. "Where is my Bird?"

Mason lifted his hand at his clear target, and pointed the gun back at Robbie, there was a swoosh as something shot overhead, glinted, and as his finger twitched, the axe of John Lox hit him square in the chest and sent him backwards with the force, the gun fired into the air.

Mason looked shocked as he hit the wall and teetered just for a second with the huge axe firmly implanted almost to the hilt, and then with a gurgle he slipped backwards and fell off the wall.

Morgan le Fey screamed with hate and pain, as she looked at the scene on her knees and watched the snow white hair of Mason flap in the breeze as he tumbled over the wall, her eyes wide and filled with tears of fear and pain.

Rune walked across the top of the platform and looked down at Morgan at the bottom of the steps as she wept. Morgan looked up her red eyes glowing with hate.

"This will not end here; you mark my words Flower Girl." Rune opened her cloak to reveal the blue black raven Rajani, Morgan trembled as more tears filled her eyes. "Don't hurt her, she is all I have, I beg you spare her."

Rune looked at her with no compassion at all. "Why should she live, why should you live? You have killed and maimed and tortured your way through life, there are no number of lost souls that have died by your hand. Merlin gave you the chance to do something good in this life, and you betrayed him and turned to the evil that you spread throughout this world. Tell me Morgana, how many did you spare in compassion?"

Rune looked to Robbie who was still reeling at seeing Mason die. "It is no longer safe here, all of you must leave." A bright blue window opened and the remaining Specialist's, who were slightly dazed by the moment, moved quickly into it, they ran through on to the road at the side of the Village Hall. Robbie hesitated.

"Rune there are still a lot of men here, I cannot leave you." Steph touched his arm.

"Go Robbie, I will be with her."

He looked unsure, and she smiled. "We are safe; this final task is not ours." He looked confused, Steph turned and looked out over the wall, where a figured robed in a black tattered hooded cloak, walked slowly down the hill towards the large wall, he lifted his hand and smiled. "Talented little wonder is that green eyed nymph." He flicked his hand and the green bright barrier disappeared in the gateway.

Robbie gave a nod, he was not happy, but he understood. He turned and walked into Sapphire's window and it closed behind him, Rune looked at the stunned soldiers.

"You are free to leave, or fight choose now."

On the wall behind Morgan stood hundreds of fighters, and they did not move, Rune shook her head. "It is not necessary to die, leave and go live your lives in peace." They drew out their swords, and she gave a sigh.

"So be it."

A violet window opened above them in the air, and thousands of arrows came hurtling out. No sooner than they had looked up, they fell to the ground leaving Morgan, Steph, and Runestone alone.

The White Lord Albanlin cloaked in tattered black, walked up the steps to the side of Runestone and came into view, Morgan began to weep and tremble more as she saw him, his hood gave a slight twitch. "Hand me the bird and leave, your task here is over little red stone."

Rune handed him the Raven, and it squawked to life as his transparent hand took it, the figure turned to Morgan as Rune's window opened and she stepped through it back into Loxley with Steph. Albanlin gave a sigh.

"So much darkness, for one small soul, I see within you how you have mutilated the essence of who you once were. Stand up, and come forward Little Black One, stand before your Lord and be judged, for it is finally time."

On trembling legs, she lifted herself up, and Albanlin handed her the bird. "You shall be judged as one, here take the part of your soul you cut away and hold it close."

With shaking hands Morgan took Rajani and pulled her close in a loving embrace, holding her close to her heart. Albanlin lifted his hands to his hood and slid it slowly down to reveal himself to her. Morgan looked into the eyes of the White Lord, and saw the vastness of eternity and the truth of the Merle.

Morgan's eyes open wide with horror, and she screamed at the top of her lungs with absolute terror as she saw the true face of the white lord. Across the way in Loxley, as Robbie stood on the platform next to Henry holding Rune in his arms, surrounded by the Specialists, they all shuddered as they heard the screams of blood curdling terror from Morgan. Many on the walls and below on the ground fell to their knees, hid their faces, and covered their ears in fear.

As the scream died with a gurgle, all of them stood as the wall began to crumble into dust and fall to the earth, Robbie squeezed Rune tight. "Is it finally over?" Rune snuggled into him.

"The source of the Merle has been broken, but there are still many in this world that were tainted by its corrupt power, evil deeds will still be done, but there will never be deeds as evil as those of the ravens."

Across the valley, the wall disappeared completely, and Robbie saw the flash of blue and white as windows opened for the rest of the Woodland Forces. Robbie gave a sigh.

"We have guests coming, brave men who should be honoured, we need to prepare."

All across the land walls fell, in some areas they remained, as Mason had built a few of his own, but in York, Tintagel, and all across London, walls crumbled to dust around the dazed freedom fighters and enslaved members of Mason's Empire.

High on the mountains of Saxony, Albanlin walked into the circular room of the castle of Berengar, and stood before the tall crystal tube that encased Branna, on his shoulder sat the large raven Roack. He ran his finger down the tube, and it crumbled revealing the bloodied Branna, he looked at her and gave a sigh, then reached out and gripped her limp body. She saw the raven and stretched out a weak arm to it, as Albanlin lifted her up. "You my darkest of all ravens, are coming with me."

The travelling people of Cezar watched for a second time, as the beam of pure white light shot into the sky, and within seconds they rejoiced as the crude ugly castle of Berengar crumbled away to dust, and for the first time in many lifetimes, they understood, that now they were truly free to go home to their ancient lands. Later as they danced in their camp round the fire, a lone figure walked down the track, and as the old lady sat on the steps of her caravan saw her, she gave a broad smile. The figure walked over to her and hugged her. "I am back Crina."

"Welcome home Ena my child."

CHAPTER FORTY

OTHER CIRCLES OPEN

The day after the fall of the Dark One, Robbie organised a giant clean-up operation across the valley. Allowing Harry to drive one of the large earth movers, a huge grave was created to bury the thousands of dead soldiers of Mason. Runestone asked her lord and grandfather to help the lost souls of each man, and once the grave was covered, she marked the grave as she had those in Carlisle, and since that day, it has been covered with the red flowers of the wild strawberry leaved Potentilla.

Little is known of the soldiers from Mason's army who lived. The site of the battle and for several miles in every direction was littered with discarded black vests and weapons. There were some who wanted them hunted down and imprisoned for their part in the Great War, but Robbie declined stating that his aim was always to create a country of free men. In his mind, the memory of their times as soldiers to the black army, would last them a lifetime, and he hoped because of it, they would live their lives in peace as better men.

On his return to Loxley, Robbie took off the Sword of Destiny, and hung it on the wall behind his desk in the village hall, he handled it only one more time, and that was the day he brought it to his rebuilt house at Robbie's Mere, where he placed it beside the scorched recovered white staff belonging to Ruby, next to his desk in his new loft office. He has never used a sword since, although to this day he remains a bowman of unnatural talent.

Life in Loxley had the giant task of returning to normal, a task that for the lord of Loxley would take years. The Specialists had not realised that their last meeting at the house of Robbie's Mere had been their last one ever. On the grass outside the Village Hall, set back a little from the path, a special garden was created. The garden was a perfect circle of space surrounded by seating, and in the very centre

of it was placed a beautiful carved tree stump in the shape of a hooded man
holding up his bow. Mr Perkins as Robbie expected, had created a fitting tribute
to everyone who had lost their lives fighting the tyranny of Mason Knox. Over the
years to come Robbie was seen often sitting there alone in deep thought. On the
long back wall of the Village Hall, below the crest of a carved Wolves Head, the
names of every person lost in the fight were added, and at the very bottom of the
wall, painted in large words was the inscription. 'Freedom is the sole possession of
those who have the courage to defend it.'(Pericles.)

Ariel resided in Loxley for a further five weeks, before returning home. She
had great knowledge in healing, and spent a great deal of time with Alice teaching
her new cures to help the men who had been wounded in battle. She returned
home at Gleefall accompanied by Tila, Crystal, and Sapphire, where she was met
on the steps by Master Elgin and Bade.

As she walked up the steps towards him, Bade fell to his knees and cried. Ariel
embraced him and lifted him up, and beside Master Elgin, they walked into the
House of Scribes to talk. Bade asked her many times to marry him over the
years, but Ariel always refused, she knew deep down inside that even though
foolish, no one would ever replace that wild dark haired girl she had lived with in
Avalon. Bade remained at her side for the rest of his life as her greatest friend and
companion.

Big John who in the final moments of the battle, had been hit in the leg with
an infected arrow, returned to his post beside Jess on the farm. He was a good
manager, and a big help on the farm, even though he limped for the rest of his life.
He finally married the bar maid in the hotel and had a son, who he named Martin
after his friend and Specialist fighting partner.

Old Joe died a few years later when his still exploded, and Robert Thorn
married Michelle (Rags). Four years after they were married, they became the
proud parents of a daughter, who they named Mary Sian. Melissa married Jaz and
moved to the Isle of Skye, Una continued to live in Loxley and became a teacher
at the school. Woody finally plucked up the courage to ask her to marry him, ten
years after the big battle.

William took a long time to recover, but three years after the last battle, he
was finally crowned the first king of a new age. He married Judith, and in a twist
of irony, a Knox finally made it to the throne of England. They had two children;
Arthur followed three years later by Marion. Skip gave up his seat as Duke, to his
cousin Rupert, and moved to Morbihan where he married Citrine, and spent his
time sailing his own boat between London and home, as he took on the role as

educator and advisor of the King, a role he shared with Bear.

Fuse was old when he entered Loxley, and enjoyed his retirement; he often could be seen sat at the Mere with his fishing rod. One morning in the summer of 2043, Rune felt him and walked to see him, when she arrived, he had passed into the other realm with a smile. She sat for a long time at his side with tears in her eyes, and told him of the love she felt for him, and thanked him for all he had done for them. He was buried with great honour in the Lox family plot.

Jacques and Alice married, and due to the fact that his brother Brett had been crippled and was blind, he took on the role of rebuilding York. Jessica Sapphire grew to be a beautiful woman, and spent a great deal of her time with Sapphire. Alice and Jacques had a son in 2044 named Michael Henry Phillips.

Saucers, aka Jimmy Perkins, finally made it into the Bowmen of Loxley; he worked hard dedicating his life to the protection of Loxley in the service of his lord, making the rank of commander, and was appointed to the court of William.

Stephanie and Peter returned to their family home and ran Trinkets and Trousers. Smokes built her a new bike from scraps and old bikes he found at Harry's place, and they would often be seen, or heard, riding at speed on the old roads along the moors, although it was often noted that Steph would disappear for weeks at a time.

Amethyst had her child, and true to her word she named her Vivian. James doted on her and spent many hours swimming with her in the Mirrored Waters each day. Shortly after the last battle, the White Lord visited the realm of Ofmoon, where he personally cleansed every member of the Fae Ofmoon to ensure none of them were tainted further by the Merle. Enaria's star is still situated in the centre of the realm Ofmoon, where it is said to ensure no Merle ever finds its way back into the realm.

Branna's parents had already died, but not in prison. Her brother Mondale dedicated the rest of his life to documenting ways in which to fight the darkness. No one knows what happened to Branna, it has been rumoured Albanlin took her to the deepest part of the Merle, where she hangs limp and unable to move, floating through time and staring into the darkness.

Luminaria was finally allowed back to Avalon, where she visited her brother Fagan, and spent two months living with him. Her sons who took the roles of

Makers in Avalonia were regular visitors. One evening Luminaria was summoned before Queen Amethyst, where she was given back her position as Commander of the Avalonia Marshals, and her record was cleared of all wrong doings.

Gwynne and Rayne returned to the farm on the outskirts of Avalon. True to his word Rayne had returned to Gwynne, although the damage to his eye was unrepairable, and he spent the rest of his days wearing a pale blue eye patch, much to the delight of Tila when she visited, as she had spent some of her time in Loxley reading books about Pirates. Crystal kept her promise, and when she returned with Tila to Florae, her and Tila headed to their room with wine and dried fruits. Crystal froze the lock on the door much to the delight of Tila, and they spent a whole week alone together.

Harry and Maggs returned to honey hill with Bob and his family, and rebuilt the farm. Harry died in 2048, when he put the wrong alcohol in his fuel tank, and blew himself up whilst riding to market on his favourite motor bike. Little remained, as the explosion was as fierce as a burning tanker, apart from one smoking cowboy boot. Maggs whilst grief stricken, did comment that it was a fitting way for her Harry to enter his cosmic rebirth.

Running the farm without Beth was a difficult task for Jess, so Blades and Todd moved into the house of Beth when Alice moved to York, and took care of John who continued to work in his forge. Over the next three years he repaired and rebuilt the gates, and the parts of the wall that had been blown down. To this day in the forge above the door, hangs the axe that killed Mason Knox. Many of the children sneak in to peep at it, and the dark patches on the blade, as it still bears the blood stains from that gruesome fight.

Jay took over the cheese shop after the death of Agatha Patterdale, when she accidentally choked on a freshly cooked biscuit whilst gossiping. Anne and Alice ran the Bakery shop for many more years, living to the ripe old age of 90, and 96 years old. Whenever Lord Loxley walked down the street, Alice would scurry out of her shop, and hand him a bag of freshly baked scones. Father Warren returned to his church at Hathersage, and spent the rest of his life administering to the many faiths that surrounded the new growing community. Bishop Stevens served as Arch Bishop for a further five years, crowning William at York, and died peacefully in his sleep.

Crystal continued as Ambassador to Florae, much to the joy of Tila, who worked exclusively with Ariel on transcribing Enaria's notes. In her spare time at home, she slowly translated the First and Second book of Branna, as Rune still had a copy held within her table of power, which she gifted to her.

Gaynor stayed close to William, and eventually married an advisor to the court named Frank, both of them worked tirelessly helping William rebuild the country, and as a result they had no children. It has often been said that Gaynor had chosen to stay childless, to ensure the curse of her line ended with her.

Louisa Married Doc of the Outlaws, and spent the rest of her life travelling the country and exploring. Beavis/Ox died whilst defending Gwynne in the last battle, and Robbie had a special stone carved and placed in his memory in Badger's Bank deep in Loxley woods. Rigger and his sister Dove left the area and have not been seen since, much to the disappointment of Jay.

Opal was right, and eventually Keith returned to Settle, the place where he was raised by his father. Whilst out for a walk near his woodland home, he met a young woman with long auburn hair named Petal. He was captivated at first sight, and they lived together in his cabin happily, and more in love than he had ever thought possible. Petal was an expert at wild flowers and potions, and had an uncanny resemblance to Sapphire.

Jett Amber became Queen of Caerleon, and eventually married Rafe. It took a while, but eventually they had a daughter they named Pandora, which everyone appeared to understand and never questioned, she did not disappoint and was often seen at the hotel in Loxley in her later years, out drinking with the boys and laughing with wild abandon. Robbie gave Rafe the house on the street in Loxley as a wedding gift, that way Jett always had two homes, ensuring she never felt alone again, and always had family close to her.

Jade gave birth to her daughter Yvee in the spring of 2040, and a few years later had a son who Rowan named Frayne. Four years later came Grover, followed two years later by Willow. Rowan played a huge role in Loxley life, and was one of the most respected members of the family. After the death of Joe Whitmore, he took on the role of forester to the Loxley estate. Mason had bull dozed a great part of the valley, and Rowan planted a wall of trees where his tall black ugly wall had once stood. Over the years the trees produced seed, and today the whole area is now one massive, dense, and beautiful forest.

Two days after the last battle, Tila arrived with Gwynfor, and began to rebuild the house at the Mere. It took thirty carpenters a year to build, and when it was completed, it was almost identical to Rune's first house. There were very few changes, due mainly to the fact that she had loved it so much, she could not stand to live in anything different. The only changes noticeable, was Gwynfor did a lot of runic carvings around the place, he said at the time it had been a wonderful experience, and had felt like a long working holiday for him.

Iona and Halbert returned to live in Loxley and grew up at the Mere, where they were soon joined by sisters, Tegan, Fern and Gailania. They all loved happily playing in the woodland around the Mere, and spending time with their aunt Jade. It was often noted how Runestone and Robbie would disappear for long periods visiting Rune's Grandfather, and also spending time with Old Fagan in the Forest of Time. Gailania was a slender girl with long red hair and sapphire blue eyes; many said she was the absolute likeness of her mother.

After the liberation of the south, as the parties involved celebrated, the strange figure known only as The Sage disappeared with his young companion Ben. For years rumours of a man with a tree like face helping people circulated, but no one could say for sure if it was the mysterious Sage. Martin and Dutch were awarded for their work and given roles within the court of the king, and served as part of his protection detail for many years.

As the walls all across the country fell, a great deal of the evil of Mason was revealed. One of the biggest shocks for Ester was how many orphanages existed, where thousands of children had been bred for Mason's Army. A great deal of young healthy women, had been enslaved to provide new children for the world that Mason had planned after the conquest of Loxley. Ester spent several years gathering together the enslaved women who had no family, and organising them to provide new schools and housing for all the children. One of William's first tasks as the new king was to help provide aide to Ester in her task of ensuring every enslaved woman, and orphaned child was given a safe home and a full education.

Dana Knox disappeared completely after the last battle, although it was rumoured that a Countess Le Fey had travelled throughout France down to Spain. She died mysteriously when she went for a walk on the beach one night, and after a strange blue light was seen near the edge of the water, the Countess washed up on the beach dead with her throat cut.

Her step son Lance suffered a similar fate, when he was stopped on the road late one night by a group wearing hooded cloaks; he was later found shot to death with violet feather tipped arrows, through his ear was a long bumblebee tipped hair pin. Nadia's son Victor lived an active life, when on his thirtieth birthday he collapsed, and he died within minutes from an exploded heart, it shocked everyone, as he had always been healthy and rarely sick.

Shortly after her fourth birthday, Iona Violet became ill and slipped into a feverish dream state. Isolde and Robbie were frightened and panicked. That night as she sat at her table of power with Robbie and Jade, Runestone explained that she was not afraid, as she understood that Iona was in a dream state created by her Fae powers. Sweeping her hand across her table, she pulled the pictures of a small child with violet eyes, handing over the violet stones to Victor Thorson the sword maker at Dunnottar. Rune smiled as she explained, Iona was fine, she had just left for a while to help save her father.

On the day of her eighteenth birthday, Iona Violet who had been trained in Loxley and at Callanish, was escorted by Isolde to Florae, where during a massive celebration, Robbie and Runestone and their children watched her be crowned Queen of the Fae of Earth. She grew to be a very fair minded and powerful member of the Fae line, and it was noted how at times she emulated the rule of not just Bridget Violet, but also Gwendolyn. Her greatest friend apart from Sapphire was Ariel, who also taught her a great deal about the power of the Fae of old.

Not much has been recorded of the life of Sapphire, she came and went and lived a reclusive life when not instructing Iona Violet. She never married or settled down, but there were rumours that she had the companionship of many in her long life, but without the knowledge of Agatha Patterdale in the local town, her life remained as mysterious as her sudden appearances.

Life once back to normal went on as usual and the war of Mason faded into the past, as more and more towns grew and reached out to each other. Loxley became a centre for trade, and the market place increased in size. With each generation the stories told late at night, spoke of dark witches and wizards, and men who looked like trees, or had a face that was made of bark. This occasionally was stirred, when talk of a pure white stag being spotted in the woodland was the talk of the town, but aside from that, life was normal and ordinary for most folks, and the years ticked on in peace for just about everyone.

It was some time later, when things out of the ordinary happened.

The Sage lifted the plate and scraped off the last few scraps of food. "Will you be alright?"

Ben lifted the large stack of bundled twigs on to his back. "You worry too much; I am not a ten year old now." He gave his usual cheeky smile, as he shook his shoulder to even the large load. The Sage smiled.

"I'm sorry, it's been such a long time now; I suppose I forget how big you have grown." He paused for a second in thought and Ben looked down on the white faced old man he had known for the largest part of his thirty years. The Sage looked back up at him. "You know that to me you are a son don't you? I mean

it's been just over twenty years, and I have had the pleasure of watching you grow, we have been through so much together that in my heart you are the son I always wanted."

Ben who had indeed grown into a tall and strong man, had never said the words, but in his heart, he knew that the man who now was starting to show his late middle age, sat before him was in every way the father figure he had always wanted. Ben loved the Sage with all his heart, he had no idea of the death that was meant for him had been averted by the Sage all those years ago; he just knew the bond between them was unbreakable and would last forever. He looked at the man he admired and respected above all others.

"Are you alright? I know of the dreams that have kept you awake this past week. You know I don't have to go today, there are three other markets this week and we are well stocked for the moment."

The Sage waved his hand. "I am fine, I know I have not slept well of late, but I am fine honestly, you go, I am sure that Miss Reilly on the jam stall would never forgive me if I held you here on market day." He gave a large smile and his blue eyes in his lined pale face that looked birch like twinkled. "Bring me a large jar of her finest damson if you remember whilst busy trying to talk her into living in that cabin you are building." Ben gave a bright white smile and nodded.

"I will do that; I will be back by night fall, stay close to the camp." The Sage gave a nod and watched as Ben turned and walked into the trees to begin his journey back down the high rock, towards the busy market town below in the shadow of the old castle.

The Sage sat back against the rock and lifted his cup. The sun was now rising up almost level with the tops of the buttery yellow leaves of the Birch and Field Maple, as the early autumnal sun marked the start of the new day. He gave a sigh and watched as the birds now decreasing in number, flew franticly above the new trees; it was going to be cool again. His mind moved from his thoughts of his friend and companion, to the disturbed dreams he had suffered the night before, what was it that they were trying to tell him? It had been two weeks now, and he still had not worked it out.

It was quiet and still as his thoughts drifted through his mind, he still had the feeling of the night in him, and he could not decide what he should do, his senses told him to stay in the camp, and so he had told Ben that he had to remain while he went alone to market, it was the first time in twenty years.

The sense of something was growing inside him and building all the time, it felt frustrating not being able to know why. "Jesus Billy get a grip." His voice seemed strange to him as he spoke his thoughts out loud.

He stood up and collected the plates and washed them out to the side of the high wall, and then packed them into his bag, at the side of the wide opening that they had used for cover at night in the years of rainstorms known to the region. The feeling in his stomach intensified and he felt his gut twist, goose bumps ran along his arms and up his back. There was no mistaking there was danger, but from where and who?

The Sage turned back to watch the trees, he suddenly felt nervous, his pale blue eyes darted from left to right, but the woodland on the edge of the high cliff was as it always was, more out of instinct than anything else he bent down, and stretched out his arm to his bow and quiver, he rose up and saw the tall hooded stranger stood just outside of the cover of the trees.

His cloak was long and pale, and the hood covered his face, he was broad and stocky, stood silent and unmoving, he held a long bow across his front and the feathers of his arrows in his quiver stood proud at his shoulder. The Sage gave a courteous nod. "Greetings woodsman, would you have business with me, or are you passing by this way, there is hot coffee if you would care to be warmed on this chilly morning?"

The woodsman stood silent for a moment, and then lifted his hand to the top of his hood. He pulled it back, and the front rose revealing his tanned face, and deep brown eyes, he too showed the signs of a man his age. "It's been a long time Master Sage, or should I say Billy? Like all men trained in Loxley, you have not been easy to find." Robbie's hood fell down his back, as his dark eyes met the cool blue of Billy's.

In the tall trees around a lost and quiet space deep within Loxley woodland, the breeze softly stroked the mists close to the ragged grass and sorrel of the leafy floor. As the birds sang high in the branches to mark the coming to an end of the summer season, somewhere out of sight came the new sound of soft leather boots on the damp floor.

The mist separated between two mighty Oaks, and swirled around the slender figure wrapped in a long cloak of black. The figure moved slowly as if in search of something on the woodland floor. Leaves fluttered down, as three squirrels above in the branches were startled, and ran along the long branches, and jumped to other trees. The cloaked figure stopped for a second, frozen by the sudden disturbance, before moving on into the clearing in front of them.

In the centre of the clearing the figure stopped, the cloak folded on the ground, as the figure softly sunk to their knees, before a small patch of dark bare earth. The patch of bare earth was just a few inches across in a perfectly formed circle, and was nothing that would look normally out of place, except in this particular part of the woodland, all the growth was lush, and covered every square inch but this one.

The cloak parted, and a soft almost bleached white, elegant hand slipped out, bearing a golden ring set with an onyx black stone. Inlaid in the stone was the shape of a hovering bird of gold. The hand rested a few inches above the exposed circle of soil, and a soft yet cold titter came from below the hood of the cloak.

The ground gave a pulse and began to vibrate, causing the soil to shake and rise in the centre, almost reaching the hand above, before it shook sideways and tumbled back to the floor at the edge of the circle. The tiny particles shook, until up through the centre of what looked like a cone of softly shaking soil, came a long shard of a black glass like material. The hand lifted and the soil fell still, as it rose to meet the other white hand that had appeared from below the folds of the black cloak. The figure that was clearly a woman, gave another soft titter, as she flung back the hood, and long strands of sleek black hair tinted with hues of a deep blue-black fell to the soft green of the woodland floor.

There was a sparkle in the jet black eyes, set within a whiter than white face, with a smile of bright red lips. The figure reached back down and lifted the shard of black glass up towards her face to examine it. Raven Merle held it before her face, as the pale sun beat down upon it, and yet it did not sparkle, or glint as any normal glass would, the figure gave a long exhale of breath.

"Found you. The rest of you may be buried deep under the water of that wretched moon fairy, but you are all I need for now. Long have I waited for this moment, for you my little piece of precious darkness, are the key to unlocking the past and the truth of my line, you are the key to the rising again of the new raven of darkness."

Far away in another realm, next to a large stone table baring the crest of a golden tree, set on a background of pale blue, and circled by twelve golden stars, the Queen of Fae of Earth stood alone with her eyes closed, as she focused on the new feeling growing within her. Her thoughts pondered the moment, and then she focused her mind.

"Hear me mother... She has finally revealed herself."

More Author's
From
Violet Circle Publishing

Mike Beale. (Children's Book)

Crumble's Adventures.
ISBN: 978-1-910299-06-7
Digital ISBN: 978-1-910299-08-1

Colin Smith (Play)

Heaven knows I'm Miserable Now
ISBN: 978-1-910299-16-6
Digital ISBN: 978-1-910299-23-4

Ted Morgan. (Poetry and verse)

Wordsmith's Wanderings.
ISBN: 978-1-910299-04-3
Digital ISBN: 978-1-910299-09-8
Peregrinations of the Wordsmith
ISBN: 978-1-910299-18-0
Digital ISBN: 978-1-910299-21-0
Silhouette Soldiers
ISBN: 978-1-910299-19-7
Digital ISBN: 978-1-910299-22-7
A Menu of Memories
Digital ISBN: 978-1-910299-32-6
Digital ISBN: 978-1-910299-33-3

Robin John Morgan. (Fiction/Fantasy/Slice of Life)

Heirs to the Kingdom.

Book One, The Bowman of Loxley.
ISBN: 978-1-910299-00-5
Digital ISBN: 978-1-910299-10-4
Book Two, The Lost Sword of Carnac.
ISBN: 978-1-910299-01-2
Digital ISBN: 978-1-910299-11-1
Book Three, The Darkness of Dunnottar.
ISBN: 978-1-910299-02-9
Digital ISBN: 978-1-910299-12-8
Book Four, Queen of the Violet Isle.
ISBN: 978-1-910299-03-6
Digital ISBN: 978-1-910299-13-5
Book Five, Crystals of the Mirrored Waters.
ISBN: 978-1-910299-05-0
Digital ISBN: 978-1-910299-14-2
Book Six, Last Arrow of the Woodland Realm.
ISBN: 978-1-910299-07-4
Digital ISBN: 978-1-910299-15-9
Book Seven, Bridge Of Sequana.
ISBN: 978-1-910299-17-3
Digital ISBN: 978-1-910299-20-3
Book Eight, The Circle of Darkness.
ISBN: 978-1-910299-26-5
Digital ISBN: 978-1-910299-29-6

The Curio Chronicles.

Part One, Abigail's Summer.
ISBN: 978-1-910299-27-2
Part Two, Curio's Summer.
ISBN: 978-1-910299-34-0
Digital ISBN: 978-1-910299-35-7
Part Three, Curio's Christmas.
ISBN: 978-1-910299-38-8
Digital ISBN: 978-1-910299-39-5

Other Works.

Rise Of The Raven
ISBN: 978-1-910299-30-2
Digital ISBN: 978-1-910299-31-9
The Countess Of Darkness
ISBN: 978-1-910299-40-1
Digital ISBN: 978-1-910299-41-8

Han's Cottage.
ISBN: 978-1-910299-36-4
Digital ISBN: 978-1-910299-37-1

Find out more about our authors and their books at
www.violetcirclepublishing.co.uk